Susan Croft

Susan is a writer, historian, curator and researcher. She worked in the USA with the Omaha Magic Theatre in the early 1980s, returning to Britain to work as a dramaturg with small-scale theatre companies and founding New Playwrights Trust, of which she was Director from 1986-89.

She taught Creative Arts (Performance) at Nottingham Trent University and then was Senior Research Fellow in Performance Arts at Manchester Metropolitan University to 1996. From 1997-2005 she was Curator of Contemporary Performance at the Theatre Museum where she worked on the National Video Archive of Performance. She also curated four major exhibitions including *Let Paul Robeson Sing!* and *Architects of Fantasy* and pioneered a range of initiatives to record the history of black and Asian theatre in Britain.

She has written extensively on women playwrights, including: *...She Also Wrote Plays: an International Guide to Women Playwrights from the 10th to the 21st Century* (Faber and Faber, 2001). She is working on a Critical Bibliography of Plays Published by Women Playwrights in English to 1914 for Manchester University Press and a major anthology *Staging the New Woman*, with Sherry Engle.

She also runs the project *Unfinished Histories: Recording the History of Alternative Theatre*, with Jessica Higgs, a major initiative to record oral histories and preserve archives of the alternative theatre movement from the 1960s to the 1980s. See www.susan.croft.btinternet.co.uk for further details.

She lives in London with her partner and two children.

Other classic plays

Lysistrata - the sex strike by Germaine Greer after Aristophanes
ISBN 09536757 -0-X £7.99

A Christmas Carol by Charles Dickens adapted by Neil Duffield
ISBN 978-09551566-8-7 £8.99

The Classic Fairytales, retold for the stage by Charles Way
ISBN 09542330 0-X £11.50

The Classic Fairytales 2, retold for the stage by Charles Way
ISBN 978-09551566-7-0 £11.99

Merlin and the Cave of Dreams by Charles Way
ISBN 09551566-0-2 £7.99

Forthcoming:

Classic Plays by Women ed. Susan Croft
ISBN 978-1-906582-00-5 £12.99

Available from www.aurorametro.com and all good bookstores.

Votes for Women
and other plays

edited and introduced
by
Susan Croft

Votes for Women
Elizabeth Robins

A Change of Tenant
Helen Margaret Nightingale

At the Gates
Alice Chapin

How the Vote was Won
Cicely Hamilton and Chris St John

The Apple
Inez Bensusan

In the Workhouse
Margaret Wynne Nevinson

Jim's Leg
L.S. Phibbs

AURORA METRO PRESS

This volume first published in Great Britain 2009 by Aurora Metro Publications Ltd, 67 Grove Avenue, Twickenham, TW1 4HX www.aurorametro.com © 2009 Aurora Metro Publications: info@aurorametro.com
Cover photo: Dorothy Newell © 2009 Corbis.com
Production editors: Gillian Wakeling & Carmel Walsh
With thanks to: Aidan Jenkins, Neil Gregory, Gabriele Maurer, Simon Bennett, Rebecca Mordan, Naomi Paxton, Sam Walters, Megan Dobson
Introduction, Compilation, Chronology and Bibliography © 2009 Susan Croft
How the Vote was Won First published 1909 by The Woman's Press, © 1909, 1913, 1985, 2009 The Cecily Hamilton Estate c/o Lady Bower
Votes for Women First published in 1907 by Mills and Boon Ltd. © 1907, 1985, 2009 c/o Independent Age

Printed and bound in Great Britain by CPI Antony Rowe, Eastbourne and Chippenham
ISBN 978-1-906582-01-2

Contents

Introduction
Susan Croft

This anthology brings together satirical sketches, comic monologues and powerful plays written to support the campaign for Votes For Women and performed by members of the Actresses' Franchise League over a century ago.

To celebrate the radical campaigning work of the Actresses' Franchise League, this new edition aims to highlight some of the lesser known plays alongside the seminal works which, despite numerous productions both professional and amateur since their creation, are now mostly out of print.[i]

This anthology includes Cicely Hamilton and Chris St John's hilarious and perennially popular *How the Vote Was Won*, Inez Bensusan's moving short drama *The Apple* and Elizabeth Robins' powerful full-length classic, *Votes for Women*. It also seeks to supplement our understanding of the range of suffrage plays by introducing some pieces which have not been reprinted before: Alice Chapin's *At the Gates*, Helen Nightingale's *A Change of Tenant*, and Margaret Wynne Nevinson's *In the Workhouse*.[ii]

The choice of what to include, what not, was difficult as space was limited and there were so many plays to draw from. Readers who want to track down these and many other suffrage plays can turn to the detailed **Chronology of Plays Addressing or Supporting Suffrage Issues 1907-1914**, which gives publication and production details of numerous other suffrage plays.

Since 1985 new research has begun to reveal just how many works in dramatic form were produced and/or published in support of the women's suffrage movement, along with some of those satirical or campaigning works which opposed women's suffrage or mocked its adherents.

The scripts included here draw on some of that research and, while they are published in honour of the AFL, they are not limited to scripts which directly related to or were necessarily produced by the AFL. Robins' play, for example, pre-dates the AFL's formation. This selection is however restricted to plays that were staged or printed as part of the suffrage campaign or, like Nevinson's, directly related to campaigns for legislative change in other aspects of women's status[iii]. This anthology also includes plays staged by other suffrage-related groups, like the Pioneer Players.

The Pioneer Players' early work grew out of and overlapped its founders, Edith (Edy) Craig's and Chris St John's, involvement in the AFL and Women Writers' Suffrage League (WWSL).

The Actresses' Franchise League

One hundred years ago, under the elaborate gold-tooled ceiling of the Criterion Restaurant in Piccadilly, nearly 400 actresses came together to pledge their support for the formation of the Actresses' Franchise League (AFL). It was a splendid gathering. As well as numerous rank and file actresses, there were major names from the business including Gertrude Forbes-Robertson (Chair), the sisters Eva and Decima Moore, Irene and Violet Vanbrugh, Lillah McCarthy and Adeline Bourne, who became the AFL's first Secretary, and Dame Madge Kendal (President). All were prepared to lend the authority of their names and standing as well-known professional women to support the cause of Votes for Women. Among the many who signed up were Ellen Terry, producers Lena Ashwell and Gertrude Kingston, Gertrude Elliott, Lily Langtry and young actresses Athene Seyler and Sybil Thorndike.

Under the leadership of Winifred Mayo and Simé Seruya, they pledged themselves to convince members of the acting profession to support women's suffrage and to work towards it through:

I) Propaganda Meetings

II) Sale of Literature

III) Propaganda Plays

IV) Lectures

They also aimed "To assist all other Leagues wherever possible." They stated that only actresses were to be eligible for the Executive Committee though membership was open to all those currently or formerly connected with any branch of the theatrical profession with a joining fee of one shilling. The AFL was "strictly neutral in regard to Suffrage Tactics".

Over the next six years, the AFL played a highly active role: training fellow suffragists in public speaking, organising events, providing speakers, advising on the costuming and choreography of large-scale demonstrations. Membership grew from an initial 360 to about 900 members in 1914. The outbreak of war in that year redirected the energies of the suffrage movement.

In later years, a men's group was formed allowing male actors and dramatists to show their support.

Maintaining, sometimes with difficulty, a stance of independence, the AFL resisted aligning itself specifically with either the suffragists who believed in peaceful lobbying and campaigning, or alignment to the so-called 'suffragettes' of the Women's Social and Political Union (WSPU), led by Emmeline and Christabel Pankhurst. Suffragettes used direct action in pursuit of the Vote, smashing windows, chaining themselves to railings, setting fire to mail boxes and seeking arrest. In the case of Emily Wilding Davis, who threw herself under the hooves of the King's horse at the Derby, martyrdom for the Cause may have been her objective. [iv]

The AFL endeavoured to offer its services to both branches of the movement. Yet within a campaign, the most prominent members of which had espoused performance as a means of drawing public attention to female disenfranchisement, it was perhaps inevitable that many in the profession identified with the theatrical actions of the suffragettes, while others were members of the suffragist National Union for Women's Suffrage or bodies affiliated to specific political parties like actress and playwright Bertha Graham who was active in the Conservative and Unionist Women's Franchise Association. Many members of the AFL were also supporters of the WSPU. In Chris St John's June 1909 dialogue, *A Defence of the Fighting Spirit*, in the WSPU journal *Votes for Women,* the character of Diana, her name evoking the huntress goddess, defends the violence of the suffragettes and identifies with the biblical David in his fight against the Philistines.

Relatively few of the AFL membership went to gaol for the Cause: exceptions being actress Kitty Marion, who was force-fed, Vera (Jack) Holme who was imprisoned for stone-throwing and Alice Chapin, who served time in Holloway for pouring ink into a ballot-box. Imprisonment could be both disruptive and detrimental to insecure careers. Others were arrested but not charged like St John who, taken up for wilful obstruction, successfully pleaded that she was there as a dramatist not as a suffragette.

Others, like Chapin, director Edith Craig, and Bessie Hatton, Secretary to the Women Writers Suffrage League, joined the Women's Freedom League (WFL), led by Charlotte Despard. The WFL was also radical in its politics and tactics, but with a wider set of concerns and analysis of women's oppression. It went beyond the focus on suffrage as the solution to the question of women's exclusion from power and entrapment in narrow roles. The WFL saw women's emancipation in broader terms and engaged with social, economic, cultural, and sexual issues. This manifesto appealed to women who were self-supporting economically. It also appealed culturally to those whose work, whether in melodramas of female victimisation or Ibsenite dramas of ideas, daily addressed the dilemmas and conflicts of women's position.

Over the years of its existence the AFL expanded its areas of activity. Beyond the issue of the vote itself, the AFL sought to educate its members and others and involve them in debating vital issues. They organised monthly 'At Homes' at the Criterion Restaurant with prominent speakers from the Church, Army, Law and medical profession, as well as prominent writers like popular American poet Ella Wheeler Wilcox, Jerome K Jerome and writer and feminist Evelyn Sharp.

At a 1911 meeting (tickets one or two shillings) chaired by Sir Arthur Conan Doyle, President of the Divorce Law Reform Union, a discussion was held on marriage and divorce laws. On Friday June 6th, 1913 a Meeting "for Women Only", was addressed by Miss Abadam on "White Slaves – Supply and Demand". At smaller gatherings at the New Reform Club motions debated included those questioning the state of their own art form and profession: "that a knowledge of politics is not injurious to dramatic art" and "that the State conception of Woman is conventional and inadequate".

In Edinburgh, Glasgow, Liverpool and Eastbourne, provincial branches were set up and local Honorary Secretaries provided a link between touring AFL members visiting or playing in the area and the needs of local suffrage groups to whom they offered their skills in reciting, singing or speaking.

The AFL was increasingly active in poorer districts like the East End of London. Local Labour M.P. George Lansbury encouraged them to provide free performances in Bow and Poplar for working-class women and to build connections locally through Settlements and Girls' Clubs. Members attended demonstrations and pickets, liaised with other suffrage societies, spoke at public rallies and drawing-room meetings, and supported deputations.

On May 10, 1912 the AFL organised their own Deputation of Professional and Self-supporting women to Ramsay McDonald, who had been elected Chairman of the Parliamentary Labour Party in 1911. They organised classes to train fellow suffragists in public speaking. Socially, they hosted an Annual Birthday Party at the Criterion Restaurant, to mark the founding of the League, and raised funds through Fancy Dress balls, Receptions and Matinees and social 'At Homes' in private houses and arts centres.

Plays for the Suffrage Movement

Between 1908 to 1914 the production of plays in support of women's suffrage was central to the activities of the League. Under the leadership of Inez Bensusan[v], and working with the Women Writers' Suffrage League (WWSL)[vi], the AFL Play Department commissioned, cast and co-ordinated the production of numerous short campaigning plays and the publication and distribution of scripts. Such work was to be staged locally by actresses connected to provincial theatres or by local suffrage campaign groups. Essentially these plays served either or both of two purposes: fundraising and propaganda.

Fundraising centred on programmes of work performed at suffrage events in the larger cities. These events tended to feature suffrage comedies like Hamilton and St John's *How the Vote Was Won* which on the final day of the WSPU's Women's Suffrage Exhibition at the Princes' Skating Rink, Knightsbridge 'was played three times running, only a few minutes elapsing between each performance'[vii]. The AFL programmed fourteen days of performances for the Exhibition with new material including Gertrude Jennings's *A Woman's Influence*, alongside previously tried suffrage plays, songs and popular recitations like *Enery Brown* and amusing duologues like Muriel Stobart's *Meringues*[viii], which though witty and contemporary, did not address a suffrage theme.

Alongside these theatre pieces audience members could experience other performance events including a life-size re-creation of a Holloway cell where WSPU members took turns as prisoners or wardresses[ix]. Many plays on suffrage themes were comedies, designed to expose the contradictions and absurdities of the anti-suffragist position, as in *How the Vote Was Won*, and Beatrice Harraden's *Lady Geraldine's Speech*, H.M. Paull's *Anti Suffrage Monologue* or Evelyn Glover's *Miss Appleyard's Awakening*. These were highly popular at suffrage meetings and the AFL duly provided entertainments, designed to rally and inspire the converted or convert the undecided.

The AFL audience included organisations as various as the Civil Service Suffrage Society, Banstead and Walton Suffrage Society, the New Constitutional Society, the Association of Women Clerks and Secretaries, the Free Church League as well as the NUWSS and local WSPU and WFL meetings.

Other AFL plays were serious dramas like Bensusan's *The Apple*, Gertrude Mouillot's *The Master*, and Bessie Hatton's *Before Sunset*, which addressed the issue of male syphilis and its impact on women kept in sexual ignorance[x]. Still others were allegorical in form like Gertrude Vaughan's *The Woman with the Pack*, or Vera Wentworth's *An Allegory* which features Woman as a traveller towards the City of Progress, impeded by Prejudice and Fear. One of the most frequently staged pieces was Cicely Hamilton's *A Pageant of Great Women*, a feminist variation on a popular contemporary form, familiar within amateur theatricals and tableaux that provided a structure which could readily be filled with content celebrating empire, lost arcadia, local history or the co-operative movement[xi]. Hamilton's play had the particular virtue of offering numerous assorted parts – Saintly Women, Artists, Rulers, Warriors etc. – to large groups, without the requirement of learning lines (with the exception of actress Nance Oldfield who, played by Ellen Terry in the original AFL production, demands the right to speak for herself.) The characters are all introduced by Woman as part of an argument to Justice against the claims of Prejudice.

A Pageant of Great Women was staged in towns across the country, both to campaign for the vote and to raise funds for the movement and was a great personal success for Edy Craig who, as its first director, was called upon to recreate it in numerous contexts. The AFL's own joint matinee with the WWSL at the Scala was successful enough financially to enable them to open an office at 2 Robert St, Strand.

Beyond the AFL: Other Suffrage Plays

While the AFL /WWSL works and the professional actresses and writers who produced them, are central to the body of drama produced by the suffrage movement, they were not its only exponents. Plays in support of women's suffrage by other members of the movement, male and female, were common and recent research by Susan Carlson, Katharine Cockin and myself has brought to light some of the dramatic dialogues and short sketches which were published in newspapers and journals such as

Votes for Women, The Common Cause and *The Vote.*

Beyond those suffrage journals other plays can be found in modernist magazines like *The New Age,* some supportive, some satirical, or even more mainstream organs like *Cornhill Magazine* (see Chronology for details of all those found). Doubtless many more songs, sketches and narrations by members of individual suffrage societies were written and performed at meetings. Artist and suffragist Emily Ford performed her monologues to Cambridge Women's Suffrage Association in 1913[xii]; but they do not appear to have survived. (Her earlier self-published feminist plays from the 1890s have survived.)

Local suffrage meetings drew on well-known apposite extracts or pieces from popular collections, reflecting a society where amateur theatricals were a central activity of the middle class, and recitations, monologues and songs were staples of public entertainments.

The relationship between campaigning theatricals is clear in the publication *Duologues for Drawing Room and Platform* (1913) edited by Emily (Mrs Ernest) Pertwee following her husband's two similar volumes [xiii]. Both husband and wife were teachers of elocution. She was a suffragist and sister of the prominent actress-vocalists and AFL members Eva and Decima Moore, and organised several musical entertainments for the suffrage cause including the musical section of the 1911 AFL procession and the AFL's first Birthday Tea Party. Her anthology included sketches by her sister Bertha Moore and by AFL playwright Beatrice Harraden and it is likely that such material may have been performed at suffrage events.

In addition the AFL had close relationships and overlapping membership with a number of existing independent theatre societies, within which many women were prominent members. This relationship led to the formation of at least two others: the Women's Theatre, started by Inez Bensusan, and the Pioneer Players, led by Edy Craig and Chris St John.

There is still much to be done to trace the complex network of stage societies of the period, but lists of board members and councils and descriptions of plays presented show close relationships between them and many of their concerns. J.T. Grein, the critic and director of the Independent Theatre Society, which had in earlier decades produced many feminist plays, attended the AFL's launch, expressed his support and published the article 'Why I am a Suffragist'[xiv]. Another key society whose membership and concerns linked closely with those of the AFL was The Play Actors which had been established by members of the Actors' Association, the forerunner of British Actors' Equity; its Council included Winifred Mayo, Inez Bensusan, Cicely Hamilton and prominent activist Rose Mathews. There was a close relationship between women's activism within the nascent union and growing suffrage activism, further fuelled by the Association's narrow vote, on its founding in 1907, to exclude women from its ruling Council[xv].

Mathews played artist Angelica Kauffman in the AFL's first production of *A Pageant of Great Women*, written by Hamilton and directed by Edith Craig. Her own play, *The Parasites*, performed at the Scala in 1908 (together with Cicely Hamilton's *The Sergeant of Hussars*), aimed to draw attention to the "steamy side of stage life," highlighting the exploitation of actresses by unscrupulous agents and their exclusion from roles by well-heeled amateurs who paid for the privilege of appearing on stage. Other Play Actors' plays include those by Elizabeth Baker, *Esther Garthorpe* and *John Malone's Love Story* by Mrs E.S. Willard (produced in 1909 with Bensusan and Mayo in the cast), and Bertha Graham's *Oop at Kierstenan's*.

Graham is listed in company material as a supporter of the Pioneer Players and was an actress and playwright whose other plays include *Under Canvass* co-written for the Holborn (Finsbury) branch of the Conservative party and 'presented to Central Office for general use' which demonstrates to volunteers the right way and the wrong way to canvass.

The Play Actors also performed George Paston and Henriette Corkran's *The Picture of the Year* (King's Hall, 1908). Paston was a member and Vice-President of the WWSL, listed under her real name Emily Morse Symonds. She was a member of the Women's Theatre General Committee and her play, *Stuffing*, was produced by the AFL/WWSL in 1911.

Bensusan and other feminists were also active in The Oncomers' Society, another independent theatre company which produced new works at matinee performances. The Oncomers' Society performed Bensusan's *Nobody's Sweetheart*, a folkloric piece, on 29 May 1911 at the Little Theatre. While *Nobody's Sweetheart* and the other three pieces in the bill were not specifically focused on suffrage[xvi], one was by Gladys B. Stern who went on to write plays exploring women's relationship to power in the post-war era[xvii], another was co-written by a woman and a man[xviii], and the third, H.F Maltby's *What Some Men Don't Know* 'would do better at a suffrage matinee' according to *The Stage* review[xix].

Annie Horniman, founder of the Gaiety Theatre in Manchester, was an AFL supporter who spoke on the League's behalf at a Mass Meeting in Platt Fields, Manchester in 1912[xx]. Horniman staged plays like P.R. Bennett's *Mary Edwards* (1911) and other feminist works such as *Edith* by Elizabeth Baker both of which were produced by the AFL. Plays and translations by Chris St John and Antonia Williams on feminist themes were produced by the Pioneer Players. The Abbey Theatre in Dublin staged feminist plays by playwrights active in the suffrage movement, reflecting an overlap of nationalist and feminist political interest, instanced by playwrights such as Eva Gore-Booth.

Elsewhere women active in the AFL continued to produce their own feminist work like Janette Steer's *The Sphinx* (Court, 1914). The heroine Mary, is an artist, married to a philandering husband who doesn't understand her need for artistic fulfilment and independence. (One of the leads was played by the suffrage activist Kitty Marion).

The Woman's Theatre

In 1913, Inez Bensusan wrote to a number of other suffrage organisations including the London Society for Women's Suffrage to persuade them to join a Co-operative scheme to underwrite a season of suffrage plays at a larger theatre which the AFL would set up. The AFL would guarantee to purchase a number of tickets for the season which they would sell on to their members at a profit. The LSWS under Philippa Strachey did not take up the idea. "It was franchise first and drama afterwards with them"[xxi]. Inez Bensusan saw the season as an outgrowth of her work with the AFL and a context in which the League could "widen its sphere of propaganda still further by establishing a permanent season for the presentation of dramatic works dealing with the Women's Movement".

It seems clear that Bensusan was frustrated by the limited repertoire of short plays, many of them hugely popular and therefore staged over and over again, but with a tendency to the formulaic – anti-suffragist man or woman comes to realise the error of his or her ways. While the formula made for highly effective entertainment, many of them were light comedies, dramatically limiting. Descriptions of membership response to the Woman's Theatre, and debates like those at the New Reform Club, suggest that other AFL members shared her frustration and desire for more demanding dramatic fare that could not be critically dismissed and might offer more challenging roles to actresses. They wished to empower other women in theatre and devised a season: "it was to be run entirely by women... The whole business management and control will be in the hands of women... there will be women business and stage managers, producers and so on"[xxii].

Bensusan had previously shown a desire to create innovative dramaturgical contexts where new work could be performed outside the enduringly popular *How the Vote Was Won* et al. She had set up a series of triple bills of new pieces, trying out their effectiveness. She was excited by the May 1913 production of Alison Garland's four-act role reversal comedy, *The Better Half*, in which women hold the reins of power and men want a vote.

The plan for the Woman's Theatre expresses a similar desire to do more sophisticated work beyond the confines of the tried and tested. Its extensive General Committee inevitably included many associated with the AFL including Emily Pertwee and Madeleine Lucette Ryley and playwrights Joan Dugdale, Evelyn Glover, Bessie Hatton, Janette Steer, Gertrude Vaughan and Ruth Young, as well as others who were involved with the Pioneer Players including Constance Campbell, Cicely Hamilton and Mrs Herbert (Jennie) Cohen, all of whom later had plays produced by the Pioneers.

The Woman's Theatre staged Brieux's *La Femme Seule* and Bjornson's *A Gauntlet* in repertoire at the Coronet in December 1913. A critical and financial success, as Holledge establishes (pp 93-96), the season did however attract criticism for using male playwrights for their presentation of women as victims: "it is very good of M.Brieux and others to champion the women's cause, but I do wish they would do it in a more optimistic spirit and be a little less lavish in their pity" and "I wish some woman playwright would write a play showing the real spirit of the Suffragette. It has never been done yet and I do not believe that a male dramatist will ever do it"[xxiii].

Plans for a further season opening 30th November, 1914 were made, focusing on an adaptation with Cicely Hamilton of Elizabeth Robins's white slavery novel *Where Are You Going To...?* but the outbreak of war intervened[xxiv] and Bensusan redirected her and the company's energy into war work setting up the Women's Theatre Camps Entertainments. By 20 Oct 1916 the Women's Theatre Camps Entertainments had given 634 performances.

The Pioneer Players

The other key initiative that had its beginnings in the work of the AFL (and WWSL) was the Pioneer Players. The various companies represented partially intersecting circles of friendship and political commitment but took differing aesthetic directions over time. At its formation in 1911, with Ellen Terry as President, the work of the Pioneer Players was closely focused on the suffrage movement and other related feminist issues, 'propaganda plays, chiefly those dealing with the women's movement, as that is at present the most important', according to the WSPU newspaper *Votes for Women*[xxv].

It is in this context that Margaret Wynne Nevinson's play *In the Workhouse*, republished here, was performed. The Chronology lists those plays produced by Pioneer Players through 1913 during the period where they paralleled AFL activity. By 1914, the company is visibly developing its direction as an experimental company, bringing innovative new work to its audiences, often translations of European and rediscovered plays.

After 1914, the Pioneer Players' relationship to the feminist movement, becomes more oblique. But in the early years the work of Edy Craig as stage-manager, performer, producer, designer and director and that of her partner since 1899 Chris St John, are bound up with that of the AFL. Craig published the script of *How the Vote was Won* and bought production rights to many of the AFL plays, giving her a professional and financial interest in their success to complement her personal commitment to their subject.

While the AFL repertoire was dominated by the comic and the celebratory pageant, and is inevitably largely focused on the specific issue of the vote, the first Pioneer Players' productions address wider areas of feminism. Chris St John's *The First Actress* describes the life of Margaret Hughes, the first woman to perform on the Restoration stage. Faced with opposition to her profession, she is prevented from losing heart by the vision of those women who will follow her into the theatre.

Margaret Wynne Nevinson's *In the Workhouse* addresses legal inequalities between married men and women. Cicely Hamilton's

Jack and Jill and a Friend confronts economic inequalities through the envy, prejudice and sense of inadequacy felt by Jack. Jack is a struggling author who plans to marry Jill on the proceeds of the literary prize for which he has been short-listed. Jack objects when Jill wins the award and suggests they marry on *her* winnings.

The Pioneer Players went on in 1911-12 to produce plays on a growing range of subjects. The trial of Caroline of Brunswick for adultery is examined in Housman's *Pains and Penalties*. Disarmament and the abuses of capitalism were explored in *The Coronation* (St John and Thursby) which was banned from public production by the Lord Chamberlain. Vegetarianism and hygiene were the subjects of Hobson's *A Modern Crusader*. These were the beginnings of a developing dramatic enquiry which would lead to an increasing emphasis on aesthetic experiment allied to political exploration. Productions of plays like Antonia Williams' *The Street* (Little Theatre, 20 Nov 1913) describing the struggle of a young woman forced into prostitution, dramatised through highly symbolic lighting effects, connect to a post-war repertoire encompassing Glaspell, Claudel, Heijermans, Chekhov and others.

How to use this book

This book is designed for both study and production. It makes a range of plays from the suffragette period available in an accessible edition together with an introduction to each play and a biography of the author. From the forceful drama of *Votes for Women* to the ebullient satire of *How the Vote Was Won,* via the formally innovative *At the Gates,* all the plays are highly stage-worthy and were produced in theatres of varying sizes at the time; most have been re-tested in production by subsequent generations. Each is published with a brief introduction and biographical information about its author.

This book also includes an extensive Chronology which details for the first time just how extensive the use of drama was within the suffrage movement. It draws together information compiled from events' listings and accounts of branch meetings in *The Vote* and *Votes for Women* together with details gleaned from accounts of Suffrage Fairs and Exhibitions, and adverts for large and small-scale events all over the country. There is still much work to extend and develop this Chronology with investigations into the activities of local branches, reports of individual women in the local press and archives, and an exploration of women's theatre initiatives like The Propaganda Players or the Indian Tableaux presented by Indian women in 1912. The stories of women like Kate Harvey, Winifred St Clair and Helen MacLachlan remain to be told.

This anthology is published in association with the launch of an innovative arts and education project celebrating the centenary of the suffragette movement and highlighting the work of the Actresses' Franchise League. As part of this project, an educational website has also been established encouraging production of the original plays and the creation of new plays addressing issues related to the suffragettes. It is a context where research can be shared, and where information and workshop exercises aimed at a range of different ages can be made available. Users of this book are encouraged to participate in sharing and extending their explorations and research of the suffragettes in their local communities via the website **www.suffragettes.org.uk,** building a resource that celebrates and explores the crucial work of these pioneering women.

---

[i] With the exception of *The Apple* which is in Pfisterer (ed. 1999) The plays are available in a scholarly reprint edited by Cockin, Norquay and Park. *Women's Suffrage Literature* (vols 1 and 3) but it is very expensive and not readily accessible.

[ii] *In the Workhouse* is also in Cockin, Norquay and Park, but has not previously been reprinted in an accessible edition.

[iii] Beyond the suffrage campaign, many plays by women were written and produced at this time around issues of women's work and education, marriage, war and peace, the arts, domestic violence, as explored in the forthcoming anthology *Staging the New Woman* ed. Susan Croft and Sherry Engle.

[iv] It has never been conclusively proved that Davis meant to kill herself for the Cause: evidence like her purchase of a return rail ticket to Epsom that day has been read to suggest the contrary.

[v] For detailed discussion of Bensusan, see Susan Bradley-Smith's essay in Schafer and Bradley Smith ed., 2003 and also her research on Bensusan in her doctoral thesis (under the name Susan Pfisterer) Australian Suffrage Theatre (1996)

[vi] WWSL members included Beatrice Harraden, Violet Hunt, Ethel Hill, Vera Hill, Beryl Margetson, Mrs Israel Zangwll and Evelyn Sharp, President: Elizabeth Robins.

[vii] *Votes for Women*, 4 June 1909, p752

[viii] See Chronology for publication and production details of plays and playwrights mentioned here.

[ix] See detailed coverage of the Exhibition in *Votes for Women*.

[x] The subject of Christabel Pankhurst's 1913 book *The Great Scourge and How to End it*.

[xi] See for example *Merrier England: a Pageant of Progress* by Kate Murray, London: Co-partnership Publishers, 1912 and for examples of imperial pageants in Canada and Australia see Croft, 2003 or the work of Sophie Lomas and Frank Lascelles who organised the Pageant of London at the Festival of London and Imperial Exhibition 1911. Women like Edy Craig, Gwen Lally, Ethel Atkinson and Mary Kelly were central as writers and directors to the growth of pageants in the inter-war years.

[xii] According to her entry in Crawford. I am grateful to Jill Liddington for bringing this to my notice.

[xiii] *A Little Book of Twentieth Century Duologues for Drawing Room and Platform* (1911) and *The Reciter's Treasury of Prose and Drama* (1912) ed. Ernest Pertwee, and *A Second Little Book of Twentieth Century Duologues for Drawing Room and Platform* ed. Mrs Ernest (Emily) Pertwee, (1913) All, London: Routledge and Sons Ltd.

[xiv] In *Votes for Women* 16 April 1909

[xv] See *The Actor's Right to Act* by Joseph Macleod, London: Lawrence and Wishart, 1981 for general history of the Association

[xvi] And are therefore not included in the Chronology

[xvii] See entry in Croft, 2001. Stern's play at this matinee was 'For One Night Only' about a touring theatre company.

[xviii] *The Blind God* by Olive Lethbridge and Gerald Fitzgerald.

[xix] Quoted in Pfisterer, p244

[xx] AFL Annual Report 1912-1913, p7

[xxi] Quoted in Hirshfield, 1995, p125

[xxii] *Votes for Women*, 23 May 1913, p498

[xxiii] *The Suffragette*, 12 Dec 1913, quoted in Holledge, p 96

[xxiv] See Pfisterer p 203. The play was also objected to by the Lord Chamberlain: Nicholson quotes the Reader's Report describing it as 'a glorified penny-dreadful' and 'an earnest but wildly-directed attack upon the methods and possibilities of the White Slave Traffic ... not less painful than well-meaning, especially in its highly imaginative sketch of the lurid proceedings in a procuress's prison'.

[xxv] Quoted in Cockin

Votes for Women

Votes for Women

The play presents a brittle, upper-class society of respectable, devoted wives living sheltered and supportive lives with husbands who are committed to busy careers. For both groups, these are only partial truths. While the women are gently mocked for their superficiality, they are actually organising to create a charitable hostel for homeless women whereas the men, who seem morally upright, have hidden pasts. The events of the play are set at that moment when the suffragettes have turned to militant action and are being condemned as having totally discredited their cause.

The play juxtaposes two women: Jean Dunbarton, a young idealistic heiress, engaged to ambitious MP Geoffrey Stonor, and Vida Levering, the feminist with a hidden past. The influence is evident, in the structure of the piece, of both conventional sentimental melodrama: (cf. Mary Elizabeth Braddon's *Lady Audley's Secret*, Wilde's *A Woman of No Importance* and Ibsen's *A Doll's House)* where a protected woman has to confront the realities of society and human behaviour.

Jean's eyes are opened, first to the humanity and integrity of the suffragettes, and then to the power of their arguments, as she realises there are double standards regarding the behaviour of women and men. The final awakening is that her fiance Stonor was the father of Vida Levering's unborn child. Where a conventional plot would demand that he make personal reparation, Vida rejects this and the old pretence, 'that to marry *at all costs* is every woman's dearest ambition till the grave closes over her'. Instead she demands that the reparation he make be political — giving his support to the suffrage cause.

Robins challenges the stereotype of the dowdy, unattractive feminist and the conventional demand that the fallen woman be made to suffer for her sins. Robins creates a complex, intelligent and outspoken character, contributing to her wish to create more challenging roles for actresses. The piece is also remarkable in its command of the large open-air crowd scene, (the rally of Act 2) which Robins conducts with theatrical skill, making it the context of the revelation of Stonor's past with Levering, and the collision of public and private spheres to which women were still supposed to confine themselves.

See also: Gates, 1994; Robins, 1940; Stowell; intro. to Gardner and Fitzsimmons; intro. to Kelly, John, 1995; www.jsu.edu/depart/english/robins

Votes for Women

Elizabeth Robins, 1907

CHARACTERS

Lord John Wynnstay
Lady John Wynnstay, His Wife
Mrs Heriot, Sister of Lady John
Miss Jean Dunbarton*, Niece to Lady John and Mrs Heriot
The Hon. Geoffrey Stonor, Unionist M. P. Affianced To Jean
    Dunbarton
Mr St John Greatorex, Liberal M. P.
The Hon. Richard Farnborough
Mr Freddy Tunbridge
Mrs Freddy Tunbridge
Mr Allen Trent
Miss Ernestine Blunt, A Suffragette
Mr Pilcher, A Working Man
A Working Woman
Miss Vida Levering
Persons in the Crowd
Servants in the two houses

Act One Wynnstay House in Hertfordshire
Act Two Trafalgar Square, London
Act Three Eaton Square, London

The entire action of the play takes place between Sunday noon and six o'clock in the evening of the same day.

---

*Reviews and cast list name her a Miss Beatrice Dunbarton (see Kelly for edition based on prompt script)
Originally published Mills and Boon Ltd.

ACT ONE
Scene One

Hall of Wynnstay House.
Twelve o'clock, Sunday morning, end of June. With the rising of the
curtain, enter the Butler. As he is going with majestic port to answer
the door, enter briskly from the garden, by the lower French window,
Lady John Wynnstay, flushed, and flapping a garden hat to fan
herself. She is a pink-cheeked woman of fifty-four, who has plainly
been a beauty, keeps her complexion, but is 'gone to fat.'

LADY JOHN   Has Miss Levering come down yet?

BUTLER *(pausing)* I haven't seen her, m'lady.

LADY JOHN *(almost sharply as Butler turns left)* I won't have her
disturbed if she's resting. *(to herself as she goes to the writing
table)* She certainly needs it.

BUTLER   Yes, m'lady.

LADY JOHN *(sitting at the writing table, her back to the front door)*
But I want her to know the moment she comes down that the new
plans have arrived by the morning post.

BUTLER *(pausing nearly at the door)* Plans, m'la –

LADY JOHN   She'll understand. There they are. *(glancing at
the clock)* It's very important she should have them in time to look
over before she goes – *(Butler opens the door left. Over her
shoulder)* Is that Miss Levering?

BUTLER   No, m'lady. Mr Farnborough.

Exit Butler.
Enter the Hon. R. Farnborough. He is twenty-six; reddish hair, high-
coloured, sanguine, self-important.

FARNBOROUGH   I'm afraid I'm scandalously early. It didn't take
me nearly as long to motor over as Lord John said.

LADY JOHN *(shaking hands)* I'm afraid my husband is no authority
on motoring – and he's not home yet from church.

FARNBOROUGH   It's the greatest luck finding *you*. I thought
Miss Levering was the only person under this roof who was ever
allowed to observe Sunday as a real Day of Rest.

LADY JOHN   If you've come to see Miss Levering –

FARNBOROUGH   Is she here? I give you my word I didn't know it.

LADY JOHN *(unconvinced)* Oh?

FARNBOROUGH   Does she come every weekend?

LADY JOHN   Whenever we can get her to. But we've only known her a couple of months.

FARNBOROUGH   And I have only known her three weeks! Lady John, I've come to ask you to help me.

LADY JOHN *(quickly)* With Miss Levering? I can't do it!

FARNBOROUGH   No, no – all that's no good. She only laughs.

LADY JOHN *(relieved)* Ah! – she looks upon you as a boy.

FARNBOROUGH *(firing up)* Such rot! What do you think she said to me in London the other day?

LADY JOHN   That she was four years older than you?

FARNBOROUGH   Oh, I knew that. No. She said she knew she was all the charming things I'd been saying, but there was only one way to prove it – and that was to marry someone young enough to be her son. She'd noticed that was what the *most* attractive women did – and she named names.

LADY JOHN *(laughing) You* were too old!

FARNBOROUGH *(nods)* Her future husband, she said, was probably just entering Eton.

LADY JOHN   Just like her!

FARNBOROUGH *(waving the subject away)* No. I wanted to see you about the Secretaryship.

LADY JOHN   You didn't get it, then?

FARNBOROUGH   No. It's the grief of my life.

LADY JOHN   Oh, if you don't get one you'll get another.

FARNBOROUGH   But there is only one.

LADY JOHN   Only one vacancy?

FARNBOROUGH   Only one man I'd give my ears to work for.

LADY JOHN *(smiling)* I remember.

FARNBOROUGH *(quickly)* Do I always talk about Stonor? Well, it's a habit people have got into.

LADY JOHN   I forget, do you know Mr Stonor personally, or *(smiling)* are you just dazzled from afar?

FARNBOROUGH   Oh, I know him. The trouble is he doesn't know me. If he did he'd realise he can't be sure of winning his election without my valuable services.

LADY JOHN   Geoffrey Stonor's re-election is always a foregone conclusion.

FARNBOROUGH   That the great man shares that opinion is precisely his weak point. *(smiling)* His only one.

LADY JOHN   You think because the Liberals swept the country the last time –

FARNBOROUGH   How can we be sure any Conservative seat is safe after – *(as Lady John smiles and turns to her papers)* Forgive me, I know you're not interested in politics *qua* politics. But this concerns Geoffrey Stonor.

LADY JOHN   And you count on my being interested in him like all the rest of my sex.

FARNBOROUGH *(leans forward)* Lady John, I've heard the news.

LADY JOHN   What news?

FARNBOROUGH   That your little niece – the Scotch heiress – is going to become Mrs Geoffrey Stonor.

LADY JOHN   Who told you that?

FARNBOROUGH   Please don't mind my knowing.

LADY JOHN *(visibly perturbed)* She had set her heart upon having a few days with just her family in the secret, before the flood of congratulations breaks loose.

FARNBOROUGH   Oh, that's all right. I always hear things before other people.

LADY JOHN   Well, I must ask you to be good enough to be very circumspect. I wouldn't have my niece think that I –

FARNBOROUGH   Oh, of course not.

LADY JOHN   She will be here in an hour.

FARNBOROUGH *(jumping up delighted)* What? Today? The future Mrs Stonor!

LADY JOHN *(harassed)* Yes. Unfortunately we had one or two people already asked for the weekend –

FARNBOROUGH   And I go and invite myself to luncheon! Lady John, you can buy me off. I'll promise to remove myself in five minutes if you'll –

LADY JOHN   No, the penalty is you shall stay and keep the others amused between church and luncheon, and so leave me free. *(takes up the plan)* Only *remember* –

FARNBOROUGH   Wild horses won't get a hint out of me! I only mentioned it to you because – since we've come back to live in this part of the world you've been so awfully kind – I thought, I hoped maybe you – you'd put in a word for me.

LADY JOHN   With – ?

FARNBOROUGH   With your nephew that is to be. Though I'm *not* the slavish satellite people make out, you can't doubt –

LADY JOHN   Oh, I don't doubt. But you know Mr Stonor inspires a similar enthusiasm in a good many young –

FARNBOROUGH   They haven't studied the situation as I have. They don't know what's at stake. They don't go to that hole Dutfield as I did just to hear his Friday speech.

LADY JOHN   Ah! But you were rewarded. Jean – my niece – wrote me it was 'glorious.'

FARNBOROUGH *(judicially)* Well, you know, *I* was disappointed. He's too content just to criticise, just to make his delicate pungent fun of the men who are *grappling* – very inadequately, of course – still grappling with the big questions. There's a carrying power *(gets up and faces an imaginary audience)* – some of Stonor's friends ought to point it out – there's a driving power in the poorest constructive policy that makes the most brilliant criticism look barren.

LADY JOHN *(with good-humoured malice)* Who told you that?

FARNBOROUGH   You think there's nothing in it because I say it. But now that he's coming into the family, Lord John or somebody really ought to point out – Stonor's overdoing his role of magnificent security.

LADY JOHN   I don't see even Lord John offering to instruct Mr Stonor.

FARNBOROUGH   Believe me, that's just Stonor's danger! Nobody saying a word, everybody hoping he's on the point of adopting some definite line, something strong and original that's going to fire the public imagination and bring the Tories back into power.

LADY JOHN   So he will.

FARNBOROUGH *(hotly)* Not if he disappoints meetings – goes calmly up to town – and leaves the field to the Liberals.

LADY JOHN   When did he do anything like that?

FARNBOROUGH   Yesterday *(with a harassed air)*. And now that he's got this other preoccupation –

LADY JOHN   You mean –
FARNBOROUGH   Yes, your niece – that spoilt child of Fortune.
  Of course! *(stopping suddenly)* She kept him from the meeting last
  night. Well! *(sits down)* If that's the effect she's going to have it's
  pretty serious!
LADY JOHN *(smiling) You* are!
FARNBOROUGH   I can assure you the election agent's more so.
  He's simply tearing his hair.
LADY JOHN *(more gravely and coming nearer)* How do you know?
FARNBOROUGH   He told me so himself – yesterday. I scraped
  acquaintance with the agent just to see if – if –
LADY JOHN   It's not only here that you manoeuvre for that
  Secretaryship!
FARNBOROUGH *(confidentially)* You can never tell when your
  chance might come! That election chap's promised to keep me
  posted..

The door flies open and Jean Dunbarton rushes in.

JEAN   Aunt Ellen – here I –
LADY JOHN *(astonished)* My dear child! *(they embrace)*

*Enter Lord John from the garden – a benevolent, silver-haired despot
of sixty-two.*

LORD JOHN   I thought that was you running up the avenue.
JEAN *(greets her uncle warmly)*
LADY JOHN   How did you get here so early?
JEAN   I knew you'd be surprised – wasn't it clever of
  me to manage it? I don't deserve all the credit.
LADY JOHN   But there isn't any train between –
JEAN   Yes, wait till I tell you.
LADY JOHN   You walked in the broiling sun – ?
JEAN   No, no.
LADY JOHN   You must be dead. Why didn't you telegraph? I
  ordered the carriage to meet the 1.10. Didn't you say the 1.10? Yes,
  I'm sure you did – here's your letter.
LORD JOHN *(has shaken hands with Farnborough and speaks
  through the torrent)* Now they'll tell each other for ten minutes that
  she's an hour earlier than we expected.

Lord John leads Farnborough towards the garden.

FARNBOROUGH   The Freddy Tunbridges said *they* were coming to you this week.

LORD JOHN   Yes, they're dawdling through the park with the Church Brigade.

FARNBOROUGH   Oh! *(with a glance back at Jean)* I'll go and meet them.

Exit Farnborough.

LORD JOHN *(as he turns back)* That discreet young man will get on.

LADY JOHN *(to Jean)* But *how* did you get here?

JEAN *(breathless)* He motored me down.

LADY JOHN   Geoffrey Stonor? *(Jean nods)* Why, where is he, then?

JEAN   He dropped me at the end of the avenue and went on to see a supporter about something.

LORD JOHN   You let him go off like that without –

LADY JOHN *(taking Jean's two hands)* Just tell me, my child, is it all right?

JEAN   My engagement? *(radiantly)* Yes, absolutely.

LADY JOHN   Geoffrey Stonor isn't going to be – a little too old for you?

JEAN *(laughing)* Bless me, am I such a chicken?

LADY JOHN   Twenty-four used not to be so young – but it's become so.

JEAN   Yes, we don't grow up so quick. *(gaily)* But on the other hand we *stay* up longer.

LORD JOHN   You've got what's vulgarly called 'looks', my dear, and that will help to *keep* you up!

JEAN *(smiling)* I know what Uncle John's thinking. But I'm not the only girl who's been 'left' what's vulgarly called 'money.'

LORD JOHN   You're the only one of our immediate circle who's been left so beautifully much.

JEAN   Ah, but remember Geoffrey could – everybody *knows* he could have married anyone in England.

LADY JOHN *(faintly ironic)* I'm afraid everybody does know it – not excepting Mr Stonor.

LORD JOHN   Well, how spoilt is the great man?

JEAN Not the least little bit in the world. You'll see! He so wants to know my best-loved relations better. *(another embrace)* An orphan has so few belongings, she has to make the most of them.

LORD JOHN *(smiling)* Let us hope he'll approve of us on more intimate acquaintance.

JEAN *(firmly)* He will. He's an angel. Why, he gets on with my grandfather!

LADY JOHN *Does* he? *(teasing)* You mean to say Mr Geoffery Stonor isn't just a tiny bit – 'superior' about Dissenters.

JEAN *(stoutly)* Not half as much as Uncle John and all the rest of you! My grandfather's been ill again, you know, and rather difficult – bless him! *(radiantly)* But Geoffrey – *(clasps her hands)*

LADY JOHN He must have powers of persuasion! – to get that old Covenanter to let you come in an abhorred motor car – on Sunday, too!

JEAN *(half whispering)* Grandfather didn't know!

LADY JOHN Didn't know?

JEAN I honestly meant to come by train. Geoffrey met me on my way to the station. We had the most glorious run. Oh, Aunt Ellen, we're so happy! *(embracing her)* I've so looked forward to having you to myself the whole day just to talk to you about –

LORD JOHN *(turning away with affected displeasure)* Oh, very well –

JEAN *(catches him affectionately by the arm)* You'd find it dreffly dull to hear me talk about Geoffrey the whole blessed day!

LADY JOHN Well, till luncheon, my dear, you mustn't mind if I – *(to Lord John as she goes to the writing table)* Miss Levering wasn't only tired last night, she was ill.

LORD JOHN I thought she looked very white.

JEAN Who is Miss – You don't mean to say there are other people?

LADY JOHN One or two. Your uncle's responsible for asking that old cynic St. John Greatorex, and I –

JEAN *(gravely)* Mr. Greatorex – he's a Radical, isn't he?

LORD JOHN *(laughing)* Jean! Beginning to 'think in parties'?

LADY JOHN It's very natural now that she should –

JEAN I only meant it was odd he should be here. Naturally at my grandfather's —

LORD JOHN   It's all right, my child. Of course we expect now that you'll begin to think like Geoffrey Stonor, and to feel like Geoffrey Stonor, and to talk like Geoffrey Stonor. And quite proper too.

JEAN *(smiling)* Well, if I do think with my husband and feel with him – as, of course, I shall – it will surprise me if I ever find myself talking a tenth as well – *(following her uncle to the French window)* You should have heard him at Dutfield. *(stopping short, delighted)* Oh! The Freddy Tunbridges. What? Not Aunt Lydia! Oh – h! *(looking back reproachfully at Lady John, who makes a discreet motion 'I couldn't help it')*

Enter the Tunbridges. Mr Freddy: of no profession and of independent means, well-groomed, pleasant-looking, of few words. A 'nice man' who likes 'nice women', and has married one of them. Mrs Freddy is thirty. An attractive figure, delicate face, intelligent grey eyes, over-sensitive mouth, and naturally curling dust-coloured hair.

MRS FREDDY   What a delightful surprise!
JEAN *(shaking hands warmly)* I'm so glad. How d'ye do, Mr Freddy?

Enter Lady John's sister, Mrs Heriot – smart, pompous, fifty – followed by Farnborough.

MRS HERIOT   My dear Jean! My darling child!
JEAN   How do you do, aunt?
MRS HERIOT *(sotto voce)* I wasn't surprised. I always prophesied –
JEAN   Sh! *Please!*
FARNBOROUGH   We haven't met since you were in short skirts. I'm Dick Farnborough.
JEAN   Oh, I remember. *(They shake hands)*
MRS FREDDY *(looking round)* Not down yet – the Elusive One?
JEAN   Who is the Elusive One?
MRS FREDDY   Lady John's new friend.
LORD JOHN *(to Jean)* Oh, I forgot you hadn't seen Miss Levering; such a nice creature! *(to Mrs Freddy)* – don't you think?
MRS FREDDY   Of course I do. You're lucky to get her to come so often. She won't go to other people.
LADY JOHN   She knows she can rest here.
MRS FREDDY *(who has joined Lady John near the writing table)*

What does she do to tire her?

LADY JOHN   She's been helping my sister and me with a scheme of ours.

MRS HERIOT   She certainly knows how to inveigle money out of the men.

LADY JOHN   It would sound less equivocal, Lydia, if you added that the money is to build baths in our Shelter for Homeless Women.

MRS FREDDY   Homeless women?

LADY JOHN   Yes, in the most insanitary part of Soho.

MRS FREDDY   Oh – a – really.

FARNBOROUGH   It doesn't sound quite in Miss Levering's line!

LADY JOHN   My dear boy, you know as little about what's in a woman's line as most men.

MR FREDDY (*laughing*) Oh, I say!

LORD JOHN (*indulgently to Mr Freddy and Farnborough*) Philanthropy in a woman like Miss Levering is a form of restlessness. But she's a *nice* creature; all she needs is to get some 'nice' fella to marry her.

MRS FREDDY (*laughing as she hangs on her husband's arm*) Yes, a woman needs a balance wheel – if only to keep her from flying back to town on a hot day like this.

LORD JOHN   Who's proposing anything so –

MRS FREDDY   The Elusive One.

LORD JOHN   Not Miss—

MRS FREDDY   Yes, before luncheon!

Exit Farnborough to the garden

LADY JOHN   She must be in London by this afternoon, she says.

LORD JOHN   What for in the name of –

LADY JOHN   Well, *that* I didn't ask her. But (*consults her watch*) I think I'll just go up and see if she's changed her plans ...

Exit Lady John Wynnstay.

LORD JOHN   Oh, she must be *made* to. Such a nice creature! All she needs –

Voices outside. Enter fussily, talking and gesticulating, St John

Greatorex, followed by Miss Levering and Farnborough. Greatorex is sixty, wealthy, a county magnate, and Liberal MP. He is square, thick-set, square-bearded. His shining bald pate has two strands of coal-black hair trained across his crown from left ear to right and securely pasted there. He has small, twinkling eyes and a reputation for telling good stories after dinner when ladies have left the room. He is carrying a little book for Miss Levering. She (parasol over shoulder), is an attractive, essentially feminine, and rather 'smart' woman of thirty-two, with a somewhat foreign grace; the kind of whom men and women alike say, 'What's her story? Why doesn't she marry?'

GREATOREX   I protest! Good Lord! What are the women of this country coming to? I *protest* against Miss Levering being carried off to discuss anything so revolting. Bless my soul! what can a woman like you *know* about it?

MISS LEVERING *(smiling)* Little enough. Good morning.

GREATOREX *(relieved)* I should think so indeed!

LORD JOHN *(aside)* You aren't serious about going –

GREATOREX *(waggishly breaking in)* We were so happy out there in the summer-house, weren't we?

MISS LEVERING   Ideally.

GREATOREX   And to be haled out to talk about Public *Sanitation* forsooth! *(hurries after Miss Levering as she advances to speak to the Freddys and company)* Why, God bless my soul, do you realise that's *drains*?

MISS LEVERING   I'm dreadfully afraid it is!
(Holds out her hand for the small book Greatorex is carrying. Greatorex returns Miss Levering's book open; he has been keeping the place with his finger. She opens it and shuts her handkerchief in.)

GREATOREX   And we in the act of discussing Italian literature! Perhaps you'll tell me that isn't a more savoury topic for a lady.

MISS LEVERING   But for the tramp population less conducive to savouriness, don't you think, than baths?

GREATOREX   No, I can't understand this morbid interest in vagrants. *You're* much too – leave it to the others.

JEAN   What others?

GREATOREX *(with smiling impertinence)* Oh, the sort of woman who smells of india rubber. The typical English spinster. *(to Miss Levering) You* know – Italy's full of her. She never goes anywhere without a mackintosh and a collapsible bathrubber. When you look at her, it's borne in upon you that she doesn't only smell of rubber. *She's* rubber too.

LORD JOHN *(laughing)* This is my niece, Miss Jean Dunbarton, Miss Levering.

JEAN   How do you do? *(they shake hands)*

GREATOREX *(to Jean)* I'm sure *you* agree with me.

JEAN   About Miss Levering being too –

GREATOREX   For that sort of thing – *much* too –

MISS LEVERING   What a pity you've exhausted the more eloquent adjectives.

GREATOREX   But I haven't!

MISS LEVERING   Well, you can't say to me as you did to Mrs Freddy: 'You're too young and too happily married – and too – *(glances round smiling at Mrs Freddy, who, oblivious, is laughing and talking to her husband and Mrs Heriot)*

JEAN   For what was Mrs Freddy too happily married and all the rest?

MISS LEVERING *(lightly)* Mr Greatorex was repudiating the horrid rumour that Mrs Freddy had been speaking in public about Women's Trade Unions – wasn't that what you said, Mrs Heriot?

LORD JOHN *(chuckling)* Yes, it isn't made up as carefully as your aunt's parties usually are. Here we've got Greatorex *(takes his arm)* who hates political women, and we've got in that mild and inoffensive looking little lady – *(Motion over his shoulder towards Mrs Freddy)*

GREATOREX *(shrinking downstage in comic terror)* You don't mean she's *really* –

JEAN *(simultaneously and gaily rising)* Oh, and you've got me!

LORD JOHN *(with genial affection)* My dear child, he doesn't hate the charming wives and sweethearts who help to win seats. *(Jean makes her uncle a discreet little signal of warning)*

MISS LEVERING   Mr Greatorex objects only to the unsexed creatures who – a –

LORD JOHN *(hastily to cover up his slip)* Yes, yes, who want to act independently of men.

MISS LEVERING   Vote, and do silly things of that sort.

LORD JOHN *(with enthusiasm)* Exactly.

MRS HERIOT   It will be a long time before we hear any more of *that* nonsense.

JEAN   You mean that rowdy scene in the House of Commons?

MRS HERIOT   Yes, no decent woman will be able to say 'Suffrage' without blushing for another generation, thank Heaven!

MISS LEVERING *(smiling)* Oh? I understood that so little I almost imagined people were more stirred up about it than they'd ever been before.

GREATOREX *(with a quizzical affectation of gallantry)* Not people like you.

MISS LEVERING *(teasingly)* How do you know?

GREATOREX *(with a start)* God bless my soul!

LORD JOHN   She's saying that only to get a rise out of you.

GREATOREX   Ah, yes, your frocks aren't serious enough.

MISS LEVERING   I'm told it's an exploded notion that the Suffrage women are all dowdy and dull.

GREATOREX   Don't you believe it!

MISS LEVERING   Well, of course we know you've been an authority on the subject for – let's see, how many years is it you've kept the House in roars whenever Woman's Rights are mentioned?

GREATOREX *(flattered but not entirely comfortable)* Oh, as long as I've known anything about politics there have been a few discontented old maids and hungry widows –

MISS LEVERING   'A few!' That's really rather forbearing of you, Mr Greatorex. I'm afraid the number of the discontented and the hungry was 96,000 – among the mill operatives alone. *(hastily)* At least the papers said so, didn't they?

GREATOREX   Oh, don't ask me; that kind of woman doesn't interest me, I'm afraid. Only I am able to point out to the people who lose their heads and seem inclined to treat the phenomenon seriously that there's absolutely nothing new in it. There have been women for the last forty years who haven't had anything more pressing to do than petition Parliament.

MISS LEVERING *(reflectively)* And that's as far as they've got.

LORD JOHN (*turning on his heel*) It's as far as they'll ever get. (*Meets the group coming down.*)

MISS LEVERING (*chaffing Greatorex*) Let me see, wasn't a deputation sent to you not long ago? (*sits*)

GREATOREX   H'm! (*irritably*) Yes, yes.

MISS LEVERING (*as though she has just recalled the circumstances*) Oh, yes, I remember. I thought at the time, in my modest way, it was nothing short of heroic of them to go asking audience of their arch opponent.

GREATOREX (*stoutly*) It didn't come off.

MISS LEVERING (*innocently*) Oh! I thought they insisted on bearding the lion in his den.

GREATOREX   Of course I wasn't going to be bothered with a lot of –

MISS LEVERING   You don't mean you refused to go out and face them!

GREATOREX (*with a comic look of terror*) I wouldn't have done it for worlds. But a friend of mine went and had a look at 'em.

MISS LEVERING (*smiling*) Well, did he get back alive?

GREATOREX   Yes, but he advised me not to go. 'You're quite right,' he said. 'Don't you think of bothering,' he said. 'I've looked over the lot,' he said, 'and there isn't a weekender among 'em.'

JEAN (*gaily precipitates herself into the conversation*) You remember Mrs Freddy's friend who came to tea here in the winter? (*to Greatorex*) He was a member of Parliament too – quite a little young one – he said women would never be respected till they had the vote! (*Greatorex snorts, the other men smile and all the women except Mrs Heriot*)

MRS HERIOT (*sniffing*) I remember telling him that he was too young to know what he was talking about.

LORD JOHN   Yes, I'm afraid you all sat on the poor gentleman.

LADY JOHN (*entering*) Oh, *there* you are! (*Greets Miss Levering*)

JEAN   It was such fun. He was flat as a pancake when we'd done with him. Aunt Ellen told him with her most distinguished air she didn't want to be 'respected.'

MRS FREDDY (*with a laugh of remonstrance*) My *dear* Lady John!

FARNBOROUGH   Quite right! Awful idea to think you're *respected!*

MISS LEVERING (*smiling*) Simply revolting.

LADY JOHN (*at writing-table*) Now, you frivolous people, go away. We've only got a few minutes to talk over the terms of the late Mr Soper's munificence before the carriage comes for Miss Levering –

MRS FREDDY (*to Farnborough*) Did you know she'd got that old horror to give Lady John £8,000 for her charity before he died?

MRS FREDDY   Who got him to?

LADY JOHN   Miss Levering. He wouldn't do it for me, but she brought him round.

MR FREDDY   Yes. Bah – ee Jove! I expect so.

MRS FREDDY (*turning enthusiastically to her husband*) Isn't she wonderful?

LORD JOHN (*aside*) Nice creature. All she needs is – .

Mr and Mrs Freddy and Farnborough stroll off to the garden. Lady John is on the far side of the writing-table. Mrs Heriot is at the top. Jean and Lord John on the left.

GREATOREX (*on divan centre, aside to Miss Levering*) Too 'wonderful' to waste your time on the wrong people.

MISS LEVERING   I shall waste less of my time after this.

GREATOREX   I'm relieved to hear it. I can't see you wheedling money for shelters and rot of that sort out of retired grocers.

MISS LEVERING   You see, you call it rot. We couldn't have got £8,000 out of *you*.

GREATOREX (*very low*) I'm not sure.

Miss Levering looks at him

GREATOREX   If I gave you that much – for your little projects – what would you give me?

MISS LEVERING (*speaking quietly*) Soper didn't ask that.

GREATOREX (*horrified*) Soper! I should think not!

LORD JOHN (*turning to Miss Levering*) Soper? You two still talking Soper? How flattered the old beggar'd be!

GREATOREX (*lower*) Did you hear what Mrs Heriot said about him? 'So kind, so munificent – so *vulgar*, poor soul, we couldn't know him in London – *but we shall meet him in heaven.*'

Greatorex and Lord John go off laughing.

LADY JOHN (*to Miss Levering*) Sit over there, my dear. (*indicating chair in front of the writing table*) You needn't stay, Jean. This won't interest you.

MISS LEVERING (*in the tone of one agreeing*) It's only an effort to meet the greatest evil in the world?

JEAN (*pausing as she's following the others*) What do you call the greatest evil in the world? (*looks between Mrs Heriot and Lady John*)

MISS LEVERING (*without emphasis*) The helplessness of women ... (*Jean stands still*)

LADY JOHN (*rising and putting her arm about the girl's shoulder*) Jean, darling, I know you can think of nothing but (*aside*) him – so just go and –

JEAN (*brightly*) Indeed, indeed, I can think of everything better than I ever did before. He has lit up everything for me – made everything vivider, more – more significant.

MISS LEVERING (*turning round*) Who has?

JEAN Oh, yes, I don't care about other things less but a thousand times more.

LADY JOHN You *are* in love.

MISS LEVERING Oh, that's it! (*smiling at Jean*) I congratulate you.

LADY JOHN (*returning to the outspread plan*) Well – *this,* you see, obviates the difficulty you raised.

MISS LEVERING Yes, quite.

MRS HERIOT But it's going to cost a great deal more.

MISS LEVERING It's worth it.

MRS HERIOT We'll have nothing left for the organ at St Pilgrim's.

LADY JOHN My dear Lydia, we're putting the organ aside.

MRS HERIOT (*with asperity*) We can't afford to 'put aside' the elevating effect of music.

LADY JOHN What we must make for, first, is the cheap and humanely conducted lodging-house.

MRS HERIOT There are several of those already, but poor St Pilgrim's –

MISS LEVERING There are none for the poorest women.

LADY JOHN No, even the excellent Soper was for

multiplying Rowton Houses. You can never get men to realise – you
can't always get women –

MISS LEVERING   It's the work least able to wait.

MRS HERIOT   I don't agree with you, and I happen to have
spent a great deal of my life in works of charity.

MISS LEVERING   Ah, then you'll be interested in the girl I saw
dying in a Tramp Ward a little while ago. *Glad* her cough was worse
– only she mustn't die before her father. Two reasons. Nobody but
her to keep the old man out of the workhouse – and 'father is so
proud'. If she died first, he would starve; worst of all he might hear
what had happened up in London to his girl.

MRS HERIOT   She didn't say, I suppose, how she happened to
fall so low.

MISS LEVERING   Yes, she had been in service. She lost the train
back one Sunday night and was too terrified of her employer to dare
ring him up after hours. The wrong person found her crying on the
platform.

MRS HERIOT   She should have gone to one of the Friendly
Societies.

MISS LEVERING   At eleven at night?

MRS HERIOT   And there are the Rescue Leagues. I myself
have been connected with one for twenty years –

MISS LEVERING (*reflectively*) 'Twenty years!' Always arriving 'after
the train's gone' – after the girl and the Wrong Person have got to
the journey's end ... (*Mrs Heriot's eyes flash.*)

JEAN   Where is she now?

LADY JOHN   Never mind.

MISS LEVERING   Two nights ago she was waiting at a street
corner in the rain.

MRS HERIOT   Near a public-house, I suppose.

MISS LEVERING   Yes, a sort of 'public-house'. She was plainly
dying – she was told she shouldn't be out in the rain. 'I mustn't go in
yet,' she said. '*This* is what he gave me,' and she began to cry. In her
hand were two pennies silvered over to look like half-crowns.

MRS HERIOT   I don't believe that story. It's just the sort of
thing some sensation-monger trumps up – now, who tells you such –

MISS LEVERING   Several credible people. I didn't believe them
till –

JEAN   Till – ?

MISS LEVERING   Till last week I saw for myself.

LADY JOHN   *Saw?* Where?

MISS LEVERING   In a low lodging-house not a hundred yards from the church you want a new organ for.

MRS HERIOT   How did you happen to be there?

MISS LEVERING   I was on a pilgrimage.

JEAN   A pilgrimage?

MISS LEVERING   Into the Underworld.

LADY JOHN   *You* went?

JEAN   How *could* you?

MISS LEVERING   I put on an old gown and a tawdry hat – *(turns to Lady John)* You'll never know how many things are hidden from a woman in good clothes. The bold, free look of a man at a woman he believes to be destitute – you must *feel* that look on you before you can understand – a good half of history.

MRS HERIOT *(rises)* Jean!

JEAN   But where did you go dressed like that?

MISS LEVERING   Down among the homeless women – on a wet night looking for shelter.

LADY JOHN *(hastily)* No wonder you've been ill.

JEAN *(under her breath)* And it's like that?

MISS LEVERING   No.

JEAN   No?

MISS LEVERING   It's so much worse I dare not tell about it – even if you weren't here I couldn't.

MRS HERIOT *(to Jean)* You needn't suppose, darling, that those wretched creatures feel it as we would.

MISS LEVERING   The girls who need shelter and work aren't all serving-maids.

MRS HERIOT *(with an involuntary flash)* We know that all the women who – *make mistakes* aren't.

MISS LEVERING *(steadily)* That is why every woman ought to take an interest in this – every girl too.

JEAN   Yes – oh, yes!

LADY JOHN *(simultaneously)* No. This is a matter for us older …

MRS HERIOT *(with an air of sly challenge)* Or for a person who has some special knowledge. *(significantly)* We can't pretend to have access to such sources of information as Miss Levering.

MISS LEVERING *(meeting Mrs Heriot's eye steadily)* Yes, for I can give you access. As you seem to think, I have some first-hand knowledge about homeless girls.

LADY JOHN *(cheerfully turning it aside)* Well, my dear, it will all come in convenient. *(tapping the plan)*

MISS LEVERING   It once happened to me to take offence at an ugly thing that was going on under my father's roof. Oh, *years* ago! I was an impulsive girl. I turned my back on my father's house –

LADY JOHN *(for Jean's benefit)* That was ill-advised.

MRS HERIOT   Of course, if a girl does that –

MISS LEVERING   That was what all my relations said *(with a glance at Jean)* and I couldn't explain.

JEAN   Not to your mother?

MISS LEVERING   She was dead. I went to London to a small hotel and tried to find employment. I wandered about all day and every day from agency to agency. I was supposed to be educated. I'd been brought up partly in Paris; I could play several instruments, and sing little songs in four different tongues. *(slight pause)*

JEAN   Did nobody want you to teach French or sing the little songs?

MISS LEVERING   The heads of schools thought me too young. There were people ready to listen to my singing, but the terms – they were too hard. Soon my money was gone. I began to pawn my trinkets. *They* went.

JEAN   And still no work?

MISS LEVERING   No but by that time I had some real education – an unpaid hotel bill, and not a shilling in the world. *(slight pause)* Some girls think it hardship to have to earn their living. The horror is not to be allowed to –

JEAN *(bending forward)* What happened?

LADY JOHN *(rises)* My dear *(to Miss Levering)* have your things been sent down? Are you quite ready?

MISS LEVERING   Yes, all but my hat.

JEAN   Well?

MISS LEVERING   Well, by chance I met a friend of my family.

JEAN   That was lucky.

MISS LEVERING   I thought so. He was nearly ten years older than I. He said he wanted to help me. *(pause)*

JEAN   And didn't he? *(Lady John lays her hand on Miss Levering's shoulder)*

MISS LEVERING   Perhaps, after all he did. *(with sudden change of tone)* Why do I waste time over myself? I belonged to the little class of armed women. My body wasn't born weak, and my spirit wasn't broken by the *habit* of slavery. But, as Mrs Heriot was kind enough to hint, I do know something about the possible fate of homeless girls. I found there were pleasant parks, museums, free libraries in our great rich London – and not one single place where destitute women can be sure of work that isn't killing or food that isn't worse than prison fare. That's why women ought not to sleep o' nights till this Shelter stands spreading out wide arms.

JEAN   No, no –

MRS HERIOT *(gathering up her gloves, fan, prayer-book, etc)* Even when it's built – you'll see! Many of those creatures will prefer the life they lead. They *like* it.

MISS LEVERING   A woman told me – one of the sort that knows – told me many of them 'like it' so much that they are indifferent to the risk of being sent to prison. *'It gives them a rest,'* she said.

LADY JOHN   A rest! *(Miss Levering glances at the clock as she rises to go upstairs. Lady John and Mrs Heriot bend their heads over the plan, covertly talking.)*

JEAN *(intercepting Miss Levering)* I want to begin to understand something of – I'm horribly ignorant.

MISS LEVERING *(looks at her searchingly)* I'm a rather busy person –

JEAN *(interrupting)* I have quite a special reason for wanting not to be ignorant. *(impulsively)* I'll go to town tomorrow, if you'll come and lunch with me.

MISS LEVERING   Thank you – I *(catches Mrs Heriot's eye)* – I must go and put my hat on.

Exit upstairs.

MRS HERIOT *(aside)* How little she minds all these horrors!

LADY JOHN   They turn me cold. Ugh! *(rising, harassed)* I wonder if she's signed the visitors' book!

MRS HERIOT   For all her Shelter schemes, she's a hard woman.

JEAN   Miss Levering is?

MRS HERIOT   Oh, of course *you* won't think so. She has angled very adroitly for your sympathy.

JEAN   She doesn't look hard.

LADY JOHN *(glancing at Jean and taking alarm)* I'm not sure but what she does. Her mouth – always like this as if she were holding back something by main force!

MRS HERIOT *(half under her breath)* Well, so she is.

Exit Lady John into the lobby to look at the visitors' book.

JEAN   Why haven't I seen her before?

MRS HERIOT   Oh, she's lived abroad. *(debating with herself)* You don't know about her, I suppose?

JEAN   I don't know how Aunt Ellen came to know her.

MRS HERIOT   That was my doing. But I didn't bargain for her being introduced to you.

JEAN   She seems to go everywhere. And why shouldn't she?

MRS HERIOT *(quickly)* You mustn't ask her to Eaton Square.

JEAN   I have.

MRS HERIOT   Then you'll have to get out of it.

JEAN *(with a stubborn look)* I must have a reason. And a very good reason.

MRS HERIOT   Well, it's not a thing I should have preferred to tell you, but I know how difficult you are to guide ... so I suppose you'll have to know. *(lowering her voice)* It was ten or twelve years ago. I found her horribly ill in a lonely Welsh farmhouse. We had taken the Manor for that August. The farmer's wife was frightened, and begged me to go and see what I thought. I soon saw how it was – I thought she was dying.

JEAN   *Dying!* What was the –

MRS HERIOT   I got no more out of her than the farmer's wife did. She had had no letters. There had been no one to see her except a man down from London, a shady-looking doctor – nameless, of course. And then this result. The farmer and his wife, highly respectable people, were incensed. They were for turning the girl out.

JEAN   *Oh!* but –

MRS HERIOT   Yes. Pitiless some of these people are! I insisted they should treat the girl humanely, and we became friends ... that is, 'sort of'. In spite of all I did for her –

JEAN   What did you do?

MRS HERIOT   I – I've told you, and I lent her money. No small sum either.

JEAN   Has she never paid it back?

MRS HERIOT   Oh, yes, after a time. But I *always* kept her secret – as much as I knew of it.

JEAN   But you've been telling me!

MRS HERIOT   That was my duty – and I *never* had her full confidence.

JEAN   Wasn't it natural she – ?

MRS HERIOT   Well, all things considered, she might have wanted to tell me who was responsible.

JEAN   Oh! Aunt Lydia!

MRS HERIOT   All she ever said was that she was ashamed – *(losing her temper and her fine feeling for the innocence of her auditor)* – ashamed that she 'hadn't had the courage to resist' – not the original temptation but the pressure brought to bear on her 'not to go through with it,' as she said.

JEAN *(wrinkling her brows)* You are being so delicate – I'm not sure I understand.

MRS HERIOT *(irritably)* The only thing you need understand is that she's not a desirable companion for a young girl. *(pause)*

JEAN   When did you see her after – after –

MRS HERIOT *(with a slight grimace)* I met her last winter at the Bishop's. *(hurriedly)* She's a connection of his wife's. They'd got her to help with some of their work. Then she took hold of ours. Your aunt and uncle are quite foolish about her, and I'm debarred from taking any steps, at least till the Shelter is out of hand.

JEAN   I do rather wonder she can bring herself to talk about – the unfortunate women of the world.

MRS HERIOT   The effrontery of it!

JEAN   Or ... the courage! *(puts her hand up to her throat as if the sentence had caught there.)*

MRS HERIOT   Even presumes to set *me* right! Of course I don't *mind* in the least, poor soul ... but I feel I owe it to your dead mother to tell you about her, especially as you're old enough now to know something about life –

JEAN *(slowly)* – and since a girl needn't be very old to suffer for her ignorance. *(moves a little away)* I *felt* she was rather wonderful.

MRS HERIOT Wonderful!

JEAN *(pausing)* To have lived through *that* when she was how old?

MRS HERIOT *(rising)* Oh, nineteen or thereabouts.

JEAN Five years younger than I. To be abandoned and to come out of it like this!

MRS HERIOT *(laying her hand on the girl's shoulder)* It was too bad to have to tell you such a sordid story today of all days.

JEAN It is a very terrible story, but this wasn't a bad time. I feel very sorry today for women who aren't happy. *(motor horn heard faintly. Jumping up.)* That's Geoffrey!

MRS HERIOT Mr Stonor! What makes you think ...?

JEAN Yes, yes. I'm sure, I'm sure –

Checks herself as she is flying off. Turns and sees Lord John entering from the garden. Motor horn louder.

LORD JOHN Who do you think is motoring up the drive?

JEAN *(catching hold of him)* Oh, dear! How am I ever going to be able to behave like a girl who isn't engaged to the only man in the world worth marrying?

MRS HERIOT You were expecting Mr Stonor all the time!

JEAN He promised he'd come to luncheon if it was humanly possible; but I was afraid to tell you for fear he'd be prevented.

LORD JOHN *(laughing as he crosses to the lobby)* You felt we couldn't have borne the disappointment.

JEAN I felt I couldn't.

The lobby door opens. Lady John appears radiant, followed by a tall figure in a dustcoat, etc., no goggles. He has straight, firm features, a little blunt, fair skin, high-coloured; fine, straight hair, very fair, grey eyes, set somewhat prominently and heavy when not interested; lips full, but firmly moulded. Geoffrey Stoner is heavier than a man of forty should be, but otherwise in the pink of physical condition. The Footman stands waiting to help him off with his motor coat.

LADY JOHN   Here's an agreeable surprise!

Jean has gone forward only a step, and stands smiling at the approaching figure.

LORD JOHN   How do you do? (*As he comes between them and briskly shakes hands with Stonor. Farnborough appears at the French window.*)

FARNBOROUGH   Yes, by Jove! (*turning to the others clustered round the window*) What gigantic luck!

Those outside crane and glance, and then elaborately turn their backs and pretend to be talking among themselves, but betray as far as manners permit the enormous sensation the arrival has created.

STONOR   How do you do?

Shakes hands with Mrs Heriot, who has rushed up to him with both hers outstretched. He crosses to Jean, who meets him half way. They shake hands, smiling into each other's eyes.

JEAN   Such a long time since we met!

LORD JOHN (*to Stonor*) You're growing very enterprising. I could hardly believe my ears when I heard you'd motored all the way from town to see a supporter on Sunday.

STONOR   I don't know how we covered the ground in the old days. (*to Lady John*) It's no use to stand for your borough any more. The American, you know, he 'runs' for Congress. By and by we shall all be flying after the thing we want. (*Smiles at Jean*)

JEAN   Sh! (*smiles and then glances over her shoulder and speaks low*) All sorts of irrelevant people here.

FARNBOROUGH (*unable to resist the temptation, comes forward*) How do you do, Mr Stonor?

STONOR   Oh – how d'you do.

FARNBOROUGH   Some of them were arguing in the smoking-room last night whether it didn't hurt a man's chances going about in a motor.

GREATOREX   Yes, we've been hearing a lot of stories about the unpopularity of motor cars – among the class that hasn't got 'em, of course. What do you say?

LADY JOHN   I'm sure you gain more votes by being able to reach so many more of your constituency than we used –

STONOR   Well, I don't know – I've sometimes wondered whether the charm of our presence wasn't counterbalanced by the way we tear about smothering our fellow-beings in dust and running down their pigs and chickens, not to speak of their children.

LORD JOHN *(anxiously)* What on the whole are the prospects? *(Farnborough cranes forward.)*

STONOR *(gravely)* We shall have to work harder than we realised.

FARNBOROUGH   Ah! *(retires towards group.)*

JEAN *(in a half-aside as she slips her arm in her uncle's and smiles at Geoffrey)* He says he believes I'll be able to make a real difference to his chances. Isn't it angelic of him?

STONOR *(in a jocular tone)* Angelic? Macchiavelian. I pin all my hopes on your being able to counteract the pernicious influence of my opponent's glib wife.

JEAN   You want me to have a *real* share in it all, don't you, Geoffrey?

STONOR *(smiling into her eyes)* Of course I do.

Farnborough drops down again on pretence of talking to Mrs Heriot.

LORD JOHN   I don't gather you're altogether sanguine. Any complication? *(Jean and Lady John stand close together, the girl radiant, following Stonor with her eyes and whispering to the sympathetic elder woman.)*

STONOR   Well, *(taking Sunday paper out of pocket)* there's this agitation about the Woman Question. Oddly enough, it seems likely to affect the issue.

LORD JOHN   Why should it? Can't you do what the other four hundred have done?

STONOR *(laughs)* Easily. But, you see, the mere fact that four hundred and twenty members have been worried into promising support – and then once in the House have let the matter severely alone –

LORD JOHN *(to Stonor)* Let it alone! Bless my soul, I should think so indeed.

STONOR   Of course. Only it's a device that's somewhat worn.

Enter Miss Levering, with hat on, gloves and veil in her hand.

LORD JOHN   Still if they think they're getting a future
Cabinet Minister on their side –

STONOR   It will be sufficiently embarassing for the
Cabinet Minister. *(Stonor turns to speak to Jean. He stops dead
seeing Miss Levering.)*

JEAN *(smiling)* You know one another?

MISS LEVERING *(looking at Stonor with intentness but quite
calmly)* Everybody in this part of the world knows Mr Stonor, but he
doesn't know me.

LORD JOHN   Miss Levering ... *(they bow.)*

*Enter Greatorex , sidling in with an air of giving Mrs Freddy a wide
berth.*

JEAN *(to Miss Levering with artless enthusiasm)* Oh, have you been
hearing him speak?

MISS LEVERING   Yes, I was visiting some relations near
Dutfield. They took me to hear you.

STONOR   Oh – the night the Suffragettes made their
customary row.

MISS LEVERING   The night they asked you –

STONOR *(flying at the first chance of distraction, shakes hands with
Mrs Freddy)* Well, Mrs Freddy, what do you think of your friends
now?

MRS FREDDY   My friends?

STONOR *(offering her the Sunday paper)* Yes, the disorderly women.

MRS FREDDY *(with dignity)* They are not my friends, but I don't
think you must call them –

STONOR   Why not? *(laughs)* I can forgive them for
worrying the late Government. But they *are* disorderly.

MISS LEVERING *(quietly)* Isn't the phrase consecrated to a different
class?

GREATOREX *(who has got hold of the Sunday paper)* He's perfectly
right. How do you do? Disorderly women! That's what they are!

FARNBOROUGH *(reading over his shoulder)* Ought to be locked up!
Every one of 'em.

GREATOREX *(assenting angrily)* Public nuisances! Going about with
dog whips and spitting in policemen's faces.

MRS FREDDY *(with a harassed air)* I wonder if they did spit?

GREATOREX *(exulting)* Of course they did.

MRS FREDDY *(turns on him)* You're no authority on what they do. *You* run away.

GREATOREX *(trying to turn the laugh)* Run away? Yes. *(backing a few paces)* And if ever I muster up courage to come back, it will be to vote for better manners in public life, not worse than we have already.

MRS FREDDY *(meekly)* So should I. Don't think that I defend the Suffragette methods.

JEAN *(with cheerful curiosity)* Still, you *are* an advocate of the Suffrage, aren't you?

MRS FREDDY Here? *(shrugs)* I don't beat the air.

GREATOREX *(mocking)* Only policemen.

MRS FREDDY *(plaintively)* If you cared to know the attitude of the real workers in the reform, you might have noticed in any paper last week we lost no time in dissociating ourselves from the little group of hysterical – *(catches her husband's eye, and instantly checks her flow of words.)*

MRS HERIOT They have lowered the whole sex in the eyes of the entire world.

JEAN *(joining Geoffrey Stonor)* I can't quite see what they want – those Suffragettes.

GREATOREX Notoriety.

FARNBOROUGH What they want? A good thrashin' – that's what I'd give 'em.

MRS HERIOT *(murmurs)* Spirited fellow!

LORD JOHN Well, there's one sure thing – they've dished their goose. *(Greatorex chuckles, still reading the account.)* I believe these silly scenes are a pure joy to you.

GREATOREX Final death-blow to the whole silly business!

JEAN *(mystified, looking from one to the other)* The Suffragettes don't seem to *know* they're dead.

GREATOREX They still keep up a sort of death-rattle. But they've done for themselves.

JEAN *(clasping her hands with fervour)* Oh, I hope they'll last till the election's over.

FARNBOROUGH *(stares)* Why?

JEAN Oh, we want them to get the working man to –

(stumbling and a little confused) – to vote for ... the Conservative candidate. Isn't that so?

Looking round for help. General laughter.

LORD JOHN   Fancy, Jean – !

GREATOREX   The working man's a good deal of an ass, but even he won't listen to –

JEAN *(again appealing to the silent Stonor)* But he does listen like anything! I asked why there were so few at the Long Mitcham meeting, and I was told, 'Oh, they've all gone to hear Miss–'

STONOR   Just for a lark, that was.

LORD JOHN   It has no real effect on the vote.

GREATOREX   Not the smallest.

JEAN *(wide-eyed to Stonor)* Why, I thought you said –

STONOR *(hastily, rubbing his hand over the lower part of his face and speaking quickly)* I've a notion a little soap and water wouldn't do me any harm.

LORD JOHN   I'll take you up. You know Freddy Tunbridge.

Stonor pauses to shake hands. All three exit.

JEAN *(perplexed, as Stonor turns away, says to Greatorex)* Well, if women are of no importance in politics, it isn't for the reason you gave. There is now and then a weekender among them.

GREATOREX *(shuffles about uneasily)* Hm – Hm. *(finds himself near Mrs Freddy)* Lord! The perils that beset the feet of man! *(with an air of comic caution, moves away, left.)*

JEAN *(to Farnborough aside, laughing)* Why does he behave like that?

FARNBOROUGH   His moral sense is shocked.

JEAN   Why, I saw him and Mrs Freddy together at the French Play the other night – as thick as thieves.

MISS LEVERING   Ah, that was before he knew her revolting views.

JEAN   What revolting views?

GREATOREX   Sh! Sunday. *(as Greatorex sidles cautiously further away.)*

JEAN *(laughing in spite of herself)* I can't believe women are so helpless when I see men so afraid of them.

GREATOREX   The great mistake was in teaching them to read and write.

JEAN *(over Miss Levering's shoulder, whispers)* Say something.

MISS LEVERING *(to Greatorex smiling)* Oh no, that wasn't the worst mistake.

GREATOREX   Yes, it was.

MISS LEVERING   No. Believe me. The mistake was in letting women learn to talk.

GREATOREX   *Ah! (wheels about with sudden rapture)* I see now what's to be the next great reform.

MISS LEVERING *(holding up the little volume)* When women are all dumb, no more discussions of the 'Paradiso'.

GREATOREX *(with a gesture of mock rapture)* The thing itself. *(aside)* That's a great deal better than talking about it, as I'm sure *you* know.

MISS LEVERING   Why do you think I know?

GREATOREX   Only the plain women are in any doubt.

Jean joins Miss Levering.

GREATOREX   Wait for me, Farnborough. I cannot go about unprotected.

Farnborough and Greatorex exit.

MRS FREDDY   It's true what that old cynic says. The scene in the House has put back the reform a generation.

JEAN   I wish I'd been there.

MRS FREDDY   I *was*.

JEAN   Oh, was it like the papers said?

MRS FREDDY   Worse. I've never been so moved in public. No tragedy, no great opera ever gripped an audience as the situation in the House did that night. There we all sat breathless – with everything more favourable to us than it had been within the memory of women. Another five minutes and the Resolution would have passed. Then ... all in a moment –

LORD JOHN *(to Mrs Heriot)* Listen – they're talking about the female hooligans.

MRS HERIOT   No, thank you! *(Sits apart with the 'Church Times'.)*

MRS FREDDY *(excitedly)* All in a moment a horrible dingy little flag

was poked through the grille of the Woman's Gallery – cries –
insults – scuffling – the police – the ignominious turning out of the
women – *us* as well as the – Oh, I can't *think* of it without – *(jumps
up and walks to and fro. Pauses)* Then the next morning! The
people gloating. Our friends antagonised – people who were
wavering – nearly won overall thrown back – heart breaking! Even
my husband! Freddy's been an angel about letting me take my share
when I felt I must – but of course I've always known he doesn't
really like it. It makes him shy. I'm sure it gives him a horrid twist
inside when he sees my name among the speakers on the placards.
But he's always been an angel about it before this. After the
disgraceful scene he said, 'It just shows how unfit women are for any
sort of coherent thinking or concerted action.'

JEAN   To think that it should be women who've given
the Cause the worst blow it ever had!

MRS FREDDY   The work of forty years destroyed in five
minutes!

JEAN   They must have felt pretty sick when they woke
up the next morning – the Suffragettes.

MRS FREDDY   I don't waste any sympathy on *them*. I'm
thinking of the penalty *all* women have to pay because a handful of
hysterical –

JEAN   Still I think I'm sorry for them. It must be
dreadful to find you've done such a lot of harm to the thing you care
most about in the world.

MISS LEVERING   Do you picture the Suffragettes sitting in
sackcloth?

MRS FREDDY   Well, they can't help realising *now* what
they've done.

MISS LEVERING *(quietly)* Isn't it just possible they realise they've
waked up interest in the Woman Question so that it's advertised in
every paper and discussed in every house from Land's End to John
O'Groats? Don't you think *they* know there's been more said and
written about it in these ten days since the scene, than in the ten
years before it?

MRS FREDDY   You aren't saying you think it was a good way
to get what they wanted?

MISS LEVERING *(shrugs)* I'm only pointing out that it seems not such a bad way to get it known they *do* want something – and *(smiling)* 'want it bad'.

JEAN *(getting up)* Didn't Mr Greatorex say women had been politely petitioning Parliament for forty years?

MISS LEVERING   And men have only laughed.

JEAN   But they'd come round. *(she looks from one to the other.)* Mrs Tunbridge says, before that horrid scene, everything was favourable at last.

MISS LEVERING   At last? Hadn't it been just as 'favourable' before?

MRS FREDDY   No. We'd never had so many members pledged to our side.

MISS LEVERING   I thought I'd heard somebody say the Bill had got as far as that, time and time again.

JEAN   Oh no. Surely not …

MRS FREDDY *(reluctanctly)* Y-yes. This was only a Resolution. The Bill passed a second reading thirty-seven years ago.

JEAN *(with wide eyes)* And what difference did it make?

MISS LEVERING   The men laughed rather louder.

MRS FREDDY   Oh, it's got as far as a second reading several times – but we never had so many friends in the House before –

MISS LEVERING *(with a faint smile)* 'Friends'!

JEAN   Why do you say it like that?

MISS LEVERING   Perhaps because I was thinking of a funny story – he said it was funny – a Liberal Whip told me the other day. A Radical Member went out of the House after his speech in favour of the Woman's Bill, and as he came back half an hour later, he heard some Members talking in the Lobby about the astonishing number who were going to vote for the measure. And the Friend of Woman dropped his jaw and clutched the man next to him: 'My God!' he said, 'you don't mean to say they're going to give it to them!'

JEAN   Oh!

MRS FREDDY   You don't think all men in Parliament are like that!

MISS LEVERING   I don't think all men are burglars, but I lock my doors.

JEAN *(below her breath)* You think that night of the scene – you think the men didn't *mean* to play fair?

MISS LEVERING (*her coolness in contrast to the excitement of the others*) Didn't the women sit quiet till ten minutes to closing time?

JEAN Ten minutes to settle a question like that!

MISS LEVERING (*quietly to Mrs Freddy*) Couldn't you see the men were at their old game?

LADY JOHN (*coming forward*) You think they were just putting off the issue till it was too late?

MISS LEVERING (*in a detached tone*) I wasn't there, but I haven't heard anybody deny that the women waited till ten minutes to eleven. Then they discovered the policeman who'd been sent up at the psychological moment to the back of the gallery. Then, I'm told, when the women saw they were betrayed once more, they utilised the few minutes left, to impress on the country at large the fact of their demands – did it in the only way left them. (*sits leaning forward reflectively smiling, chin in hand*) It does rather look to the outsider as if the well-behaved women had worked for forty years and made less impression on the world then those fiery young women made in five minutes.

MRS FREDDY Oh, come, be fair!

MISS LEVERING Well, you must admit that, next day, every newspaper reader in Europe and America knew there were women in England in such dead earnest about the Suffrage that the men had stopped laughing at last, and turned them out of the House. Men even advertised how little they appreciated the fun by sending the women to gaol in pretty sober earnest. And all the world was talking about it.

Mrs Heriot lays down the 'Church Times' and joins the others.

LADY JOHN I have noticed, whenever the men aren't there, the women sit and discuss that scene.

JEAN (*cheerfully*) I shan't have to wait till the men are gone. (*leans over Lady John's shoulder and says half aside.*) He's in sympathy.

LADY JOHN How do you know?

JEAN He told the interrupting women so.

Mrs Freddy looks mystified. The others smile.

LADY JOHN Oh!

Mr Freddy and Lord John appear by the door they went out of.

They stop to talk.

MRS FREDDY   Here's Freddy! *(lower, hastily to Miss Levering.)* You're judging from the outside. Those of us who have been working for years – we all realise it was a perfectly lunatic proceeding. Why, *think*! The only chance of our getting what we want is by *winning* over the men. *(her watchful eye, leaving her husband for a moment, catches Miss Levering's little involuntary gesture.)* What's the matter?

MISS LEVERING   'Winning over the men' has been the woman's way for centuries. Do you think the result should make us proud of our policy? Yes? Then go and walk in Piccadilly at midnight. *(The older women glance at Jean.)* No, I forgot –

MRS HERIOT *(with majesty)* Yes, it's not the first time you've forgotten.

MISS LEVERING   I forgot the magistrate's ruling. He said no decent woman had any business to be in London's main thorough-fare at night unless she has *a man with her*. I heard that in Nine Elms, too. 'You're obliged to take up with a chap!' was what the woman said.

MRS HERIOT *(rising)* Jean! Come!

She takes Jean by her arm and draws her to the window, where she signals Greatorex and Farnborough. Mrs Freddy joins her husband and Lord John.

LADY JOHN *(kindly, aside to Miss Levering)* My dear, I think Lydia Heriot's right. We oughtn't to do anything *or say* anything to encourage this ferment of feminism, and I'll tell you why: it's likely to bring a very terrible thing in its train.

MISS LEVERING   What terrible thing?

LADY JOHN   Sex antagonism.

MISS LEVERING *(rising)* It's here.

LADY JOHN *(very gravely)* Don't say that. *(Jean has quietly disengaged herself from Mrs Heriot and the group at the window returns and stands behind Lady John, looking up into Miss Levering's face.)*

MISS LEVERING *(to Lady John)* You're so conscious it's here, you're afraid to have it mentioned.

LADY JOHN *(turning and seeing Jean. Rising hastily)* If it's here, it is the fault of those women agitators.

MISS LEVERING *(gently)* No woman *begins* that way. *(leans forward with clasped hands looking into vacancy)* Every woman's in a state of natural subjection *(smiles at Jean)* – no, I'd rather say allegiance to her idea of romance and her hope of motherhood. They're embodied for her in man. They're the strongest things in life – till man kills them. *(rousing herself and looking into Lady John's face)* Let's be fair. Each woman knows why that allegiance died.

Lady John turns hastily, sees Lord John coming down with Mr Freddy and meets them at the foot of the stairs. Miss Levering has turned to the table looking for her gloves, etc., among the papers; unconsciously drops the handkerchief she had in her little book.

JEAN *(in a low voice to Miss Levering)* All this talk against the wicked Suffragettes – it makes me want to go and hear what they've got to say for themselves.

MISS LEVERING *(smiling with a non-committal air as she finds the veil she's been searching for)* Well, they're holding a meeting in Trafalgar Square at three o'clock.

JEAN   This afternoon? But that's no use to people out of town – unless I could invent some excuse.

LORD JOHN *(benevolently)* Still talking over the Shelter plans?

MISS LEVERING   No. We left the Shelter some time ago.

LORD JOHN *(to Jean)* Then what's all the chatterment about?

Jean a little confused, looks at Miss Levering

MISS LEVERING   The latest thing in veils. *(ties hers round her hat)*

GREATOREX   The invincible frivolity of woman!

LORD JOHN *(genially)* Don't scold them. It's a very proper tonic.

MISS LEVERING *(whimsically)* Oh, I was afraid you'd despise us for it.

BOTH MEN *(with condescension)* Not at all – not at all.

JEAN *(to Miss Levering as Footman appears)* Oh, they're coming for you. Don't forget your book. *(Footman holds out a salver with a telegram on it for Jean)* Why, it's for me!

MISS LEVERING   But it's time I was – *(she crosses to the table.)*

JEAN *(opening the telegram)* May I? *(reads, and glances over the paper at Miss Levering.)* I've got your book. *(crosses to Miss*

Levering, and, looking at the back of the volume) Dante!
Whereabouts are you? *(opening at the marker)* Oh, the 'Inferno'.

MISS LEVERING   No. I'm in a worse place.

JEAN   I didn't know there was a worse.

MISS LEVERING   Yes, it's worse with the Vigliacchi.

JEAN   I forget. Were they Guelf or Ghibelline?

MISS LEVERING *(smiling)* They weren't either, and that was why
Dante couldn't stand them. *(more gravely)* He said there was not
place in Heaven nor in Purgatory – not even a corner in Hell – for
the souls who had stood aloof from strife. *(looking steadily into the
girl's eyes.)* He called them 'wretches who never lived,' Dante did,
because they'd never felt the pangs of partizanship. And so they
wander homeless on the skirts of limbo among the abortions and
off-scourings of Creation.

JEAN *(a long breath after a long look. When Miss Levering has
turned away to make her leisurely adieux, Jean's eyes fall on the
open telegram)* Aunt Ellen, I've got to go to London.

Stonor, re-entering, hears this, but pretends to talk to Mr Freddy, etc.

LADY JOHN   My dear child!

MRS HERIOT   Nonsense! Is your grandfather worse?

JEAN *(folding the telegram)* No-o. I don't think so. But it's necessary I
should go, all the same.

MRS HERIOT   Go away when Mr Stonor –

JEAN   He said he'd have to leave directly after
luncheon.

LADY JOHN   I'll just see Miss Levering off, and then I'll
come back and talk about it.

LORD JOHN *(to Miss Levering)* Why are you saying goodbye as if
you were never coming back?

MISS LEVERING *(smiling)* One never knows. Maybe I shan't come
back. *(to Stonor)* Goodbye.

*Stonor bows ceremoniously. The others go up laughing. Stonor comes
down.*

JEAN *(impulsively)* There mayn't be another train! Miss Levering –

STONOR *(standing in front of her)* What if there isn't? I'll take you
back in the motor.

JEAN *(rapturously)* Will you? *(inadvertently drops the telegram)*

I must be there by three!

STONOR (*picks up the telegram and a handkerchief lying near, glances at the message*) Why, it's only an invitation to dine – Wednesday!

JEAN   Sh! (*takes the telegram and puts it in her pocket*)

STONOR   Oh, I see! (*lower, smiling*) It's rather dear of you to arrange our going off like that. You *are* a clever little girl!

JEAN   It's not that I was arranging. I want to hear those women in Trafalgar Square – the Suffragettes.

STONOR (*incredulous, but smiling*) How perfectly absurd! (*looking after Lady John*) Besides, I expect she wouldn't like my carrying you off like that.

JEAN   Then she'll have to make an excuse and come too.

STONOR   Ah, it wouldn't be quite the same –

JEAN (*rapidly thinking it out*) We could get back here in time for dinner.

Geoffrey Stonor glances down at the handkerchief still in his hand, and turns it half mechanically from corner to corner.

JEAN (*absent-mindedly*) Mine?

STONOR (*hastily, without reflection*) No. (*he hands it to Miss Levering as she passes*) Yours.

Miss Levering, on her way to the lobby with Lord John seems not to notice.

JEAN (*takes the handkerchief to give it to her, glancing down at the embroidered corner, stops.*) But that's not an L! It's V! (*Geoffrey Stonor suddenly turns his back and takes up the newspaper.*)

LADY JOHN (*from the lobby*) Come Vida, since you will go.

MISS LEVERING   Yes, I'm coming.

Exit Miss Levering.

JEAN   *I* didn't know her name was Vida, how did you?

Stonor stares silently over the top of his paper.

ACT TWO
Scene One
The north side of the Nelson Column in Trafalgar Square.
The Curtain rises on an uproar. The crowd, which suddenly increases,
is composed chiefly of weedy youths and wastrel old men. There are a
few decent artisans; a few 'beery' out-o'-works; three or four young
women of the domestic servant or Strand restaurant cashier class;
one aged woman in rusty black peering with faded, wondering eyes,
consulting the faces of men and laughing nervously and apologetically
from time to time; one or two quiet-looking, business-like women,
thirty to forty; two middle-class men, who stare and whisper and
smile. A quiet old man with a lot of unsold Sunday papers under one
arm stands in an attitude of rapt attention, with the free hand round
his deaf ear. A brisk-looking woman of forty-five or so, wearing pince
-nez, goes round with a pile of propagandist literature on her arm.
Many of the men are smoking cigarettes, the old ones pipes. On the
outskirts of this crowd, of several hundred, a couple of smart men in
tall shining hats hover a few moments, monocle up, then saunter off.

   Against the middle of the Column, where it rises above the stone
platform, is a great red banner, one supporting pole upheld by a
grimy sandwichman, the other by a small, dirty boy of eight. If prac-
ticable only the lower portion of the banner need be seen, bearing the
words – 'VOTES FOR WOMEN!' in immense white letters. It will be
well to get, to the full, the effect of the height above the crowd of the
straggling group of speakers on the pedestal platform.

   As the Curtain rises, a working-class woman is waving her arms
and talking very earnestly, her voice for the moment blurred in the
uproar. She is dressed in brown serge and looks pinched and sallow.
At her side is the Chairman urging that she be given a fair hearing.
Allen Trent is a tall, slim, brown-haired man of twenty-eight, with a
slight stoop, an agreeable aspect, well-bred voice, and the gleaming
brown eye of the visionary. Behind these two, looking on or talking
among themselves, are several other carelessly dressed women; one,
better turned out than the rest, is quite young, very slight and grace-
fully built, with round, very pink cheeks, full, scarlet lips, naturally
waving brown hair, and an air of childish gravity. She looks at the
unruly mob with imperturbable calm. The Chairman's voice is
drowned out.

WORKING WOMAN *(with lean, brown finger out and voice raised shriller now above the tumult)* I've got boys o' me own and we laugh at all sorts o' things, but I should be ashymed and so would they if ever they was to be'yve as you're doin' to-d'y . *(in laughter the noise dies)* ... People 'ave been sayin' this is a middle-class woman's movement. It's a libel. I'm a workin' woman myself, the wife of a working man. *(Voice:* 'Pore devil!'*)* I'm a Poor Law Guardian and a –

NOISY YOUNG MAN Think of that, now – gracious me!

Laughter and interruption.

OLD NEWS VENDOR *(to the noisy young man near him.)* Oh, shut up, cawn't yer?

NOISY YOUNG MAN Not fur *you*!

VOICE Go 'ome and darn yer old man's stockens!

VOICE Just clean yer *own* doorstep!

WORKING WOMAN It's a pore sort of 'ousekeeper that leaves 'er doorstep till Sunday afternoon. Maybe that's when you would do *your* doorstep. I do mine in the mornin' before you men are awake.

OLD NEWSVENDOR It's true wot she says! – every word.

WORKING WOMAN You say we women 'ave got no business servin' on boards and thinkin' about politics. Wot's politics?. *(a derisive roar)* ... It's just 'ousekeepin' on a big scyle. 'Oo among you working men 'as the most comfortable 'omes? Those of you that gives yer wives yer wyges.

Loud laughter and jeers.

VOICES That's it! Wantin' our money ... Lord 'Igh 'Ousekeeper of England.

WORKING WOMAN If it wus only to use fur *our* comfort, d'ye think many o' you workin' men would be found turnin' over their wyges to their wives? No! Wot's the reason thousands do – and the best and the soberest? Because the workin' man knows that wot's a pound to 'im is twenty shillin's to 'is wife. And she'll myke every penny in every one o' them shillin's tell. She gets more fur 'im out of 'is wyges than wot 'e can! Some o' you know wot the 'omes is like where the men don't let the women manage. Well, the Poor Laws and the 'ole Government is just in the same muddle because the men 'ave tried to do the national 'ousekeepin' without the women. *(roars)* But, like

I told you before, it's a libel to say it's only the well-off women wot's wantin' the vote. Wot about the 96,000 textile workers? Wot about the Yorkshire tailoresses? I can tell you wot plenty o' the poor women think about it. I'm one of them, and I can tell you we see there's reforms needed. *We ought to 'ave the vote (jeers), and we know 'ow to appreciate the other women 'oo go to prison fur tryin' to get it fur us!*

With a little final bob of emphasis and a glance over shoulder at the old woman and the young one behind her, she seems about to retire, but pauses as the murmur in the crowd grows into distinct phrases.

OTHER VOICES   They get their 'air cut free.
Naow they don't, that's only us!
Silly Suffragettes! Stop at 'ome!
Inderin policemen – mykin' rows in the streets!
VOICE *(louder than the others)* They sees yer ain't fit t'ave –
OTHER VOICES   Ha, ha! Shut up! Keep quiet, cawn't yer?

General uproar.

CHAIRMAN   You evidently don't know what had to be done by men before the extension of the Suffrage in '67. If it hadn't been for demonstrations of violence. *(his voice is drowned)*
WORKING WOMAN *(coming forward again, her shrill note rising clear)* You s'y woman's plyce is 'ome! Don't you know there's a third of the women o' this country can't afford the luxury of stayin' in their 'omes? They got to go out and 'elp make money to p'y the rent and keep the 'ome from bein' sold up. Then there's all the women that 'aven't got even miseerable 'omes. They 'aven't got any 'omes at all.
NOISY YOUNG MAN You said you got one. W'y don't you stop in it?
WORKING WOMAN Yes, that's like a man. If one o' you is all right, he thinks the rest don't matter. We women –
NOISY YOUNG MAN The lydies! God bless 'em!

Voices drown out her and the Chairman.

OLD NEWS VENDOR *(to Noisy Young Man)* Oh, take that extra 'alf pint 'ome and *sleep it off!*
WORKING WOMAN P'raps *your* 'omes are all right. P'raps you

aren't livin', old and young, married and single, in one room. I come from a plyce where many fam'lies 'ave to live like that if they're to go on livin' *at all.* If you don't believe me, come and let me show you! *(she spreads out her lean arms)* Come with me to Canning Town! – come with me to Bromley – come to Poplar and to Bow! No. You won't even think about the overworked women and the underfed children and the 'ovels they live in. And you want that we shouldn't think neither –

A VAGRANT   We'll do the thinkin'. You go 'ome and nuss the byby.

WORKING WOMAN I do nurse my byby! I've nursed seven. What 'ave you done for yours? P'r'aps your children never goes 'ungry, and maybe you're satisfied – though I must say I wouldn't a' thought it from the look o' you.

VOICE   Oh, I s'y!

WORKING WOMAN But we women are not satisfied. We don't only want better things for our own children. We want better things for all. Every child is our child. We know in our 'earts we oughtn't to rest till we've mothered 'em every one.

VOICE   Women – children – wot about the men? Are they all 'appy?. *(derisive laughter.)*

VOICES   No! no! Not precisely.'Appy? Lord!

WORKING WOMAN No, there's lots o' you men I'm sorry for, *(Shrill Voice: 'Thanks awfully!'),* an' we'll 'elp you if you let us.

VOICE   'Elp us? You tyke the bread out of our mouths. You women are blackleggin' the men!

WORKING WOMAN W'*y* does any woman tyke less wyges than a man for the same work? Only because we can't get anything better. That's part the reason w'y we're yere to-d'y. Do you reely think we tyke them there low wyges because we got a *lykin'* for low wyges? No. We're just like you. We want as much as ever we can get.

VOICES   'Ear! 'Ear! *(laughter)*

WORKING WOMAN We got a gryte deal to do with our wyges, we women has. We got the children to think about. And w'en we got our rights, a woman's flesh and blood won't be so much cheaper than a man's that employers can get rich on keepin' you out o' work, and sweatin' us. If you men only could see it, we got the *syme* cause, and if you 'elped us you'd be 'elpin yerselves.

VOICES　　　　　　　Rot! Drivel.
OLD NEWS VENDOR　True as gospel!

*She retires against the banner with the others. There is some
applause.*

A MAN *(patronisingly)* Well, now, that wusn't so bad, fur a woman.
ANOTHER　　　　　Nnaw. *Not fur a woman.*
CHAIRMAN *(speaking through this last)* Miss Ernestine Blunt will
　　now address you ...

*Applause. Chiefly ironic, laughter, a general moving closer and
knitting up of attention. Ernestine Blunt is about twenty-four, but
looks younger. She is very downright, not to say pugnacious. There is
something amusing and attractive about her, as it were, against her
will, and the more fetching for that. She has no conventional gestures,
and none of any sort at first. As she warms to her work she uses her
slim hands to enforce her emphasis, but as though unconsciously. Her
manner of speech is less monotonous than that of the average woman
speaker, but she, too, has a fashion of leaning all her weight on the
end of the sentence. She brings out the final word or two with an
effort of underscoring, and makes a forward motion of the slim body
as if the better to drive the last nail in. She evidently means to be
immensely practical – the kind who is pleased to think she hasn't a
grain of sentimentality in her composition, and whose feeling, when it
does all but master her, communicates itself magnetically to others.*

MISS ERNESTINE BLUNT Perhaps I'd better begin by explaining a
　　little about our 'tactics'.
VOICES *(cry out)*　　Tactics! We know! Mykin' trouble! Public
　　scandal!
MISS ERNESTINE BLUNT To make you understand what we've
　　done, I must remind you of what others have done. Perhaps you
　　don't know that women first petitioned Parliament for the Franchise
　　as long ago as 1866.
VOICE　　　　　　　How do you know?

*She pauses a moment, taken off her guard by the suddenness of the
attack.*

VOICE　　　　　　　You wasn't there!

VOICE That was the trouble. Haw! haw!

MISS ERNESTINE BLUNT And the petition was presented –

VOICE Give 'er a hearin' now she 'as got out of 'er crydle.

MISS ERNESTINE BLUNT – presented to the House of Commons by that great Liberal, John Stuart Mill.

VOICE Mill? Who is he when he's at home?

MISS ERNESTINE BLUNT Bills or Resolutions have been before the House on and off for the last thirty-six years. That, roughly, is our history. We found ourselves, towards the close of the year 1905, with no assurance that if we went on in the same way any girl born into the world in this generation would live to exercise the rights of citizenship, though she lived to be a hundred. So we said all this has been in vain. We must try some other way. How did the working man get the Suffrage, we asked ourselves? Well, we turned up the records, and we *saw* –

VOICES Not by scratching people's faces! ...
Disraeli give it 'em! Dizzy? Get out!
Cahnty Cahncil scholarships!
Oh, Lord, this education!
Chartists riots, she's thinkin' of!
(Noise in the crowd)

MISS ERNESTINE BLUNT But we don't *want* to follow such a violent example. We would much rather not – but if that's the only way we can make the country see we're in earnest, we are prepared to show them.

VOICE An' they'll show you! – Give you another month 'ard.

MISS ERNESTINE BLUNT Don't think that going to prison has any fears for us. We'd go *for life* if by doing that we could get freedom for the rest of the women.

VOICES Hear, hear!
Rot! W'ye don't the men 'elp yer to get your rights?

MISS ERNESTINE BLUNT Here's someone asking why the men don't help. It's partly they don't understand yet – they *will* before we've done! *(laughter)* Partly they don't understand yet what's at stake –

RESPECTABLE OLD MAN *(chuckling)* Lord, they're a 'educatin' of us!

VOICE Wot next?

MISS ERNESTINE BLUNT – and partly that the bravest man is afraid of ridicule. Oh, yes. We've heard a great deal all our lives about the timidity and the sensitiveness of women. And it's true. We *are* sensitive. But I tell you, ridicule crumples a man up. It steels a woman. We've come to know the value of ridicule. We've educated ourselves so that we welcome ridicule. We owe our sincerest thanks to the comic writers. The cartoonist is our unconscious friend. Who cartoons people who are of no importance? What advertisement is so sure of being remembered?

POETIC YOUNG MAN I admit that.

MISS ERNESTINE BLUNT If we didn't know it by any other sign, the comic papers would tell us we've *arrived*! But our greatest debt of gratitude we owe, to the man who called us female hooligans ... *(the crowd bursts into laughter)* ... We aren't hooligans, but we hope the fact will be overlooked. If everybody said we were nice, well-behaved women, who'd come to hear us? *Not the men. (roars)* Men tell us it isn't womanly for us to care about politics. How do they know what's womanly? It's for women to decide that. Let the men attend to being manly. It will take them all their time.

VOICE Are we down-'earted? Oh no!

MISS ERNESTINE BLUNT And they say it would be dreadful if we got the vote, because then we'd be pitted against men in the economic struggle. But that's come about already. Do you know that out of every hundred women in this country eighty-two are wage-earning women? It used to be thought unfeminine for women to be students and to aspire to the arts – that bring fame and fortune. But nobody has ever said it was unfeminine for women to do the heavy drudgery that's badly paid. That kind of work had to be done by *somebody* – and the men didn't hanker after it. Oh, no.

Laughter and interruption.

A MAN ON THE OUTER FRINGE She can talk – the little one can.

ANOTHER Oh, they can all 'talk'.

A BEERY, DIRTY FELLOW OF FIFTY I wouldn't like to be 'er 'usban'. Think o' comin' 'ome to *that*!

HIS PAL I'd soon learn 'er!

MISS ERNESTINE BLUNT *(speaking through the noise)* Oh, no!

Let the women scrub and cook and wash. That's all right! But if they want to try their hand at the better paid work of the liberal professions – oh, very unfeminine indeed! Then there's another thing. Now I want you to listen to this, because it's very important. Men say if we persist in competing with them for the bigger prizes, they're dreadfully afraid we'd lose the beautiful protecting chivalry that – Yes, I don't wonder you laugh. We laugh.
(Bending forward with lit eyes.)
But the women I found at the Ferry Tin Works working for five shillings a week – I didn't see them laughing. The beautiful chivalry of the employers of women doesn't prevent them from paying women ten pence a day for sorting coal and loading and unloading carts – doesn't prevent them from forcing women to earn bread in ways worse still. So we won't talk about chivalry. It's being over-sarcastic. We'll just let this poor ghost of chivalry go – in exchange for a little plain justice.

VOICE   If the House of Commons won't give you justice, why don't you go to the House of Lords?

MISS ERNESTINE BLUNT What?

VOICE   Better 'urry up. Case of early closin' ...

Laughter, a man at the back asks the speaker something.

MISS ERNESTINE BLUNT *(unable to hear)* You'll be allowed to ask any question you like at the end of the meeting.

NEWCOMER *(boy of eighteen)* Oh, is it question time? I s'y, Miss, 'oo killed cock robin?

She is about to resume, but above the general noise the voice of a man at the back reaches her indistinct but insistent. She leans forward trying to catch what he says. While the indistinguishable murmur has been going on Geoffrey Stonor has appeared on the edge of the crowd, followed by Jean and Lady John in motor veils.

JEAN *(pressing forward eagerly and raising her veil)* Is she one of them? That little thing!

STONOR *(doubtfully)* I – I suppose so.

JEAN   Oh, ask someone, Geoffrey. I'm so disappointed. I did so hope we'd hear one of the – the worst.

MISS ERNESTINE BLUNT *(to the interrupter, on the other side)*

What? What do you say? *(She screws up her eyes with the effort to hear, and puts a hand up to her ear. A few indistinguishable words between her and the man)*

LADY JOHN *(who has been studying the figures on the platform through her lorgnon, turns to a working man beside her)* Can you tell me, my man, which are the ones that make the disturbances?

WORKING MAN   Don't you be took in, Miss.

MISS ERNESTINE BLUNT Oh, yes – I see. There's a man over here asking –

A YOUNG MAN   *I've* got a question, too. Are – you – married?

ANOTHER *(sniggering)* Quick! There's yer chawnce. 'E's a bachelor ... *(laughter)*

MISS ERNESTINE BLUNT *(goes straight on as if she had not heard)*

MAN *(asking)* If the women get full citizenship, and a war is declared, will the women fight?

POETIC YOUNG MAN   No, really – no, really, now!

The Crowd: 'Haw! Haw!' 'Yes!' 'Yes, how about that?'

MISS ERNESTINE BLUNT *(smiling)* Well, you know, some people say the whole trouble about us is that we *do* fight. But it is only hard necessity makes us do that. We don't *want* to fight – as men seem to – just for fighting's sake. Women are for peace.

VOICE   Hear, hear.

MISS ERNESTINE BLUNT And when we have a share in public affairs there'll be less likelihood of war. But that's not to say women can't fight. The Boer women did. The Russian women face conflicts worse than any battlefield can show. *(her voice shakes a little, and the eyes fill, but she controls her emotion gallantly, and dashes on.)* But we women know all that is evil, and we're for peace. Our part – we're proud to remember it – our part has been to go about after you men in war time, and – *pick up the pieces! (a great shout)* Yes – seems funny, doesn't it? You men blow them to bits, and then we come along and put them together again. If you know anything about military nursing, you know a good deal of our work has been done in the face of danger – *but it's always been done.*

OLD NEWS VENDOR   That's so. That's so.

MISS ERNESTINE BLUNT You complain that more and more we're taking away from you men the work that's always been yours. You can't any longer keep women out of the industries. The only question is upon what terms shall she continue to be in? As long as she's in on bad terms, she's not only hurting herself – she's hurting you. But if you're feeling discouraged about our competing with you, we're willing to leave you your trade in war. *Let* the men take life! We *give* life! *(her voice is once more moved and proud)* No one will pretend ours isn't one of the dangerous trades either. I won't say any more to you now, because we've got others to speak to you, and a new woman helper that I want you to hear.

She retires to the sound of clapping. There's a hurried consultation between her and the Chairman.

VOICES IN THE CROWD   The little 'un's all right. Ernestine's a corker, *etc.*

JEAN *(looking at Stonor to see how he's taken it)* Well?

STONOR *(smiling down at her)* Well –

JEAN   Nothing reprehensible in what *she* said, was there?

STONOR *(shrugs)* Oh, reprehensible!

JEAN   It makes me rather miserable all the same.

STONOR *(draws her hand protectingly through his arm)* You mustn't take it as much to heart as all that.

JEAN   I can't help it – I can't indeed, Geoffrey. I shall *never* be able to make a speech like that!

STONOR *(taken aback)* I hope not, indeed.

JEAN   Why, I thought you said you wanted me –?

STONOR *(smiling)* To make nice little speeches with composure – so I did! So I – *(seems to lose his thread as he looks at her.)*

JEAN *(with a little frown)* You *said* –

STONOR   That you have very pink cheeks? Well, I stick to that.

JEAN *(smiling)* Sh! Don't tell everybody.

STONOR   And you're the only female creature I ever saw who didn't look a fright in motor things.

JEAN *(melted and smiling)* I'm glad you don't think me a fright.

CHAIRMAN   I will now ask *(name indistinguishable)* to address the meeting.

JEAN (*as she sees Lady John moving to one side*) Oh, don't go yet,
Aunt Ellen!

LADY JOHN   Go? Certainly not. I want to hear another.
(*craning her neck*) I can't believe, you know, she was really one of
the worst.

*A big, sallow Cockney has come forward. His scanty hair grows in
wisps on a great bony skull.*

VOICE   That's Pilcher.

ANOTHER   'Oo's Pilcher?

ANOTHER   If you can't afford a bottle of Tatcho, w'y don't
you get yer 'air cut.

MR PILCHER (*not in the least discomposed*) I've been addressin' a
big meetin' at 'Ammersmith this morning, and w'en I told 'em I was
comin' 'ere this awfternoon to speak fur the women – well – then
the usual thing began! (*an appreciative roar from the crowd*) In
these times if you want peace and quiet at a public meetin' – (*the
crowd fills in the hiatus with laughter*) There was a man at
'Ammersmith, too, talkin' about women's sphere bein' 'ome. 'Ome
do you call it? You've got a kennel w'ere you can munch your
tommy. You've got a corner w'ere you can curl up fur a few hours till
you go out to work again. No, my man, there's too many of you ain't
able to *give* the women 'omes fit to live in, too many of you in that
fix fur you to go on jawin' at those o' the women 'oo want to myke
the 'omes a little decenter ...

VOICE   If the vote ain't done us any good, 'ow'll it do
the women any good?

MR PILCHER   Looke 'ere! Any men here belongin' to the
Labour Party? (*shouts and applause*) Well, I don't need to tell these
men the vote 'as done us *some* good. They know it. And it'll do us a
lot more good w'en you know 'ow to use the power you got in your
'and.

VOICE   Power! It's those fellers at the bottom o' the
street that's got the power.

MR PILCHER   It's you, and men like you, that gave it to 'em.
You carried the Liberals into Parliament Street on your own
shoulders. (*complacent applause*) You believed all their fine words.
You never asked yourselves, 'Wot's a Liberal, anyw'y?'

VOICE   He's a jolly good fellow. *(cheers and booing)*

MR PILCHER   No, 'e ain't, or if 'e is jolly, it's only because 'e thinks you're such silly codfish you'll go swellin' his majority again. *(laughter, in which Stonor joins)* It's enough to make any Liberal jolly to see sheep like you lookin' on, proud and 'appy, while you see Liberal leaders desertin' Liberal principles. *(Voices in agreement and protest)* You show me a Liberal, and I'll show you a Mr Fycing-both-W'ys. Yuss. *(Stonor moves closer with an amused look)* 'E sheds the light of 'is warm and 'andsome smile on the working man, and round on the other side 'e's tippin' a wink to the great land-owners. That's to let 'em know 'e's standin' between them and the Socialists. Huh! Socialists ... Yuss, Socialists! *(general laughter, in which Stonor joins)* The Liberal, 'e's the judicial sort o'chap that sits in the middle –

VOICE   On the fence!

MR PILCHER   Tories one side – Socialists the other. Well it ain't always so comfortable in the middle. You're like to get squeezed. Now, I s'y to the women, the Conservatives don't promise you much but what they promise they do!

STONOR *(to Jean)* This fellow isn't half bad.

MR PILCHER   The Liberals – they'll promise you the earth, and give yer ... the whole o' nothing ...

Roars of approval.

JEAN   Isn't it fun? Now, aren't you glad I brought you?

STONOR *(laughing)* This chap's rather amusing!

MR PILCHER   We men 'ave seen it 'appen over and over. But the women can tyke a 'int quicker 'n what we can. They won't stand the nonsense men do. Only they 'aven't got a fair chawnce even to agitate fur their rights. As I wus comin' up 'ere I 'eard a man sayin', 'Look at this big crowd. W'y, we're all *men*! If the women want the vote w'y ain't they 'ere to s'y so?' Well, I'll tell you w'y. It's because they've 'ad to get the dinner fur you and me, and now they're washin' up the dishes.

VOICE   D'you think *we* ought to st'y 'ome and wash the dishes?

MR PILCHER *(laughs good-naturedly)* If they'd leave it to us once or twice per'aps we'd understand a little more about the Woman Question. I know w'y *my* wife isn't here. It's because she *knows* I ain't much use round the 'ouse, and she's 'opin' I can talk to some purpose. Maybe she's mistaken. Any'ow, here I am to vote for her and all the other women.

VOICES Hear! hear!, Oh – h!

MR PILCHER And to tell you men what improvements you can expect to see when women 'as the share in public affairs they ought to 'ave!

VOICE What do you know about it? You can't even talk grammar.

MR PILCHER (*is dashed a fraction of a moment, for the first and only time*) I'm not 'ere to talk grammar but to talk Reform. I ain't defendin' my grammar – but I'll say in pawssing that if my mother 'ad 'ad 'er rights, maybe my grammar would have been better .

Stonor and Jean exchange smiles. He takes her arm again and bends his head to whisper something in her ear. She listens with lowered eyes and happy face. The discreet love-making goes on during the next few sentences.

Interruption. One voice insistent but not clear. The speaker waits only a second and then resumes.

MR PILCHER Yes, if the women –

He cannot instantly makes himself heard. The boyish Chairman looks harassed and anxious. Miss Ernestine Blunt alert, watchful.

MR PILCHER Wait a bit – 'arf a minute, my man!
VOICE 'Oo yer talkin' to? I ain't your man.
MR PILCHER Lucky for me! There seems to be a *gentleman* 'ere who doesn't think women ought to 'ave the vote.
VOICE One? Oh – h! (*laughter*)
MR PILCHER P'raps 'e doesn't know much about women? (*indistinguishable repartee*) ... Oh, the gentleman says 'e's married. Well, then, fur the syke of 'is wife we mustn't be too sorry 'e's ere. No doubt she's s'ying: 'Eaven by prysed those women are mykin' a Demonstrytion in Trafalgar Square, and I'll 'ave a little peace and quiet at 'ome for one Sunday in my life.'

Laughter. There are jeers for the interruptor and at the speaker.

MR PILCHER (*pointing*) Why, you're like the man at 'Ammersmith this morning. 'E was awskin' me: 'Ow would you like men to st'y at 'ome and do the family washin'?' Laughter ... I told 'im I wouldn't advise it. I 'ave too much respect fur – me clo'es.

VAGRANT   It's their place – the women ought to do the washin'.

MR PILCHER   I'm not sure you ain't right. For a good many o' you fellas, from the look o' you – you cawn't even wash yerselves ... (*laughter*)

VOICE (*threatening*) 'Oo are you talkin' to?

Chairman more anxious than before – movement in the crowd.

THREATENING VOICE   Which of us d'you mean?

MR PILCHER (*coolly looking down*) Well, it takes about ten of your sort to myke a man, so you may take it I mean the lot of you ...

Angry indistinguishable retorts and the crowd sways. Miss Ernestine Blunt who has been watching the fray with serious face, turns suddenly, catching sight of someone just arrived at the end of the platform. Miss Blunt goes right with alacrity, saying audibly to Pilcher as she passes:

MISS ERNESTINE BLUNT   Here she is.

She proceeds to offer her hand helping someone to get up the improvised steps. Laughter and interruption in the crowd.

LADY JOHN   Now, there's another woman going to speak.

JEAN   Oh, is she? Who? Which? I do hope she'll be one of the wild ones.

MR PILCHER (*speaking through this last. Glancing at the new arrival whose hat appears above the platform*) That's all right, then. (*turns to the left*) When I've attended to this microbe that's vitiating the air on my right –

Laughter and interruptions from the crowd.

Geoffrey Stonor stares, one dazed instant, at the face of the new arrival – his own changes. Jean withdraws her arm from his and quite suddenly presses a shade nearer the platform. Stonor moves forward and takes her by the arm.

STONOR	We're going now.
JEAN	Not yet – oh, please not yet. *(breathless, looking back)* Why I– I do believe –

STONOR *(to Lady John, with decision)* I'm going to take Jean out of this mob. Will you come?

LADY JOHN What? Oh yes, if you think – *(another look through her glasses)* But isn't that – *surely* it's – !!!

Vida Levering comes forward. She wears a long, plain, dark green dust cloak. She stands talking to Ernestine Blunt and glancing a little apprehensively at the crowd.

JEAN Geoffrey!

STONOR *(trying to draw Jean away)* Lady John's tired –

JEAN But you don't see who it is, Geoffrey! *(looks into his face and is arrested by the look she finds there.)*

Lady John has pushed in front of them amazed, transfixed, with glass up.

Geoffrey Stonor restrains a gesture of annoyance and withdraws behind two big policemen. Jean from time to time turns to look at him with a face of perplexity.

MR PILCHER *(resuming through a fire of indistinct interruption)* I'll come down and attend to that microbe while a lady will say a few words to you *(raises his voice)* – if she can myke erself 'eard.

Pilcher retires in the midst of booing and cheers.

CHAIRMAN *(harassed and trying to create a diversion)* Someone suggests – and it's such a good idea, I'd like you to listen to it *(noise dies down)* that a clause shall be inserted in the next Suffrage Bill that shall expressly reserve to each Cabinet Minister, and to any respectable man, the power to prevent the Franchise being given to the female members of his family on his public declaration of their lack of sufficient intelligence to entitle them to vote.

VOICES Oh! Oh.

CHAIRMAN Now, I ask you to listen, as quietly as you can, to a lady who is not accustomed to speaking – a – in Trafalgar Square – or a – a matter of fact, at all.

VOICES   A dumb lady. Hooray! Three cheers for the dumb lady!

CHAIRMAN   A lady who, as I've said, will tell you, if you'll behave yourselves, her impressions of the administration of police court justice in this country .

Jean looks wondering at Stonor's sphinx-like face as Vida Levering comes to the edge of the platform.

MISS LEVERING   Mr Chairman, men and women –

VOICES *(off)* Speak up ...

Miss Levering flushes, comes quite to the edge of the platform and raises her voice a little.

MISS LEVERING   I just wanted to tell you that I was – I was – present in the police court when the women were charged for creating a disturbance.

VOICE   Y' oughtn't t' get mixed up in wot didn't concern you.

MISS LEVERING   I – I – *(stumbles and stops)*

VOICES *(talking and laughing increases)* Wot's 'er name? Mrs or Miss? 'Ain't seen this one before.

CHAIRMAN *(anxiously)* Now, see here, men – don't interrupt.

A GIRL *(shrilly)* I don't like this one's 'at. Ye can see she ain't one of 'em.

MISS LEVERING *(trying to recommence)* I –

VOICE   They're a disgrace – them women be'ind yer.

A MAN WITH A FATHERLY AIR It's the w'y they goes on as mykes the Government keep ye from gettin' yer rights.

CHAIRMAN *(losing his temper)* It's the way you go on that – *(noise increases.)*

Chairman drowned, waves his arms and moves his lips. Miss Levering discouraged, turns and looks at Ernestine Blunt and pantomimes: 'It's no good. I can't go on.' Ernestine Blunt comes forward, says a word to the Chairman, who ceases gyrating, and nods.

MISS ERNESTINE BLUNT *(facing the crowd)* Look here. If the Government withhold the vote because they don't like the way some of us ask for it – *let them give it to the Quiet Ones.* Does the Government want to punish *all* women because they don't like the manners of a handful? Perhaps that's you men's notion of justice. It isn't women's.

VOICES   Haw! haw!

MISS LEVERING   Yes. Thi-this is the first time I've ever 'gone on,' as you call it, but they never gave me a vote.

MISS ERNESTINE BLUNT *(with energy)* No! And there are one – two – three – four women on this platform. Now, we all want the vote, as you know. Well, we'd agree to be disfranchised all our lives, if they'd give the vote to all the other women.

VOICE   Look here, you made one speech, give the lady a chawnce.

MISS ERNESTINE BLUNT *(retires smiling)* That's *just* what I wanted *you* to do!

MISS LEVERING   Perhaps you – you don't know – you don't know –

VOICE *(sarcastic)* 'Ow 're we goin' to know if you can't tell us?

MISS LEVERING *(flushing and smiling)* Thank you for that. We couldn't have a better motto. How *are* you to know if we can't somehow manage to tell you? *(with a visible effort she goes on)* Well, I certainly didn't know before that the sergeants and policemen are instructed to deceive the people as to the time such cases are heard. You ask, and you're sent to Marlborough Police Court instead of to Marylebone.

VOICE   They ought ter sent yer to 'Olloway – do y' good.

OLD NEWS VENDOR You go on, Miss, don't mind 'im.

VOICE   Wot d'you expect from a pig but a grunt?

MISS LEVERING   You're told the case will be at two o'clock, and it's really called for eleven. Well, I took a great deal of trouble, and I didn't believe what I was told. *(warming a little to her task)* Yes, that's almost the first thing we have to learn – to get over our touching faith that, because a man tells us something, it's true. I got to the right court, and I was so anxious not to be late, I was too early. The case before the women's was just coming on. I heard a noise. At the door I saw the helmets of two policemen, and I said to myself: 'What sort of crime shall I have to sit and hear about? Is this a burglar coming along between the two big policemen, or will it be a murderer? What sort of felon is to stand in the dock before the women whose crime is they ask for the vote?' But, try as I would, I couldn't see the prisoner. My heart misgave me. Is it a woman, I wondered? Then the policemen got nearer, and I saw – *(she waits an instant)* a little, thin, half-starved boy. What do you think he was charged with? Stealing. What had he been stealing – that small criminal? *Milk.* It seemed to me as I sat there looking on, that the men who had the affairs of the world in their hands from the beginning, and who've made so poor a business of it –

VOICES   Oh! Oh! Pore benighted man! Are we down – 'earted? *Oh,* no!

MISS LEVERING   – so poor a business of it as to have the poor and the unemployed in the condition they're in today – when your only remedy for a starving child is to hale him off to the police court because he had managed to get a little milk – well, I *did* wonder that the men refuse to be helped with a problem they've so notoriously failed at. I began to say to myself: 'Isn't it time the women lent a hand?'

A VOICE   Would you have women magistrates?

She is stumped by the suddenness of the demand.

VOICES   Haw! Haw! Magistrates!
ANOTHER   Women! Let 'em prove first they deserve –
A SHABBY ART STUDENT *(his hair longish, soft hat, and flowing tie)* They study music by thousands – where's their Beethoven? Where's their Plato? Where's the woman Shakespeare?
ANOTHER   Yes – what 'a' they ever *done*?

The speaker clenches her hands, and is recovering her presence of mind, so that by the time the Chairman can make himself heard with, 'Now men, give this lady a fair hearing – don't interrupt.' She, with the slightest of gestures, waves him aside with a low: 'It's all right'

MISS LEVERING *(steadying and raising her voice)* These questions are quite proper! They are often asked elsewhere and I would like to ask in return: Since when was human society held to exist for its handful of geniuses? How many Platos are there here in this crowd?
A VOICE *(very loud and shrill)* Divil a wan! *(laughter)*
MISS LEVERING   Not one. Yet that doesn't keep you men off the

register. How many Shakespeares are there in all England today? Not one. Yet the State doesn't tumble to pieces. Railroads and ships are built, homes are kept going, and babies are born. The world goes on! *(bending over the crowd)* It goes on *by virtue of its common people.*

VOICES *(subdued)* Hear! hear!

MISS LEVERING   I am not concerned that you should think we women can paint great pictures, or compose immortal music, or write good books. I am content that we should be classed with the common people – who keep the world going. But *(straightening up and taking a fresh start)* I'd like the world to go a great deal better. We were talking about justice. I have been inquiring into the kind of lodging the poorest class of homeless women can get in this town of London. I find that only the men of that class are provided for. Some measure to establish Rowton Houses for women has been before the London County Council. They looked into the question 'very carefully', so their apologists say. And what did they decide? They decided that *they could do nothing.*

LADY JOHN *(having forced her way to Stonor's side)* Is that true?

STONOR *(speaking through Miss Levering's next words)* I don't know.

MISS LEVERING   Why could that great, all-powerful body do nothing? Because, if these cheap and decent houses were opened, they said, the homeless women in the streets would make use of them! You'll think I'm not in earnest. But that was actually the decision and the reason given for it. Women that the bitter struggle for existence has forced into a life of horror –

STONOR *(sternly to Lady John)* You think this is the kind of thing – *(a motion of the head towards Jean.)*

MISS LEVERING   – the outcast women might take advantage of the shelter these decent, cheap places offered. But the *men,* I said! Are all who avail themselves of Lord Rowton's hostels, are *they* all angels? Or does wrong-doing in a man not matter? Yet women are recommended to depend on the chivalry of men.

The two policemen, who at first had been strolling about, have stood during this scene in front of Geoffrey Stonor. They turn now and walk away, leaving Stonor exposed. He, embarrassed, moves uneasily, and Vida Levering's eye falls upon his big figure. He still has the collar of his motor coat turned up to his ears. A change passes over her face, and her nerve fails her an instant.

MISS LEVERING   Justice and chivalry!! *(she steadies her voice and hurries on)* – they both remind me of what those of you who read the police court news – (I have begun only lately to do that) – but you've seen the accounts of the girl who's been tried in Manchester lately for the murder of her child. Not pleasant reading. Even if we'd noticed it, we wouldn't speak of it in my world. A few months ago I should have turned away my eyes and forgotten even the headline as quickly as I could. But since that morning in the police court, I read these things. This, as you'll remember, was about a little working girl – an orphan of eighteen – who crawled with the dead body of her new born child to her master's back door, and left the baby there. She dragged herself a little way off and fainted. A few days later she found herself in court, being tried for the murder of her child. Her master – a married man – had of course reported the 'find' at his back door to the police, and he had been summoned to give evidence. The girl cried out to him in the open court, 'You are the father!' He couldn't deny it. The Coroner at the jury's request censured the man, and regretted that the law didn't make him responsible. But he went scot-free. And that girl is now serving her sentence in Strangeways Gaol.

Murmuring and scraps of indistinguishable comment in the crowd, through which only Jean's voice is clear.

JEAN *(who has wormed her way to Stonor's side)* Why do you dislike her so?
STONOR   I? Why should you think –
JEAN *(with a vaguely frightened air)* I never saw you look as you did – as you do.
CHAIRMAN   Order, please – give the lady a fair –
MISS LEVERING *(signing to him 'It's all right')* Men make boast that an English citizen is tried by his peers. What woman is tried by hers? *(A sombre passion strengthens her voice and hurries her on)* A woman is arrested by a man, brought before a man judge, tried by a jury of men, condemned by men, taken to prison by a man, and by a man she's hanged! Where in all this were *her* 'peers'? Why did men so long ago insist on trial by 'a jury of their peers'? So that

justice shouldn't miscarry – wasn't it? A man's peers would best
understand his circumstances, his temptation, the degree of his
guilt. Yet there's no such unlikeness between different classes of
men as exists between man and woman. What man has the knowledge that makes him a fit judge of woman's deeds at that time of
anguish – that hour – *(lowers her voice and bends over the crowd)*
that hour that some woman struggled through to put each man here
into the world. I noticed when a previous speaker quoted the Labour
Party you applauded. Some of you here – I gather – call yourselves
Labour men. Every woman who has borne a child is a Labour
woman. No man among you can judge what she goes through in her
hour of darkness –

JEAN *(with frightened eyes on her lover's set, white face, whispers)*
Geoffrey –

MISS LEVERING *(catching her fluttering breath, goes on very low)*
– in that great agony when, even under the best conditions that
money and devotion can buy, many a woman falls into temporary
mania, and not a few go down to death. In the case of this poor little
abandoned working girl, what man can be the fit judge of her deeds
in that awful moment of half-crazed temptation? Women know of
these things as those know burning who have walked through fire.

*Stonor makes a motion towards Jean and she turns away fronting the
audience. Her hands go up to her throat as though she suffered a
choking sensation. It is in her face that she 'knows'. Miss Levering
leans over the platform and speaks with a low and thrilling
earnestness.*

MISS LEVERING   I would say in conclusion to the women here,
it's not enough to be sorry for these unfortunate sisters. We must get
the conditions of life made fairer. We women must organise. We
must learn to work together. We have all, rich and poor, happy and
unhappy, worked so long and so exclusively for men, we hardly
know how to work for one another. But we must learn. Those who
can, may give money –

VOICES *(grumbling)* Oh, yes – Money! Money!

MISS LEVERING   Those who haven't pennies to give – even those
people aren't so poor they can't give some part of their labour –
some share of their sympathy and support. *(turns to hear something*

the Chairman is whispering to her.)
JEAN *(low to Lady John)* Oh, I'm glad I've got power!
LADY JOHN *(bewildered)* Power! – *you?*
JEAN   Yes, all that money –

Lady John tries to make her way to Stonor.

MISS LEVERING *(suddenly turning from the Chairman to the crowd)* Oh, yes. I hope you'll all join the Union. Come up after the meeting and give your names.
LOUD VOICE   You won't get many men.
MISS LEVERING *(with fire)* Then it's to the women I appeal!

She is about to retire when, with a sudden gleam in her lit eyes, she turns for the last time to the crowd, silencing the general murmur and holding the people by the sudden concentration of passion in her face.

MISS LEVERING   I don't mean to say it wouldn't be better if men and women did this work together – shoulder to shoulder. But the mass of men won't have it so. I only hope they'll realise in time the good they've renounced and the spirit they've aroused. For I know as well as any man could tell me, it would be a bad day for England if all women felt about all men *as I do.*

She retires in a tumult. The others on the platform close about her. The Chairman tries in vain to get a hearing from the excited crowd. Jean tries to make her way through the knot of people surging round her.

STONOR *(calls)* Here – Follow me!
JEAN   No – no – I –
STONOR   You're going the wrong way.
JEAN   This is the way I must go.
STONOR   You can get out quicker on this side.
JEAN   I don't *want* to get out.
STONOR   What! Where are you going?
JEAN   To ask that woman to let me have the honour
of working with her.

She disappears in the crowd.

Curtain.

ACT THREE
Scene One

The drawing room at old Mr Dunbarton's house in Eaton Square. Six o'clock the same evening. As the Curtain rises the door opens and Jean appears on the threshold. She looks back into her own sitting room, then crosses the drawing room, treading softly on the parquet spaces between the rugs. She goes to the window and is in the act of parting the lace curtains when the folding doors are opened by the Butler.

JEAN *(to the Servant)* Sh! *(She goes softly back to the door she has left open and closes it carefully. When she turns, the Butler has stepped aside to admit Geoffrey Stonor, and departed, shutting the folding doors. Stonor comes rapidly forward. Before he gets a word out.)* Speak low, please.

STONOR *(angrily)* I waited about a whole hour for you to come back.

She turns away as though vaguely looking for the nearest chair.

STONOR   If you don't mind leaving *me* like that you might have considered Lady John.

JEAN *(pausing)* Is she here with you?

STONOR   No. My place was nearer than this, and she was very tired. I left her to get some tea. We couldn't tell whether you'd be here, or *what* had become of you.

JEAN   Mr Trent got us a hansom.

STONOR   Trent?

JEAN   The Chairman of the meeting.

STONOR   'Got us'?

DUNBARTON   Miss Levering and me.

STONOR *(incensed)* Miss L –

BUTLER *(opens the door and announces)* Mr Farnborough ...

Enter Mr Richard Farnborough – more flurried than ever.

FARNBOROUGH *(seeing Stonor)* At last! You'll forgive this incursion, Miss Dunbarton, when you hear – *(turns abruptly back to Stonor)* They've been telegraphing you all over London. In despair they set me on your track.

STONOR   Who did? What's up?

FARNBOROUGH (*lays down his hat and fumbles agitatedly in his breast pocket*) There was the devil to pay at Dutfield last night. The Liberal chap tore down from London and took over your meeting!

STONOR   Oh! Nothing about it in the Sunday paper I saw.

FARNBOROUGH   Wait till you see the Press tomorrow morning! There was a great rally and the beggar made a rousing speech.

STONOR   What about?

FARNBOROUGH   Abolition of the Upper House –

STONOR   They were at that when I was at Eton!

FARNBOROUGH   Yes. But this new man has got a way of putting things! – the people went mad. (*pompously*) The Liberal platform as defined at Dutfield is going to make a big difference.

STONOR (*drily*) You think so.

FARNBOROUGH   Well, your agent says as much. (*opens telegram*)

STONOR   My – (*taking telegram*) 'Try find Stonor' – Hm! Hm!

FARNBOROUGH (*pointing*) 'tremendous effect of last night's Liberal manifesto ought to be counteracted in tomorrow's papers.' (*Very earnestly*) – You see, Mr Stonor, it's a battle cry we want.

STONOR (*turns on his heel*) Claptrap!

FARNBOROUGH (*a little dashed*) Well, they've been saying we have nothing to offer but personal popularity. No practical reform. No –

STONOR   No truckling to the masses, I suppose. (*walks impatiently away.*)

FARNBOROUGH (*snubbed*) Well, in these democratic days – (*turns to Jean for countenance*) I hope you'll forgive my bursting in like this. (*struck by her face*) But I can see you realise the gravity – (*lowering his voice with an air of speaking for her ear alone*) It isn't as if he were going to be a mere private member. Everybody knows he'll be in the Cabinet.

STONOR (*drily*) It may be a Liberal Cabinet.

FARNBOROUGH   Nobody thought so up to last night. Why, even your brother – but I am afraid I'm seeming officious. (*takes up his hat.*)

STONOR (*coldly*) What about my brother?

FARNBOROUGH   I met Lord Windlesham as I rushed out of the Carlton.

STONOR Did he say anything?

FARNBOROUGH I told him the Dutfield news.

STONOR *(impatiently)* Well?

FARNBOROUGH He said it only confirmed his fears.

STONOR *(half under his breath)* Said that, did he?

FARNBOROUGH Yes. Defeat is inevitable, he thinks, unless – *(Pause. Geoffrey Stonor who has been pacing the floor, stops but doesn't raise his eyes)* unless you can 'manufacture some political dynamite within the next few hours.' Those were his words.

STONOR *(resumes his walking to and fro, raises his head and catches sight of Jean's white, drawn face. Stops short)* You are very tired.

JEAN No. No.

STONOR *(to Farnborough)* I'm obliged to you for taking so much trouble. *(shakes hands by way of dismissing Farnborough)* I'll see what can be done.

FARNBOROUGH *(offering the reply-paid form)* If you'd like to wire I'll take it.

STONOR *(faintly amused)* You don't understand, my young friend. Moves of this kind are not rushed at by responsible politicians. I must have time for consideration.

FARNBOROUGH *(disappointed)* Oh well, I only hope someone else won't jump into the breach before you. *(watch in hand)* I tell you *(to Jean)* I'll find out what time the newspapers go to press on Sunday. Good bye. *(to Stonor)* I'll be at the Club just *in case* I can be of any use.

STONOR *(firmly)* No, don't do that. If I should have anything new to say –

FARNBOROUGH *(feverishly)* B-b-but with our party, as your brother said – 'heading straight for a vast electoral disaster'.

STONOR If I decide on a counterblast I shall simply telegraph to headquarters. Good bye.

FARNBOROUGH Oh-a-G-Good bye. *(a gesture of: 'The country's going to the dogs.')*

Jean rings the bell. Exit Farnborough.

STONOR *(studying the carpet)* 'Political dynamite', eh? *(pause)* After all … women are much more conservative than men – aren't they?

(Jean looks straight in front of her, making no attempt to reply.)
Especially the women the property qualification would bring in. *(he glances at Jean as though for the first time conscious of her silence.)*
You see now – *(he throws himself into the chair by the table)*
one reason why I've encouraged you to take an interest in public affairs. Because people like us don't go screaming about it, is no sign we don't (some of us) see what's on the way. However little they want to, women of our class will have to come into line. All the best things in the world – everything that civilisation has won will be in danger if – when this change comes – the only women who have practical political training are the women of the lower classes. Women of the lower classes, and *(his brows knit heavily)* – women inoculated by the Socialist virus.

JEAN   Geoffrey.

STONOR *(draws the telegraph form towards him)* Let us see, how we shall put it – when the time comes – shall we?

He detaches a pencil from his watch chain and bends over the paper, writing. Jean opens her lips to speak, moves a shade nearer the table and then falls back upon her silent, half-incredulous misery.

STONOR *(holds the paper off, smiling)* Enough dynamite in that! Rather too much, isn't there, little girl?

JEAN   Geoffrey, I know her story.

STONOR   Whose story?

JEAN   Miss Levering's.

STONOR   *Whose?*

JEAN   Vida Levering's.

Stonor stares speechless. Slight pause.

JEAN *(the words escaping from her in a miserable cry)* Why did you desert her?

STONOR *(staggered)* I!– I?

JEAN   Oh, why did you do it?

STONOR *(bewildered)* What in the name of – What has she been saying to you?

JEAN   Someone else told me part. Then the way you looked when you saw her at Aunt Ellen's – Miss Levering's saying you didn't know her – then your letting out that you knew even the curious name on the handkerchief – Oh, I pieced it together –

STONOR *(with recovered self-possession)* Your ingenuity is
    undeniable!

JEAN   – and then, when she said that at the meeting
    about 'the dark hour' and I looked at your face – it flashed over me.
    – Oh, *why* did you desert her?

STONOR   I *didn't* desert her.

JEAN   Ah-h! *(puts her hands before her eyes.)*

*Stoner makes a passionate motion towards her, is checked by her
muffled voice saying:*

JEAN   I'm glad – I'm glad!

*He stares bewildered. Jean drops her hands in her lap and steadies
her voice.*

JEAN   She went away from you, then?'

STONOR   You don't expect me to enter into –

JEAN   She went away from you?

STONOR *(with a look of almost uncontrollable anger)* Yes!

JEAN   Was that because you wouldn't marry her?

STONOR   I couldn't marry her, and she knew it.

JEAN   Did you want to?

STONOR *(an instant's angry scrutiny and then turning away his
    eyes)* I thought I did – *then*. It's a long time ago.

JEAN   And why 'couldn't' you?

STONOR *(a movement of strong irritation cut short)* Why are you
    catechising me? It's a matter that concerns another woman.

JEAN   If you're saying that it doesn't concern me,
    you're saying – *(her lip trembles)* that *you* don't concern me.

STONOR *(commanding his temper with difficulty)* In those days I – I
    was absolutely dependent on my father.

JEAN   Why, you must have been thirty, Geoffrey.

STONOR *(slight pause)* What? Oh – thereabouts.

JEAN   And everybody says you're so clever.

STONOR   Well, everybody's mistaken.

JEAN *(drawing nearer)* It must have been terribly hard *(Stonor turns
    towards her)* for you both. *(he arrests his movement and stands
    stonily)* that a man like you shouldn't have had the freedom that
    even the lowest seem to have.

STONOR	Freedom?
JEAN	To marry the woman they choose.
STONOR	She didn't break off our relations because I

couldn't marry her.

JEAN	Why was it, then?
STONOR	You're too young to discuss such a story. *(half*

turns away.)

JEAN   I'm not so young as she was when –

STONOR *(wheeling upon her)* Very well, then, if you will have it! The truth is, it didn't seem to weigh upon her as it seems to on you, that I wasn't able to marry her.

JEAN	Why are you so sure of that?
STONOR	Because she didn't so much as hint such a

thing when she wrote that she meant to break off the – the –

JEAN   What made her write like that?

STONOR *(with suppressed rage)* Why *will* you go on talking of what's so long over and ended?

JEAN   What reason did she give?

STONOR   If your curiosity has so got the upper hand – ask her.

JEAN *(her eyes upon him)* You're afraid to tell me.

STONOR *(putting pressure on himself to answer quietly)* I still hoped – at that time – to win my father over. She blamed me because *(goes to the window and looks blindly out and speaks in a low tone)* if the child had lived it wouldn't have been possible to get my father to – to overlook it.

JEAN *(faintly)* You wanted it *overlooked?* I don't underst –

STONOR *(turning passionately back to her)* Of course you don't. *(he seizes her hand and tries to draw her to him.)* If you did, you wouldn't be the beautiful, tender, innocent child you are –

JEAN *(has withdrawn her hand and shrunk from him with an impulse – slight as is its expression – so tragically eloquent, that fear for the first time catches hold of him.)* I am glad you didn't mean to desert her, Geoffrey. It wasn't your fault after all – only some misunderstanding that can be cleared up.

STONOR	*Cleared up?*
JEAN	Yes. Cleared up.

STONOR *(aghast)* You aren't thinking that this miserable old affair I'd as good as forgotten –

JEAN *(in a horror struck whisper, with a glance at the door which he doesn't see.)* Forgotten!

STONOR   No, no. I don't mean exactly forgotten. But you're torturing me so I don't know what I'm saying. *(He goes closer.)* You aren't – Jean! You – you aren't going to let it come between you and me!

JEAN *(presses her handkerchief to her lips, and then, taking it away, answers steadily)* I can't make or unmake what's past. But I'm glad, at least, that you didn't mean to desert her in her trouble. You'll remind her of that first of all, won't you? *(moves to the door.)*

STONOR   Where are you going? *(raising his voice.)* Why should I remind anybody of what I want only to forget?

JEAN *(finger on lip)* Sh!

STONOR *(with eyes on the door)* You don't mean that she's –

JEAN   Yes. I left her to get a little rest …
  (he recoils in an excess of uncontrollable rage. She follows him. Speechless, he goes to get his hat.) Geoffrey, don't go before you hear me. I don't know if what I think matters to you now – but I hope it does. *(with tears)* You can still make me think of you without shrinking – if you will.

STONOR *(fixes her a moment with his eyes. Then sternly)* What is it you are asking of me?

JEAN   To make amends, Geoffrey.

STONOR *(with an outburst)* You poor little innocent!

JEAN   I'm poor enough. But *(locking her hands together)* I'm not so innocent but what I know you must right that old wrong now, if you're ever to right it.

STONOR   You aren't insane enough to think I would turn round in these few hours and go back to something that ten years ago was ended for ever! Why, it's stark, staring madness!

JEAN   No. *(catching on his arm)* What you did ten years ago – *that* was mad. This is paying a debt.

STONOR   Look here, Jean, you're dreadfully wrought up and excited – tired too –

JEAN   No, not tired – though I've travelled so far today. I know you smile at sudden conversions. You think they're hysterical – worse – vulgar. But people must get their revelation how they can. And, Geoffrey, if I can't make you see this one of mine – I shall know your love could never mean strength to me. Only weakness. And I shall be afraid. So afraid I'll never dare to give you the *chance* of making me loathe myself. I shall never see you again.

STONOR   How right *I* was to be afraid of that vein of fanaticism in you. *(moves towards the door)*

JEAN   Certainly you couldn't make a greater mistake than to go away now and think it any good ever to come back. *(he turns)* Even if I came to feel different, I couldn't *do* anything different. I should know all this couldn't be forgotten. I should know that it would poison my life in the end. Yours too.

STONOR *(with suppressed fury)* She has made good use of her time! *(with a sudden thought)* What has changed her? Has *she* been seeing visions too?

JEAN   What do you mean?

STONOR   Why is she intriguing to get hold of a man that, ten years ago, she flatly refused to see, or hold any communication with?

JEAN   'Intriguing to get hold of?' She hasn't mentioned you!

STONOR   *What!* Then how in the name of Heaven do you know that she wants – what you ask?

JEAN *(firmly)* There can't be any doubt about that.

STONOR *(with immense relief)* You absurd, ridiculous child! Then all this is just your own unaided invention. Well – I could thank God! *(falls into the nearest chair and passes his handkerchief over his face.)*

JEAN *(perplexed, uneasy)* For what are you thanking God?

STONOR *(trying to think out his plan of action)* Suppose, *I'm not going to risk it* – but suppose – *(he looks up and at the sight of Jean's face a new tenderness comes into his own. He rises suddenly.)* Whether I deserve to suffer or not – it's quite certain *you* don't. Don't cry, dear one. It never was the real thing. I had to wait till I knew you before I understood.

JEAN *(lifts her eyes brimming)* Oh, is that true? *(checks her movement towards him)* Loving you has made things clear to me I didn't dream of before. If I could think that because of me you were able to do this –

STONOR *(seizes her by the shoulders and says hoarsely)* Look here!
  Do you seriously ask me to give up the girl I love – to go and offer to
  marry a woman that even to think of –
JEAN   You cared for her once. You'll care about her
  again. She is beautiful and brilliant – everything. I've heard she
  could win any man she set herself to –
STONOR *(pushing Jean from him)* She's bewitched you!
JEAN   Geoffrey, Geoffrey, you aren't going away like
  that. This isn't the *end!*
STONOR *(darkly – hesitating)* I suppose even if she refused me,
  you'd –
JEAN   She won't refuse you.
STONOR   She did once.
JEAN   She didn't refuse to marry you –

Jean is going to the door.

STONOR *(catches her by the arm)* Wait! a – *(hunting for some
  means of gaining time)* Lady John is waiting all this while for the
  car to go back with a message.
JEAN   *That's* not a matter of life and death–
STONOR   All the same –I'll go down and give the order.
JEAN *(stopping quite still on a sudden)* Very well. *(sits)* You'll come
  back if you're the man I pray you are. *(breaks into a flood of silent
  tears, her elbows on the table, her face in her hands.)*
STONOR *(returns, bends over her, about to take her in his arms)*
  Dearest of all the world –

*Door opens softly and Vida Levering appears. She is arrested at the
sight of Stonor, and is in the act of drawing back when, upon the slight
noise, Stonor looks round. His face darkens, he stands staring at her
and then with a look of speechless anger goes silently out. Jean, hearing
him shut the door, drops her head on the table with a sob. Vida Levering
crosses slowly to her and stands a moment silent at the girl's side.*

MISS LEVERING   What is the matter?
JEAN *(lifting her head, drying her eyes)* I – I've been seeing Geoffrey.
MISS LEVERING *(with an attempt at lightness)* Is this the effect
  seeing Geoffrey has?
JEAN   You see, I know now as *(Miss Levering looks*

quite uncomprehending) – how he *(drops her eyes)* –how he
spoiled someone else's life.

MISS LEVERING *(quickly)* Who tells you that?

JEAN   Several people have told me.

MISS LEVERING   Well, you should be very careful how you
believe what you hear.

JEAN *(passionately)* You *know* it's true.

MISS LEVERING   I know that it's possible to be mistaken.

JEAN   I see! You're trying to shield him –

MISS LEVERING   Why should I – what is it to me?

JEAN *(with tears)* Oh – h, how you must love him!

MISS LEVERING   Listen to me –

JEAN *(rising)* What's the use of your going on denying it? *(Miss
Levering, about to break in, is silenced)* Geoffrey doesn't ... *(Jean,
struggling to command her feelings, goes to window. Vida
Levering relinquishes an impulse to follow, and sits left centre.
Jean comes slowly back with her eyes bent on the floor, does not
lift them till she is quite near Vida. Then the girl's self-absorbed
face changes.)* Oh, don't look like that! I shall bring him back to
you! *(drops on her knees beside the other's chair.)*

MISS LEVERING   You would be impertinent *(softening)* if you
weren't a romantic child. You can't bring him back.

JEAN   Yes, he –

MISS LEVERING   But there's something you can do –

JEAN   What?

MISS LEVERING   Bring him to the point where he recognises
that he's in our debt.

JEAN   In *our* debt?

MISS LEVERING   In debt to women. He can't repay the one he
robbed –

JEAN *(wincing and rising from her knees)* Yes, yes.

MISS LEVERING *(sternly)* No, he can't repay the dead. But there are
the living. There are the thousands with hope still in their hearts
and youth in their blood. Let him help *them*. Let him be a Friend to
Women.

JEAN *(rising on a wave of enthusiasm)* Yes, yes – I understand. That
too!

The door opens. As Stonor enters with Lady John, he makes a slight gesture towards the two as much as to say, 'You see'.

JEAN *(catching sight of him)* Thank you!

LADY JOHN *(in a clear, commonplace tone to Jean)* Well, you rather gave us the slip. Vida, I believe Mr Stonor wants to see you for a few minutes *(glances at watch)* – but I'd like a word with you first, as I must get back. *(to Stonor)* Do you think the car – your man said something about re-charging.

STONOR *(hastily)* Oh, did he? I'll see about it ...

As Stonor is going out he encounters the Butler. Exit Stonor.

BUTLER　　　　　　Mr Trent has called, Miss, to take Miss Levering to the meeting.

JEAN　　　　　　Bring Mr Trent into my sitting room. I'll tell him you can't go tonight.

Exit Butler centre, Jean left.

LADY JOHN *(hurriedly)* I know, my dear, *you're* not aware of what that impulsive girl wants to insist on.

MISS LEVERING　　Yes, I am aware of it.

LADY JOHN　　　　But it isn't with your sanction, surely, that she goes on making this extraordinary demand.

MISS LEVERING *(slowly)* I didn't sanction it at first, but I've been thinking it over.

LADY JOHN　　　　Then all I can say is I am greatly disappointed in you. You threw this man over years ago for reasons – whatever they were – that seemed to you good and sufficient. And now you come between him and a younger woman – just to play Nemesis, so far as I can make out!

MISS LEVERING　　Is that what he says?

LADY JOHN　　　　He says nothing that isn't fair and considerate.

MISS LEVERING　　I can see he's changed.

LADY JOHN　　　　And you're unchanged – is that it?

MISS LEVERING　　I've changed even more than he.

LADY JOHN　　　　But *(pity and annoyance blended in her tone)* – you care about him still, Vida?

MISS LEVERING　　No.

LADY JOHN　　　　I see. It's just that you wish to marry somebody –

MISS LEVERING   Oh, Lady John, there are no men listening.

LADY JOHN *(surprised)* No, I didn't suppose there were.

MISS LEVERING   Then why keep up that old pretence?

LADY JOHN   What pre –

MISS LEVERING   That to marry *at all costs* is every woman's
dearest ambition till the grave closes over her. You and I *know* it
isn't true.

LADY JOHN   Well, but – Oh! it was just the unexpected
sight of him bringing it back – *That* was what fired you this
afternoon! *(with an honest attempt at sympathetic understanding)*
Of course. The memory of a thing like that can never die – can never
even be dimmed – *for the woman.*

MISS LEVERING   I mean her to think so.

LADY JOHN *(bewildered)* Jean! *(Miss Levering nods.)*

LADY JOHN   And it *isn't so?*

MISS LEVERING   You don't seriously believe a woman with
anything else to think about, comes to the end of ten years still
absorbed in a memory of that sort?

LADY JOHN *(astonished)* You've got over it, then!

MISS LEVERING   If the newspapers didn't remind me I shouldn't
remember once a twelvemonth that there was ever such a person as
Geoffrey Stonor in the world.

LADY JOHN *(with unconscious rapture)* Oh, I'm *so glad!*

MISS LEVERING *(smiles grimly)* Yes, I'm glad too.

LADY JOHN   And if Geoffrey Stonor offered you – what's
called 'reparation' – you'd refuse it?

MISS LEVERING *(smiles a little contemptuously)* Geoffrey Stonor!
For me he's simply one of the far back links in a chain of evidence.
It's certain I think a hundred times of other women's present
unhappiness, to once that I remember that old unhappiness of mine
that's past. I think of the nail and chain makers of Cradley Heath.
The sweated girls of the slums. I think of the army of ill-used women
whose very existence I mustn't mention –

LADY JOHN *(interrupting hurriedly)* Then why in Heaven's name do
you let poor Jean imagine –

MISS LEVERING *(bending forward)* Look – I'll trust you, Lady
John. I don't suffer from that old wrong as Jean thinks I do, but I
shall coin her sympathy into gold for a greater cause than mine.

LADY JOHN   I don't understand you.

MISS LEVERING   Jean isn't old enough to be able to care as much about a principle as about a person. But if my half-forgotten pain can turn her generosity into the common treasury –

LADY JOHN   What do you propose she shall do, poor child?

MISS LEVERING   Use her hold over Geoffrey Stonor to make him help us!

LADY JOHN   Help you?

MISS LEVERING   The man who served one woman – God knows how many more – very ill, shall serve hundreds of thousands well. Geoffrey Stonor shall make it harder for his son, harder still for his grandson, to treat any woman as he treated me.

LADY JOHN   How will he do that?

MISS LEVERING   By putting an end to the helplessness of women.

LADY JOHN *(ironically)* You must think he has a great deal of power–

MISS LEVERING   Power? Yes, men have too much over penniless and frightened women.

LADY JOHN *(impatiently)* What nonsense! You talk as though the women hadn't their share of human nature. *We* aren't made of ice any more than the men.

MISS LEVERING   No, but all the same we have more self-control.

LADY JOHN   Than men?

MISS LEVERING   You know we have.

LADY JOHN *(shrewdly)* I know we mustn't admit it.

MISS LEVERING   For fear they'd call us fishes!

LADY JOHN *(evasively)* They talk of our lack of self-control, but it's the last thing they *want* women to have.

MISS LEVERING   Oh, we know what they want us to have. So we make shift to have it. If we don't, we go without hope – sometimes we go without bread.

LADY JOHN *(shocked)* Vida – do you mean to say that you ...

MISS LEVERING   I mean to say that men's vanity won't let them see it but the thing's largely a question of economics.

LADY JOHN *(shocked)* You never loved him, then!

MISS LEVERING   Oh yes, I loved him – once. It was my helplessness turned the best thing life can bring, into a curse for both of us.

LADY JOHN   I don't understand you –

MISS LEVERING   Oh, being 'understood!' – that's too much to expect. When people come to know I've joined the Union –

LADY JOHN   But you won't –

MISS LEVERING   – who is there who will resist the temptation to say, 'Poor Vida Levering! What a pity she hasn't got a husband and a baby to keep her quiet'? The few who know about me, they'll be equally sure that it's not the larger view of life I've gained – my own poor little story is responsible for my new departure. *(leans forward and looks into Lady John's face)* My best friend, she will be surest of all, that it's a private sense of loss, or, lower yet, a grudge – ! But I tell you the only difference between me and thousands of women with husbands and babies is that I'm free to say what I think. *They aren't.*

LADY JOHN *(rising and looking at her watch)* I must get back – my poor ill-used guests.

MISS LEVERING *(rising)* I won't ring. I think you'll find Mr Stonor downstairs waiting for you.

LADY JOHN *(embarrassed)* Oh – a – he will have left word about the car in any case....

Miss Levering has opened the door. Allen Trent is in the act of saying goodbye to Jean in the hall.

MISS LEVERING   Well, Mr Trent, I didn't expect to see you this evening.

TRENT *(comes and stands in the doorway)* Why not? Have I ever failed?

MISS LEVERING   Lady John, this is one of our allies. He is good enough to squire me through the rabble from time to time.

LADY JOHN   Well, I think it's very handsome of you, after what she said today about men. *(shakes hands)*

TRENT   I've no great opinion of most men myself. I might add – or of most women.

LADY JOHN   Oh! Well, at any rate I shall go away relieved to think that Miss Levering's plain speaking hasn't alienated *all* masculine regard.

TRENT   Why should it?

LADY JOHN   That's right, Mr. Trent! Don't believe all she says in the heat of propaganda.

TRENT   I do believe all she says. But I'm not cast down.

LADY JOHN *(smiling)* Not when she says –

TRENT *(interrupting)* Was there never a misogynist of my sex who ended by deciding to make an exception?

LADY JOHN *(smiling significantly)* Oh if *that's* what you build on!

TRENT   Well, why shouldn't a man-hater on your side prove equally open to reason?

MISS LEVERING   That part of the question doesn't concern me. I've come to a place where I realise that the first battles of this new campaign must be fought by women alone. The only effective help men could give – amendment of the law – they refuse. The rest is nothing.

LADY JOHN   Don't be ungrateful, Vida. Here's Mr Trent ready to face criticism in publicly championing you.

MISS LEVERING   It's an illusion that I as an individual need Mr Trent. I am quite safe in the crowd. Please don't wait for me, and don't come for me again.

TRENT *(flushes)* Of course if you'd rather –

MISS LEVERING   And that reminds me. I was asked to thank you and to tell you, too, that they – the women of the Union – they won't need your chairmanship any more – though that, I beg you to believe, has nothing to do with any feeling of mine.

TRENT *(hurt)* Of course, I know there must be other men ready – better known men –

MISS LEVERING   It isn't that. It's simply that they find a man can't keep a rowdy meeting in order as well as a woman. *(he stares)*

LADY JOHN   You aren't serious?

MISS LEVERING *(to Trent)* Haven't you noticed that all their worst disturbances come when men are in charge?

TRENT   Well – a – *(laughs a little ruefully as he moves to the door)* I hadn't connected the two ideas. Good bye.

MISS LEVERING   Good bye.

Jean takes him downstairs, right centre.

LADY JOHN *(as Trent disappears)* That nice boy's in love with you. *(Levering simply looks at her)* Good bye. *(they shake hands)* I wish you hadn't been so unkind to that nice boy!

MISS LEVERING   Do you?

LADY JOHN   Yes, for then I would be more certain of your telling Geoffrey Stonor that intelligent women don't nurse their wrongs and lie in wait to punish them.

MISS LEVERING   You are *not* certain?

LADY JOHN *(goes close up to Vida)* Are you?

Levering stands with her eyes on the ground, silent, motionless. Lady John, with a nervous glance at her watch and a gesture of extreme perturbation, goes hurriedly out. Vida shuts the door. She comes slowly back, sits down and covers her face with her hands. She rises and begins to walk up and down, obviously trying to master her agitation. Enter Geoffrey Stonor.

MISS LEVERING   Well, have they primed you? Have you got your lesson *(with a little broken laugh)* by heart at last?

STONOR *(looking at her from immeasurable distance)* I am not sure I understand you. *(pause)* However unpropitious your mood may be – I shall discharge my errand. *(Pause. Her silence irritates him)* I have promised to offer you what I believe is called 'amends.'

MISS LEVERING *(quickly)* You've come to realise, then – after all these years – that you owed me something?

STONOR *(on the brink of protest, checks himself)* I am not here to deny it.

MISS LEVERING *(fiercely)* Pay, then – *pay*.

STONOR *(a moment's dread as he looks at her, his lips set. Then stonily)* I have promised that, if you exact it. I will.

MISS LEVERING   Ah! If I insist you'll 'make it all good'! *(quite low)* Then don't you know you must pay me in kind?

STONOR   What do you mean.

MISS LEVERING   Give me back what you took from me: my old faith. Give me that.

STONOR   Oh, if you mean to make phrases – *(a gesture of scant patience)*

MISS LEVERING *(going closer)* Or give me back mere kindness – or even tolerance. Oh, I don't mean *your* tolerance! Give me back the power to think fairly of my brothers – not as mockers – thieves.

STONOR   I have not mocked you. And I have asked you –

MISS LEVERING   Something you knew I should refuse!

Or *(her eyes blaze)* did you dare to be afraid I wouldn't?

STONOR   I suppose, if we set our teeth, – we could –

MISS LEVERING   I couldn't – not even if I set my teeth. And you wouldn't dream of asking me, if you thought there was the smallest chance.

STONOR   I can do no more than make you an offer of such reparation as is in my power. If you don't accept it – *(he turns with an air of 'That's done.')*

MISS LEVERING   Accept it? No! ... Go away and live in debt! Pay and pay and pay – and find yourself still in debt! – for a thing you'll never be able to give me back. *(lower)* And when you come to die, say to yourself, "I paid all creditors but one."

STONOR   I'm rather tired, you know, of this talk of debt. If I hear that you persist in it I shall have to –

MISS LEVERING   What? *(she faces him)*

STONOR   No. I'll keep to my resolution. *(turning to the door)*

MISS LEVERING *(intercepting him)* What resolution?

STONOR   I came here, under considerable pressure, to speak of the future – not to re-open the past.

MISS LEVERING   The Future and the Past are one.

STONOR   You talk as if that old madness was mine alone. It is the woman's way.

MISS LEVERING   I know. And it's not fair. Men suffer as well as we by the woman's starting wrong. We are taught to think the man a sort of demigod. If he tells her: 'go down into Hell' – down into Hell she goes.

STONOR   Make no mistake. Not the woman alone. *They go down together.*

MISS LEVERING   Yes, they go down together, but the man comes up alone. As a rule. It is more convenient so – for him. And for the Other Woman ... *(the eyes of both go to Jean's door)*

STONOR *(angrily)* My conscience is clear. I know – and so do you – that most men in my position wouldn't have troubled themselves. I gave myself endless trouble.

MISS LEVERING *(with wondering eyes)* So you've gone about all these years feeling that you'd discharged every obligation.

STONOR   Not only that. I stood by you with a fidelity that was nothing short of Quixotic. If, woman like, you must recall the Past – I insist on your recalling it correctly.

MISS LEVERING *(very low)* You think I don't recall it correctly?

STONOR   Not when you make other people believe that I deserted you. *(with gathering wrath)* It's a curious enough charge when you stop to consider – *(checks himself, and with a gesture of impatience sweeps the whole thing out of his way)*

MISS LEVERING   Well, when we *do* – just for five minutes out of ten years – when we do stop to consider –

STONOR   We remember it was *you* who did the deserting! Since you had to rake the story up, you might have had the fairness to tell the facts.

MISS LEVERING   You think 'the facts' would have excused you! *(she sits)*

STONOR   No doubt you've forgotten them, since Lady John tells me you wouldn't remember my existence once a year if the newspapers didn't –

MISS LEVERING   Ah, you minded that!

STONOR *(with manly spirit)* I minded your giving false impressions. *(she is about to speak, he advances on her)* Do you deny that you returned my letters unopened?

MISS LEVERING *(quietly)* No.

STONOR   Do you deny that you refused to see me – and that, when I persisted, you vanished?

MISS LEVERING   I don't deny any of those things.

STONOR   Why, I had no trace of you for years!

MISS LEVERING   I suppose not.

STONOR   Very well, then. What *could* I do?

MISS LEVERING   Nothing. It was too late to do anything.

STONOR   It wasn't too late! You knew – since you 'read the papers' – that my father died that same year. There was no longer any barrier between us.

MISS LEVERING   Oh yes, there was a barrier.

STONOR   Of your own making, then.

MISS LEVERING   I had my guilty share in it but the barrier *(her voice trembles)* – the barrier was your invention.

STONOR   It was no 'invention'. If you had ever known my father –

MISS LEVERING   Oh, the echoes! The echoes! How often you used to say, if I 'knew your father!' But you said, too *(lower)* – you called the greatest barrier by another name.

STONOR   What name?

MISS LEVERING *(very low)* The child that was to come.

STONOR *(hastily)* That was before my father died. While I still hoped to get his consent.

MISS LEVERING *(nods)* How the thought of that all-powerful personage used to terrorise me! What chance had a little unborn child against 'the last of the great feudal lords', as you called him.

STONOR   You *know* the child would have stood between you and me!

MISS LEVERING   I know the child did stand between you and me!

STONOR *(with vague uneasiness)* It *did* stand –

MISS LEVERING   Happy mothers teach their children. Mine had to teach me.

STONOR   You talk as if –

MISS LEVERING   – teach me that a woman may do a thing for love's sake that shall kill love.

A silence.

STONOR *(fearing and putting from him fuller comprehension, rises with an air of finality)* You certainly made it plain you had no love left for me.

MISS LEVERING   I had need of it all for the child.

STONOR *(stares – comes closer, speaks hurriedly and very low)* Do you mean then that, after all – it lived?

MISS LEVERING   No, I mean that it was sacrificed. But it showed me no barrier is so impassable as the one a little child can raise.

STONOR *(a light dawning)* Was that why you ... was *that* why?

MISS LEVERING *(nods, speechless a moment)* Day and night there it was! – between my thought of you and me. *(he sits again, staring at her)* When I was most unhappy I would wake, thinking I heard it cry. It was my own crying I heard, but I seemed to have it in my arms. I suppose I was mad. I used to lie there in that lonely farmhouse pretending to hush it. It was so I hushed myself.

STONOR   I never knew –

MISS LEVERING   I didn't blame you. You couldn't risk being
with me.

STONOR   You agreed that for both our sakes –

MISS LEVERING   Yes, you had to be very circumspect. You were
so well known. Your autocratic father, your brilliant political future–

STONOR   Be fair. *Our* future – as I saw it then.

MISS LEVERING   Yes, it all hung on concealment. It must have
looked quite simple to you. You didn't know that the ghost of a child
that had never seen the light, the frail thing you meant to sweep
aside and forget – have *swept* aside and forgotten – you didn't know
it was strong enough to push you out of my life. *(lower with added
intensity)* It can do more.*(leans over him and whispers)* It can push
that girl out. *(Stonor's face changes)* It can do more still.

STONOR   Are you threatening me?

MISS LEVERING   No, I am preparing you.

STONOR   For what?

MISS LEVERING   For the work that must be done. Either with
your help – or *that girl's*. *(Stonor lifts his eyes a moment)* One of
two things. Either her life, and all she has, given to this new service
– or a Ransom, if I give her up to you.

STONOR   I see. A price. Well – ?

MISS LEVERING *(looks searchingly in his face, hesitates and
shakes her head)* Even if I could trust you to pay – no, it would be a
poor bargain to give her up for anything you could do.

STONOR *(rising)* In spite of your assumption – she may not be your tool.

MISS LEVERING   You are horribly afraid she is! But you are
wrong. Don't think it's merely I that have got hold of Jean
Dunbarton.

STONOR *(angrily)* Who else?

MISS LEVERING   The New Spirit that's abroad. *(Stonor turns
away with an exclamation and begins to pace, sentinel-like, up and
down before Jean's door)* How else should that inexperienced girl
have felt the new loyalty and responded as she did?

STONOR *(under his breath)* 'New' indeed – however little loyal.

MISS LEVERING   Loyal above all. But no newer than electricity
was when it first lit up the world. It had been there since the world
began – waiting to do away with the dark. *So has the thing you're
fighting.*

STONOR *(his voice held down to its lowest register)* The thing I'm
fighting is nothing more than one person's hold on a highly sensitive
imagination. I consented to this interview with the hope – *(a
gesture of impotence)* It only remains for me to show her your true
motive is revenge.

MISS LEVERING　　　Once say that to her and you are lost! *(Stonor
motionless: his look is the look of a man who sees happiness
slipping away)* I know what it is that men fear. It even seems as if it
must be through fear that your enlightenment will come. That is
why I see a value in Jean Dumbarton far beyond her fortune.
(Stonor lifts his eyes dully and fixes them on Vida's face) More than
any girl I know – if I keep her from you – that gentle, inflexible
creature could rouse in men the old half-superstitious fear –

STONOR　　　'Fear?' I believe you are mad.

MISS LEVERING　　　'Mad.' 'Unsexed.' These are the words of today.
In the Middle Ages men cried out 'Witch!' and burnt her – the
woman who served no man's bed or board.

STONOR　　　You want to make that poor child believe –

MISS LEVERING　　　She sees for herself we've come to a place
where we find there's a value men see in them. You teach us not to
look to you for some of the things we need most. If women must be
freed by women, we have need of such as – *(her eyes go to Jean's
door)* – who knows? She may be the new Joan of Arc.

STONOR *(aghast)* That *she* should be the sacrifice!

MISS LEVERING　　　You have taught us to look very calmly on the
sacrifice of women. Men tell us in every tongue it's 'a necessary evil'.
(Stoner stands rooted, staring at the ground) One girl's happiness,
against a thing nobler than happiness for thousands – who can
hesitate? – Not Jean.

STONOR　　　Good God! Can't you see that this crazed
campaign you'd start her on – even if it's successful, it can only be
so through the help of men? What excuse shall you make your own
soul for not going straight to the goal?

MISS LEVERING　　　You think we wouldn't be glad to go straight to
the goal?

STONOR　　　I do. I see you'd much rather punish me and
see her revel in a morbid self-sacrifice.

MISS LEVERING　　　You say I want to punish you only because, like

most men, you won't take the trouble to understand what we do
want – or how determined we are to have it. You can't kill this new
spirit among women. *(going nearer)* And you couldn't make a
greater mistake than to think it finds a home only in the exceptional,
or the unhappy. It's so strange, Geoffrey, to see a man like you as
much deluded as the Hyde Park loafers who say to Ernestine Blunt,
'Who's hurt *your* feelings?' Why not realise *(going quite close to
him)* this is a thing that goes deeper than personal experience?
And yet *(lowering her voice and glancing at the door)* if you take
only the narrowest personal view, a good deal depends on what you
and I agree upon in the next five minutes.

STONOR *(bringing her farther away from the door)* You recommend
my realising the larger issues. But in your ambition to attach that
girl to the chariot wheels of 'Progress', you quite ignore the fact that
people fitter for such work – the men you look to enlist in the end –
are ready waiting to give the thing a chance.

MISS LEVERING   Men are ready! What men?

STONOR *(avoiding her eyes, picking his words)* Women have
themselves to blame that the question has grown so delicate that
responsible people shrink – for the moment – from being implicated
in it.

MISS LEVERING   We have seen the 'shrinking'.

STONOR   Without quoting any one else. I might point
out that the New Antagonism seems to have blinded you to the small
fact that I, for one, am not an opponent.

MISS LEVERING   The phrase *has* a familiar ring. We have heard
it from four hundred and twenty others.

STONOR   I spoke, if I may say so, of someone who would
count. Someone who can carry his party along with him – or risk a
seat in the Cabinet.

MISS LEVERING *(quickly)* Did you mean you are ready to do that?

STONOR   An hour ago I was.

MISS LEVERING   Ah! ... an hour ago.

STONOR   Exactly. You don't understand men. They can
be led. They can't be driven. Ten minutes before you came into the
room I was ready to say I would throw in my political lot with this
Reform.

MISS LEVERING   And now ...?

STONOR Now you block my way by an attempt at coercion. By forcing my hand you give my adherence an air of bargain – driving for a personal end. Exactly the mistake of the ignorant agitators of your 'Union,' as you call it. You have a great deal to learn. This movement will go forward, not because of the agitation, but in spite of it. There are men in Parliament who would have been actively serving the Reform today … as actively as so vast a constitutional change –

MISS LEVERING (*smiles faintly*) And they haven't done it because –

STONOR Because it would have put a premium on breaches of decent behaviour. (*he takes a crumpled piece of paper out of his pocket*) Look here!

MISS LEVERING (*flushes with excitement as she reads the telegram*) This is very good. I see only one objection.

STONOR Objection!

MISS LEVERING You haven't sent it.

STONOR *That* is your fault.

MISS LEVERING When did you write this?

STONOR Just before you came in – when – (*he glances at the door*)

MISS LEVERING Ah! It must have pleased Jean – that message. (*Offers him back the paper. Stonor astonished at her yielding it up so lightly, and remembering Jean had not so much as read it. He throws himself heavily into a chair and drops his head in his hands.*) I could drive a hard and fast bargain with you, but I think I won't. If *both* love and ambition urge you on, perhaps – (*she gazes at the slack, hopeless figure with its sudden look of age – goes over silently and stands by his side*) After all, life hasn't been quite fair to you. (*he raises his heavy eyes*) You fall out of one ardent woman's dreams into another's.

STONOR You may as well tell me – do you mean to – ?

MISS LEVERING To keep you and her apart? No.

STONOR (*for the first time tears come into his eyes. After a moment he holds out his hand*) What can I do for you? (*Vida shakes her head, speechless*) For the real you. Not the Reformer, or the would-be politician – for the woman I so unwillingly hurt. (*as she turns away, struggling with her feelings, he lays a detaining hand on her arm*) You may not believe it, but now that I understand, there is almost nothing I wouldn't do to right that old wrong.

MISS LEVERING   There's nothing to be done. You can never give me back my child.

STONOR (*at the anguish in Vida's face his own has changed*) Will that ghost give you no rest?

MISS LEVERING   Yes, oh, yes. I see life is nobler than I knew. There is work to do.

STONOR (*stopping her as she goes towards the folding doors*) Why should you think that it's only you, these ten years have taught something to? Why not give even a man credit for a willingness to learn something of life, and for being sorry – profoundly sorry – for the pain his instruction has cost others? You seem to think I've taken it all quite lightly. That's not fair. All my life, ever since you disappeared, the thought of you has hurt. I would give anything I possess to know you – were happy again.

MISS LEVERING   Oh, happiness!

STONOR (*significantly*) Why shouldn't you find it still?

MISS LEVERING (*stares an instant*) I see! She couldn't help telling about Allen Trent – Lady John couldn't.

STONOR   You're one of the people the years have not taken from, but given more to. You are more than ever ... You haven't lost your beauty.

MISS LEVERING   The gods saw it was so little effectual, it wasn't worth taking away. (*she stands looking out into the void*) One woman's mishap? – what is that? A thing as trivial to the great world as it's sordid in most eyes. But the time has come when a woman may look about her, and say, 'What general significance has my secret pain? Does it "join on" to anything?' And I find it does. I'm no longer merely a woman who has stumbled on the way. I'm one (*she controls with difficulty the shake in her voice*) who has got up bruised and bleeding, wiped the dust from her hands and the tears from her face, and said to herself not merely, 'Here's one luckless woman! but – here is a stone of stumbling to many. Let's see if it can't be moved out of other women's way.' And she calls people to come and help. No mortal man, let alone a woman, *by herself,* can move that rock of offence. But (*with a sudden sombre flame of enthusiasm*) if many help, Geoffrey, the thing can be done.

STONOR (*looks at her with wondering pity*) Lord! how you care!

MISS LEVERING (*touched by his moved face*) Don't be so sad. Shall I tell you a secret? Jean's ardent dreams needn't frighten you, if she has a child. *That* – from the beginning, it was not the strong arm – it was the weakest – the little, little arms that subdued the fiercest of us. *(Stonor puts out a pitying hand uncertainly towards her. She does not take it, but speaks with great gentleness)* You will have other children, Geoffrey – for me there was to be only one. Well, well – *(she brushes her tears away)* since men alone have tried and failed to make a decent world for the little children to live in – it's as well some of us are childless. *(quietly taking up her hat and cloak)* Yes, *we* are the ones who have no excuse for standing aloof from the fight.

STONOR   Vida!

MISS LEVERING What?

STONOR   You've forgotten something. *(as she looks back he is signing the message) This ...*

She goes out silently with the 'political dynamite' in her hand ...

Curtain.

The end.

Elizabeth Robins (1862-1952)

Born in Louisville, Kentucky, and educated at Putnam Female seminary in Ohio she became an actress with the Boston Museum Company, where she played almost three hundred parts in Boston and on tour. In 1885, she married an actor, George Parks, who killed himself two years later. In 1889, Robins moved to London where she established herself as a major actress and soon became active in the movement to bring Ibsen's plays to Britain, working with her close friend the critic William Archer. In *Ibsen and the Actress* (1928), Robins writes of the life-changing experience of seeing *A Doll's House* and her determination, with fellow American actress Marion Lea, to produce *Hedda Gabler* themselves when the managers expressed indifference and loathing towards it. She performed leading roles in many Ibsen plays and produced the work of other playwrights including fellow Norwegian Alfhild Agrell's *Karin*, (Vaudeville, 1892) translated by Florence Bell. Bell was Robins' close friend and co-author on the controversial play *Alan's Wife* (1893), dealing with infanticide, which they produced and published anonymously.

Fifteen novels followed, many with theatrical themes (some under the pseudonym C.E. Raimond) including *The Coming Woman* (1892), *George Mandeville's Husband* (1894), and *The Open Door* (1898). Several were adapted for the stage or from her stage plays, like *The Convert*, based on *Votes For Women*, which was one of the first plays directly about the suffrage campaign in Britain (both 1907).

Robins was a prominent member of the WSPU and first President of the WWSL. She lived for many years with Octavia Wilberforce, the doctor and feminist, with whom she adopted a child.

In 1913, many of her speeches, lectures and articles on the Suffrage Movement were published in volume form as *Way Stations*. These and many of her novels are now available online. Later, *Theatre and Friendship*, her correspondence with Henry James was published. Further (unpublished) plays include: *Mirkwater*, *The Silver Lotus* (1895) *Benvenuto Cellini* (1899/1900), *Judith,* (c1906), *The Bowarra* (1909) and *Where Are You Going To...?*, originally written for Bensusan's Women's Theatre (also known as *My Little Sister*), *Evangeline* (1914) and *The Secret that Was Kept* or *Fear*[1].

---

[1]   Robins' unpublished works are in the New York University Fales Library.

A Change of Tenant

A Change of Tenant

The play examines the reasons why Squire Brooks has decided to evict his long-standing tenant of 30 years, a widow, Mrs Basset, despite the fact that she is an industrious, reliable tenant who pays her rent on time and looks after his property well.

The Squire reluctantly agrees to her visit to plead her case. He reveals that the insuperable problem is her sex. Not having a vote, she will not be able to support his son in winning a highly marginal election. In the meeting that follows with his prospective new tenant, John Smith, the Squire is forced to question the wisdom of the 'Mrs Bassets' being disenfranchised when the 'John Smiths' of the world have a say in government. John Smith is a drinker and a fool, in debt and ignorant, and when he has bothered to vote at all, he has spoiled his voting papers.

The piece is weakened by the stereotypical portrayal of both John Smith and Mrs Basset. In choosing to make Basset unremarkable, merely the embodiment of reasonable ordinary civic virtue, the author bases her argument on justice: she is visibly no less worthy of a vote than a similar man in her circumstances, no less worthy than was her husband. She is a version of a virtuous, suffering (albeit middle-aged) heroine, victimised by the heartless squire. Her ordinary virtues: concern for her neighbours, maintaining and improving the property, are contrasted to Smith's fecklessness and selfishness. However, she also reveals more dynamic virtues in her response to the situation – a determination to be given the reasons for her removal and an intelligence and adaptability. She understands the processes of political persuasion 'talking to people, giving away papers', in contrast to Smith, and is willing to earn more, take in washing rather than keep chickens, if required, but finally these cannot make up for her inability to vote.

She is sent away for 'a vote is a vote, and nothing else however good and necessary can make up for the lack of a vote'. It is only when faced with Smith's record of rent arrears that the Squire relents in his decision.

A Change of Tenant

Helen Margaret Nightingale (1908)

CHARACTERS

Squire Brooks
Mrs Basset
John Smith
Servant

Scene One

A Room at the Hall. Squire Brooks discovered reading paper.
Enter servant.

SERVANT   Mrs Basset wishes to speak to you, sir.

SQUIRE *(laying aside paper)* Mrs Basset! What Mrs Basset?

SERVANT   From Hillside cottage, sir.

SQUIRE   Oh–ah–yes. Tell her I'm busy, Keen.

SERVANT   Yes, sir. *(exit)*

SQUIRE   The Widow Basset, I suppose. Lorden spoke to me about her last week. He said she had been thirty years at Hillside, and there would probably be a bit of a bother when she heard she'd got to turn out. Can't be helped, though – Bob will need every vote he can scrape if he's to get in at the next election. We can't afford to have any voteless tenants on this estate. *(takes up paper again)*

Re-enter Servant.

SERVANT   Beg pardon, sir, but Mrs Basset says her business is very important, and she won't detain you more than a few minutes.

SQUIRE *(testily)* I told you to say I was engaged, Keen.

Servant goes towards the door.

SQUIRE	Keen!
SERVANT	Yes, sir.
SQUIRE	Ask her if she can't send a message.

Exit Servant.

SQUIRE   Yes, Bob will have a stiff fight for it, and elections have been lost by one vote before now. No, no, we can't afford to run any risks of that sort in this constituency.

Re-enter Servant.

SERVANT   Mrs. Basset's very sorry, sir, but she can't explain in a message, and she'll call again tomorrow if that will be more convenient to you.

SQUIRE   Confound it! No, it won't be convenient. *(rises)* Why can't the woman understand that I don't want to see her? It won't do the slightest good. *(hesitates)* Still, perhaps, I'd better see her. If there is to be a scene, we'd better get it over. *(to Servant)* Very well, I'll see her, Keen.

Exit Servant.

SQUIRE   It won't do the slightest good, though. Lorden says he can put his finger on a new tenant now – one that will be entirely satisfactory from Bob's point of view. 'Entirely satisfactory' from Bob's, and 'fairly satisfactory' from mine were his actual words, by the way. I wonder what he meant by that? Still, one can't have everything in this world.

Enter Mrs Basset, who curtseys.

SQUIRE	Oh, good evening, Mrs Basset, sit down.
MRS BASSET	Thank you, sir. *(both sit. Pause.)*
MRS BASSET	I'm very sorry to intrude, sir, when you're so busy. *(stops)*

SQUIRE   Oh, I can spare you a few minutes, Mrs Basset. You sent me a message that your business was important.

MRS BASSET   Yes, sir, most important – at least, to me, that's been thirty years at Hillside, and my father before me.

SQUIRE *(aside)* As I thought. *(aloud)* Quite so, quite so, and, no doubt, you have become attached to the place. I do not doubt that for a moment, Mrs Basset.

MRS BASSET   Yes, indeed, sir, and especially since Martin died there. He was ill close upon four months in the room over the porch, and from his bed he could just see the old cherry tree by the gate. When he fell ill it was just the bare tree, but while he lay there the little green shoots came, and then the flowers, like a cloud all white and pink. He suffered cruel with the rheumatics, sir, and he said it minded him of himself, all bent and gnarled, and he hoped the Almighty would give our poor old bodies a beautiful resurrection like the trees. The Resurrection Tree I always calls it, and every spring – *(wipes her eyes)*

SQUIRE   Yes, yes, Mrs Basset. I can quite understand your feelings. As you say, old associations can do much to increase the attractions of a place, but still –

MRS BASSET   I beg pardon, sir. I'm sure I'd no intention of saying so much. *(feels in her bag and produces paper)* If you'll be kind enough to look at this paper, sir, you'll see what I've come about.

Squire takes paper. Silence while he reads it.

SQUIRE   This is a letter from my agent, Mr Lorden, saying that Hillside cottage will be required after Lady Day. The lease signed by your late husband expires then, Mrs Basset?

MRS BASSET   Yes, sir, but I didn't think as there'd be any difficulty about renewing it. *(proudly)* I'm a poor woman, sir, but Mr Lorden knows I've paid the rent regular ever since Martin died, and I'll go on doing it as long as I'm spared, please God.

SQUIRE   Yes, yes – Mrs Basset. There is no question as to that I believe. I have never heard any complaint in the past; it is with regard to the future ...

MRS BASSET   Well, sir, I had hoped as you'd have seen your way to leaving things as they are since Martin's gone and I'm a lone woman but if it's a question of raising the rent – well, I'm strong, still, and I'll manage that too, sooner than leave Hillside.

SQUIRE   I'm afraid that is not the point either, Mrs Basset, your willingness to undertake –

MRS BASSET   You needn't be afraid, sir, that I'll undertake what I can't perform. If you'll give me the chance I'll find the ways and the means to keep Hillside, never you fear.

SQUIRE   I am sorry, Mrs Basset, but if it were merely a question of rent there would be no difficulty. There is no idea of raising the rent to you or any other tenant, I believe.

MRS BASSET   Then, sir – it must be that there's something amiss with the place since Martin's gone, and I don't give satisfaction as a tenant. I'm not as young as I used to be, and a woman can't be like a man, I know, but I've done my best to keep the place like – like it used to be and I hoped I'd managed it, sir, though it's been hard work at times; there's the little shed at the side and the bit of fence behind the cabbages as I've had new and been so proud of but it's all no use, since Martin's gone. *(wipes her eyes again)*

SQUIRE   I assure you, Mrs. Basset, you are quite mistaken. Neither Mr Lorden nor I have any fault to find with you as a tenant. I understand that Hillside is quite as well looked after as in your husband's time.

MRS BASSET   Then, sir, what is it? Have any of the neighbours been finding fault? There's the fowls, of course, will stray once in a while, and a hen did get into Mr Green's last week. I didn't think as he'd have gone behind my back like this, but if it's that, why sooner than leave Hillside I'll get rid of the fowls and take a bit of washing instead!

SQUIRE   No complaint has been made by anyone, as far as I know, Mrs Basset. The reason why we cannot – er – renew your lease is a little difficult to explain, especially to a lady.

MRS BASSET   Oh, don't mind me, sir. Thirty years I've been at Hillside, and I think – begging your pardon, sir – as I've a sort of claim to know why I'm to be turned out now.

SQUIRE   Quite so, Mrs Basset. I agree with you. The facts of the matter are briefly these. My son, Mr Robert, whom you know, intends to contest this constituency at the next Parliamentary election. Last time, as you may remember, the seat was won by a narrow, an exceedingly narrow, majority, and next time we shall want every vote we can influence. Elections have been lost before now by a single vote. We must feel on the polling-day that we have done everything we possibly can, and we should not be able to feel that if we had allowed voteless tenants on the estate.

MRS BASSET   I – I don't understand, sir.

SQUIRE   I'm afraid it is a little difficult to explain, Mrs Basset but the point is this: we must have a tenant at Hillside who will be able to vote at the next election. You, as a woman, have no vote – I will not express an opinion as to the right or wrong of that; the fact remains. As a tenant we have no fault to find with you, as a constituent you are unfortunately quite valueless. It is, in fact, as though Hillside were empty from that point of view.

MRS BASSET   But Martin voted regular, sir.

SQUIRE   Quite so, and had Mr Basset been living still, this unfortunate difficulty would not have arisen. Mr Basset voted as a man, however, and, as I said before, you as a woman cannot do so. The tenant's vote for Hillside is at present non-existent.

MRS BASSET   But I pay the same rent, sir, and, as far as I can, I do the same work. Why, you said yourself just now that the place is as well kept up as when Martin was here.

SQUIRE   I know I did, Mrs Basset, and I meant it only, unfortunately, it does not touch the point. The law, just or unjust, is still the law, and at present the law does not allow women to vote. Some day it may be otherwise, but in the meantime I dare not imperil my son's chances by retaining voteless tenants on the estate.

MRS BASSET   But if I can't vote, sir, can't I help Mr Robert in either ways? Surely even a poor old woman like me can do something – talking to people, or giving away papers, or something? If only you'll give me a chance to keep Hillside there's nothing I wouldn't do, only *(clasping her hands)* give me a chance to keep Hillside.

SQUIRE   I'm very sorry – very sorry, indeed, Mrs Basset – but you see it's not quite the same thing. Speeches and bills and canvassing are all very well – very good and absolutely necessary, of course, but on the actual polling-day it is votes that count. A vote is a vote, and nothing else, however good and necessary, can make up for the lack of a vote.

MRS BASSET   Then nothing I can do will be of any good! You say I give satisfaction as a tenant, and you won't take more rent, and it's all no use – no use at all. *(puts her handkerchief to her eyes.)*

SQUIRE   There, there, Mrs Basset, I'm extremely sorry, but it can't be helped, and there are plenty of other cottages beside Hillside, you know.

MRS BASSET   Thirty years I've been at Hillside, and now I've got to leave it all – the Resurrection Tree, and the little new shed and the bit of fence. *(suddenly)* Oh, you can't mean it, sir! You aren't really going to turn me out?

SQUIRE   Come, come, my good woman, we're not turning you out. Your lease is up, and you've plenty of time to look round. We want to show you every consideration and if there is, anything I can do – a reference for your new landlord, for instance. Why apply to me, of course.

MRS BASSET   And that's your last word, sir? – there's nothing I can do?

SQUIRE   Nothing, Mrs Basset. The cause is, unfortunately beyond the control of either you or me. I must think of my son. *(rises)*

MRS BASSET *(rising also)* And I'm to leave Hillside—me that's there thirty years, and my father before me – all because I'm a woman and haven't got a vote?

She exits weeping. Squire watches her go then sits down heavily.

SQUIRE   Unpleasant, deuced unpleasant but what's to be done? Can't run any risks for Bob, and one vote or a hundred short comes to the same thing on a polling day. *(pauses)* Why the deuce hasn't she got a vote, I'd like to know? She's got as much right to it as most of them, as far as I can see, and–

Enter Servant.

SERVANT   A gentleman to see you sir – Mr John Smith.

SQUIRE   John Smith! Never heard of him. What does he want?

SERVANT   I'll inquire sir.

Exit Servant.

SQUIRE   Now who's this I wonder? Am I never to have a minute to myself?

Re-enter Servant.

SERVANT   Please sir, he says he's the new tenant for Hillside cottage, and he wants to see you about some alterations before he signs the lease.

SQUIRE   Confound his impertinence! Tell him I'm engaged; he must go to Mr Lorden. Oh and, by the way, Keen, what sort of a person is he?

SERVANT   Well, sir, begging your pardon, I should call him a party myself.

SQUIRE   Oh! A party. What was that Lorden said? 'Fairly satisfactory from my point of view'? Perhaps I'd better see him.

(turning to Servant) Very well, Keen, tell him I'll see him for a few minutes, but he must be brief, I'm a busy man.

SERVANT   Yes, sir.

Exit Servant.

SQUIRE   Yes, I'd better see him, decidedly I'd better see him. The mere fact of his having a vote doesn't guarantee much when all's said and done, and I haven't forgotten that tipsy Tom Taylor. He went into the church porch on the polling day, where the table of forbidden degrees was hanging up, and put his cross against his grandmother. Said he thought he'd voted for Col. Grandison. Ha! ha! ha! I never was quite sure that Tom was as drunk as Grandison's agent made out but all the same it is a joke that doesn't want repeating on this estate.

Enter John Smith, twirling a somewhat battered hat.

SQUIRE *(aside)* Good Lord! *(aloud)* Er – Mr Smith, I believe. Sit down.

Both sit. Smith thrusting out his legs and looking round the room.

SQUIRE *(clearing his throat)* I believe my agent, Mr Lorden, mentioned you to me. You are thinking of taking Hillside cottage, on my estate?

JOHN SMITH   That's so, Squire, if we can come to terms but there's one or two little things I should like to straighten out first.

SQUIRE   Excuse me, Mr Smith, but my agent always attends to such matters. I never interfere.

JOHN SMITH   And, excuse me, Squire, but I never deals with hagents. I don't hold with hagents; nasty, prying things they be, with no feelins for a pore man. I goes to the fountain 'ead, I does, so to speak.

SQUIRE   Well, Mr Smith, it is quite contrary to my usual custom but as you have come on purpose, I will hear what you wish to suggest, though I can make no promises, of course.

JOHN SMITH   No, no, very proper, sir, them's my sentiments – never make no promises unless you know you can get out of them fairly easy!

SQUIRE   That was not exactly my meaning. Still, it will pass. And before we go further, Mr Smith, there is just one thing I might mention to you. Do you take any interest in politics? You are in the habit of recording your vote at elections, I hope? *(aside)* Lorden said that would be all right but after that remark about promises I think I had better investigate a little on my own.

JOHN SMITH   Oh! That'll be all right. Your hagent gave me the tip, and I twigged right enough, never you fear. I puts my cross and writes 'John Smith, his mark' after it, like a dook.

SQUIRE   What!

JOHN SMITH *(nodding)* Yes, indeed, them crosses is all very well for them what's 'ad no heddication but my mother learned me to write, and I lets them electioneering fellers know it, I does.

SQUIRE *(aside)* Great Scott! *(aloud)* But, Mr Smith, you misunderstand entirely. The idea of putting a cross is not intended as a reflection on the education of the electors, but to preserve the secrecy of the ballot.

JOHN SMITH   Lor' bless you, I don't want no secrecy. I votes square and above board, I does – when I votes at all, that is.

SQUIRE *(aside)* And his fathers possibly went to gaol to get him the ballot. It would be quite lost upon him to call his attention to that fact, I suppose and what did he say, "when he votes at all" *(aloud)* Do I understand, Mr Smith, that you do not always exercise your privilege? *(aside)* I might as well have a tenant that can't vote as one that won't.

JOHN SMITH   Well, you see Squire, last time it was like this. There comes to me a man, and he sez: "See here, you vote for old Weeks, and you'll get two loaves for what you pay for one now." So I sez, "Right you are" but the next day there comes another chap, and he sez: "If you're such a silly juggins as to vote for old Weeks you'll no loaf at all." So I sez, "That so?" and he sez it was so in the end I voted no way at all, for I thought things had better stay as they were, not being so bad but they might be worse.

SQUIRE   Quite so, Mr Smith. There is a great deal of sense in your remarks, and I am glad you take such an intelligent interest in the affairs of the country. I always like my tenants to take an interest in politics. *(aside)* He's not one of my tenants yet, by the way.

JOHN SMITH   Why, bless your heart, Squire – politics is the most interestin' things in the world, and many's the laugh I've had out of them. Ha! *(leans forward)* Why the other day there comes to me a little ferrety man what wanted me to vote for someone or other, I forget the party's name just now, and he sez very solemn like : "here's one good Bill he'll help to bring in if he gets in himself."

And I sez, "what's that?" and he sez "The Deceased Wife's Sister's Bill." I sez, "Who's she?" and he sez: "Well, you see, it's like this: if anything happens to your missus you can't marry her sister, to look after the little 'uns. See?" And, I sez, "Yes, I knows that." "Well," he sez, "This Bill'll make it all right for you to do so" and I sez, "No, it will not. Not all the Lords and Commons, nor the Harchbishop, nor the King hisself, God bless him – can do that!" And he sez, testy like, "Oh, nonsense, my good man, you mustn't let narrow-minded, old-fashioned people – parsons and such like – mislead you; there's nothing against it." And I sez, "I ain't a-going by no parsons, I'm a-going by the laws o' nature – my missus ain't got no sister!" Ha! ha! ha! ha! Real ratty that made the little man for a minute then he sez, "But we musn't think only of ourselves because we don't want a thing doesn't prove that other people don't want it. Other people have got deceased wives' sisters, if you haven't, and you ought to think of them." But I wasn't takin' any – not much – wasn't good enough. I'm not a-goin' helping other people get what I don't want myself – I'm not such a muggins.

SQUIRE *(aside)* Thinks imperially, evidently.

JOHN SMITH Bills what won't do John Smith no good ain't in John Smith's line o' business. I don't want no deceased wife's sister, and I don't see what other folks want with her, what's more.

SQUIRE Still the fact that you didn't feel any hardship under the old law isn't exactly an argument that no one else did, Mr Smith. *(aside)* If he's as selfish as a tenant as he seems to be as a politician, it's a bad look-out for his landlord! *(aloud)* By the way, where have you been living until now, Mr Smith?

JOHN SMITH *(fidgeting)* Well, you see, sir, it's this way. Me and Lord Greyling's hagent 'as 'ad a bit of a breeze – 'orrid mean man that hagent – no feelins for a pore man what finds the rent a bit heavy. I never did hold with hagents; as I said afore, and –

SQUIRE Do I understand, then, Mr Smith, that– you are leaving Lord Greyling's estate on account of your rent being in arrears?

JOHN SMITH *(uneasily)* Well, I am and I aren't, so to speak. The rent was the beginning of the trouble, but the pigs were the end of it.

SQUIRE The pigs!

JOHN SMITH Y-e-s. 'Orrid mean man that hagent, and he comes pokin' round my place just afore the spring cleanin' was done.

After that bit of rent he was, 'orrid mean, and no gentleman like yourself, sir, but I makes bold to ask him for a new pigsty for the pigs. And *(with emphasis)* he sez, sez he, "Bring 'em in here along with you, there ain't much to choose between one sty and t'other." Those were his very words – most improper and unbecomin' from one gent to another. So I up and sez, riled, as was but natural – I sez, "Git out yourself, then, and make room for one of them!"

SQUIRE *(rising)* Really, Mr Smith, I don't wonder that there was a slight breeze as you call it, between yourself and Lord Greyling's agent. In fact I'm afraid, if you came to live on this estate, there would probably be something more than a breeze, a hurricane in fact, between you and my own agent.

JOHN SMITH   Oh, that'll be all right, Squire, never you fear. Just you give him a word to leave me alone, and I won't worry him. I don't 'old with no hagents – I goes to the fountain 'ead.

SQUIRE   Yes, yes, Mr Smith, and I'll look into it myself. I promise you that. *(aside)* His lease isn't signed yet, thank the Lord! *(aloud)* Now I must ask you to excuse me – I'm a busy man.

JOHN SMITH *(rising)* Yes, and I must be gettin' along myself. Mike Ross'll be waiting for me at the Plough and Furrow. *(goes towards door)* Good night and thank you kindly, sir. Always pays to go to the fountain 'ead.

He exits. Squire watches him go, then rings bell.
Enter Servant.

SQUIRE   Ask Giles to ride over to Mr Lorden's and tell him to take no further steps about the lease of Hillside cottage until he hears from me again. Tell him to go at once.

SERVANT   Very good, sir.

Servant exits.

SQUIRE   Well, all I can say is it's a deuced silly law that says that John Smith's more fit to have a vote than Mrs Basset but things being as they are, I'm not going to do such a deuced silly thing as to give him a cottage as well! Bob must take his chance. Because John Bull's an old fool is no reason why Squire Brooks should be another!

The end.

Helen Margaret Nightingale (?-1921)

Little is known of Nightingale apart from her two romantic novels *Savile Gilchrist M.D.* (1906) and *The Choir at Newcommon Road* (1909) together with the collected poems *The Men in Blue and Other Poems*, which were published in her memory in Reigate in 1922. Many of the poems were first published in the 'Gazette of the 3rd L.G.H', most deal with the war, including one titled 'Demobilised', which suggests that Nightingale worked as a nursing auxiliary:

> "Never more
> Shall stand outside the Matron's door,
> And wonder if my cap is straight"

Two other poems refer to the nursing and recovery of her (female) lover.

A Change of Tenant was published with the author accredited as a 'Miss H. M. Nightingale', but it has often gone unrecognised. It was published by the Woman Citizen Publishing Company and is undated though the Bodleian Library gives it as 1908. Originally entered as a work by 'anonymous' at The British Library and recorded with the author as H. M. Nightingale in *The Players Library* (British Drama League,1950).

The play was toured by the AFL in 1910 and produced by other suffrage organisations. Elizabeth Crawford records that the feminist and novelist Isabella Ford performed in a production of *A Change of Tenant* at the Leeds Women's Suffrage Society. The AFL Report of 1909-1910 lists productions of *A Change of Tenant* for the Sevenoaks Branch of the National Union for Women's Suffrage, (along with Cicely Hamilton's *Pot and Kettle* and *How the Vote was Won*) and another production at Battersea Arts Centre. On 21st April 1911, it was performed in aid of the NUWS, with Graham Moffat's *The Maid and the Magistrate*.

At the Gates
being a twentieth century episode

At the Gates

At the Gates dates from and is based on the events of the same year when the Women's Freedom League picketed the House of Commons from July 5th to October 28th, 1909: "an example of patient endurance which should go far to silence the foolish cry of "hysteria" as applied to the Suffrage Movement". Chapin was actually in prison when the play was first scheduled to be performed at the Albert Hall in December 1909. However, it was cancelled due to the "lateness of the hour" following a long programme.

Based on the experience of a young woman's 540 hour picket, it presents a series of encounters between her and various passers by, a male sympathiser, an embarrassed waiter, two well-disposed policemen, ardently interested in politics, cynical about most of their rulers and one of them a great theatre-goer who likes serious drama. Others include: small boys and grown men who jeer; a drunk (who boasts that he has the vote while she does not); a seamstress (who works in a sweatshop and is battered by her husband) and who supports the suffragists as a means to gain the power, it is implied, to change her circumstances; an elderly, self-described "womanly woman", who attacks the male sympathiser with her umbrella.

The line: "These *Antis* are so militant", spoken by the heroine, was added to the play between the submission of the manuscript to the Lord Chamberlain's office and the play's publication.

It is interesting dramaturgically in its attempt to give theatrical form to a durational experience and find a theatrical language to describe an experience of multiple brief encounters, rather than a defining dramatic collision of different viewpoints. The piece makes reference to the biblical Book of Esther comparing the arbitrary exercise of power by the tyrannical King Ahasuerus who ordered the slaughter of the Jews of Persia to that of the government of the day – but "Ahasuerus was a gentleman. He did hold out his sceptre... He didn't keep her waiting either".

The published play is rare and has attracted little critical attention.

At The Gates
being a twentieth century episode

Alice Chapin

CHARACTERS

Suffragette
1st Officer
2nd Officer
Sympathizer
Waiter
Seamstress
Old Lady
Drunken Man
Member of Parliament
Various passers-by

Scene One

The iron fence and one post, by the exit gate of the House of Commons. Only a little of the driveway can be seen, but carriages can be heard from time to time as if rolling through. The police are stationed as usual.

The Suffragette is standing by her post, wearing her colours. Her bag, mackintosh and umbrella are hanging on railings, a larger bag is on the ground by the gate. She holds her petition and a bundle of handbills and literature.

The police show signs of animation when they stroll in her direction. She occasionally bows as if to someone in one of the passing carriages.

1st OFFICER You must have been pretty tired this morning, Miss. What time did you get home?

SUFFRAGETTE Not till five o'clock.

1st OFFICER I suppose you don't have to get up very early.

SUFFRAGETTE No, I slept till noon.

1st OFFICER Sleeping in the day time doesn't do you half the good a night's rest does. I'd rather have four hours at night than eight in the day.

SUFFRAGETTE Oh, I feel very fit. I don't mind when I sleep so long as I get the rest.

1st OFFICER It won't be so late a sitting tonight. It's Arson's Dove-cote Bill. They won't talk so much over it. Last night the budget ran away with them.

SUFFRAGETTE I wish it had run so far that they couldn't find their way back.

2nd OFFICER (*strolls up*) Bit nippy tonight, don't you think?

SUFFRAGETTE Yes, it seems frosty.

2nd OFFICER It's wonderful how cold it gets down here. The wind over the river, I suppose.

1st OFFICER (*resenting the advent of No. 2*) You won't be able to stand the really cold weather, Miss. It is too much for us sometimes.

SUFFRAGETTE Unless a sense microbe penetrates to the brain of one in authority, I shall have to stand it.

1st OFFICER You can't. It will be a physical impossibility.

2nd OFFICER This rotten Government will be turned out before the very cold weather arrives.

1st OFFICER It will take a lot of turning.

2nd OFFICER Ho, a rotten lot like this?

SUFFRAGETTE (*hastily*) There goes Gainstone Kirksick.

2nd OFFICER (*allowing himself to be tempted from a political discussion*) He's actually walking tonight.

SUFFRAGETTE Too much visiting. Hard up after tipping foreign waiters.

2nd OFFICER He would tip foreigners. English men aren't good enough for him.

1st OFFICER What I say is that he is a smart man.

2nd OFFICER Smart man, he? Why, he hasn't the brains of a fly.

1st OFFICER   No, perhaps not. But he has the brains of a man. A very clever man too.

2nd OFFICER   Well, I have travelled a good deal, I have seen service in foreign parts, and I–

1st OFFICER   Don't know a clever man when you see one.

SUFFRAGETTE (*interposing while No. 2 is still speechless with indignation*) It's curious how opinions differ about the same person, isn't it? Of course, Kirksick has his following.

1st OFFICER   That he has, and a big following too.

2nd OFFICER   A few brainless idiots.

1st OFFICER   That's what you think, but let me tell you that, with all your service in foreign parts -

SUFFRAGETTE (*still hoping to keep the peace*) And there goes Foursome.

2nd OFFICER   Ah, that's the man. (*Suffragette bows.*) See there. He always bows and looks civil. Wait till we have him in again.

1st OFFICER   That is just what you will do.

2nd OFFICER   What?

1st OFFICER   Wait.

2nd OFFICER   "Pride goeth before a fall," let me tell you. And them as is too sure now may have a big surprise at the elections.

1st OFFICER   I have no fears. Would the country exchange such men as Kirksick, Merrypebble, and Poter Jones for Foursome?

2nd OFFICER   That they would and gladly.

SUFFRAGETTE (*to 1st Officer*) Do you mean to tell me that you approve of Merrypebble?

1st OFFICER   Not altogether, Miss. It's a good liberal name though, isn't it?

SUFFRAGETTE   Tarnished, disgraced by its present possessor. Why, when his policy rouses a storm he doesn't dare to face the music himself. He leaves a Secretary to do it for him. He has not even the courage of his convictions.

2nd OFFICER   Quite true, now if Foursome –

1st OFFICER   Foursome?–I am not upholding Merrypebble, because he doesn't deserve it. This young lady knows that I sympathize with her and her cause, but when you tell me Foursome, with his puny brain—

2nd OFFICER   What? He has more brains in his little finger than any of the rest of them have in their whole bodies.

SUFFRAGETTE   What a funny place to carry one's brains in.

2nd OFFICER   It's a common enough expression as I take it.

Enter a Male Sympathizer.

SYMPATHIZER   Are you ready for a little food, and some tea or coffee? You must need something warm. Standing is chilly work.

Police move away, still arguing.

SUFFRAGETTE   You have arrived just in time. I have offended one of my friends.

SYMPATHIZER   Oh, I am sorry to hear that. He will forgive you though I am sure. What is he arguing about?

SUFFRAGETTE   The political situation. Those two men always row. One is an ardent Liberal and the other a red hot Conservative.

VOICE OF PASSER-BY (*mockingly*) Votes for Women, I don't think.

SUFFRAGETTE (*sweetly*) No, you look as if you didn't.

SYMPATHIZER   There. Put that in your pipe and smoke it.

VOICE OF SMALL BOY Yah, yah, Suffragette.

Suffragette stops Sympathizer who makes a move as if to chastise them. Little Boy runs away.

SUFFRAGETTE   You musn't. They are not worth noticing.

SYMPATHIZER   They are worth thumping.

SUFFRAGETTE   They get a lot of that, I dare say. Probably that's what is the matter with them.

SYMPATHIZER   It's Pip, isn't it, who complains that the outward application of whitewash to the skull, by having one's head banged into the wall, has a hardening effect?[1]

SUFFRAGETTE   Yes, I believe so.

VOICE   Go 'ome. Go 'ome and wash the baby.

More derisive cries. Sympathizer grows restive.

SYMPATHIZER   It is disgraceful that you should be forced to put up with this vulgar abuse.

SUFFRAGETTE   It's disgraceful that we are placed in such a position. I have no quarrel with the rabble who don't know any better. My quarrel is with those who have made and who maintain this whole strained situation. They are responsible for everything.

SYMPATHIZER   I was talking with a fellow yesterday who said Absolute couldn't give you the vote, even if he wanted to.

SUFFRAGETTE *(truculently)* He can at least discuss the subject. His present attitude of ignoring us is insulting. As for his inability to give us the vote, he can bring the measure forward, can't he? If he understood human nature as well as I do, he would exert himself, and do something. I want to be one thing or the other, either a citizen or a rebel. I'm sick of being a hybrid.

1st Officer has appeared and listens to this outburst.

1st OFFICER   Is that what you call yourself?

SUFFRAGETTE   What else am I? I've no say as a citizen in the making of the laws. I am only worth jibing at when I demand my right as a thinking creature. What would you do, officer, if I smashed that beastly light up there?

1st OFFICER *(uneasily)* Don't talk in that way, Miss. You know I would have to arrest you. But it ain't my fault.

SUFFRAGETTE   Did I ever say it was?

1st OFFICER   But you ain't going to smash that glass; it would be foolish, so why–?

SUFFRAGETTE   As things are at present I am ready to do anything. This position – the knowledge that that Government in there have encouraged outrage, and violence amounting to torture – Oh, you can't imagine how I feel. And I try to restrain myself, try to be lady-like, and quiet, and properly subdued, and all the while I – I – Oh, it is too hard ...

Sympathizer and Officer both look as uncomfortable as men can when they see a woman on the verge of tears.

SUFFRAGETTE *(gulping down the lump in her throat)* I've read the papers, of course. I've read of the laughter of fools. *(With a glare of contempt towards the House.)* I have read, too, remarks deploring the violence of "these women." Does anybody deplore the fact that we have been laughed at, baited, insulted? Treated like wild beasts on show, left standing here day in and day out, night in and night out, when the simple courtesy of taking this thing *(she waves her petition)* is all that is required. That wouldn't give us votes. That would only mean: I – Mr. Absolute – hereby acknowledge that you are a human being with certain rights and privileges, and out of my valuable time I will try to extract a single half-hour in which I will condescend to listen to your very humble request. *(Abruptly changing)* Did you ever read the Book of Esther?

SYMPATHIZER *(taken aback, stammers)* Yes, I believe so. At school or somewhere.

1st OFFICER   I never read it.

SUFFRAGETTE   Well, there is in it a poor young queen. And when she has a request to make of the king, she puts on her best rig out and stands where he can see her. If he is in a good temper, he holds out his sceptre. She touches it, and then she can go ahead and talk. If, on the other hand, the king is in a bad temper, he doesn't hold out the sceptre, and – whisk – "Off with her head – so much for – a queen."

1st OFFICER   Those stories have to do with people who lived a long time ago. Foreigners, all of them.

SUFFRAGETTE   I feel like that poor Jewish girl. Here I stand. Absolute sees me. Bad temper – "Away with her" – Police Court. Offence? "Obstruction." "40 shillings or 7 days." After the 7 days here I am again. Absolute passes. Better temper. "Stand there if you like, but you mustn't worry me. Don't be silly." Oh, yes, Queen Esther did live a long time ago, but Ahasuerus was a gentleman. He did hold out his sceptre.

1st OFFICER   I'm glad of that.

SUFFRAGETTE   He didn't keep her waiting either. Decidedly he was a gentleman.

1st OFFICER   Why can't Absolute take the paper, as the young lady says? It wouldn't hurt anybody.

SYMPATHIZER   Oh, no, but it would infer a sentiment of real respect for a woman, and that is something he cannot show.

SUFFRAGETTE   Maintain a judicial calm, my friend, you'll need it. *(pulls herself together and laughs bitterly.)* We can cheer our souls by reflecting that we are making history.

SYMPATHIZER   Yes, and some who hold a high position today will not go down to posterity with shining records.

SUFFRAGETTE   No, I suppose they will be judged much as we judge Lord North or Grenville.

SYMPATHIZER   But we are forgetting all about your food. It is nearly 11.30; there are weary hours before you yet. One of the officers said two might see the finish. You were here this afternoon, weren't you?

SUFFRAGETTE   Yes, for a couple of hours. We are awfully short today. Some of our people are ill. Not from over work, but from over standing. They will be back next week.

SYMPATHIZER   Which shall it be, tea or coffee?

SUFFRAGETTE   Can I have tea? I think I would prefer it tonight.

SYMPATHIZER   Yes, of course you can. I will order it from Lombardis.

He exits hastily.

1st OFFICER   I went to the theatre last night, Miss.

SUFFRAGETTE   I thought I missed you.

1st OFFICER   It was my night off.

SUFFRAGETTE   What did you see?

1st OFFICER   'The Haughty Patriarch'.

SUFFRAGETTE   Oh, did you like it?

1st OFFICER   Can't say I did. It seemed to me just a bit obscure. And there was too much lying in it.

SUFFRAGETTE   Oh, really?

1st OFFICER   Yes. I don't like such a lot of deception. I don't say that it is not permissible sometimes, but in this case it didn't seem right.

SUFFRAGETTE   Do you go much to theatres?

1st OFFICER   I'm pretty regular at them. I try to see most of the serious dramas. I am specially fond of operas. I don't care so much about funny plays, the people will laugh so much.

SUFFRAGETTE   After all that is natural, isn't it? Do you want them to cry?

1st OFFICER   I want them to keep quiet. It does annoy me when folks applaud and make a fuss. Why can't they keep still? If it is funny can't the audience just smile quietly? There's no need to laugh so loud that they interfere with your hearing the next thing said on the stage. I never applaud.

SUFFRAGETTE   Isn't that rather hard on the actors?

1st OFFICER   Oh, I don't fancy so. I should think they would prefer it. When I leave the theatre I think it all over, and I say to myself, "That was a very funny play," or "That was a good strong drama," as the case may be. But I make no disturbance while there.

SUFFRAGETTE   Still, I can't help thinking that the actors prefer a little applause just as a sign that the audience is sympathetic.

Enter Sympathizer followed by a Waiter bearing a tray containing tea things, cake, etc. Suffragette pours tea, eats cake, and sips tea. Waiter looks distinctly uncomfortable. Officer looks hungry. Suffragette quite unconcerned. Pours herself out more tea. Regards Officer wickedly.

SUFFRAGETTE   Nice and hot, isn't it?

1st OFFICER   It looks so.

SUFFRAGETTE   Do you like tea?

1st OFFICER   Very much indeed.

SUFFRAGETTE   What a pity that I've only one cup. I might offer you some.

1st OFFICER   Don't let it worry you. *(meaningly)* Are you noticing those who are going out?

SUFFRAGETTE   I am. Not one has escaped me. Five have bowed.

SYMPATHIZER   Five? Oh, that's something.

SUFFRAGETTE   Yes, they will learn manners in time. At least some of them will. Some still find it amusing to see a woman standing at these gates. They evidently forget that we pay taxes for the upkeep of all this, and that we are seriously influenced by some of their stupid laws. Still, five remember us. We can afford to be hopeful.

> Five little gentlemen
> We can count on now.
> Five little gentlemen
> Who don't forget to bow.

SYMPATHIZER *(wickedly)* Perhaps they didn't bow, only ducked.

SUFFRAGETTE *(indignantly)* I don't throw things?

SYMPATHIZER   There are others. *(hastily, as fearing another outburst.)* I only said that in fun. You used to be able to take a joke.

SUFFRAGETTE   And l can now. Thanks so much for the tea. I have enjoyed it.

Waiter, who has not enjoyed standing with it, makes haste to depart with tray.

1st OFFICER   I say, Miss, we ought to provide you with
  tables.
SUFFRAGETTE   Quite right, and hooks to hang my things on –
  and a hammock.
1st OFFICER   I'll mention it at Headquarters.
SUFFRAGETTE   Do.

Enter a Seamstress, not of the better Class, but a poor, disfigured woman, who has known sweated labour and also man's chivalry to the weak and helpless.

SEAMSTRESS   There you are, Miss – I'm with you, but I ain't
  no account.
SUFFRAGETTE   Oh, don't say that.
SEAMSTRESS   I know. I'm poor and wore out. Likewise
  knocked out by a beauty I married. He did that for me. *(motions to her disfigured face)* Made me a nice object, didn't he? The magistrate was awfully pally with 'im. Rather cottoned to him so I thought.
SUFFRAGETTE   Didn't he send him to prison?
SEAMSTRESS   Prison? –Lor, bless you, no. Prison? – not he.
  Told him not to do it again, and let him off with a fine. Of course he did do it again, only worse, and that's why I'm such a pretty thing to look at. *(laughs drearily)* My fault though. He was my second. I ought to have known that I was a fool to try my luck again. The first was pretty fair, I might have left it at that. I was tired out with trying to keep going with two children on my hands. He said he'd help me. He was a lovely liar.
SUFFRAGETTE   What sort of work do you do?
SEAMSTRESS   Blouse making. Work all day long in a filthy,
  dirty room, with a lot of other women, or work at home, day and night, to make enough to keep soul and body together. Not always enough for that. Either way it's no great cop. I spoiled my eye-sight in a workroom.
SUFFRAGETTE   It all sounds so horrible. I have never been in a
  sweating den.
SEAMSTRESS   Don't you never go. The smell would sicken
  you. My only hope is that the folks who buys the things we have to

make there will get some disease from them. I do hope it. Straight,
I do.

SUFFRAGETTE   And has life always meant just this to you, just
what it means today, nothing else?

SEAMSTRESS   No, not always. My first husband, he was all
right. Only he never would think for the future. Never would lay by
nothing for me and the babies. "Bless you, I'm a young man," says
he, when anybody would say a word for insurance or anything like
that. "Time enough for that," says he, "when I'm past thirty." Well, I
buried 'im before he was thirty, and I was so cut up about him, and
about having to do for my two babies, and nothing to do with, that I
nigh went off my chump. I had a fever and they sent me to a
hospital, where I worried my heart out over my children.

SUFFRAGETTE   And were they all right?

SEAMSTRESS   Yes, a neighbour looked after them. Trust the
poor to help each other.

SUFFRAGETTE   You must have had a fearful struggle to make
both ends meet.

SEAMSTRESS   You're right. No worse than lots of other
women. There are hundreds just keeping alive, that's all.

SYMPATHIZER *(breaking in suddenly)* Do you ever go on strike?

SEAMSTRESS *(laughs)* Strike? What, with children to feed? Strike,
with no Union back of you? No fear.

SYMPATHIZER   No, of course. not, I never thought. You
couldn't. You simply have to take what you can get.

SEAMSTRESS   You've hit it. We have to take what we can get,
and we get many a cuff with it, I can tell you. That's why I'm so keen
for your sort. *(to Suffragette)* We can't fight fair. We've got no
Trades Unions, worth the name. We can't have, till you get the vote
for us. Maybe some of us wouldn't be voters, but it would make a lot
of difference. It would turn us from no account creatures to having
the same rights that the men have.

SUFFRAGETTE   Yes, that's what I believe.

SEAMSTRESS   I'm sure of it. Some men like to talk large
about helping you. They'll help a lot more when you can give them a
lift in return.

SUFFRAGETTE   And women could do so much more for each
other. *(with kindling earnestness)* That is what nerves us to go

ahead. So that we don't mind sneers, nor even prison itself, if it brings us nearer to victory.

SEAMSTRESS Don't you give way or be discouraged. We depend on you. Good night.

She goes slowly away.

SUFFRAGETTE No, I won't be discouraged. You have given me new strength just when I needed it most. *(turning to Sympathizer)* Isn't it great to feel that we are going to help poor women like that?

Voice from The House crying "Division".

SUFFRAGETTE What, again? That's the third division in forty minutes.

SYMPATHIZER Here, Officer, how many "divisions" must they get through tonight?

2nd Officer strolls up.

2nd OFFICER I can't tell you that exactly, sir. I did hear it was to last till two, but at this rate they may finish in another half-hour.

SUFFRAGETTE Oh, dear. I got that tea under false pretences.

SYMPATHIZER I'll go down to St. Stephen's, they may have news there.

An Elderly Woman, with a somewhat firm expression, and carrying an umbrella, appears. She walks past the Suffragette, who offers her a handbill which she refuses with haughty disdain. The Sympathizer, who has turned before going, to have a final word with the Suffragette thinks it incumbent upon him to reason with her.

SYMPATHIZER *(with an ingratiating smile)* Oh surely, Madam, you would like to read about the Suffrage movement.

The Elderly Lady glares at him in speechless disgust.

SYMPATHIZER *(moving reckless to his doom)* You will take a bill, won't you? It tells –

OLD LADY I am a womanly woman.

She hits him firmly over the head with her umbrella, crushing his hat down over his eyes, and sails majestically away. The Officer and

Suffragette rush to the assistance of the misguided enthusiast, and he is helped to a cab.

SUFFRAGETTE *(as he departs)* These *Antis* are so militant.

A drunken man appears and comes slowly toward the Suffragette.

MAN   "Votes for Women" is it? I think not. Oh, I think not.

Officer returns.

SUFFRAGETTE *(to Officer)* I've heard something like that remark before.

MAN   What I want to know is, why do you grind us down? That's what I want to know. Why do you grind us down? You take the bread out of our mouths. You leave us the butter. Look at me – can I get work? No. Why? You have taken it out of my very hands. Yes, you have. I know what I am talking about. I am a clever man, I am. You don't think so? Ah, indeed. Let me tell you one thing and perhaps you will alter your opinion. I know what keeps you going. That makes you open your eyes, does it? Well open them again. Everybody knows. *(in a husky whisper)* Inquire at the Carlton Club. You won't? Then I will tell you. You are paid. Paid to stand here. Look at your clothes. Look at your hat. One guinea a night is what you get. One guinea a night, and here am I with empty pockets. Look at 'em. *(proceeds to turn them inside out)* Nice things to feed babies on, ain't they? Empty. While yours are filled with Tory gold. I am a man, too. You are not a man.

SUFFRAGETTE *(desperately, half to herself)* Thank God for that!

MAN   What are you muttering about? Don't be afraid to speak out. Can you walk over Westminster Bridge at five in the morning? *(staggers back with the air of one who has delivered a poser)*

SUFFRAGETTE *(to Officer, who is regarding Man with strong disfavour)* I dare say I could if I put my whole mind to it.

MAN   Can you? I wait for your answer. You can't? What can you do? Can you sweep a floor or dust a ceiling? What you should do is to go home and wash shirts.

SUFFRAGETTE   Thanks. I'd rather not.

MAN   Too proud? That's it. Too proud. What right have you to be proud, when a man stands idle before you? A man, I say. All you want is to grind us down. And let me tell you this, my old Missus can wash shirts.

SUFFRAGETTE *(who is growing restive)* Then I wish she would wash yours. Do go away.

MAN I know my place. I am talking to you as a gentleman should. P'raps you would listen if you got more money for doing it. You can't fool me. That's an expensive fur you are wearing. Look at your hat, you couldn't buy that for a guinea.

2nd OFFICER Come now, that will do. Move on.

1st Officer comes into view.

MAN *(with elaborate politeness)* Move on, is it? Oh, very well. *(staggers up to 1st Officer and falls affectionately upon his chest)* He's moving me on. Moving me on, because I was talking to her. *(becomes most effusive)* I'll tell you a secret. I am a gentleman, I am – and I am a voter. She can't vote, and while I have my way, she shan't.

Staggers off.

1st OFFICER Nice specimen that of the free and independent voter.

SUFFRAGETTE Yes, I wonder which party he belongs to.

2nd OFFICER To the one that gives him the most beer.

The two Officers move into the yard. Suffragette stamps to keep warm. Bows suddenly and holds up petition.

SUFFRAGETTE Ah, dear me. A closed motor this time.

Drunken Man staggers on again.

MAN I want to ask you one question, my lady, before you grind us down. You've nothing to say? Before I would stain my hands with Tory gold –

2nd Officer appears.

2nd OFFICER I thought I told you to move on.

MAN No offence, guvnor, p'raps you did. P'raps you did not.

2nd OFFICER Yes, perhaps I did, and the sooner you go the better it will be for you.

MAN   I suppose that to question this young woman about her hat is not a case for the police.

2nd OFFICER   I intend to make it one.

MAN   Oh, you do? You do? Has any of the gold fallen out of her pocket into –

2nd OFFICER *(sharply)* What's that you are saying?

MAN *(thinks better of it)* I thought the young lady dropped something – that's all.

2nd OFFICER   That's all, is it? Now, you move on.

MAN   Don't forget that you are addressing a voter. *(turns suddenly on Suffragette)* My old woman is a lot better looking than you are.

He exits with dignity.

SUFFRAGETTE   There goes Arson. Heavens, he bowed. He actually bowed. Which does he consider me, "A Young Hooligan," or "A brazen hussey?" Perhaps a mixture of both.

Officer laughs and strolls off. A Member of Parliament crosses in front of Suffragette. She offers him a handbill. He goes by and off without noticing her.

SUFFRAGETTE   Dear man.

Another Member appears. He smiles at her in a rather supercilious manner, but thinks he will have a chat.

MEMBER   Still faithful

SUFFRAGETTE   Is faithfulness so rare a virtue?

MEMBER   What good do you think you are doing?

SUFFRAGETTE   Proving the chivalry of the law-makers of England.

MEMBER *(nettled)* One might retort that you are proving your own obstinacy.

SUFFRAGETTE   Or someone else's.

MEMBER   Why can't you take "No" for an answer?

SUFFRAGETTE   Because this question must be answered in the affirmative.

MEMBER   "Must?" That sounds peremptory.

SUFFRAGETTE   I hope it does.

MEMBER.   Women should not try to rule by coercive tactics.

SUFFRAGETTE   Then blame those who force us to them. Don't blame us.

MEMBER   I am not altogether opposed, you know, but I am doubtful. Some of your party have gone too far.

SUFFRAGETTE   No one can deplore what has happened more than we do but there is one man in this country who alone is responsible. One man who by his crass, stupid obstinacy has raised this violent spirit of protest against what has become intolerable tyranny.

MEMBER   Well, that is going it pretty strong, isn't it?

SUFFRAGETTE   No stronger than is borne out by what has happened. Look at what has followed. Are you proud of that? Are you proud of the Home Office? When you proved to us women that there was no such thing for us as fair and simple justice, you did a dangerous thing.

MEMBER   I confess I am rather horrified at what has been done since. Still, you must admit that it is a very peculiar case. What are the authorities to do? Bow these violent women out of prison with a grand flourish and say "There is a heap of stones round the corner, we'll send a man along to teach you ladies to aim straight." Is that what you suggest?

SUFFRAGETTE   I am not holding a brief for stone throwing. I have not a word to say against the police court sentences, if the authorities would remember that we are political offenders and should be treated as such. Besides, five days' starvation is pretty heavy punishment for anybody, and no civilized Government has the right to commit an outrage.

MEMBER   It has been done before. Insane persons have been fed so.

SUFFRAGETTE   The last prisoner they tried it on died, and after that it was made illegal. Didn't the prison authorities have to ask for a special mandate from the Home Office? Pretty picture isn't it? I don't refer to the prison scene, that is revolting. What I do refer to is the protest made in that House, and the merry laughter of a lot of your Members as they conjured up the scene and enjoyed the humour of it. They are supposed to be sufficiently representative men to be sent there as law makers. You talk to me about leaving them to take care of us women, about chivalry which we are destroying. The chivalry in many of your sex today is so dead that it needs to be buried in a pit with quicklime thrown over it. It is liable to breed a pestilence.

MEMBER   Oh, come, come, come now, aren't you showing a, rather, shall we say, bitter spirit?

SUFFRAGETTE   Russian methods do not suit English women. I didn't need to have it proved to me that there are a lot of people behind those walls who are unutterable cads. I've stood here for twelve weeks, and I know. You can be sure of this, that this Government cannot wear us out; or frighten us. *(waving her hand toward the House)* It ought to have soaked into their intelligence by this time.

MEMBER   I must say that you have displayed extra-ordinary endurance. I doubt the wisdom of your course, still, I am bound to admit that you have persevered in it with a courage born of conviction.

SUFFRAGETTE   It is only because we are so convinced of the justice of our cause that we are so strong. Do you suppose that it is funny standing here in a kind of modern pillory? Do you suppose that we women who do this are enjoying it? But one thing we do know, and that is that we are working not only for the betterment of our sex but of humanity. We realize by uplifting womanhood the whole race will be ennobled, and so we are willing to face the impudent sneer of politicians, who ought to know better; the vulgar chaff of the ignorant crowd who don't know better; and the savage abuse of the narrow-minded partisans who don't want to know better. We are willing to face all this if only it can bring us a step nearer to our ultimate goal.

MEMBER   You ought to go into Parliament.

SUFFRAGETTE   Thanks. As at present constituted I shouldn't care to.

Member says Good Night, and departs. Drunken Man appears once more.

MAN *(with pathos)* Can you cross Westminster Bridge at five in the morning?

He staggers away.

The end.

Alice Chapin (1858-1924)

Born at Keene, New Hampshire, Chapin became an actress and spent her career partly in the USA, and partly in Britain. She married H.M. Ferris in 1885, by whom she had a daughter, Elsie, a suffrage activist and a son, actor/playwright Harold Chapin with whom she wrote *A Knight Errant* (Grand, Falkirk, 1906). She also co-wrote plays with others including *Shame* (1892) and the extravaganza *Dresden China* (both with E.H.C. Oliphant, both Vaudeville, 1892), *The Happy Medium* (with P. Gaye, Ladbroke Hall, 1909) and most interestingly *Outlawed* (Court, 1911) a dramatisation with Mabel Collins of Collins' and Charlotte Despard's suffrage novel of the same name.

Her other plays included *The Wrong Legs* (Ilkeston, 1896); *Sorrowful Satan* or *Lucifer's Match* (Kentish Town, 1897); *A Woman's Sacrifice* (St George's Hall, 1899) and *A Modern Medea* (Rehearsal Theatre, 1910) directed by Edith Craig.

Chapin was a suffrage activist and dedicated member of the WFL and an early and committed member of the AFL. Accounts in the suffrage press or AFL reports mention her chairing meetings such as that in Victoria Park, Manchester when the "platform was singled out by a band of rowdies, and the speakers not given a hearing", addressing a meeting in Edinburgh and chairing three meetings for the AFL in Hyde Park during 1913. A one-page version of her play appears in *The Vote* (16 Dec, 1909) before its pamphlet publication by the Woman Citizen Publishing Society.

In 1909, at the age of 51, she was arrested for pouring acid into ballot boxes, together with her fellow-protester, Alison Neilans[2]. Only Chapin was found guilty, as the acid slightly splashed and "injured" one of the tellers. Chapin was sentenced to imprisonment for four months. She later returned to the USA for some years and died in Keene.

---

[1] A reference to Charles Dickens' *Great Expectations*.

[2] See *The Ballot Box Protest, and the trial of Mrs Chapin and Miss Neilans, at the Central Criminal Court* (*Miss Neilans' Defence*) London: Women's Freedom League, 1911.

How the Vote was Won

How the Vote was Won

How the Vote Was Won was one of the most successful of the suffrage plays alongside Cicely Hamilton's *A Pageant of Great Women*. In 1909, it was a great hit at its first AFL matinee at the Royalty Theatre on 13th April, directed by Edy Craig, while numerous later performances took place all over Britain and in the US[1].

It has retained a kind of canonical status within the suffrage movement and since the 1980s it has been re-discovered and re-staged at feminist events. Originally a comic short story published in pamphlet form by the WWSL with comic illustrations by C. Hedley-Charlton, Chris St John saw the dramatic potential of adapting it as a play.

A vigorous farce, it is set in the home of Horace Cole, a Brixton clerk, and his dutiful wife. In a new campaign, women throughout Britain unite and down tools, turning for support to their nearest male relative, and causing the Government to draft in the Coldstream Guards to deal with the strike. When Horace's house fills up with a frightening parade of female relatives who demand he support them financially, he is rapidly converted to eager pro-suffragist, joining thousands of other men to march on the House of Commons.

The play was well-received by critics as well as audiences, called "vigorous", "ingenious" and "truly comic"[2] while a reviewer in *The Star* wrote that "the desolating effects of a general strike of women, as observed in operation in the home of Horace Cole, are as desolating as they are funny." *The Daily Graphic* described the audience as a "crowded house ... provoked to cheering and counter-demonstrations by the vigorous arguments".[3]

---

[1] Rachel France included the play in her anthology *A Century of Plays by American Women* (NY: Richard Rosen Press, 1979) 'because it played such a substantial role in our own suffrage activity.' (p 18)

[2] See Spender and Hayman edition for further details of reviews.

[3] See also: Hamilton, (1935), Whitelaw (1990); Holledge, Stowell; Cockin; *Cicely Hamilton on Theatre: a Preliminary Bibliography* by Sue Thomas in *Theatre Notebook* 1995, vol. 49, no2 .

How The Vote Was Won

Cicely Hamilton and Christopher St John (1909)

CHARACTERS

Horace Cole, a clerk, about 30
Ethel, his wife, 22
Winifred, her sister
Agatha Cole, Horace's sister
Molly, his niece
Madame Christine, his distant relation
Maudie Spark, his first cousin
Miss Lizzie Wilkins, his aunt
Lily, his maid-of-all-work
Gerald Williams, his neighbour

ACT ONE
Scene One

A sitting-room in Horace Cole's house at Brixton. The room is cheaply furnished in a genteel style. The window looks out on a row of little houses, all of the Cole pattern. The door leads into a narrow passage communicating at once with the front door. The fireplace has a fancy mantel border, and over it is an overmantel, decorated with many photographs and cheap ornaments. The sideboard, a small bookcase, a table, and a comfortable armchair, are the chief articles of furniture. The whole effect is modest, and quite unpleasing.

Time: Late afternoon on a spring day in any year in the future.

When the curtain rises, Mrs Horace Cole is sitting in the comfortable armchair putting a button on to her husband's coat. She is a pretty, fluffy little woman who could never be bad-tempered, but might be fretful. At this minute she is smiling indulgently, and rather irritatingly, at her sister Winifred, who is sitting by the fire when the curtain rises, but gets up almost immediately to leave. Winifred is a tall and distinguished-looking young woman with a cheerful, capable manner and an emphatic diction which betrays the public speaker. She wears the colours of the N. W. S. P. U.

WINIFRED   Well, good bye, Ethel. It's a pity you won't believe me. I wanted to let you and Horace down gently, or I shouldn't be here.

ETHEL   But you're always prophesying these dreadful things, Winnie, and nothing ever happens. Do you remember the day when you tried to invade the House of Commons from submarine boats? Oh, Horace did laugh when he saw in the papers that you had all been landed on the Hovis wharf by mistake! "By accident, on purpose!" Horace said. He couldn't stop laughing all the evening. "What price your sister, Winifred," he said. "She asked for a vote, and they gave her bread." He kept on – you can't think how funny he was about it!

WINIFRED   Oh, but I can! I know my dear brother-in-law's sense of humour is his strong point. Well, we must hope it will bear the strain that is going to be put on it today. Of course, when his female relations invade his house – all with the same story, "I've come to be supported" – he may think it excruciatingly funny. One never knows.

ETHEL   Winnie, you're only teasing me. They would never do such a thing. They must know we have only one spare bedroom, and that's to be for a paying guest when we can afford to furnish it.

WINIFRED   The servants' bedroom will be empty. Don't forget that all the domestic servants have joined the League and are going to strike, too.

ETHEL   Not ours, Winnie. Martha is simply devoted to me, and poor little Lily *couldn't* leave. She has no home to go to. She would have to go to the workhouse.

WINIFRED   Exactly where she will go. All those women who have no male relatives, or are refused help by those they have, have instructions to go to the relieving officer. The number of female paupers who will pour through the workhouse gates tonight all over England will frighten the Guardians into blue fits.

ETHEL   Horace says you'll never *frighten* the Government into giving you the vote.

WINIFRED   It's your husband, your dear Horace, and a million other dear Horaces who are going to do the frightening this time. By tomorrow, perhaps before, Horace will be marching to Westminster shouting out "Votes for Women!"

ETHEL   Winnie, how absurd you are! You know how often you've tried to convert Horace and failed. Is it likely that he will become a Suffragette just because – ?

WINIFRED   Just because –? Go on, Ethel.

ETHEL   Well, you know – all this you've been telling me about his relations coming here and asking him to support them. Of course I don't believe it. Agatha, for instance, would never dream of giving up her situation. But if they did come Horace would just tell them he *couldn't* keep them. How could he on £4 a week?

WINIFRED   How could he! That's the point! He couldn't, of course. That's why he'll want to get rid of them at any cost – even the cost of letting women have the Vote. That's why he and the majority of men in this country shouldn't for years have kept alive the foolish superstition that all women are supported by men. For years we have told them it was a delusion, but they could not take our arguments seriously. Their method of answering us was exactly that of the little boy in the street who cries "Yah – Suffragette!" when he sees my ribbon.

ETHEL   I always wish you wouldn't wear it when you come here ... Horace does so dislike it. He thinks it's unwomanly.

WINIFRED   Oh! does he? Tomorrow he may want to borrow it – when he and the others have had their object-lesson. They wouldn't listen to argument ... so we had to expose their pious fraud about woman's place in the world in a very practical and sensible way. At this very minute working women of every grade in every part of England are ceasing work, and going to demand support and the necessities of life from their nearest male relatives, however distant the nearest relative may be. I hope, for your sake, Ethel, that Horace's relatives aren't an exacting lot!

ETHEL   There wasn't a word about it in the *Daily Mail* this morning.

WINIFRED   Never mind. The evening papers will make up for it.

ETHEL   What male relative are you going to, Winnie? Uncle Joseph?

WINIFRED   Oh, I'm in the fighting line, as usual, so our dear uncle will be spared. My work is with the great army of women who have no male belongings of any kind! I shall be busy till midnight marshalling them to the workhouse ... This is perhaps the most important part of the strike. By this we shall hit men as ratepayers even when they have escaped us as relatives! Every man, either in a public capacity or a private one, will find himself face to face with the appalling problem of maintaining millions of women in idleness. Will the men take up the burden, d'ye think? Not they! *(looks at her watch)* Good heavens! The strike began ages ago. I must be off. I've wasted too much time here already.

ETHEL *(looking at the clock)* I had no idea it was so late. I must see about Horace's tea. He may be home any minute. *(rings the bell left.)*

WINIFRED   Poor Horace!

ETHEL *(annoyed)* Why "poor Horace"? I don't think he has anything to complain of. *(rings again.)*

WINIFRED   I feel some pity at this minute for all the men.

ETHEL   What can have happened to Martha?

WINIFRED   She's gone, my dear, that's all.

ETHEL   Nonsense. She's been with me ever since I was married, and I pay her very good wages.

Enter Lily, a shabby little maid-of-all-work, dressed for walking, the chief effect of the toilette being a very cheap and very smart hat.

ETHEL   Where's Martha, Lily?

LILY   She's left, m'm.

ETHEL   Left! She never gave me notice.

LILY   No, m'm, we wasn't to give no notice, but at three o'clock we was to quit.

ETHEL	But why? Don't be a silly little girl. And you mustn't come in here in your hat.
LILY	I was just goin' when you rang. That's what I've got me 'at on for.
ETHEL	Going! Where? It's not your afternoon out.
LILY	I'm goin' back to the Union. There's dozens of others goin' with me.
ETHEL	But why?
LILY	Miss Christabel – she told us. She says to us: "Now look 'ere, all of yer – you who've got no men to go to on Thursday – yer've got to go to the Union," she says; "and the one who 'angs back" – and she looked at me, she did – "may be the person 'oo the 'ole strain of the movement is restin' on, the traitor 'oo's sailin' under the 'ostile flag," she says; and I says, "That won't be me – not much!"

During this speech Winifred puts on a sandwich board which bears the inscription: "This way to the Workhouse."

WINIFRED	Well, Ethel, are you beginning to believe?
ETHEL	Oh, I think it's very unkind – very wicked. How am I to get Horace anything to eat with no servants?
WINIFRED	Cheer up, my dear. Horace and the others can end the strike when they choose. But they're going to have a jolly bad time first. Good bye.

Exit Winnie, singing "The Marseillaise."

LILY	Wait a bit, Miss. I'm comin' with yer. *(sings "The Marseillaise" too.)*
ETHEL	No, no. Oh, Lily, please don't go, or at any rate bring up the kettle first, and the chops, and the frying-pan. Please! Then I think I can manage.
LILY *(coming back into the room and speaking impressively)* There's no ill-feeling. It's an objick lesson – that's all.

Exit Lily. Ethel begins to cry weakly then lays the table, gets bread, cruet, tea, cups, etc., from the cupboard. Lily re-enters with a frying-pan, a kettle, and two raw chops.

LILY	'Ere you are – it's the best I can do. You see,

mum, I've got to be recognized by the State. I don't think I'm a criminal nor a lunatic, and I oughtn't to be treated as sich.

ETHEL   You poor little simpleton. Do you suppose that, even if this absurd plan succeeds, *you* will get a vote?

LILY   I may – you never know your luck; but that's not why I'm giving up work. It's so as I shan't stop them as ought to 'ave it. The 'ole strain's on me, and I'm goin' to the Union – so good bye, m'm.

Exit Lily.

ETHEL   And I've always been so kind to you! Oh, you little brute! What *will* Horace say? *(looking out of the window)* It can't be true. Everything looks the same as usual.

Off-stage Horace's voice outside:

HORACE   We must have at least sixteen Dreadnoughts this year.

Williams' voice off-stage:

WILLIAMS   You can't get 'em, old chap, unless you expect the blooming colonies to pay for 'em.

ETHEL   Ah, here is Horace, and Gerald Williams with him. Oh, I hope Horace hasn't asked him to tea! *(she powders her nose at the glass then pretends to be busy with the kettle.)*

Enter Horace Cole – an English master in his own house – and Gerald Williams, a smug young man stiff with self-consciousness.

ETHEL   You're back early, aren't you, Horry? How do you do, Mr. Williams?

WILLIAMS   How do you do, Mrs. Cole? I just dropped in to fetch a book your husband's promised to lend me.

Horace rummages in book-shelves.

ETHEL   Had a good day, Horry?

HORACE   Oh, much as usual. Ah, here it is – *(reading out the title)* – "Where's the Wash-tub now?" with a preface by Lord Curzon of Kedleston, published by the Men's League for Opposing Women's Suffrage. If that doesn't settle your missus, nothing will.

ETHEL   Is Mrs. Williams a Suffragette?

WILLIAMS   Rather; and whenever I say anything, all she can answer is, "You know nothing about it." Thank you, old man. I'll read it to her after tea. So long. Good bye, Mrs. Cole.

ETHEL   Did Mrs. Williams tell you anything this morning ... before you went to the City?

WILLIAMS   About Votes for Women, do you mean? Oh, no. Not allowed at breakfast. In fact, not allowed at all. I tried to stop her going to these meetings where they fill the women's heads with all sorts of rubbish, and she said she'd give 'em up if I'd give up my footer matches so we agreed to disagree. See you tomorrow, old chap. Good bye, Mrs. Cole.

Exit Gerald Williams.

HORACE   You might have asked him to stop to tea. You made him very welcome – I don't think.

ETHEL   I'm sorry; but I don't think he'd have stayed if I *had* asked him.

HORACE   Very likely not, but one should always be hospitable. Tea ready?

ETHEL   Not quite, dear. It will be in a minute.

HORACE   What on earth is all this!

ETHEL   Oh, nothing. I only thought I would cook your chop for you up here today – just for fun.

HORACE   I really think, Ethel, that so long as we can afford a servant, it's rather unnecessary.

ETHEL   You know you're always complaining of Martha's cooking. I thought you would like me to try.

HORACE   My dear child! It's very nice of you. But why not cook in the kitchen? Raw meat in the sitting-room!

ETHEL   Oh, Horry, don't!

She puts her arms round his neck and sobs. The chop at the end of the toasting fork in her hand dangles in his face.

HORACE   What on earth's the matter? Ethel, dear, don't be hysterical. If you knew what it was to come home fagged to death and be worried like this... I'll ring for Martha and tell her to take away these beastly chops. They're getting on my nerves.

ETHEL   Martha's gone.

HORACE   When? Why? Did you have a row? I suppose you had to give her a month's wages. I can't afford that sort of thing, you know.

ETHEL *(sobbing)* It's not you who afford it, anyhow. Don't I pay Martha out of my own money?

HORACE   Do you call it ladylike to throw that in my face.

ETHEL *(incoherently)* I'm not throwing it in your face ... but as it happens I didn't pay her anything. She went off without a word ... and Lily's gone, too. *(she puts her head down on the table and cries.)*

HORACE   Well, that's a good riddance. I'm sick of her dirty face and slovenly ways. If she ever does clean my boots, she makes them look worse than when I took them off. We must try and get a charwoman.

ETHEL   We shan't be able to. Isn't it in the papers?

HORACE   What *are* you talking about?

ETHEL   Winifred said it would be in the evening papers.

HORACE   Winifred! She's been here, has she? That accounts for everything. How that woman comes to be your sister I can't imagine. Of course she's mixed up with this wild-cat scheme.

ETHEL   Then you know about it!

HORACE   Oh, I saw something about "Suffragettes on Strike" on the posters on my way home. Who cares if they do strike? They're no use to anyone. Look at Winifred. What does she ever do except go round making speeches, and kicking up a row outside the House of Commons until she forces the police to arrest her. Then she goes to prison and poses as a martyr. Martyr! We all know she could go home at once if she would promise the magistrate to behave herself. What they ought to do is to try all these hysterical women in camera and sentence them to be ducked – privately. Then they'd soon give up advertising themselves.

ETHEL   Winnie has a splendid answer to that, but I forget what it is. Oh, Horry, was there anything on the posters about the nearest male relative?

HORACE   Ethel, my dear, you haven't gone dotty, have you? When you have quite done with my chair, I – *(he helps her out of the chair and sits down.)* Thank you.

ETHEL   Winnie said that not only are all the working women going to strike, but they are going to make their nearest male relatives support them.

HORACE   Rot!

ETHEL   I thought how dreadful it would be if Agatha came, or that cousin of yours on the stage whom you won't let me know, or your Aunt Lizzie! Martha and Lily have gone to *their* male relatives; at least, Lily's gone to the workhouse – it's all the same thing. Why shouldn't it be true? Oh, look, Horace, there's a cab – with luggage. Oh, what shall we do?

HORACE   Don't fuss! It's stopping next door, not here at all.

ETHEL   No, no; it's here. *(she rushes out.)*

HORACE *(calling after her)* Come back! You can't open the door yourself. It looks as if we didn't keep a servant.

Re-enter Ethel, followed after a few seconds by Agatha. Agatha is a weary-looking woman of about thirty-five. She wears the National Union colours, and is dowdily dressed.

ETHEL   It is Agatha – and such a big box. Where can we put it?

AGATHA *(mildly)* How do you do, Horace. *(kisses him)* Dear Ethel! *(kisses her)* You're not looking so well as usual. Would you mind paying the cabman two shillings, Horace, and helping him with my box? It's rather heavy, but then it contains all my worldly belongings.

HORACE   Agatha – you haven't lost your situation! You haven't left the Lewises?

AGATHA   Yes, Horace; I left at three o'clock.

HORACE   My dear Agatha – I'm extremely sorry – but we can't put you up here.

AGATHA   Hadn't you better pay the cab? Two shillings so soon becomes two-and-six.

Exit Horace.

AGATHA   I am afraid my brother doesn't realize that I have some claim on him.

ETHEL   We thought you were so happy with the Lewises.

AGATHA   So were the slaves in America when they had
kind masters. They didn't want to be free.

ETHEL   Horace said you always had late dinner with
them when they had no company.

AGATHA   Oh, I have no complaint against my late
employers. In fact, I was sorry to inconvenience them by leaving so
suddenly. But I had a higher duty to perform than my duty to them.

ETHEL   I don't know what to do. It will worry Horace
dreadfully.

Re-enter Horace.

HORACE   The cab *was* two-and-six, and I had to give a
man tuppence to help me in with that Noah's ark. Now, Agatha,
what does this mean? Surely in your position it was very unwise to
leave the Lewises. You can't stay here. We must make some
arrangement.

AGATHA   Any arrangement you like, dear, provided you
support me.

HORACE   I support you!

AGATHA   As my nearest male relative, I think you are
obliged to do so. If you refuse, I must go to the workhouse.

HORACE   But why can't you support yourself? You've
done it for years.

AGATHA   Yes – ever since I was eighteen. Now I am going
to give up work, until my work is recognized. Either my proper place
is the home – the home provided for me by some dear father, brother,
husband, cousin or uncle – or I am a self-supporting member of the
State who ought not to be shut out from the rights of citizenship.

HORACE   All this sounds as if you had become a
Suffragette! Oh, Agatha, I always thought you were a lady.

AGATHA   Yes, I was a lady – such a lady that at eighteen
I was thrown upon the world, penniless, with no training whatever
which fitted me to earn my own living. When women become
citizens I believe that daughters will be given the same chances as
sons, and such a life as mine will be impossible.

HORACE   Women are so illogical. What on earth has all
this to do with your planting yourself on me in this inconsiderate
way? You put me in a most unpleasant position. You must see,

Agatha, that I haven't the means to support a sister as well as a wife. Couldn't you go to some friends until you find another situation?

AGATHA No, Horace. I'm going to stay with you.

HORACE *(changing his tone and turning nasty)* Oh, indeed! And for how long – if I may ask?

AGATHA Until the Bill for the removal of the sex disability is passed.

HORACE *(impotently angry)* Nonsense. I can't keep you, and I won't. I have always tried to do my duty by you. I think hardly a week passes that I don't write to you. But now that you have deliberately thrown up an excellent situation as a governess and come here and threatened me – yes, threatened me – I think it's time to say that, sister or no sister, I will be master in my own house!

Enter Molly, a good-looking young girl of about twenty. She is dressed in well-cut, tailor-made clothes, wears a neat little hat, and carries some golf-clubs and a few books.

MOLLY How are you, Uncle Horace? Is that Aunt Aggie? How d'ye do? I haven't seen you since I was a kid.

HORACE Well, what have you come for?

MOLLY There's a charming welcome to give your only niece!

HORACE You know perfectly well, Molly that I disapprove of you in every way. I hear – I have never read it, of course – but I hear that you have written a most scandalous book. You live in lodgings by yourself, when if you chose you could afford some really nice and refined boarding-house. You have most undesirable acquaintances, and altogether –

MOLLY Cheer up, Uncle. Now's your chance of reforming me. I've come to live with you. You can support me and improve me at the same time.

HORACE I never heard such impertinence! I have always understood from you that you earn more than I do.

MOLLY Ah, yes; but you never *liked* my writing for money, did you? You called me "sexless" once because I said that as long as I could support myself I didn't feel an irresistible temptation to marry that awful little bounder Weekes.

ETHEL Reginald Weekes! How can you call him a

bounder! He was at Oxford.

MOLLY   Hullo, Auntie Ethel! I didn't notice you. You'll be glad to hear I haven't brought much luggage – only a night-gown and some golf-clubs.

HORACE   I suppose this is a joke!

MOLLY   Well, of course that's one way of looking at it. I'm not going to support myself any longer. I'm going to be a perfect lady and depend on my Uncle Horace – my nearest male relative – for the necessities of life. *(A motor horn is heard outside.)* Aren't you glad that I am not going to write another scandalous book, or live in lodgings by myself!

ETHEL *(at the window)* Horace! Horace! There's someone getting out of a motor – a grand motor. Who can it be? And there's no one to answer the door.

MOLLY   That doesn't matter. I found it open, and left it open to save trouble.

ETHEL   She's got luggage, too! The chauffeur's bringing in a dressing-case.

HORACE   I'll turn her into the street – and the dressing-case, too.

He goes fussily to the door and meets Madame Christine on the threshold. The lady is dressed smartly and tastefully. Age about forty, manners elegant, smile charming, speech resolute. She carries a jewel-case, and consults a legal document during her first remarks.

CHRISTINE   You are Mr. Cole?

HORACE   No! Certainly not! *(wavering)* At least, I was this morning, but –

CHRISTINE   Horace Cole, son of John Hay Cole, formerly of Streatham, where he carried on the business of a –

A motor horn sounds outside.

HORACE   I beg your pardon, but my late father's business has really nothing to do with this matter, and to a professional man it's rather trying to have these things raked up against him. Excuse me, but do you want your motor to go?

CHRISTINE   It's not my motor any longer and – yes, I do want it to go, for I may be staying here some time. I think you had one sister Agatha, and one brother Samuel, now dead. Samuel was much older than you –

AGATHA Why don't you answer, Horace? Yes, that's perfectly correct. I am Agatha.

CHRISTINE Oh, are you? How d'ye do?

MOLLY And Samuel Cole was my father.

CHRISTINE I'm very glad to meet you. I didn't know I had such charming relations. Well, Mr. Cole, my father was John Hay Cole's first cousin; so you, I think, are my second cousin, and my nearest male relative.

HORACE (*distractedly*) If anyone calls me that again I shall go mad.

CHRISTINE I am afraid you aren't quite pleased with the relationship!

HORACE You must excuse me – but I don't consider a second cousin exactly a relation.

CHRISTINE Oh, it answers the purpose. I suddenly find myself destitute, and I want you to support me. I am sure you would not like a Cole to go to the workhouse.

HORACE I don't care a damn where any of 'em go.

ETHEL (*shocked*) Horry! How can you!

CHRISTINE That's frank, at any rate; but I am sure, Cousin Horace, that in spite of your manners, your heart's in the right place. You won't refuse me board and lodging, until Parliament makes it possible for me to resume my work?

HORACE My dear madam, do you realize that my salary is £3 10s. a week – and that my house will hardly hold your luggage, much less you?

CHRISTINE Then you must agitate. Your female relatives have supported themselves up till now, and asked nothing from you. I myself, dear cousin, was, until this morning, running a profitable dress-making business in Hanover Square. In my public capacity I am Madame Christine.

MOLLY I know! I've never been able to afford you.

HORACE And do you think, Madame Christine –?

CHRISTINE Cousin Susan, please.

HORACE Do you think that you are justified in coming to a poor clerk and asking him to support you – you could probably turn over my yearly income in a single week! Didn't you come here in your own motor?

CHRISTINE   At three o'clock that motor became the property of the Women's Social and Political Union. All the rest of my property and all available cash have been divided equally between the National Union and the Women's Freedom League. Money is the sinews of war, you know.

HORACE   Do you mean to tell me that you've given all your money to the Suffragettes! It's a pity you haven't a husband. He'd very soon stop your doing such foolish things.

CHRISTINE   I had a husband once. He liked me to do foolish things – for instance, to support him. After that unfortunate experience, Cousin Horace, you may imagine how glad I am to find a man who really is a man, and will support me instead. By the way, I should *so* much like some tea. Is the kettle boiling?

ETHEL (*feebly*) There aren't enough cups! Oh, what shall I do?

HORACE   Never mind, Ethel. I shan't want any. I am going to dine in town and go to the theatre. I shall hope to find you all gone when I come back. If not, I shall send for the police.

Enter Maudie Spark, a young woman with an aggressively cheerful manner, a voice raucous from much bellowing of music-hall songs, a hat of huge size, and a heart of gold.

MAUDIE   'Ullo! 'ullo! who's talking about the police? Not my dear cousin Horry!

HORACE   How dare you come here?

MAUDIE   Necessity, old dear. If I had a livelier male relative, you may bet I'd have gone to him! But you, Horace, are the only first cousin of this poor orphan. What are you in such a hurry for?

HORACE   Let me pass! I'm going to the theatre.

MAUDIE   Silly jay! The theatres are all closed – and the halls too. The actresses have gone on strike – resting indefinitely. I've done my little bit towards that. They won't get any more work out of Maudie Spark, Queen of Comédiennes, until the women have got the vote. Ladies and fellow-relatives, you'll be pleased to hear the strike's going fine. The big drapers can't open tomorrow. One man can't fill the place of fifteen young ladies at once, you see. The duchesses are out in the streets begging people to come in and wash their kids. The City men are trying to get taxi-men in to do their typewriting. Every man, like Horry here, has his house full of females. Most of 'em thought, like Horry, that they'd go to the theatre to escape. But there's not a blessed theatre to go to! Oh, what a song it'll make. "A woman's place is in the home – I don't think, I don't think, I don't think."

HORACE Even if this is not a plot against me personally, even if there are other women in London at this minute disgracing their sex –

MAUDIE Here stop it – come off it! If it comes to that, what are you doing – threatening your womankind with the police and the workhouse.

HORACE I was not addressing myself to you.

AGATHA Why not, Horace? She's your cousin. She needs your protection just as much as we do.

HORACE I regard that woman as the skeleton in the cupboard of a respectable family but that's neither here nor there. I address myself to the more lady-like portion of this gathering, and I say that whatever is going on, the men will know what to do, and will do it with dignity and firmness.

The impressiveness of this statement is marred by the fact that Horace's hand, in emphasizing it, comes down heavily on the loaf of bread on the table.

HORACE A few exhibitions of this kind won't frighten them.

MAUDIE Oh, won't it! I like that! They're being so firm and so dignified that they're running down to the House of Commons like lunatics, and blackguarding the Government for not having given us the vote before!

Shouts outside of newsboys in the distance.

MOLLY Splendid! Have they begun already?

CHRISTINE Get a paper, Cousin Horace. I know some men never believe anything till they see it in the paper.

ETHEL The boys are shouting out something now. Listen.

Shouts outside.

NEWSBOY   Extry special. Great strike of women. Women's strike. Theatres closed. Extry special edition. Star! News! 6.30 edition!

MOLLY   You see. Since this morning Suffragettes have become women!

ETHEL *(at window)* Here, boy, paper!

Cries go on.

NEWSBOY   Extry special Star. Men petition the Government. Votes for Women. Extry special.

ETHEL   Oh, heavens, here's Aunt Lizzie!

As Ethel pronounces the name Horace dives under the table. Enter Aunt Lizzie leading a fat spaniel and carrying a birdcage with a parrot in it. Miss Elizabeth Wilkins is a comfortable, middle-aged body of a type well known to those who live in the less fashionable quarter of Bloomsbury. She looks as if she kept lodgers, and her looks do not belie her. She is not very well-educated, but has a good deal of native intelligence. Her features are homely and her clothes about thirty years behind the times.

AUNT L   Well, dears, all here? That's right. Where's Horace? Out? Just as well – we can talk more freely. I'm sorry I'm late, but animals do so hate a move. It took a long time to make them understand the strike. But I think they will be very comfortable here. You love dogs, don't you, Ethel?

ETHEL   Not Ponto. He always growls at me.

AUNT L   Clever dog! he knows you don't sympathize with the cause.

ETHEL   But I do, Aunt, only I have always said that as I was happily married I thought it had very little to do with me.

AUNT L   You've changed your mind about that today, I should think! What a day it's been! We never expected everything would go so smoothly. They say the Bill's to be rushed through at once. No more broken promises, no more talking out. Deeds, not words, at last! Seen the papers? The press are not boycotting us today, my dears. *(Madame Christine, Molly, and Maudie each take a paper)* The boy who sold them to me put the money back into

Ponto's collecting box. That dog must have made five pounds for the cause since this morning.

Horace puts his head out.

HORACE   Liar!

MOLLY   Oh, do listen to this. It's too splendid! *(reading from the paper)* "Women's Strike – Latest: Messrs. Lyons and Co. announce that by special arrangement with the War Office the places of their defaulting waitresses will be filled by the non-commissioned officers and men of the 2nd Battalion Coldstream Guards. Business will therefore be carried on as usual."

CHRISTINE   What do you think of this? *(reading)* "Latest Intelligence. – It is understood that the Naval Volunteers have been approached by the authorities with the object of inducing them to act as charwomen to the House of Commons."

AUNT L *(to Ethel)* Well, my dear! Read then, what *The Star* says.

ETHEL *(tremulously reading)* "The queue of women waiting for admission to Westminster workhouse is already a mile and a half in length. As the entire police force is occupied in dealing with the men's processions, Lord Esher has been approached with a view to ascertaining if the Territorials can be sworn in as special constables."

MAUDIE *(laughing)* This is a little bit of all right. *(reading)* "Our special representative, on calling upon the Prime Minister with the object of ascertaining his views on the situation, was informed that the Right Honourable gentleman was unable to receive him, as he was actively engaged in making his bed with the assistance of the boot-boy and a Foreign Office messenger."

AUNT L   Always unwilling to receive people, you see! Well, he must be feeling sorry now that he never received us. Everyone's putting the blame on to him. It's extraordinary how many men – and newspapers, too – have suddenly found out that they have always been in favour of woman's suffrage! That's the sensible attitude, of course. It would be humiliating for them to confess that it was not until we held a pistol to their heads that they changed their minds. Well, at this minute I would rather be the man who has been our ally all along than the one who has been our enemy. It's not the popular thing to be an "anti" any more. Any man who tries to oppose us today is likely to be slung up to the nearest lamp-post.

ETHEL *(rushing wildly to the table)* Oh, Horry! my Horry!

Horace comes out from under the table.

AUNT L	Why, bless the boy, what are you doing there?
HORACE	Oh, nothing. I merely thought I might be less in the way here, that's all.
AUNT L	You didn't hide when I came in by any chance!
HORACE	I hide from you! Aren't you always welcome in this house?
AUNT L	Well, I haven't noticed it particularly; and I'm

not calling today, you understand, I've come to stay. *(Horace, dashed and beaten, begins to walk up and down the room, and consults Ethel)* Well, well! I won't deny it was a wrench to leave 118a, Upper Montagu Place, where I've done my best for boarders, old and young, gents and ladies, for twenty-five years – and no complaints! A home from home, they call it. All my ladies had left before I started out, on the same business as all of us – but what those poor boys will do for their dinner tonight I don't know. They're a helpless lot! Well, it's all over; I've given up my boarding-house, and I depend on you, Horace, to keep me until I am admitted to citizenship. It may take a long time.

HORACE   It *must* not take a long time. I shan't allow it. It shall be done at once. Well, you needn't all look so surprised. I know I've been against it, but I didn't realize things. I thought only a few howling dervishes wanted the vote but when I find that you – Aunt – Fancy a woman of your firmness of character, one who has always been so careful with her money, being declared incapable of voting! The thing is absurd.

MAUDIE   Bravo! Our Horry's waking up.

HORACE *(looking at her scornfully)* If there are a few women here and there who *are* incapable – I mention no names, mind – it doesn't affect the position. What's going to be done? Who's going to do it? If this rotten Government think we're going to maintain millions of women in idleness just because they don't like the idea of my Aunt Lizzie making a scratch on a bit of paper and shoving it into a ballot-box once every five years, this Government have

reckoned without the men – *(general cheering)* I'll show 'em what
I've got a vote for! What do they expect? You can't all marry. There
aren't enough men to go round, and if you're earning your own
living and paying taxes you ought to have a say; it's only fair.
*(General cheering and a specially emphatic "Hear, hear" from
Madame Christine.)* The Government are narrow-minded idiots!

CHRISTINE   Hear! Hear!

HORACE   They talk as if all the women ought to stay at
home washing and ironing. Well, before a woman has a wash-tub,
she must have a home to put it in, mustn't she? And who's going to
give it her? I'd like them to tell me that. Do they expect *me* to do it?

AGATHA   Yes, dear.

HORACE   I say if she can do it herself and keep herself,
so much the better for everyone. Anyhow, who are the Government?
They're only representing *me*, and being paid thousands a year by
me for carrying out my wishes.

MOLLY   Oh, er – what ho!

HORACE *(turns on her angrily)* I like a woman to be a woman –
that's the way I was brought up; but if she insists on having a vote –
and apparently she does –

ALL   She does! she does!

HORACE   I don't see why she shouldn't have it. Many a
woman came in here at the last election and tried to wheedle me
into voting for her particular candidate. If she has time to do that –
and I never heard the member say then that she ought to be at home
washing the baby – I don't see why she hasn't time to vote. It's never
taken up much of *my* time, or interfered with my work. I've only
voted once in my life – but that's neither here nor there. I know
what the vote does for me. It gives me a status; that's what you
women want – a status.

ALL   Yes, yes; a status.

HORACE   I might even call it a *locus standi*. If I go now
and tell these rotten Cabinet Ministers what I think of them, it's my
locus standi –

MAUDIE   That's a good word.

HORACE   – that will force them to listen to me. Oh, I
know. And, by gum! I'll give them a bit of my mind. They shall hear
a few home truths for once. "Gentlemen," I shall say – well, that

won't be true of all of them to start with, but one must give 'em the benefit of the doubt – "gentlemen, the men of England are sick and tired of your policy. Who's driven the women of England into this? *You – (he turns round on Ethel, who jumps violently) –* because you were too stupid to know that they meant business – because you couldn't read the writing on the wall.

ALL   Hear, hear!

HORACE   It may be nothing to you, gentlemen, that every industry in this country is paralyzed and every Englishman's home turned into a howling wilderness –

MOLLY   Draw it mild, Uncle.

HORACE   A howling wilderness, I repeat– by your refusal to see what's as plain as the nose on your face. But I would have you know, gentlemen, that it is something to us. We aren't slaves. We never will be slaves –

AGATHA   Never, never!

HORACE   – and we insist on reform. Gentlemen, conditions have changed, and women have to work. Don't men encourage them to work, *invite* them to work?

AGATHA   Make them work.

HORACE   And women are placed in the battle of life on the same terms as we are, short of one thing, the *locus standi* of a vote.

MAUDIE   Good old *locus standi*!

HORACE   If you aren't going to give it them, gentlemen, and if they won't go back to their occupations without it, we ask you, how they're going to live? Who's going to support them? Perhaps you're thinking of giving them all old age pensions and asking the country to pay the piper! The country will see you damned first, if, gentlemen, you'll pardon the expression. It's dawning upon us all that the women would never have taken such a step as this if they hadn't been the victims of gross injustice.

ALL   Never.

HORACE   Why shouldn't they have a voice in the laws which regulate the price of food and clothes? Don't they pay for their food and clothes?

MAUDIE   Paid for mine all my life.

HORACE   Why shouldn't they have a voice in the rate of wages and the hours of labour in certain industries? Aren't they working at those industries? If you had a particle of common sense or decent feeling, gentlemen –

Enter Gerald Williams like a souvenir of Mafeking night. He shouts incoherently and in a hoarse voice. He is utterly transformed from the meek, smug being of an hour before. He is wearing several ribbons and badges and carrying a banner bearing this inscription: "The men of Brixton demand votes for women this evening."

WILLIAMS   Cole! Cole! Come on! Come on! You'll be late. The procession's forming up at the town hall. There's no time to lose. What are you slacking here for? Perhaps this isn't good enough for you. I've got twelve of them in my drawing-room. We shall be late for the procession if we don't start at once. Hurry up! Come on! Votes for Women! Where's your banner? Where's your badge? Down with the Government! Rule Britannia! Votes for Women! D'you want to support a dozen women for the rest of your life, or don't you? Every man in Brixton is going to Westminster. Borrow a ribbon and come along. Hurry up, now! Hooray! (*rushes madly out crying*) Votes for Women! Rule Britannia! Women, never, never shall be slaves! Votes for Women!

All the women who are wearing ribbons decorate Horace.

ETHEL   My hero!

She throws her arms round him.

HORACE   You may depend on me – all of you – to see justice done. When you want a thing done, get a man to do it! Votes for Women!

Agatha gives him a flag which he waves triumphantly.

Curtain tableau: Horace marching majestically out of the door, with the women cheering him enthusiastically.

The end.

Cicely Hamilton (1872-1952)

Hamilton was born in London, the daughter of an army officer, Denzill Hamill. After her mother, Maude, died (or disappeared, Hamilton is evasive in her autobiography, *Life Errant*, 1935) Cicely helped bring up and support her younger brothers and sisters. After a brief stint as a pupil teacher, she became an actress, and began writing popular fiction.

In 1906, her first play *The Sixth Commandment* was produced at Wyndham's in London. It was followed by *The Sergeant of Hussars* (Play Actors, 1907). In 1908 her play, *Diana of Dobson's*, written in the style of the "new drama" of Shaw, Granville-Barker and others, was produced at the Kingsway Theatre. It was highly successful, enjoying a long run, extensive tours and a series of revivals and introduced themes developed in her book *Marriage as Trade* (1909).

Hamilton put her public recognition to the service of the suffrage campaign, joining the WSPU, becoming a speaker at rallies and co-founding WWSL with Bessie Hatton. She also wrote *A Pageant of Women* (AFL, Scala, 1909) and the words to her friend, Ethel Smyth's anthem, *March of the Women* which became classics of the campaign.

Her later plays included numerous one-acts such as *Mrs Vance* (1907) and *Just To Get Married* (1910), *The Pot and the Kettle* (with St John, AFL, 1909), *The Home Coming* (1910) and *The Cutting of the Knot* (Glasgow Royal, 1911) *The Constant Husband* (1912), *Lady Noggs* (1913) and *Phyl* (1913) which enjoyed the distinction of being banned at Oxford University[1].

During the War, Hamilton worked as a hospital administrator and went on to organise concerts and theatre performances for the troops. She continued writing after the War, helping found the feminist magazine *Time and Tide*, with Rebecca West, Winifred Holtby and others. She also produced a history of the Old Vic with Lillian Baylis. *The Old Adam*, her last play concerns the devastation of war, and the indifference of women who tried to ignore its horrors.

---

[1] See Whitelaw on *Phyl*, Croft (2001) for publication details.

Christopher St John (1871-1960)

Christabel Marshall assumed this name upon her conversion to Catholicism and because she felt herself better suited to a man's name. She was the youngest of nine children, daughter of banker Hugh Graham Marshall and novelist, Emma Marshall who supported the family by historical fiction-writing after the bank failed. Chris grew up in the West Country, went to Oxford University and then worked as Secretary to Lady Randolph Churchill. In 1899 she met Ellen Terry and fell in love with Terry's daughter, Edith (Edy) Craig[2].

The two set up house together in Smith Square, becoming active members of the suffrage movement. They also provided a retreat and safe-house for other women at their home, the Priest's House, at Smallhythe, Kent where they were later joined by the visual artist Claire 'Tony' Atwood. Their circle grew to include other lesbians such as Vita Sackville-West, whose Sissinghurst home was close by, Gabrielle Enthoven, (whose theatre collection formed the basis of the Theatre Museum's Collection)[3] and Radclyffe Hall.

With Edith Craig, she established the Pioneer Players, an innovative theatre company which produced many of Chris's plays, as well as plays by other feminist writers and experimental works from the European repertoire.

St John's numerous plays and translations, largely unpublished include *The Decision* (1906); *The Wilson Trial* (1909); *Eriksson's Wife* (Royalty, 1904), *Macrena* (1912,) *The First Actress* (1911), *The Coronation* (1912, with Charles Thursby), and *The Plays of Roswitha* (1923), the tenth century nun and first woman playwright. St John also edited Ellen Terry's *Memoirs*, wrote music and dramatic criticism, in particular for *Time and Tide* and *The Lady*, and a biography of the composer and feminist, Ethel Smyth.

---

2 See Cockin 1998 and 2001.

3 Now the V&A Theatre Collections.

The Apple

The Apple

The Apple is a powerful indictment of inequality between the sexes and its economic consequences. It explores a family in which the grandfather has left his money to all his grandchildren, but it has been spent on the favoured son, Cyril, the 'apple' of his father's eye, to establish his position in the world. Meanwhile his sister Ann acts as unpaid housekeeper and Helen works as a typist, about which Cyril is duly superior. When Helen is subjected to sexual advances at work from her father's friend Nigel Dean, Helen determines to use her share of the money to go to Canada to make a better life. But Cyril has already made his claim for the money to buy the partnership which will allow him to marry.

Where many of the AFL plays are propaganda pieces which use a comic mode to defeat anti-suffragist arguments, *The Apple* addresses larger grievances of women's lives frustrated by lack of economic independence, the narrow options open to women in the workforce and the issue of sexual harassment.

In its account of economic drudgery it has similarities to the work of Elizabeth Baker or Cicely Hamilton. It powerfully, and still unusually for its time, creates a heroine in Helen who gives unapologetic voice to her anger at the limitations imposed on her. The author juxtaposes her with her downtrodden, self-sacrificing sister, Ann, whose only access to money, is by pawning her possessions. It remains moving and resonant in its account of the frustration and oppressiveness of family structures in which Helen demands "a glimpse of life, a taste of the joy of living, a few pence in my pocket, my rights as an individual" but remains entrapped within a scenario, dictated by her boss, which alone seems to offer any chance of these.

Inez Bensusan wrote three other plays, all unpublished, the duologue, *Perfect Ladies* (1909, now lost), *Nobody's Sweetheart*, 1911 (produced at the Little Theatre) and *The Prodigal Passes*, 1914 (Cosmopolis).

See: Stowell; Holledge; Pfisterer; Pfisterer and Pickett, Bradley-Smith

The Apple

An Episode of Today in One Act

Inez Bensusan

CHARACTERS

Helen Payson
Ann Payson, her sister
Cyril Payson, their brother (the Apple)
Nigel Dean, friend of Cyril, Ann's boss

ACT ONE
Scene One

Useful room in suburban villa. The furniture is very worn, giving the impression of poor gentlefolk trying to make a brave show. Doors right and left. Door right gives on to hall and through it is seen, if possible, staircase. Door left gives into kitchen and, if possible, shows interior with pots and pans, etc. Table left with sewing machine. Sofa right. Mirror over mantle-piece right. 2nd Armchair right, centre.

As curtain rises Ann is discovered at table left working the sewing machine. She is a slight, short-sighted girl about 27, but looks older, as though all her life she had been overworked. She wears a washed-out cotton frock and a big apron. She is an alert, active, nervous type. A noise as of opening and banging of hall door is heard, then enter Helen through door right. She is a tall, buxom type, very handsome with a fine figure, neatly dressed in tailor-made style, stiff collar, little tie, short pleated skirt, plain hat, simple but distinctly smart, the type to be met with frequently in city offices, but young with good colour and clear complexion. Ann looks up in surprise then looks at clock and back at Helen.

ANN   How awfully early you are Ellie – it's only half-past three.

Helen comes down to armchair right and resolutely throws herself into it, begins almost savagely to tear off her gloves. She looks heated and excited.

ANN I do hope you're not ill? What's the matter? I'll make you a cup of tea. *(Helen does not answer.)* You're sure you're quite well, dear? *(rises)*

HELEN Yes, there's nothing wrong with me. Don't start fussing for goodness sake. *(takes off her hat, jabs the pins into the crown, and throws it across the room on to the sofa.)*

ANN But, Ellie dear –

(Helen holds her hands before her eyes.) There! I'm sure you're ill. *(Comes to her. Helen sits up quickly.)*

HELEN Don't talk rubbish, I tell you. I'm as strong as a bullock, worse luck!

ANN Ell, what do you–

HELEN I'm excited, bad-tempered, that's all. I've been thinking hard on the way home. Too much thinking is more than my cheap brain can stand, I suppose.

ANN Then you've a headache? I was sure of it. I *will* make you some tea. *(moves towards the kitchen.)*

HELEN *(petulantly)* Oh, sit down, do! I'll get my own tea when I want it. I won't have you slaving for me. You're worked to death as it is. Do sit down!

ANN The kettle won't be a minute – *(moves up)*

HELEN *(jumps up, goes after Ann, seizes her by the shoulders and pushes her into chair by table.)* What a blessed nuisance you are Ann, always on the hop, like a jumping bean. It's bad enough the way the others make use of you, but I'm hanged if I'll allow it. *(Ann protests.)* What's this you're making? *(picks up material.)*

ANN It's Norah's dress for the Lamond's party. Isn't it sweet? *(holds it up)* The bodice is such a dear, it's going to be crossed over like this *(showing her)* and have lace and insertion and blue ribbons run through. *(Helen crosses to left of table.)* Don't you like it?

HELEN Why can't Norah make her own things? She has more spare time than you.

ANN But the poor child is so tired after her day's work. I wouldn't be a nursery governess for anything.

HELEN *(Bitterly)* She's not too tired to go to a party anyway. *(sits)*

ANN You don't grudge her that surely? I never thought Mrs. Prescott would spare her, but she said if she got up at five next morning, she might go. Poor Norah! She will be tired.

HELEN You're giving it to her of course? *(Ann nods.)* Where did you get the money?

ANN Whatever's come over you today, Ell? I'm sure you're ill.

HELEN *(firmly)* Where did you get it? Father didn't give it to you. *(Ann shakes her head.)* Mother hasn't got it to give. You've pawned something again. What?

ANN *(uncomfortably)* It wasn't a bit of good to me. I didn't want it.

HELEN *(sternly)* What?

ANN That little medallion thing. *(quickly)* I never wore it. It was no good to me.

HELEN Ann! You're awfully fond of it. How dare you!

ANN But the poor child – she had to wear something, and they pay her so badly where she is. She can't save a penny. I couldn't bear the thought that–

HELEN *(angrily)* Why didn't you ask Father?

ANN *(surprised)* What an idea!

HELEN *(bringing her hand down violently on the table)* He ought to pay for Norah's clothes – not you or me. It's a sin, a disgrace that a girl should have to – to pawn her trinkets, in order to go decently clad! Ugh! It makes me sick.

Crosses centre to armchair.

ANN You know Ellie, Father would give it if he had it to give. It isn't that he's mean – you know if –

HELEN *(sits)* I know that every penny that can be saved or squeezed out of the miserable family exchequer goes to support the Apple, instead of supporting *us*! And I consider it's high time the Apple was self-supporting. He's older than Norah or me – he's a man, a strong healthy male thing. What right has he to everything, while we girls are struggling to – to cover ourselves decently?

ANN It isn't Cyril's fault, Ellie dear. You know there are things a man must have that girls can do without.

HELEN Clubs, cigarettes, hansoms and so on? Oh yes.

Because he's the son, the apple of his parents' eyes, everything has to be sacrificed for him – everything! His own sisters' comfort – more – their very chances in life!

ANN I never heard you speak like this. Has anything happened?

HELEN Yes. The worst has happened. I've awakened to a sense of the injustice of it all. I'm going to rebel. I'm going to fight for my rights, your rights, equal rights for us all.

ANN But how? You know Father can't afford to give us pocket money and things. You know what a struggle it has always been, dear.

HELEN Oh, I'm not grumbling with Father, he's acting according to his lights I suppose. It's the gospel of the generation that everything must be done for the boy – the son – he's the rare and precious individual in a country where there are more than a million superfluous women!

Ann shakes her head mournfully; gets up and goes to kitchen door. Helen leans her elbows on her knees and takes her head in her hands. A slight pause.

HELEN What a pity we don't live in China!

ANN *(pausing at door)* Whatever for? *(Goes through, leaving door open, gets kettle, and puts on stove or gas ring.)*

HELEN *(with bitter laugh)* Superfluous girl babies there are legally and comfortably done away with directly they're born.

ANN *(horrified, drops teapot lid)* Oh! how awful – how ghastly!

HELEN It's far more merciful than letting them live to toil and moil and scrape and scratch along through the best years of their life as hundreds of us girls have to do.

Ann looks compassionately at her a moment, then bustles about getting a cup and saucer, etc. A slight pause. Helen turns round.

HELEN Have your own way then. I'll submit. You won't have me here much longer so I may as well try to be decent for the time being.

Helen crosses to table and sits at machine and commences work.

ANN *(at door)* I can't understand you, Ellie. You're so queer today.

What are you talking about? Never mind that, Ellie, I'll get along with it all right. I do wish you'd lie down. You seem so unhappy somehow, I'm quite worried.

HELEN *(working machine almost viciously)* Don't you worry, I'm all right. In luck most likely – very much in luck. I thought it would come to it some time, but I didn't expect it quite so soon, not quite. But anyway since it had to come–

Ann listens, quite at sea. She is seen inside the door cutting bread and butter. Helen takes work out of machine, shakes and turns bodice over with critical eye.

HELEN You can't get on properly with this until it's fitted – come here and try it on.

ANN It will do when I go to bed. I always fix Norah's things in front of the glass, our figures are so alike. Don't you bother.

HELEN You can't possibly fix the back on yourself.

ANN But Ellie, you know how tired you are–

HELEN . Not anything like the corpse you'll be, by bedtime.

ANN But really –

HELEN *(turns)* Let me swallow that tea, and then see whose will is strongest.

ANN I'll bring it to you. What a trial you are to be sure. *(sighs good-naturedly, brings cup in one hand, brown teapot in the other. Helen puts work down and takes cup.)* I've put the milk in. Is this strong enough? *(pouring)*

HELEN Fine. That's enough, thanks. *(drinks)*

A pause. Ann gives her a plate of bread and butter on her lap.

HELEN Awfully good. You *can* make tea, Ann – I'm glad I let you have your own way, for once. I feel better already – at least my temper does. Aren't you going to have a cup?

ANN I'm not thirsty.

HELEN Economy or honour?

ANN *(laughing)* Honour bright.

HELEN *(between her mouthfuls)* Off with your bodice then, I want to try this on.

ANN   I can do it quite well tonight, really.

HELEN *(firmly)* I'll rip it off you myself if you don't. It will take half the time my way – come on.

ANN *(protesting)* I do wish to Goodness that–

HELEN *(putting down cup)* Now then– *(rising)*

ANN *(weakly)* You really are too awful.

HELEN *(centre)* Never mind – you won't have to put up with your bully of a sister much longer. Take it off.

ANN   But someone might come.

HELEN   No fear. Mother won't matter, and there's no danger of the Apple returning just yet. He's swaggering down Pall Mall or lounging in the Park if the office is too dull for him.

ANN   You've heaps of your own things to see to.

HELEN   Heaps. More than you think, considering the journey I'm going on shortly.

ANN *(taking off blouse)* Whatever nonsense are you talking now?

HELEN *(helping her on with the other)* It's anything but nonsense. It's the solemn truth. I've been hinting at it for the last half hour, but you've taken no notice.

ANN *(turning)* Ellie! What do you mean?

HELEN   Keep still, or the pins will stick in you. *(fitting and pinning)* It means this. Today week I'm going to Canada.

ANN   Canada? *(turns sharply and squeals.)*

HELEN   In the "Cymric" with Mabel Arnott and her friends.

ANN   But how? Why? What will you do there? Where will you get the money? – Ellie –

HELEN *(firmly)* Keep still! Father will have to give me the money. He must. I mean to have a talk with him tonight. Nothing will change my determination. I mean to go. I'm sick of this life of scrape and screw – the narrow hemmed in existence. I've had enough of it.

ANN   But suppose Father can't give you the money?

HELEN   There's no suppose in it. The bit of money Grandfather left for us has so far been used to further Cyril's interests *only*. We three girls haven't had a penny of it. Cyril must go to Oxford – Cyril must belong to a fashionable club – Cyril must have a good tailor – he must keep up appearances –he must play the gentleman. Well, I don't grudge it to the Apple, but the time has come when *I* need help, consideration, money, and I mean to have it. *(all through this speech she has been fitting the bodice, pinning and adjusting in true dressmaker style.)*

ANN   When did you make up your mind to this? It's very sudden, isn't it?

HELEN   Very. This afternoon.

ANN   But why? How?

HELEN   I had a – I had words with Mr Dean. He annoyed me. I threw something at him – a ruler I think it was... I don't know exactly, anyway I put on my things, and walked out of the office there and then. I can't go back. I've got to do something. Canada's best. It's farthest away. *(crosses to table)*

ANN *(listening breathlessly)* You threw – a ruler – at Mr Dean? Mr –? Ellie! Nigel Dean, Father's *chief*! Oh, what will Father say?

HELEN *(pinning at shoulder)* I don't think Father's likely to hear anything about it.

ANN   Not? *(a pause)* What was Mr. Dean doing in your office anyway?

HELEN *(meaningly)* Ah! *(fitting again.)*

ANN   How did he annoy you?

HELEN   He kissed me.

ANN *(shocked)* Ellie! *(turns sharply and screams.)* Oh!

HELEN   I told you to keep still. *(picks out pin.)*

ANN   What an awful man. How dare he!

HELEN *(smiling)* He's not awful at all. That's the worst of it. He's rather nice.

ANN *(aghast)* But he's nearly as old as Father.

HELEN   Says he's forty-five.

ANN   And he's married!

HELEN *(laughing ironically)* Poor Ann! It's easily seen you haven't been a typist in a city office. You're so unsophisticated. *(leans her head down an instant on Ann's shoulder.)* It's my own fault I suppose. I'm cursed with some sort of attraction for that kind of man.

ANN *(after a little pause)* Poor Ellie. It's awful to think that such a vile man should be Father's chief. How could he treat you so! He always seemed such a friend of the family. *(Helen looks at her steadily.)* Perhaps he didn't *mean* anything. Don't you think he might have –

well, just felt sorry for you somehow? *(Helen smiles.)* He's always been particularly nice to you, hasn't he?

HELEN   Always.

ANN   Perhaps he only called at the office to see how you were getting on. After all it was through him speaking for you that Mr. Thatcher gave you the post. Wasn't it?

HELEN   Yes.

ANN *(cheering her)* Then it's not half as bad as you imagine, Ellie. I see it quite clearly. He called because he was interested in you – he thought you looked overworked – you are, you know. I've noticed it myself, and seeing the lines under your eyes, he felt sorry for you – so sorry that –

HELEN *(interrupting with a burst of laughter)* That he offered me anything, anything I wanted in the whole world.

ANN   Really? Ah, he meant it kindly you see.

HELEN   He did. *(with intensity.)* He is very generous, very thoughtful, very understanding.

ANN   And so fond of Father.

HELEN *(not heeding)* So concerned about my happiness... so anxious to lighten the burden... to make things easy – *(Helen sinks down at table full of thought.)*

ANN   He must be a real dear! A trump I call him. Don't you think so? *(Helen does not answer. A pause.)*
I hope you did not hurt him with the ruler? *(no answer.)*
It was rather unkind of you, don't you think? *(no answer.)*
(struggling to get out of bodice, but cannot.) I must say I think you're rather foolish to go flying off to Canada just because Mr. Dean gave you a – a *fatherly* kiss. I do really. At his age it's rather a compliment than anything else, – and to throw up your billet, and annoy Father, by asking for money, and make Mother miserable, and upset us all by having to answer all sorts of questions about you, – all because – *(struggling)* Unpin me, Ellie, I can't get out of the thing. *(comes centre to Helen.)*

Helen rouses herself and undoes pins.

HELEN   One, two, three, four, five! I'm so sorry. Five years to wait for a husband. I ought to have been more considerate.

ANN *(taking it off finally)* I don't mind that. All I care about is to see you sensible and happy. *(sees clock)* Dear, dear, the time I've wasted! I must go and put the kettle on. And Cyril's dining out this evening and wants his shoes cleaned. And I've Mother's cap to do up, and all the – *(knock heard)* Who's that? Thought this would happen if I tried it on –

Knocking repeated. Ann hurries into her things.

HELEN *(rising wearily)* I'll go.
ANN No, don't you bother. Just fasten me up. *(double knock)* Good gracious, how awful, dear, dear! Haven't you done? Do be quick. Where's my belt? *(bustles about.)*

Helen goes to door right and as she opens it Cyril comes in. He is a dapper conceited youth of twenty-three. The sort of superior bank clerk type. Very well-dressed, rather overdressed in fact. His hair is shiny and sleek; he wears a large buttonhole, fawn doeskin gloves, smart socks and immaculate shoes.

CYRIL What are you girls thinking about? Father's been knocking for the last ten minutes. Says the lock's stuck but that's rot – my key opened it right enough when I came along.

Helen seats herself again at chair right of table.

ANN I'm so sorry, Cyril. It's my fault.
CYRIL I'd advise you to take some tea in, to appease him. He's got his chief in there with him.
ANN & HELEN Nigel Dean?
CYRIL Yes. There must be something good in the wind. The Governor's all over him.
ANN *(looking at Helen but speaking to Cyril)* But how strange of Mr Dean to come here. *(goes into kitchen.)*

Cyril smoothes his hair at the glass, straightens his tie, and when perfectly approving of his appearance, throws himself full length on the sofa.

CYRIL Oh well, I can't stand the man. Thinks a jolly sight too much of himself. Conceit's a thing I bar. *(stretches himself, yawns.)*

Helen sits at table thinking. Ann busy in kitchen preparing tea. Clatter of cups, etc., heard.

CYRIL What a beastly noise you're making in there, Ann.

ANN I'm so sorry. *(nervously watching Helen.)* – I shan't be a minute now.

CYRIL *(knocking off Helen's hat which is in his way on the sofa.)* What the deuce is this?

HELEN My only hat when you're done with it.

CYRIL Shouldn't leave your things kicking around. Must teach you girls a few things. Look at the mess this room's in. There's never a decent corner in the house I can ask anyone into.

HELEN *(who has rescued her hat and is restoring it)* Why ask then? I don't suppose anyone's dying for that honour.

CYRIL That shows all you know.

HELEN Your friends can't be over particular then.

CYRIL Why not?

HELEN Need you ask? Look at yourself.

CYRIL *(sitting up)* What's wrong with me?

HELEN You've the manners of a potboy.

CYRIL *(enraged)* Manners of a – well I'm –

Ann comes in with tray.

ANN Oh please don't quarrel. Can't you see Ellie has a headache? Cyril do let her alone.

CYRIL Let her alone? I've done nothing. She's been saying the most brutal things I ever heard – finding fault with my manners, as though hers were so perfect. *(shrugging)* Manners! Wants me to model myself on the young men she comes in contact with perhaps? Fifteenth rate fellows earning their paltry twenty-five bob a week – manners indeed! A miserable typewriting girl to prate about manners, ha, ha! That's funny, damn funny!

HELEN *(flaring up)* Typewriting girl! You *would* turn up your nose – it's what one expects of you. You think it's degrading for a girl to work in an office, you and Father with your high and mighty notions of woman's sphere, and all that bosh! You'd like me to be a cipher in the house like Mother or sit at home like Ann, wearing my fingers to the bone over the housework, slaving for your comfort, with never a sixpenny piece in my pocket but for what you, in your magnanimity choose to bestow. Yes, that's your idea of how a girl ought to live. But because I choose to earn a decent living you do nothing but sneer!

Cyril attempts to interrupt, but Helen goes on heatedly. Ann meanwhile makes futile attempts to pacify both. She has the tray in her hands and goes from one to the other.

ANN He didn't mean to sneer, Ellie, did you Cyril? He only said –

HELEN If you think it's degrading to be a typist, perhaps you'll find me something better to do? Something more to your aesthetic taste? Do you think it's fun to sit stewing in a city office for hours and hours, at the beck and call of small-minded, self-satisfied men like yourself? That's where the degradation comes in. The work's all right. I don't mind the work, but it's the fact of having to knuckle under to the very men I wouldn't even wipe my boots on in the ordinary course of things – that's degrading. It's men like you, that make office work degrading to girls like me.

CYRIL *(furious)* Serve you right if you don't like it. Who asked you to go to work? Whose fault is it if you are treated like – like you deserve to be?

HELEN Whose fault indeed! Yours! Everything's yours. You've been spoiled and pampered and given into, since the day you were born. Everything's been sacrificed for you – and for what? I wouldn't mind if you were worth it, but you're not – you're just a selfish conceited jackanapes, and that's all we've been sacrificed for!

ANN Oh don't shout like this – please don't! Father will hear you. Oh! *(sees her efforts are futile, goes up, stops at door.)* Well, do stop till I open the door, please.

CYRIL Sacrificed? What damn nonsense.

ANN Cyril!

CYRIL Well, it's enough to make a fellow swear, to have a girl ragging him like this, though she is only a sister. I've done nothing. Why's she got her knife into me?

ANN She doesn't mean it – she's out of sorts. Let her alone. If you'll only be quiet for a few minutes it will all come right. Ellie, I wish you'd go and – lie down. Do, like a dear.

HELEN   Oh shut up, Ann.

A pause. Cyril goes back to the glass and tidies himself up. Ann waits a moment then goes to door right. Helen looks up to see if Cyril makes any attempt to open it, but he makes no movement.

ANN   It would be so awful if Mr Dean had heard you.

Helen rises and opens door for Ann, with an expression of utter contempt for Cyril on her face.

ANN   Why did you bother, Ellie dear? Thanks so much. Now promise me you won't –

HELEN   There's the gentleman for you! And no mistake. Manners if you like!

CYRIL   You'd like me to cavort round you all day like a circus horse perhaps?

HELEN   Don't flatter yourself. You've neither the brains nor the beauty of a circus horse.

ANN *(just going out)* Do wait till the door is shut, please! *(she exits.)*

Cyril kicks the fire irons savagely. A pause. Helen goes back to table, gives a deep sigh, and picks up work. Cyril lights another cigar. Looks round at her once or twice, and is about to speak, but changes his mind each time. In reality he is a little afraid of her. Helen puts down work and collects hat, gloves, etc., goes to door, looks out.

Dean's voice heard off: "All yes, just so, just so –"

Helen re-enters quickly and reseats herself. She has seen that the other door is open, so will not go upstairs. She goes back to armchair. Cyril calms down, throws himself full length on sofa, smacks rather savagely at the cushions. He smokes away in silence a few minutes.

Ann re-enters.

ANN   Ellie, Mr Dean's asking for you.

HELEN   Let him ask. I don't want to see him.

ANN   But Father told me to tell you –

HELEN   I'm not going, that is the long and short of it.

ANN *(changes the subject forcibly. Goes to Cyril and pats his head.)* It has been a tiring day, Cyril, hasn't it?

CYRIL   It's jolly hard luck on a fellow just when he's feeling particularly fit, to have a girl jump down his throat for nothing. It makes him feel a bit –

HELEN Sick. Naturally.

Cyril starts up. Ann quiets him. He turns to her, ignoring Helen.

CYRIL Thought I'd give you girls a treat by getting home early. I was feeling as fit as a fiddle. I had something to tell you, something interesting, and suddenly Helen goes for me like a bull at a gate.

HELEN No. Like a terrier at a rat. You need well shaking.

Cyril is about to explode again but Ann restrains him.

ANN It's only her fun, Cyril. Don't take any notice. What is the something interesting you were going to tell us?

CYRIL It will be a great surprise. *(stops)* Have you cleaned my shoes?

ANN Yes, yes, go on.

CYRIL Put the links in my dress shirt? I'm going out early.

ANN I'll have everything ready for you, dear. Now do tell me.

CYRIL *(condescendingly)* You're not at all a bad sort, Ann. I know you'll wish me luck anyway. *(Ann nods.)* Well, here goes. I'm thinking of getting married.

Both girls exclaim in surprise. They look at one another a moment, then Ann shakes him by the hand.

ANN No? Really? How exciting. Who to?
HELEN Poor girl!
CYRIL What?
HELEN No. My mistake. I meant rich girl, of course.
CYRIL How did you guess?
HELEN What has she done to deserve it?
ANN Anyone we know?
CYRIL No, no – no third-rate suburban miss for me, thanks.
ANN But what are you going to marry on?

HELEN   Her money, of course.

CYRIL (*furious*) I've stood enough of this Helen, and I'm full up. If you can't keep a civil tongue in your head perhaps you'll hold it altogether, or I'll – (*picks up something to throw at her.*)

HELEN   Temper! Temper! It's in the family, you see, Ann.

ANN   You really are awful, you two. Ellie, what is the matter?

HELEN (*roaring with laughter*) He takes himself in such deadly earnest.

ANN   Tell us about it – when did it happen? The engagement, I mean.

CYRIL (*putting himself tidy at mirror*) Oh, it hasn't exactly happened yet. But it will pretty soon – perhaps this very evening.

HELEN   Remember the adage. Pride, etc. Look out for stray pieces of banana skin.

CYRIL (*contemptuously*) Vulgarian.

ANN   Do go on, dear.

CYRIL   Not unless Helen shuts up.

HELEN   All right. I can't help it though, you're so funny. (*crosses to table and sits right chair.*)

CYRIL (*continuing, very self-importantly*) It depends of course whether she'll have me, but I don't think there's much doubt about that. Only seeing the inequality of our pecuniary positions it is only fair that I shouldn't ask her until I'm able to offer her – well something worth having.

HELEN   Yourself, for instance.

CYRIL (*ignoring her*) Any other course would be hardly honourable. Consequently I am going to buy a partnership –

ANN   You? How?

Helen turns round aghast.

CYRIL   Oh, easily managed. I've had a talk with the Governor. It's all but settled.

HELEN   Is it?

CYRIL   There's that nest egg of grandfather's – it's time it was put to same practical purpose.

HELEN   What's left of it.

CYRIL   There's really no need for me to discuss the matter with you girls at all. Father, as sole trustee, may spend it as he thinks fit, but I am inclined to let you know what is being done in the interest of all concerned.

HELEN   Just as well, considering it is ours as much as yours.

CYRIL   Quite so. Well, the important point is that my future should be considered.

HELEN   Naturally. Your future is the only thing that matters. Being a son. *(quotes)* "Where the apple reddens never pry." *(laughs a little bitterly.)*

CYRIL   I don't understand.

HELEN   You wouldn't. Go on. Only there's no Eden to lose in this case. *(sighs.)*

CYRIL   I'll need several hundred pounds. It's a great chance – a favour almost. But it's worth it. And with such good prospects my future father-in-law can't withhold his consent. Later on I can buy a still larger interest.

ANN   But I don't understand where the money is coming from?

CYRIL *(loftily)* Girls don't understand these things. It's done by mortgage. Father's estate, what he'll leave, by and by – don't you see? And with the money already in hand –

HELEN *(rises, blazing)* Part of that money is ours – it belongs to us girls, it belongs to me, and I'm going to have my share now, at once. *(Cyril stares at her thunderstruck.)* Of course you're surprised, but you'll have to get used to it. I've thrown up my job – I'm going to Canada next week, and I want my share. Don't you dare talk to Father until I've done with him – don't dare let him keep my share from me, or there'll be trouble, worse, much worse – a scandal, do you hear? *(going to him)* I want £100 before another week is out, so for once you and your prospects don't count, see? *(crosses back to table.)*

CYRIL   Are you going dotty?

ANN   No, no, it's true, Cyril. Ellie must have some money – you must help her to it.

CYRIL   Money? What does she want with money? What's all this bunkum – this talk about Canada?

HELEN   It's this. I'm going with the Arnotts next week.

There are sure to be openings there, and there are none here. I'll find work to do, only I need money to start, for my passage – for clothes, I must have it – I will!

CYRIL *(crosses to her. Sneering)* So, my career is to be jeopardised by a wild cat scheme of yours? For your pleasure, your amusement? It's abominable. The most selfish thing I ever heard.

HELEN   Selfish? Because I'm trying to go straight? Trying to help myself – to fight my way? Selfish? And what are you?

CYRIL *(stamping about, his hands in his pockets. Crosses back right.)* It's confounded cheek, I think, for you to suggest such a thing. My chances are to be flung to the winds, I suppose, my whole future ruined on your account. Very nice, I must say!

ANN *(coming centre)* Perhaps something can be arranged. It does seem such a pity that –

CYRIL *(walks about blazing with rage)* Just as everything was carefully planned out. Just as I had got over the worry, the difficulty – when not only my happiness, but hers – the girl I love –

ANN   Poor boy!

CYRIL *(continues)* Her happiness is to be ignored – by Jove! It's more than a fellow can stand.

HELEN   And what about my happiness? My future? My chances?

CYRIL   Girls don't want chances. They only want husbands. If you'd stay at home like a decent young woman, some decent man might want to marry you, but while you prefer –

HELEN   I don't want your decent husband. I want a little pleasure, a glimpse of life, a taste of the joy – of living, a few pence in my pocket, my rights as an individual–

VOICE *(off calling)* Ann, Ann!

ANN *(running off)* Yes Father, I'm coming. *(she exits.)*

CYRIL   Rights as an individual! Bosh! Twaddle! What you really want is a good hiding, and bread and water for a week.

Ann re-enters.

ANN *(anxiously)* It's for you, Ellie, Father wants you, that is –

HELEN   What for?

ANN   It's Mr Dean wants to speak to you about something.

HELEN *(tossing her head)* Let him want. I shan't come.
ANN   But Father says, it's important.
HELEN   I don't care what it is. Tell him I won't.
CYRIL   Shan't. Won't. Nice behaviour I must say. I'll
have to teach you a little obedience – a little discipline, I can see.
(going to door) See if I don't.

He exits.

ANN   Ellie! Whatever can Mr Dean want with you? I
wonder if he's told Father?
HELEN   Not likely.
CYRIL *(opens door preceding Nigel Dean)* She's here, sir. Will you
come in? Helen, here's Mr Dean. Ann, take some shaving water up
to my room. I'm just going to have a few minutes business talk with
Father. *(looking meaningly at Helen.)*

*Ann shakes hands with Nigel, goes into kitchen, looking nervously at
Helen. Cyril chuckles at Helen's discomfiture. She remains at table left,
pretending to sew, but in reality trembling with excitement.*
*Dean is a tall, good-looking man. He has a large patch of sticking
plaster on his forehead. He stands right quite composedly, as though
knowing himself master of the situation.*

CYRIL   Manners! Helen, offer Mr Dean a chair. He's
come to give you a talking to, to oblige Father. Perhaps you'll listen
to him. Aren't you going to offer him a seat?

Helen bites her lips to control herself.

DEAN   Thanks. Don't trouble.
CYRIL   Must apologise for her, she doesn't know any
better. Excuse me, won't you?
DEAN   Certainly, certainly.

*Exit Cyril very pleased with himself. Exit Ann after Cyril with shaving
water.*
*A pause. Helen does not look up. She controls her emotions with
utmost difficulty.*

DEAN   You're surprised to see me?
(she does not move.) Come, come let's have it out. I've been talking

to your father –

HELEN   Throwing dust in his eyes, you mean.

DEAN   If you like, yes. I've spoken about you–

HELEN *(looks up, sees plaster on his forehead, gives an exclamation of horror)* Oh! *(tears start to her eyes.)* Your forehead.

DEAN   What's the matter? This? Oh, it's nothing. It doesn't even throb any more.

HELEN *(weakly)* I didn't mean to – to hurt – I – I'm sorry.

DEAN *(lightly)* Not at all. I deserved it. Don't let's talk about that. I want to put things right.

HELEN *(sullenly)* They're quite right as they are, thank you. I'm not going back to the office any more. I'm going abroad.

DEAN   Abroad? Where? When?

HELEN   That's my business. *(sits)*

DEAN   Pardon me. It's mine. *(sits)* Mr Thatcher gave you the post on my recommendation. I'm responsible for you, as it were. I've already made it all right with the head clerk about today, and you'll find no difficulties in the way when you return to the office in the morning.

HELEN *(struggling with her tears)* I'm not going back.

DEAN *(softening his tone)* Yes you are, Helen. *(rising and going up to centre)* You are. You must. I've spoken to your father about you – I've been reconciling him to the fact that work is good for you – that a girl like you needs occupation. *(during this he comes above table.)*

HELEN   Occupation? It's freedom I want.

DEAN *(very low)* Freedom? You know what your answer was when I offered you that. *(she draws in her breath.)* You thought it brutal of me. So it was. But I'd like to give you a good time. No good-looking girl ought to fight for a living. I've told you this over and over again. Do you suppose I don't understand? I'd like to take you abroad, anywhere you please – show you how to enjoy life – let you revel in pretty things, buy you new hats enough to turn your head – take you to dances, theatres –

HELEN   You've said all this before.

DEAN   I know. But I mean it. *(comes down left of table.)* Well, you won't have it. Of course, quite right if you don't care for me enough. It's my misfortune that I'm married, but there you are. I'm not a villain in a melodrama, I'm a reasonable human being, I'm willing to give you what you want and you won't take it. Can't be helped. I won't worry you. I'll let you alone, that's all. *(He waits for her to speak. She keeps her head turned from him. He looks nervously towards the door once or twice then continues.)* I've done the next best thing I can think of. I've been to your father –

HELEN   About – me?

DEAN   Among other things, yes. It appears he's in some difficulty over a sum of money for –

HELEN   The Apple?

DEAN *(smiles)* Well yes, the Apple? Hmm, it's rather a case of another apple, don't you think? But I'm afraid I'm an indifferent Eve, and you're no Adam at all. *(she smiles in spite of herself.)* Ah! That's better. *(sitting right of table.)* Now, let's make up. I've promised to see your father through his difficulty – help him–

HELEN *(quickly)* With money? *(he nods, she stamps her foot.)* I won't have it. It's scandalous, it's vile of you. It's buying my silence. I won't keep it. I'll make a clean breast of everything, I'll tell Father the truth, and though I'll get all the blame, at least – he'll see you as you really are.

DEAN *(sits quite composedly)* Do just as you think best. I don't wish to come between you and that conscience of yours. It's a pretty conscience. I admire it. But remember what it will mean. Your father will have to look out for another billet, his self-respect will force him to, and billets are not so easy to find at his time of life. Then again Cyril's chances won't be worth that! *(snaps his fingers)* He won't have a sixpence to scratch himself with, and the girl's father won't hear of the match – and as for all you girls – well, is the prospect attractive?

Helen watches him with quivering lips.

HELEN *(under her breath)* I don't care, I don't care.

DEAN   Yes you do, Helen, and you know it. Now think what will happen if you're sensible. Cyril helped to a good match, which will set him on his feet commercially – and for yourself –

HELEN *(between her teeth)* Never mind about me.

DEAN   Oh, but I must. You're the crux of the whole concern. I'll keep out of the way till you've forgotten this little episode – unless you'll let me take you about a bit as usual – a luncheon, a theatre, now and again.

HELEN   Never, never!

DEAN   Nonsense. You'd never have had any pleasure at all if it hadn't been for me. You've said so again and again.

HELEN   That was different. I thought of you as a friend of the family, I liked you, I never dreamed –

DEAN   That I'd want to kiss you? I had no right, but I couldn't help it. It's your own fault, you're too good-looking.

HELEN *(impatient)* I wish you'd go. I've quite made up my mind. *(she moves to centre.)*

DEAN   Not yet. *(rises)* Not for a minute or so. *(going to Helen centre.)* I want you to tell me something. *(she calms down.)* Was it the kiss you objected to – or the principle?

HELEN *(looking at him a moment taken aback)* How – how can you! *(bursts into tears. Comes down to armchair, sits.)*

DEAN *(coming to Helen and placing his hands on her shoulders)* Hush, hush. That's all I want to know.

Pause. He moves down left.

HELEN *(fights with herself, then begins in a low hysterical voice)* I – I always blamed girls – who – who had experiences like this. I've always been so scornful. We've talked things over, compared notes, hundreds of times. I've always rebelled so against the lot of the millions of office girls like myself – felt so sorry for their dull, drab lives, the hopeless monotone of their existence. We women have such a few years to be young – hardly as many as can be counted on the fingers, we ought to enjoy those few years at any rate to the full – it's our right. We long for a little amusement – we snatch at a little fun when it offers– it's natural. A little admiration – even, a little flirting helps to kill the tedium of the day– that's why I've let you take me about – trusting you, never realising until – *(pulls herself up with a jerk and raises her hand to her face.)*

DEAN *(listening with knitted brow, coming to Helen and placing his hand on hers, half compassionate, half impatient)* You'll have forgotten all about it in a week.

HELEN   Never, never. *(crosses to fireplace right)* That's what a man can't understand. It means nothing to him. But with a girl like me – it's – it's like losing something that's best in her. Something she can never get back.

DEAN *(shakes his head indulgently)* Come, come, Helen, a kiss isn't worth the upheaval of a home, is it? *(she looks at him fixedly without speaking, he watches her.)* Think, think what it will mean to Cyril –

HELEN *(knitting her brows)* The Apple again!

Enter Ann anxiously, after obviously giving warning at the door.

ANN   I – I do hope nothing has boiled over, please excuse me, won't you.

Looks at Helen then goes into kitchen and closes door.

DEAN *(coming up)* I must be getting along. What have you decided?

Helen crosses to him and sits right of table. He holds out his hand. She does not take it.

DEAN   You aren't going to treat me like an enemy are you?

HELEN   Do you think you deserve to be a–a friend?

DEAN   Most certainly. Try me. *(she shakes her head.)* Ah well, you know best. *(moving to door)* Good bye. *(Cyril opens door just as he gets there.)* Ah, Cyril, I've administered the lecture your father wished, and I must say I congratulate you on your sister. You should be proud of her – she has character *and* common sense, a rare combination – and that common sense of hers will be more helpful to you than you imagine. *(with meaning)* Well – *(turns)* Good bye again.

Exit Cyril who returns with Dean's hat and stick.

DEAN   Till tomorrow, Helen.

HELEN *(shakes her head quickly, but controls the impulse to contradict him. He waits a moment. Then she says almost inaudibly)* Good bye.

Cyril holds door open.

CYRIL   If you care to wait a moment, Ann will call a hansom.

DEAN   Thanks, I'll walk a bit.

Dean and Cyril go out.

ANN *(comes right of table, whispering)* Well Ellie dear, what did he say? Who got the best of the argument?

HELEN *(tossing the dress over and turning the handle of the machine savagely)* Who do you think? The Apple of course!

Ann stirs the contents of the saucepan with vigour expressive of her complete satisfaction. Helen continues sewing with tears streaming down her cheeks.

Curtain.

The end.

Inez Bensusan (1871-1967)

The eldest of ten children, she was born in Sydney, Australia into a wealthy Jewish family, eight of whom survived. She appears to have wanted to act from her youth, staging recitals and entertainments for the community. Sometime after 1893 she emigrated to Britain, travelling via South Africa.

Best known for her work as journalist, writer and campaigner for women's suffrage, she was active in Australia and New Zealand Women Voters and the Jewish League for Women's Suffrage, serving on its Executive Committee. Most centrally she made a vital contribution to the work of the AFL, developing and running the Play Department and working in conjunction with the WWSL to encourage and commission women to write plays in support of women's suffrage. Bensusan also performed with and was on the Council of the Play Actors.

Later, she ventured into film, writing and starring in *True Womanhood* (1911), playing a starving woman sweatshop worker, saved from the workhouse by a suffragette fairy godmother (it also featured Decima Moore and Auriol Lee). In 1913, Bensusan went on to set up the Women's Theatre, launched at the Coronet Theatre that December, which aimed to establish a permanent season of work dealing with women's issues. She played the grandmother in Israel Zangwill's *The Melting Pot* (Court, 1914) and in 1916 produced and performed in Jennie (Mrs Herbert D.) Cohen's *The Lonely Festival* as part of an All Jewish Matinee.

During the Great War she worked with the first Women's Theatre Company to perform for the Army of Occupation in Cologne and then with the British Rhine Army Dramatic Company for three and a half years. She later converted to Christian Science and became active in the Women's Institute and on issues of child welfare. She maintained her involvement in small-scale and experimental companies serving on the committee of The 1930s Players and, as late as 1951, appearing in a House of Arts Drama Circle triple-bill, at Chiswick Town Hall.

In the Workhouse

In the Workhouse

In the Workhouse was one of the most controversial plays produced by Edy Craig's Pioneer Players as part of a triple bill with Chris St John's *The First Actress* and Cicely Hamilton's *Jack and Jill and a Friend* (King's Hall, 1911). It is an exposé of the iniquities of the Coverture Act, which decreed that a married woman had no separate legal existence from her husband and therefore meant that if her husband entered – or left – the workhouse, she and her children were obliged to go with him.

Set in a workhouse ward, where a group of mothers, married and unmarried, look after their children, it exposes the contradictions of a system where Penelope, a respectable, secure, mother of five and unmarried is freer than respectable Mrs Cleaver who returns from her appeal to the Board of Guardians to announce that legally she has no right to leave the workhouse, even though she has work to go to and a home available for herself and her children.

The play, with its refusal to condemn vice and the unmarried mother, was either condemned for offensiveness or acclaimed for its importance. *The Pall Mall Gazette* compared it to the work of Eugene Brieux "which plead for reform by painting a terrible, and perhaps overcharged, picture of things as they are ... Such is the power of the dramatic pamphlet, sincerely written and sincerely acted. There is nothing to approach it in directness and force. It sweeps all mere prettiness into oblivion".

Two years after the play was produced, the law was changed, in large measure due to Nevinson's and other suffragists' campaigns.

The play was revived in 1979 by Mrs Worthington's Daughters, a feminist theatre company, directed by Julie Holledge in a double-bill with Susannah Cibber's *The Oracle* (1752). [1]

---

[1] See interview with actress Anne Engel as part of *Unfinished Histories*, in the National Sound Archive and other collections: see www.susan.croft.btinternet.com

Preface

In writing this little play (I make no apology for its realism except that it is true) I have tried to show the parlous condition of twentieth century womanhood under the unjust Gilbertian muddle of uni-sexual legislation: "the truth shall make you free," and it seems sometimes as if the lamp of truth turned upon the dark places and cruel habitations of the earth, like radium upon some foul sore, will heal these wrongs.

For most of these wrongs the ridiculous and antiquated law of coverture is mainly responsible, and until it is wholly abolished, new reforms only seem to create new absurdities; it is merely tinkering at a rotten system and pouring new wine into old bottles. It has been said that "the four Married Women's Property Acts are a record of the hesitation and dulness of members of Parliament. Parliament tried to reform the law in accordance with ideas borrowed from equity, and some of the lawyers, by whom Parliament was guided, did not understand the principles of equity they were meant to follow."

It has ever been so. I suppose in private life our legislators claim to be gentlemen and sportsmen, but in the game of law-making for women they seem to be lost to all sense of decency and fair play, and the only excuse for the stupidity and lack of imagination in these male lawyers is that made long ago for all human dulness and brutality on the Cross of Calvary, "Father, forgive them for they know not what they do."

Under the law of coverture the wife has no separate existence whatever; like an infant, she is entirely under the custody and control of her husband. He is the sole parent and guardian of all children born in marriage, and has power to fix their religion and education; and under the Poor Law it is a common thing to see whole families dragged about at the will of a drunken, brutal and lazy male, their cries stifled in the dust.

Some three years ago, all England was startled at its own laws on reading that an able-bodied woman, willing and anxious to make her own living, and knowing a trade, was compelled to remain in the workhouse, a dead weight round the necks of the ratepayers, because the drunken scoundrel of a husband, who had brought his family there, "has power by his marital authority to detain his wife in the workhouse." Questions were asked in Parliament; distinguished lawyers wrote that such detention is an infringement of the great Law of Habeas Corpus.

(Undoubtedly that is so, for even under the Poor Law a wife cannot be compelled to enter the workhouse; but, once there, it is easy to keep her.) Suffragette tongues spread the story and the woman was allowed to leave; but the order still stands in Glen's Poor Law Orders, and no doubt in our free England up and down the country married women are still in captivity at the will of some worthless husband.

By the same law a married woman is compelled to follow her husband wherever he goes, and the Liberal Government which gave us the Children's Charter and interests itself in infant mortality, either in ignorance or indifference, still permits wives and babes to be turned out in all weathers, to wander without food or shelter, should the husband choose to leave the workhouse, sometimes nominally to look for work, sometimes merely to enjoy a day's drinking.

Under the law of coverture a woman under seventy married to an old age pensioner may not receive parish relief, though she has a separate digestive apparatus. "Relief given to the wife is relief given to the husband," and the wife must either starve till she is seventy or the husband must forfeit his pension.

On the other hand, a husband under seventy married to a State pensioner may receive parish relief, he being an independent citizen.

Under the same law British women married to foreigners are counted aliens and shut off from old age pensions, though foreign women married to Britishers receive the pension without demur.

Again, a deserted wife, not being a parent, has frequently to suffer the agony and humiliation of having her children taken away from her, protected by the Guardians, and sent away to workhouse schools. By the sin of the male, without any fault of her own, she is deprived not only of a husband but also of the children of her body.

The law of coverture, however, is quietly dropped when there is money to be got out of a woman; a wife can be compelled to contribute to the support of a lazy, drunken or dissolute husband in workhouse, infirmary or lunatic asylum.

The Liberal Government in 1908 found time to pass a law making it compulsory for married women with separate estate to support their parents, and even grandchildren, in the workhouse.

It is not legal to tax married women, for the law of 1842 has never been repealed, but the Inland Revenue has always done so, subsequently counting the wife's income as the husband's, and so increasing their revenue on the aggregate.

Mr Lloyd George is also bringing in a law waiving again the law of coverture and compelling wives to return their income for the Super Tax.

In this little play I have attempted to illustrate from life some of the hardships of the law to an unrepresented sex, the cruel punishment meted out to women, and to women only, for any breach of traditional morality, the ruin of the girl, the absolute immunity of the male, the brutality that attacks an idiot, the slavery of the married women, the singular advantage a clever woman can take of laws apparently made for the maintenance of wickedness and vice and the punishment of virtue.

No wonder the marriage rate is declining and that we hear that more and more throughout the country free unions are on the increase, particularly in the industrial parts of England. The shrewd and self-supporting younger generation hesitates before they accept wedlock on the present terms and endure the wrongs they have seen their mothers suffer. Added to this the persistent rumours of legislation limiting the work of married women in factories does not encourage the young to put their heads beneath the yoke of such tyranny. Will this be for the making of a great nation?

These facts told to a street corner audience invariably arouse great indignation, for the poor know by bitter experience that they are true; to bring them to the knowledge of our legislators is harder. If only men knew, we feel that "these laws that blaspheme and tyrannies that fetter" would be swept away and we could sing without hypocrisy "Rule Britannia," a song which sounds to many of us a hidden blasphemy of the truth.

"For the hurt of the daughter of my people am I hurt ... astonishment hath taken hold of me. Is there no balm in Gilead; is there no physician there? Why then is not the health of the daughter of my people recovered?"

Margaret Wynne Nevinson

In The Workhouse

A play in one act

Margaret Wynne Nevinson

Originally published by The International Suffrage Shop, The New Era Booklets-2.

CHARACTERS

Lily, a red-faced, Cockney girl
Wilhelmina, thin and worn, about 40
Monica, idiot girl, about 18
Mrs Jarvis, middle-aged, drunken and coarse
Ethel, refined and pretty parlour-maid
Penelope Law, a handsome, voluptuous woman, about 30
Mrs Cleaver, respectable, middle-aged matron
Infants

ACT ONE
Scene One

A workhouse ward. Yellow washed walls with a few texts about: "In everything give thanks," "Blessed are the pure in heart for they shall see God," "Little children love one another." Bedsteads and cots covered with red coverlets. Infants, Lily, Mrs Jarvis, Wilhelmina and Monica discovered. All are in pauper dress: dark blue cotton gowns, ill-fitting, with white caps and aprons. Lily is rocking her baby. Monica is standing by the window singing. She has her baby in her arms. Before the curtain rises, singing is heard:

"All things bright and beautiful,
All creatures great and small,
All things wise and wonderful,
The Lord God made them all."

As the curtain rises, Ethel with open letter in her hand, runs in and flings herself on the bed, sobbing.

"The tall tree in the green wood,
The meadows where we play,
The rushes by the water,
We gather every day."

LILY *(a coarse red-faced young woman, walks up and down the ward, trying to soothe a wailing infant; Cockney accent)* There, there, did 'ums, then! Don't cry, my beauty! We're going out tomorrow, my pet! And father's going to marry us.

WILHELMINA *(a wasted consumptive looking woman, about 40; Yorkshire accent)* Don't be too sure, my wench. There's many a slip 'twixt the cup and the lip, and fathers don't always turn up, you know, on these occasions.

LILY *(sharply)* The mission lady's seeing to it; she's bought a ring and put up the banns and H'augustus says she's promised him a sovereign if he turns up at the church door punctual at ten. She's got another lidy to mind biby too, whilst I am in church, so as not to shime me. Can't tike you to me wedding, duckie, can I now?

WILHELMINA   The sovereign may do the trick, but men are slippery cards to the like of us, as no doubt you know. I remember well how I stood in the church at Foxearth, up on the moors, waiting for my child's father, the parson in his surplice ready to make us one, and poor mother a-running up and down the street outside, a-cocking her head into all the pubs to try and find 'im. But 'e ain't turned up neither then nor since, and that is nigh on twenty year ago.

Elderly woman with twins, babies on each arm, walks up and down.

WILHELMINA   Your twins are restless tonight, Mrs Jarvis. seems cruel 'ard on a mother to bring forth a pair of superfluous twins and no father between 'em. What's the law of the land on this matter? Do you get 5s. each or are you held responsible for the extra one?

MRS JARVIS   None of your lip, Wilhelmina; I'm a married lidy, that's what I am, and I'll thank you to remember it.

WILHELMINA   I'm sure I beg your pardon, Mrs What's-a-name, only, I understood you to say as Mr Jarvis 'ad been dead some years.

MRS JARVIS   Well, and if 'e 'as? Ain't I got the ring and lines just the same? Makes all the difference, my gal, I can tell you between my position and you bad women in 'ere.

WILHELMINA There, there, keep your 'air on! Don't you know it is an unwritten law in these state-rooms that pots don't call kettles black?

MONICA *(squint-eyed and with a wide grin from ear to ear gives a shrill cry of ecstasy)* I do love my biby!

WILHELMINA That's a mercy, my dear, as no one else ain't likely to. Who's the baby's father, Monica?

MONICA *(with another broad grin)* Bill.

WILHELMINA What's the baby's name?

MONICA Bill.

WILHELMINA Got any more babies, Monica?

MONICA Ess, two bibies, two Bills, three Bills; love my Bills.

WILHELMINA And where are the other Bills?

MONICA *(with an extra grin)* I dunno.

WILHELMINA Well, I ain't a saint myself, but I do think as the propagation of idiots ought to be stopped.

MONICA *(sings to her Bill)*

"All things bright and beautiful ,
All creatures great and small,
All things wise and wonderful,
The Lord God made them all."

On a bed behind the door Ethel sits crying, her apron over her head. Lily pauses in her walk to speak to her, takes her hand kindly and tries to soothe her but her attempts at consolation meet with no result and she shrugs her shoulders and resumes her walk up and down the ward.

WILHELMINA Dear, dear! What's the matter with that poor soul?

LILY The organisation lady outside has written and told her mother where she is, and she's terrible upset. Poor Ethel! She's a different sort to us. Father's a coachman in an earl's family, and she was keeping it quiet from them, hoping her young man would marry her afore they knew but now her mother's written to 'er very cruel, and it's about broke 'er 'eart. She feels she's disgracing them – quite natural too.

WILHELMINA *(rising and going towards Ethel)* A dirty bit of busy-bodying, I call that! There, there, my wench! Don't 'ee cry, dearie; it's 'ard, I know, the first time, cruel 'ard, but we gets used to it. Don't 'ee cry dearie.

Baby in cot yells wildly. Lily picks it up and rocks the two of them

LILY   Did it want its mother, my lamb? 'Ere, Pennyloaf, take your young monkey. It's waking the crew of 'em, just as they were going off nicely.

A tall handsome woman enters the ward and takes the infant silently in her arms.

PENELOPE *(sitting down)* Aint Mrs Cleaver back yet?

LILY   Not yet; she's gone to appear afore the Board. She gave in 'er discharge two or three days ago, but 'er husband says as she's got to stop 'ere with 'im, and Master says that's the law of the land; so, not believing such nonsense, she's gone to complain on 'em both to the Board.

WILHELMINA   And a fine dose she's 'aving. I hate appearing afore them Committees; last time I went I called the lady "Sir" and the gentleman "Mum" and my 'eart went pitter-patter in my breast so that you might have knocked me down with a feather.

MONICA *(sings)*
"The purple-headed mountain
The river running by
The sunset in the evening
That brightens up the sky."

WILHELMINA   Just 'ark to that – purple-headed mountains and sunsets. Lor' child, 'old your row; turns me creepy in my insides to 'ear of such things in 'ere, we who never goes out year in year out. Doing time is better than this. Even in 'Olloway ye runs round the yard and sees a bit of sky for one hour. Lord, how it makes me think of Yorkshire 'earing that there 'ymn. Why, 'ere's Mrs Cleaver. Well, my dear, and you do look bad. Sit ye down and tell us all about it.

MRS CLEAVER *(a middle-aged woman, very over-heated sinks down on the end of a bed panting and fanning herself vigorously with her apron.)* Them Committees allus turns me dead-sick, and my boots feel too tight for me, and I goes into a perspiration and the great drops go rolling off my forehead. Well, 'e's kept 'is word and got the law and right of England behind 'im. *(sensation in the ward. The other women gather round Mrs Cleaver; infants are patted and dandled and soothed with much vigour.)* Well, I went afore the Committee and I says, "I want to take my discharge," I says. "I applied last week to Master, but mine got at 'im first, and Master up and says, "No, Mrs Cleaver, you can't go," he says; 'your 'usband can't spare you," 'e says; "wants you to keep 'im company in 'ere," he says. *(sensation and exclamations of horror.)* "Is that true, Master?" says the little man wot sits lost in a big chair. "That is so, sir," says the Master, and then 'e out with a big book and reads something very learned and brain-confusing that I did not rightly understand, as to 'ow a 'usband may detain 'is wife in the workhouse by his marital authority.

WILHELMINA Good 'eavens! Is that the law of England?

MRS CLEAVER That's what the little lady-guardian said, 'er that comes up here dressed so shabby. " 'eavens!" she says, same as you; "is that the law of England?" Then they all began talking at once most excited, and the little man in a big chair beats like a madman on the table with a 'ammer, and no one took the slightest notice but when some quiet was restored the little man asked me to tell the Board the circumstances. So I says 'ow 'e lost 'is work through being drunk on duty which was the lying tongues of the perlice, for 'is 'ead was clear, the drink allus taking 'im in the legs, like most cabmen, and the old 'oss keeps sober. It was a thick fog, and 'e'd just got off the box to lead the 'oss through the gates of the mews and the perliceman spotted 'is legs walking out in contrary directions, though 'is 'ead was clear as daylight, and so the perlice ran 'im in, and the beak took 'is licence from 'im and 'ere we are. Now I've got over my confinement, and the child safe in 'eaven after all the worrit and starvation, I thought I'd like to go out and earn my own living. I'm a dressmaker by trade, and my sister will give me a 'ome. I 'ate being 'ere living on the rates, and 'e not having done better for us than this Bastille – though I allus says as it was the lying tongue of a perliceman – it seems fair I should go free. The lady wot comes round Sundays told me I ain't got no responsibility for my children, being a married lady with the lines.

WILHELMINA   That's quite true – you can 'ear the Suffragette ladies a-saying that at any street corner.

MRS CLEAVER   Well, it is time the Guardians learnt it but the little man in the big chair flew out most violent: "Don't talk like that, my good woman, of course you have responsibility for your children, you must not believe what ignorant people tell you." Then I 'eard the tall ginger-'aired chap – 'im wot sits next the little man, as you unmarried girls go before to try and father your babies – I 'eard 'im say quite distinct: "the woman is right, sir — married women are not responsible for their children but I believe the husband is within his rights in refusing to allow her to leave the 'ouse without him". Then they told me to retire and I should know the result later. O Lord! I'm that 'ot and upset with the worry of it, I feel I'll never cool again. *(sits back on the bed, wipes her face and fans herself with her apron.)*

PENELOPE   Single life has its avantages: you with the lines ain't been as perlite as might be to us, who ain't got em but we 'as the laugh over you really. I'm taking my discharge tomorrow morning, and not one amongst them dare stop me. I don't have to appear afore boards and be worried and upset with 'usbands and Guardians and things before I can take myself off the parish and eat my bread independent.

WILHELMINA   But why weren't you married, Pennyloaf? Not for want of asking, I'll be bound.

PENELOPE   No, it wasn't for lack of asking. Fact is, I was put off marriage at a very early age. I 'ad a drunken beast of a father as spent 'is time a-drinking by day and a-beating mother by night. One night 'e overdid it and killed 'er. He got quad for life, and we was put away in them workus schools; it would 'ave been kinder of the parish to put us in the lethal chamber as they do cats and dogs as ain't wanted. But we grew up somehow, knowing as we weren't wanted, and then the parish found me a place, under-housemaid in a big 'ouse, and then I found as the young master wanted me, the first time since Mother died as any human soul had taken an interest in me, and Lord! I laughs now when I think what a 'appy time it was. Since then I've had five children and twenty-five shillings a week coming in regular besides what I can make at the cooking.

LILY   How do you manage to get the five shillings a week – the lawyer chaps don't seem to do much for us.

PENELOPE   I don't bother with lawyer chaps. I make my own arrangements and not one man has gone back on 'is promise. I lives clean and respectable – no drinking, no bad language – my children never see and 'ear what I saw and 'eard and they are mine – mine – mine. I always come into the 'ouse for confinement, liking quiet and skilled medical attention. I never gets refused; the law dare not refuse such as me – it's you married ladies as can't get in 'ere. I always leave the coming in till the last moment, then there are no awkward questions and when they begin to "enquire as to settlement" I'm far away. All the women in our street are expecting next week; their 'usbands all out of work and not a pair of sheets or the price of a pint of milk between them; all lying in one room too, as I don't consider decent, but having the lines it's precious 'ard for them to get taken in 'ere, and besides 'alf on 'em daren't even try, for fear he and someone else will sell up the 'ome whilst they are away.

MRS JARVIS   Yes, that's quite true; the law seems agin us respectable women. You remember the lady as died last week up in the lying in. Well, she told me she tried to get in 'ere weeks ago, 'er 'usband being out of work all right and she feeling very queer and low, but the Board said that she was the wife of an able-bodied man and 'e was responsible for 'er and must find work. But she got 'ere in the end spite of 'em all, for 'er 'usband swore at 'er so fearful for having twins, that the Doctor nearly fought 'im for being a brute, and he ordered 'er in 'ere out of 'is way, but what with all the upset and the starvation whilst she was carrying of 'em, it was too late to save 'er; she took fever and snuffed out like a candle, and it was fearful to 'ear 'er raving and crying out to 'im not to beat 'er till the child was born.

MRS CLEAVER   If I'd my time over again I'd not marry, not I.

LILY   What? Mrs Cleaver, you say that?

MRS CLEAVER   Yes and I means it too. The idea of keeping me 'ere with that there drunkard when I knows a trade and look how us married lidies 'as to turn out if 'e chooses to 'is tike discharge and wander about with the kiddies in the rain and snow with no clothes nor decent boots for them. I remember Mrs Page and her four children coming back looking like death last Christmas-time. Page had been out to look for work, but 'e never went further than the King of Bohemia to find it, and all day, while he was drinking, they had been shivering outside in the rain. In the old days there was the shelter of the bar, but now there ain't that any longer. Only 'Arry kept dry, being over fourteen. Mrs Page told me a gentleman stood 'er 'alf-quartern of gin, but the children 'ad nothing all day, and they was 'alf dead with cold and 'unger. Massacring of the hinnocents I call it, for all the children except 'Arry, were laid up in the Infirmary next day, the biby died the next week of bronchitus and Mrs Page took a heavy cold on 'er chest, and now she's coughing 'er poor 'eart out in the 'tysis ward with the wall taken out on one side and the winds and the fogs coming in shameful; this is the truth, for I used to scrub in the 'tysis ward.

WILHELMINA   Mrs Kemp 'ad 'em all nicely over that. Kemp wanted a day off to look for work, though being a cripple 'e ain't got no chance and when 'e took 'is discharge Master told 'er she and the children 'ad got to go too. She says as she warn't going out to wander the streets with no clothes and no 'ome, and then the Master tells 'er as she got to go, the law being that them two are one and 'e's the one and if she wouldn't go quiet she'd be put out by force. Then Mrs Kemp went off in one of 'er tantrums flying out at 'im, most fearful; "Well then, you shall 'ave the truth," she says, "which I've been keeping quiet for shame. I ain't married to Kemp – never 'ave been – my first 'usband deserting me and going off with another woman, leaving me starving at one-and-twenty with two children and another coming. Kemp offered me a 'ome then and 'e's been a sight better to me than Johnson, who went to church and swore to be faithful, but couldn't manage to keep his oath not even for three years. We'd never 'ave been in here if the motor car 'adn't run over Kemp a-crippling 'im for life, but I shan't take my children out to die of cold not for 'im nor no man, and now you know I'm a bad woman perhaps I may be left in peace." And she was.

PENELOPE   That's just what I was a-telling you. The law is all on the side of us bad 'uns. I'm going back tomorrow to my neat little 'ome, which my lidy-help is minding for me, to my dear children and my regular income, and I can't say as I envies you married lidies either your rings or your slavery.

WILHELMINA   But don't the neighbours find out, Pennyloaf?

PENELOPE Not they – they don't know as I'm a bad woman. I generally moves afore a confinement, and I 'as a 'usband on the 'igh seas. Besides that, I 'as a good connection cooking dinner parties in the West End. If your cooking's good, I find there's no nasty questions about your morals.

LILY (*walking up and down with her baby*) I think we won't get married, my pet! Better keep single, I say, after what we've 'eard tonight. What I've heard tonight is a lesson to me. I'll not get married, not I. Just look at Mrs Cleaver, an honest married woman. All 'er 'usband 'as done for 'er is to bring 'er and the kids to the 'Ouse and now they say she can't even go out to earn her living. Then look at Pennyloaf, free and rich and prosperous, and the kids 'er own. The bad 'uns wins, my pet! Vice triumphant, I says!

MONICA (*gives an ecstatic shriek*) I do love my biby.

The end.

Margaret Wynne Nevinson (1858-1932)

Nevinson grew up in a Welsh-speaking vicarage. She took a degree at St Andrew's University and then travelled and taught before marrying the journalist and *Manchester Guardian* war correspondent Henry Woodd Nevinson in 1884. They worked together in an East End settlement before moving to Hampstead where she worked as a journalist.

She served for 25 years as a school manager and later Poor Law Guardian and Justice of the Peace. She was active in the WSPU, the Tax Resistance League and especially the Women's Freedom League who published her pamphlets *Ancient Suffragettes* (1911) and *Five Year's Struggle for Freedom: a history of the suffrage movement* (1908-1912).

Her husband was also active in the Suffrage Movement, becoming a founder of the Men's Political Union for Women's Enfranchisement for which he wrote at least one dramatic sketch. Margaret Wynne Nevinson spoke several times at AFL events including on Women Under the Poor Law.

Her collection of short pieces, originally published in newspapers and journals, *Workhouse Characters*, based on interviews with sailors, drunks, dossers and attempted suicides, some of which in are in the form of dramatic monologues, was published in 1918. In 1922 she wrote *Fragments of Life*, a further volume of short autobiographical pieces and stories on social issues, and published her memoirs, *Life's Fitful Fever* in 1926.

After Margaret's death her husband remarried to her close friend and prominent suffragist, Evelyn Sharp.

Jim's Leg

Jim's Leg

Originally published in *Votes for Women*, 29 Jan 1911, *Jim's Leg* is a comedy of reversed sex roles. This device is a familiar one, most often enacted in the political realm in fantasy pieces where women are in control of the machinery of government and men struggle for respect and representation, such as Mary Cholmondeley's *Votes for Men* or Alison Garland's *The Better Half*.

In *Jim's Leg* the role reversal is anchored in believable social reality as the speaker recounts how her husband's losing his leg in an accident with a motor bus has been the best thing to happen to her. Whereas before he used to belittle her work in the home, go out drinking and come home and hit her, now, having had to stay home and look after the children while she did his job as a bottle washer, he has gained an immediate appreciation of what's involv-ed and even converts to the belief that women should have the vote.

While somewhat stereotypical in its representation of East End life, as an account of domestic grind it is vivid and believable. It also acknow-ledges the devaluation of women's work outside the home – when the speaker takes over Jim's bottle washing job, she is paid less than him for it – an issue on which the AFL was particularly active. This was largely due to their own experience as women in the acting profession, where pay was based on an individual's standing as a performer rather than on gender bias, a situation that was highly unusual in the Edwardian workplace (though unemployment was high throughout the profession).

The monologue recognizes the draining nature and thanklessness of domestic labour and childcare in a way which remains immediate and contemporary.

A short radio version was aired on BBC Radio 4 *Woman's Hour* in November 1999 as part of an item on the 90th anniversary of the AFL.

See also: Holledge, Stowell

Jim's Leg

A Monologue

L. S. Phibbs

CHARACTER

WOMAN

Scene One

A room in an East End House.

WOMAN The best thing as ever happened to me was when my Jim lost 'is leg. Afore then 'e was always a-grumbling, and saying as women wasn't of no account, and my eyes – as mother used to say was a lovely brown – was most times a nugly black, for]im was that free with 'is fists when 'e'd 'ad 'a drop too much. And, bless you, to 'ear 'im 'old forth on pollyticks and votes for women! Why according to 'im, women 'ardly deserved to be let live, and men only let 'em because of cooking dinners, and mending clothes and the like.

'What 'ave *you* to do?' he'd say. 'You can jest sit at 'ome and amoose yerself, lookin' after the kiddies and cleanin' up. Why, that's only play, that is. Where's *your* responsibilities? And 'oo's you to 'ave a vote? Thinkin' yourselves on a level with us men!'

Well, one day as 'e was a-coming out of the Red Lion, and none too steady on 'is feet, 'e was run into by a motor bus. 'E would stop in the middle of the street to argue with it, and it 'adn't any time to listen, and it went over 'is leg, and 'e was took to the 'ospital and 'is leg was took off. And there was me, with six children at 'ome, and only my eldest, Ethel Emerly – 'oo was fourteen – in service.

Well, I got took on in Jim's place: 'e was bottle washer at a brewery, and o' course they said they couldn't give me as much as 'e 'ad, 'cos I was only a woman.

'Not if I does as much work as 'e do?' say I and they only laughs and says, 'Women can't do men's work.'

'Can't they?' says I. 'You'll see.' But give me more than twelve shillin' a week they would not, not if I washed them bottles ever so, and a lick and a wipe was never my way.

Well I got Gladys Matilder, as was thirteen, a little place, and Vilet Muriel 'ad to look after the little 'uns, and we got on some'ow till Jim 'e come out 'o the 'ospital, just able to 'op about on a crutch. And when 'e come 'ome I says to 'im, 'Now you've got to take care of the 'ouse and do my work while I does yours. You says there ain't nothing for a mother of a family to do, so let's 'ope you'll find it easy.'

'That's all right,' says 'e, careless, but when I come 'ome at night 'e 'ad a different tale to tell. The 'ouse looked as if all the monkeys out the Zoo 'ad bin turned loose in it. E'd forgotten to cook any supper, the fire was out, all the children was a-crying, and 'e was sitting middle of the room with his 'ed in 'is 'ands, the very picter of misery.

''Ope you've enjoyed yer little 'oliday,' says I, perky like, and pretending to see nothing. 'Oliday,' 'e groans, 'I'd rather do a month's 'ard. The kids ain't stopped hollering, hollering all day, and the biby's the wussest of um all.'

'No wonder, with a pin sticking into the precious lamb,' says I. 'Call that dressing 'im, Every blessed thing's on wrong. Well, you've cleaned up, I s'pose?'

'Clean,' says 'e, miserable like. 'I've bin cleanin' the 'ole time and it don't seem to get nothing bur dirtier every minit.'

'You'll do better soon,' says I, 'when you've 'ad practice. You'll see 'ow nice it is to set at 'ome and do nothing, as you says. Now let's 'ave supper. Somethin 'ot and taysty, I 'ope,'

'There ain't none,' says 'e, 'I ain't 'ad time to think of it.'

"Ain't 'ad time,' says I. 'You 'ad all day jus' as much time as I 'ave'.
I couldn't 'elp feeling' pityin' in my heart, 'e did look that wretched
sittin' in a sloppy floor as 'e'd bin trying to wash, but I says, 'Things
is changed. I'm going to clean myself and take the children out. You
can set to work and put the biby to bed and 'ave things tidy when we
comes 'ome.'

'Go out and leave me,' 'e cries.

'Why not?' says I. 'You ain't done nothing all day but amoose
yourself. I'm going out after my 'ard day's work same as you used to.
There's a Sufferagette meeting as I means to attend, to learn 'ow to
stand up for my rights.'

'You don't want no learnin',' says 'e. 'You might stop and keep me
company when I've bin shut up 'ere with the kids all day.'

'Company?' says I. "Ow often 'ave you told me the children was all
the company I needed? No, a little peaceful time to think is what
you're needin',' says I, and off I goes. Poor Jim! After three days 'ed
got things in such a muddle that I scarcely knew 'ow to put up with
it, 'aving found a saucepan lid under the biby's pillow and my
stockins used as a kettle-'older. Then comes washin' day, and I 'eard
Jim a mutterin' about 'is clean collar, which indeed 'e wanted badly.

"Oo's goin' to do the washin'?' he asks as 'e sees me going out as
usual.

'Why, you are, of course,' says I. "Oo else?'

'Me?' says 'e. 'Me do the washin', with only one leg?'

'Bless the man,' says I. 'You don't wash with your legs you wash with
your 'ands. And then there's the manglin', and next day the starchin'
and ironin', and I 'ope you'll like the job. I'm sendin' Vilet Muriel

round to 'elp 'er aunt a bit 'as 'ad the collect cruel, so you must look after the little 'uns extry speshul. Good bye.'

'Well, 'ave you finished the wash?' says I that evening.

'The wash 'as finished me,' says 'e a-gaspin', and indeed 'e looked like it.' ''Ow you ever gets done', says 'e, 'I don't know. Them things 'ave bin bilin' and bilin', and don't get no cleaner.'

You should have seen the way 'ed washed 'em! All biled up, on my saucepans, and no rinsin' nor nothin' and as to 'is manglin' – well, mangled they was indeed. The poor children 'adn't a pinny 'ole among 'em, and my lace curtains jus' fell to pieces when you touched 'em like a spider's web. But the ruinin' of them clothes and things was the makin' of Jim. 'E began to see for the fust time in 'is life what a woman's work meant, and by the time 'e could go back to 'is bottle washin', 'e was a changed man. 'Andy 'e could never be, and sometimes I wished 'e'd lost an arm instead of a leg – 'e'd 'ave missed it less. But one night 'e 'opped along of me to a Sufferagette meeting and comin' out 'e says, says 'e, 'Esther,' says 'e, 'I'm a goin' to be a Sufferagette myself. As soon as I gets my noo leg I'll join. One 'as to be an 'ole man to be up to them women. And you did ought to 'ave a vote, Esther,' says 'e. 'Bottle washin' is play to biby mindin' and 'ome work what ain't never over. And if I ever gives you a black eye again, well –'

'I'll give you one back with your own noo leg,' says I smilin' friendly-like. But lor', there ain't bin no need to. And we're all Sufferagettes and the children too, bless their hearts down to the noo biby as is an 'owling 'er precious 'ed off, as tho' to say, 'I won't be 'appy till I gets it.'

The end.

L.S. Phibbs (Dates unknown)

No information has been traced about L.S. Phibbs though she may well be the same person as Mrs Harlow Phibbs, who wrote another AFL piece, *The Mothers' Meeting*. This play too is a monologue about a working-class woman, spoken by Mrs Puckle who, in search of the mothers' meeting of the title, stumbles instead on an anti-suffrage meeting. There, she becomes so outraged by the absurdities of Lady Clementina Pettigrew's speech that she stands up and tells her that she's talking nonsense and fills her in on the realities of life – the hardship and suffering women undergo equally with men and she finds herself condemning the iniquities of taxation without representation.

The working-class woman who trounces the upper-class anti-suffrage woman was a favourite device of AFL plays (see also Glover) though it is probable that Phibbs, like most other AFL playwrights, was herself middle-class.

A further one-act play by Mrs Phibbs, *The Rack,* was presented at the Rehearsal Theatre in 1912 with Madeleine Lucette Ryley[1] in the cast.

---

1. Ryley was a Vice-President of the AFL, prominent actress and playwright with a career in both Britain and the US. See Engle 2007 for reprinted interview with Ryley from *The Vote*.

Chronology of Plays addressing or supporting Suffrage Issues 1907-1914

Before and after the founding of the Actresses' Franchise League in 1908 numerous plays by women were written, produced or published on issues relating to women's rights. Some of these plays were produced professionally, others were performed at rallies, fundraisers, or as Sunday matinees. They appeared in suffrage journals and magazines, or were published by small presses including those directly associated with the suffrage movement.

It was a time of burgeoning amateur theatre activity in Britain and its colonies and the issue of women's rights was one of the burning questions of the day. This issue was touched on directly or indirectly in numerous plays of the period, as well as in skits, romantic comedies, farces and musicals, both amateur and professional.

The following list includes more than 120 plays focusing primarily on works written by active suffragists and women's rights campaigners, on or closely related to the topic of suffrage, and/or produced by suffrage groups or at suffrage rallies. The list includes early productions by Edith Craig and Chris St John's Pioneer Players, before their focus moved beyond campaigning work (see Cockin, 1998). There are, no doubt, many others to discover among the welter of unpublished scripts in the Lord Chamberlain's Play collection at the British Library – and elsewhere.

I have not included plays from the wider culture on suffrage themes and women's rights, unless they were part of a campaign or reviewed as suffragist in the press. Crawford also includes a number of these in her list Plays[1] (pp 554-557). The numerous plays of the period on women's rights in general, including female education, careers, relationships etc. are also not included unless they were specifically performed at suffrage meetings[2].

Plays are listed chronologically by production date, when known, or publication date, if they were unproduced. Sources for information are given for those plays for which only accounts in listings or reviews remain. All theatres are in London unless otherwise indicated.

---

* I would be interested to hear via my web site: www.susan.croft.btinternet.co.uk or via www.suffragettes.org.uk of additions to this Chronology or if published versions of listed plays exist.

Abbreviations:

n.d. – no date

n.p. –no publisher and/or no place of publication

ETMM – Ellen Terry Memorial Museum.

LCP – Lord Chamberlain's Plays, Manuscript Rm, British Library.

NYPL – New York Public Library.

pseud. – pseudonym of

SM – Stage Manager

The Vote – the newspaper of the WFL.

VfW – *Votes for Women*, weekly newspaper of WSPU

WFL – Women's Freedom League.

WL – Women's Library.

WSPU – Women's Social and Political Union.

WWW – *Who Was Who in Theatre*.

1907 – 1908

Elizabeth Robins, *Votes for Women,* 9th April 1907, Court Theatre. Published London: Mills & Boon, 1907 and in Hayman & Spender and in Kelly and in Cockin, Norquay and Park v1. *(See this volume)*

Oswald Saint Clair, *Ladies' Logic: a dialogue between a suffragette and a mere man* Published London: Digby, Long & Co., 1907. Dialogue between an engaged couple, he anti-, she pro-suffrage, the piece comes out in favour of establishing a separate, elected parliamentary House of Ladies.

George Dance, *The Suffragette*, 1907. Unpublished, in LCP. Farce with songs in which a man is driven by his wife's and mother's suffrage activities into the arms of his lover.

Cicely Hamilton, *Anti-Suffrage waxworks*, March/April 1908.

Shown at various AFL events inc. in Croydon, Redhill and WFL pageant, Swansea 1910. Unpublished. See Crawford.

E.A.Crawley, *The Suffragette*, Birmingham, 18 April 1908. Unpublished, in LCP. 'Quick change knockabout farce' in which a suffragette invades the Home Secretary's office, is serially thrown out and comes back in an array of guises.

Lavinia King, *The Suffragette,* a farce in *The New Age*, May 1908. Similar farce to above which ends with the Home Secretary arrested as a suffragette.

Mary (Mrs James) Ward, *Man and Woman*, London, May 1908, then by Hammersmith WSPU at Brondesbury House on 14 Jan 1909. Published Cambridge: Heffer and Sons, c1911. Advert in *Votes for Women*, 19 Jan 1912 states that it deals "with all the main arguments for *Votes for Women*, in all classes and conditions". Oddly described by Nicoll as a 'folk play'. Crawford states it 'proved very popular with suffrage societies throughout the country over the next few years' eg in Cambridge 26 Oct 1911.

Christiana Jane Herringham and **Caroline Hodgson,** *Granny's Decision: a duologue*, WFL bazaar, c1908. Unpublished. Hodgson was a founder member of the WFL. Herringham was an artist and founder of the Women's Franchise League. See Crawford.

1909

Anon, *A Woman's Vote* 13 Jan 1909, Corn Exchange, Thrapston. Unpublished, in LCP. Comedy featuring a suffragette doll (played by a girl) that screams 'Votes for Women', the play's ending is ambivalent in support as schoolgirl Molly opines women will always get their way with or without the vote.

Inez Bensusan, *The Apple* AFL, Court, 14 Mar 1909. Published London: AFL, 1911 and in Hayman & Spender, and in Gardner, and in Pfisterer, and in Cockin, Norquay and Park. *(See this volume)*

Cicely Hamilton and **Christopher St John,** *How The Vote Was Won*, Royalty Theatre 13 April 1909. Published London: The Woman's Press, 1909 (second edition, published Edith Craig, 1913), in Hayman & Spender, in France, in Spender & Todd, in France and in Cockin,

Norquay and Park. *(See this volume)*

Edith Craig, *Famous Women of History*, Green, White and Gold Fair, Caxton Hall, 17 April 1909. Unpublished. See Gandolfi.

Beatrice Harraden, *Lady Geraldine's Speech*, AFL, Princes' Skating Rink, Knightsbridge for WSPU's Women's Suffrage Exhibition, 13-26 May 1909. Later produced 15 July 1909 at Guildhall School of Music, reviewed *VfW* (28 May 1909).Published in *VfW*, 2 Apr 1909 and in Hayman & Spender and in Gardner.

Gertrude Jennings, *A Woman's Influence*. As above 13-26 May, 1909. Published AFL, 1913 and in Gardner and in Spender and Hayman and in Cockin, Norquay and Park. Reviewed *VfW* (28 May 1909). See Stowell. Much performed examination of women's wiles versus rational influence.

Rita Milman, *A Suffrage Episode*. As above 13-26 May, 1909. Sketch, unpublished. Milman is listed as an AFL member.

Mabel Annie St Clair Stobart, *Meringues: A Drawing Room Duologue*, as above, 25 May 1909. Published London: Samuel French, circa 1909. Production info given at top of published script. Stobart later became famous as 'the lady on the Black Horse' for her wartime exploits in Serbia.

Rita Milman, *Thus It Was*, as above 26 May, 1909. Sketch, unpublished See *VfW*, 4 June 1909, p752.

Christopher St John, *A Defence of the Fighting Spirit* in *VfW*, 18 June 1909. Dialogue defending violent tactics.

George Bernard Shaw, *Press Cuttings*, Court Theatre, Civic and Dramatic Guild, 9 Jul 1909. Later Gaiety, Manchester and AFL various. Directed by Edith Craig. Published London: Constable, 1909. The play was banned for some time by the Lord Chamberlain.

Inglis Allen, *The Suffragette's Redemption*, Royalty, Glasgow 17th Aug 1909. Published London: Samuel French, 1913 (according to Nicoll). Husband and suffragette wife argue about why he paid her fine to keep her out of jail. Not anti-suffrage per se though exposes her contradictions and jealousy.

Cicely Hamilton, *A Pageant of Great Women*, produced for WWSL

by the AFL, Scala Theatre, 10 Nov 1909. Directed by Edith Craig.
Published London: The International Suffrage Shop, 1910, and in
Gardner, and in Cockin, Norquay and Park. As *VfW* saw it, the great
women presented 'appear to dispute with the silent testimony of their
lives and work, the contention of Prejudice that woman is not fit for
freedom' (12 Nov 1909). Craig re-created it in towns across the country.
See Cockin 1998.

Cicely Hamilton and **Chris St John**, *The Pot and the Kettle*,
AFL/WWSL matinee, Scala 12 Nov 1909. Published N.p: n.p, 1909
(Copy in NYPL). Review *The Era*, 20 Nov 1909, p15.

W.H.Margetson, *A Suffrage Tableau*, AFL/WWSL matinee, Scala, 12
Nov 1909. Unpublished.

Gertrude Mouillot, *The Master*, AFL/WWSL matinee, Scala, 12 Nov
1909. Unpublished, in LCP. Review *VfW* 19 Nov, 1909, p117. Mouillot
was a Vice-President of the AFL and a supporter of Inez Bensusan's
Women's Theatre.

Beatrice Harraden and **Bessie Hatton**, *The Outcast* AFL/WWSL
matinee at the Scala, 12 Nov 1909. Unpublished, in LCP. Review *VfW*.

Netta Syrett, *Might is Right*, Haymarket (ran for 18 performances),
13 Nov 1909. Unpublished, in LCP. Reviewed in *VfW* (19 Nov, 1909). It
featured the Women's Marseillaise and a plot where highly militant
suffragettes kidnap the prime minister who falls in (mutual) love with
one of them and agrees to support them if she marries him.

Graham Moffatt, *The Maid and the Magistrate*, Glasgow Men's
League for Women's Suffrage, 'At Home' Nov 1909. London: AFL, 1913.
Later performed at WSPU Christmas Bazaar 1911 and in several other
towns to 1913. His *Bunty Pulls the Strings* was reviewed with great
approval in *The Vote*. The Moffatts were active in the women's
movement in Scotland. Mrs Moffatt was a suffrage worker and had
gone to prison.

Mary Cholmondeley, *Votes For Men: a dialogue* in *Cornhill
Magazine*, Dec. 1909 pp 747-755. Role reversal comedy.

Arthur M. Heathcote, *A Junction duologue,* AFL, Walter's Rd
Schoolroom, Holloway for WFL, 1 Dec 1909. Published London, AFL,

1913. See AFL report 1909-1910, Crawford states it played in Battersea 1910.

Mrs George Norman (pseud. Melesina Mary Mackenzie), *Green Cushions*, National Union and London Societies for Women's Suffrage event, Kensington Town Hall 6 Dec 1909. Published in *Living Age*, 256, Feb 29, 1908 (reprinted from *Pall Mall Magazine*). The play, a gentle satire, was performed as part of the general programme of sketches and recitations prior to the AFL programme. The author performed in the piece under her real name.

Inez Bensusan, *Perfect Ladies*, AFL programme for National Union and London Societies for Women's Suffrage event, Kensington Town Hall 6 Dec 1909. Unpublished, lost duologue, performed with Jennings' *A Woman's Influence* and Hamilton and St John's *How the Vote was Won* and the popular dialogue *'Enery Brown*. See Bradley-Smith.

Janette Steer, *A duologue*, as above Kensington Town Hall, 6 Dec 1909. Unpublished. Steer was an American feminist writer, director and a member of the Executive Committee of the AFL, she wrote several other feminist plays. The duologue was performed and possibly written by Steer.

Bessie Hatton, *Before Sunrise*, Albert Hall, for the Women's Freedom League, 11 Dec 1909. Published AFL, n.d. and in Gardner, and in Cockin, Norquay and Park. Hatton was Secretary of WWSL. See Stowell.

Alice Chapin, *At The Gates*, billed for performance at the Albert Hall on 11 Dec 1909 but cancelled due to the 'lateness of the hour'. Published London: Woman Citizen Publishing Society, 1909. A one-page version appears in *The Vote* 16 Dec, 1909. *(See this volume)*

Angela Cudmore and **Peter Davey**, *We Dine at Seven: a sketch for 2 ladies*. Published London: Samuel French, 1909. Nicoll wrongly names Cudmore as Cadman and dates it 1916. The two struggle to cook for themselves after the servants have all gone to a suffragette meeting.

1910

Louis Cowen, *Unexpected Circumstances*, AFL 1910. Unpublished. Cowen collaborated with Israel Zangwill on another play. *The Vote* 14

May 1910 lists it as *Unforeseen Circumstances.*

Henry Arncliffe Sennett, *An Englishwoman's Home*, Glasgow Suffrage Exhibition, 1910. Published AFL, n.d. and in Cockin, Norquay and Park. A popular piece, repeated elsewhere inc. as part of a programme in Bow and Poplar, East London 1911 organised by George Lansbury.

H.M. (Harry Major) Paull, *An Anti-Suffragist* or *The Other Side*, 1910. Published AFL, n.d. and in Gardner and in Cockin, Norquay and Park. Paull collaborated with Laurence Housman on another play and wrote many individually, generally not feminist.

John Austin, *How One Woman Did It*. N.p: n.p, n.d and in Cockin, Norquay and Park. Gandolfi lists this under 1910, Cockin gives no date.

Irene Rutherford Macleod, *The Reforming of Augustus*, Rehearsal Theatre, 15 Jan 1910. Also Greenwich Borough Hall on 25th Feb 1911. "A light fantastic comedy". Published Streatham: Woman's Press, 1910. *VfW* 25 March, 1910, p406. Actress Macleod married Aubrey De Selincourt from a pro-suffragist family (see 1912) Source *WWW*

George Grossmith, *The Suffrage Girl*, Court Theatre, Mar 1910. Unpublished. A 'dainty musical comedy... all allusions to the Suffrage are quite sympathetic'. *VfW* 10 Mar 1910 – see Crawford. Grossmith's wife was a suffragist.

L.Morton (pseud. Josephine Harvey), *Deeds Not Words*, Glasgow WSPU Exhibition, also Hampstead April 1910. Unpublished. Miss Josephine Harvey was a member of the AFL. (see Mar 1911)

W.Pett Ridge, *A Good-By Election*, in *VfW*, 8 April 1910, p441 and in Cockin, Norquay and Park.

Henry V. Esmond, *Her Vote*, Playhouse Theatre, 18 May 1910. Published London: Samuel French, 1910. Husband of AFL supporter Eva Moore, one of five actor/singer sisters, all active suffragists.

Miss Nelson, *Trial by Jury*, WFL branch meeting, Swansea, 18 May 1910. Unpublished. 'A man Suffragist is on trial before the opposite sex for daring to demonstrate in favour of the enfranchisement of men.' (*The Vote* 4 June 1910)

Rose Mathews, *The Smack*, Suffrage Atelier, Court Theatre 27 May 1910. Unpublished, in LCP. One-act play, announced in *The Vote*, 28 May 1910 as preceding Housman's plays. Mathews was a member of the AFL, WFL and active in the Actors' Association, the forerunner of Equity, and the Play Actors.

Laurence Housman, *A Likely Story* and *The Lord of the Harvest*, Suffrage Atelier, Court Theatre, 27 May 1910. Published *A Likely Story* in *Five One Act Plays of Village Characters*, London: Village Drama Society Plays, 1928. Bessie Hatton was in the cast.

Alice Chapin, *A Modern Medea* and *Shame*, Rehearsal Theatre in aid of Women's Freedom League, 8 July 1910. Directed by Edith Craig. Unpublished. See *The Vote* 16 July 1910 p137. Elsie Chapin, daughter of Alice, jointly organised the event. *The Vote* later reviewed Gilbert Murray's translation of Euripides' *Medea* with AFL organiser Adeline Bourne in the title-role.

Laurence Housman, *Lysistrata*, Little Theatre, 11 Oct 1910. Published London: Woman's Press, 1911. 'Clever and up-to-date paraphrase of Aristophanes'. (*VfW*, 17 Mar 1911)

Cicely Hamilton, *The Home Coming*, AFL/WWSL, Aldwych, 18 Nov 1910. Unpublished, in LCP. Whitelaw states the play was later presented as *After Twenty Years*. Reviewed *VfW* 26 Nov 1910.

George Paston (pseud. Emily Morse Symonds), *Stuffing*, AFL/WWSL, Aldwych,18 Nov 1910. Published London: Samuel French, 1912. Programme also included *A Pageant of Great Women* and a scene from *Lysistrata*.

Israel Zangwill, *A Prologue*, Croydon WSPU, later AFL, Lyceum, 1911. Published AFL 1911 and in Gardner. Author and radical Zangwill's *The Next Religion*, with AFL organiser Adeline Bourne in the cast, was presented by The New Players and reviewed in *The Vote*.

Dame Elizabeth Wordsworth, *Belinda in the Twentieth Century* (c1910), Lady Margaret Hall, Oxford c1910. Published in *Poems and Plays*, Oxford: Oxford University Press, Humphrey Milford, 1931. Play on women's education, features two suffragettes. Wordsworth, Principal of the college, was ambivalent about supporting women's suffrage.

Helen Margaret Nightingale, *A Change of Tenant*, Sevenoaks and toured by AFL and produced by other suffrage organisations, 1910. Published London: Woman Citizen Publishing Company, n.d. [1908]. *(See this volume)*

1911

L.S. Phibbs, *Jim's Leg* in *VfW*, 29 Jan 1911 and in Holledge. *(See this volume)*

Gwendolen Watkinson, *Women and Suffrage*, Lady Margaret Hall, Oxford, Michaelmas Term 1911. Published in *The Common Cause*, 2 Feb 1911, pp 701-3 & in Cockin, Norquay & Park. Watkinson was a student at Lady Margaret Hall.

Percy Nash, *A Suffrage Girl*, St Andrews Church, W. Kensington, 6 Feb 1911. Unpublished, in LCP. Originally called *A Woman's Vote*. Set in future: the heroine has casting vote and elects her father, the plot is otherwise very conventional and her declarations of independence are not expressed in action.

Bertha Moore, *The Woman Wins*, Portman Rooms, 18 Feb 1911. Unpublished, 5 pages of a marked copy of the play are in Vera (Jack) Holmes's papers in WL. See: AFL Play Department's Half-Yearly Report. Programme also included musical items arranged by Mrs Emily Pertwee (née Moore).

James Barrie, *The Twelve Pound Look*, AFL, York for WSPU, 28 Feb 1911. Published London: Hodder and Stoughton, 1914 and AFL Play Department's Half-Yearly Report, 1911. First of several AFL productions of Barrie's play. (Originally prod. Duke of Yorks, 1 Mar 1910.)

Harold Rubinstein, *Her Wild Oats*, Rehearsal Theatre 7 Mar 1911, part of double-bill first of a series of 'trial performances for propaganda plays'. Unpublished. Rubinstein's play was later given at a Drawing Room Entertainment of the Kensington WSPU at Mrs Lowy's, 76 Holland Park. The Lowys were active suffragists and connected by friendship and marriage to Mrs Herbert Cohen

John Kidd, *Restitution*. Rehearsal Theatre, 7 Mar 1911, part of a double-bill in first of a series of 'trial performances for propaganda plays'. Unpublished. Also listed as produced in 1913-14 in Bensusan's AFL annual report.

Cicely Hamilton, *The Cutting of the Knot*, Glasgow Royal, 13 Mar 1911, (re-staged London, as *A Matter of Money*, 9 Feb 1912). Bensusan was in the London cast. Unpublished.

Vera Wentworth, *An Allegory*, Rehearsal Theatre, 25 April 1911, part of a triple-bill in second of a series of 'trial performances for propaganda plays'. Published London: AFL, 1913 and in Gardner. Source: Crawford, AFL Play Department's Half-Yearly Report. It may have been the same play under the title *The Awakening* that was put on at the WSPU Christmas bazaar in 1911. It was also staged by prisoners in Holloway, Mar 1912, directed by Mrs Pethick-Lawrence.

Maurice Hunter, *The Eclectics Club*, Rehearsal Theatre, 25 April 1911, part of a triple-bill in second of a series of 'trial performances for propaganda plays'. Unpublished. Source: AFL Play Department's Half-Yearly Report.

M.Slieve McGowan, *Trimmings*, Rehearsal Theatre, 25 April 1911, part of a triple-bill in second of a series of 'trial performances for propaganda plays'. Unpublished. Source: AFL Play Department's Half-Yearly Report and reviewed *The Vote* 6 May 1911. McGowan was in the WFL and a regular contributor to *The Vote*.

Mrs Kate Harvey, *Baby*, Small Public Hall, Croydon, Pioneer Players for WFL, 29 Mar 1911. Unpublished. Harvey also organised garden parties and other events for the Cause. Cockin, 2001 dates production as Nov at venue listed, Gandolfi as Mar at unknown location. She lived in Bromley, was Hon Sec of WFL, designed and organised the International Suffrage Fair Nov 1912 and went on a lengthy tax resistance strike.

Jerome K. Jerome, *The Master of Mrs Chilvers*, King's, Glasgow, 10 April 1911. Published London: Fisher Unwin, c1911. Main characters all defined in relation to the Women's Parliamentary Suffrage League and similar groups. Pregnancy reinforces husband/wife bond.

Marion Cunningham, *Out of the Storm* and *The Laugh Against the Lawyers*, Men's Political Union for Women's Enfranchisement, Court Theatre 28 Apr 1911. Both unpublished, in LCP. Reviewed in *The Vote*,

6 May 1911. Alice Chapin and her daughter Elsie were in the cast. *Out of the Storm* is a melodrama where poverty is the 'grim, ghastly foe' that leads to murder. In *The Laugh Against the Lawyers* a woman dresses as a male legal clerk to get information on the solicitor uncle who is fleecing her.

P.R. Bennett, *Mary Edwards,* 'an anachronism' in one act. Gaiety, Manchester, 8 May 1911 then by AFL Aldwych, June, 1912 Published AFL, 1911 and in Gardner. Produced by Annie Horniman's company.

Christopher St John, *The First Actress*, King's Hall, Pioneer Players' inaugural triple bill 8 May 1911. Published N.p.: n.p., 1911 and in Cockin, Norquay and Park. Celebrates women's history of actresses on eve of Restoration actress, Margaret Hughes first stage appearance.

Cicely Hamilton, *Jack and Jill and a Friend*, King's Hall, Pioneer Players' as above, 8 May 1911. Published London: Samuel French, 1911 and in Shay.

Margaret Wynne Nevinson, *In the Workhouse*, King's Hall, Pioneer Players' as above, 8 May 1911. Published London: The International Suffrage Shop, 1911, and in Cockin, Norquay and Park. *(See this volume)*

Evelyn Glover, *Mrs Appleyard's Awakening*, Rehearsal Theatre, 20 Jun 1911. Published London: AFL, 1911 and in Hayman & Spender. Mrs A realises that her interest in politics is incompatible with her anti-suffragism.

Graham Moffatt, *Bunty Pulls the Strings*, Playhouse, 4 July 1911. *The Vote* saw this play as having suffrage at its centre, though not the topic of the piece. 'Bunty was a Suffragette, or rather she would have been one, had she lived today' according to Moffatt, *The Vote* 5 May 1913. Published London: Samuel French 1932.

Isabel Tippett, *The Stuff That 'Eroes Are Made Of*, Beau Site Hotel, Cannes, Jan 1912, later (Nov 1912) at International Suffrage Fair, Chelsea Town Hall. Published in *The Vote* 19 Aug 1911, pp 207-9 and in Cockin, Norquay and Park. Source: report in *The Vote*, 3 Feb 1912. A cousin of Charlotte Despard, the author was mother of composer Sir Michael Tippett and an ardent suffragist, imprisoned for her activism. The second production of her play, directed by Miss St Clair, was by

The Propaganda Players, a group set up to offer performances to suffrage branches.

Laurence Housman, *Alice in Ganderland,* Grand AFL fundraising matinee, Lyceum, 27 Oct 1911. Published London: Woman's Press, 1911 Presented with a *Pageant of the Leagues,* later popular with local branches.

Alice Chapin and **Mabel Collins,** *Outlawed,* Royal Court, 23 Nov 1911. Unpublished, in LCP. Three act play, based on novel by Collins and WFL leader, Charlotte Despard. Heroine is wrongfully imprisoned, mistaken for her double and comes to identify with outcasts and outlaws and chooses to work for women's freedom.

Laurence Housman, *Pains and Penalties: the Defence of Queen Caroline,* Pioneer Players, Savoy, 26 Nov 1911. Published London: Sidgwick & Jackson, 1911.

Gertrude Vaughan, *The Woman with the Pack,* Portman Rooms, Baker St, 8 Dec 1911. Published London: W. J. Ham-Smith, 1912, and in Cockin, Norquay and Park. Review of book in *The Vote* 20 July 1911

Edith M Baker, *Our Happy Home* in *The Vote* 30th Dec 1911 and in Cockin, Norquay and Park.

Emily Pertwee (née Moore) Musical entertainments for the suffrage cause inc. the musical section of the AFL procession,1911. Unpublished. Ethel Smyth was at the head of the march. Emily was sister to well-known actresses and AFL activists Eva and Decima Moore.

Bertha N Graham and **Frank Vernon,** *Under Canvass: a sketch.* Published London: Conservative Central Office, 1911.Written for the Holborn (Finsbury) branch of the party and presented to Central Office for general use, it discusses suffrage via 2 women canvassers. Graham was an actress, also SM for the 6 Dec 1909 suffrage event.

1912

Suffragette Burns' Night, Edinburgh, 25 Jan 1912. Unpublished. Programme included Trafalgar Square scene from Robins's *Votes for Women* and a Shakespeare pageant, *The Vote* 2 Feb, 1912.

Christopher St John and **Charles Thursby**, *The Coronation*, Savoy, 28 Jan 1912. Published London: The International Suffrage Shop, 1912, and in Cockin, Norquay and Park. In aid of the International Suffrage Shop. Directed by Edith Craig. The Lord Chamberlain sought to ban the play. Shown 'to an invited audience at the Savoy Theatre under the polite fiction that they were not the public' (*The Vote*, 3 Feb 1912). See also Gandolfi.

Elizabeth Baker, *Edith*, AFL for WWSL matinee at Prince's Theatre, 9 Feb 1912. Published London: Sidgwick and Jackson, 1927. Presented with *A Pageant of Shakespeare's Heroines*. Janette Steer played Edith. Pageant was arranged by Bessie Hatton and Beatrice Harraden, also performed was the Trafalgar Square scene from Robins's *Votes for Women* (*The Vote* 17 Feb).

Fred Murray and **Chas Hilburn**, *The Suffragette*, Ardwick Empire, Manchester 19 Feb 1912. Unpublished, in LCP. Sketch: a hen-pecked husband violently turns the tables on wife, threatening a hiding if she goes to suffrage meeting.

Mrs Harlow Phibbs, *The Rack*, Rehearsal Theatre, 20 Feb 1912. Unpublished, in LCP. Sources: Nicoll, review in *The Vote* 2 Mar. 1912.

Evelyn Glover, *A Chat with Mrs Chicky,* Rehearsal Theatre, 20 Feb 1912. Published AFL, 1912 and in Hayman & Spender and in Gardiner.

Indian Tableaux by Indian Women Outside Royal Court, Sloane Square 1-2 Mar 1912, see *The Vote* 9 Mar 1912.

Helen MacLachlan, *The Mad Hatter's Tea Party Up To Date*, Hard-Up Social, Edinburgh 29 Mar 1912. Published in *The Vote* 20 April 1912, p11, and in Cockin, Norquay and Park. Helen MacLachlan M.A. was Assistant Secretary of the Edinburgh WFL. Produced with three dramatic sketches from J.M.Barrie's *Window in Thrums*. Review *The Vote* 13 Apr 1912. See: Carlson.

Christopher St John, *Macrena*, King's Hall, Pioneer Players, 21 April 1912. Unpublished, in ETMM. See Cockin, 2001. In a triple bill with Dorynne's play below and H.Hamilton Fyfe's Race Suicide.

Jess Dorynne, *The Surprise of His Life*, King's Hall, Pioneer Players 21 April 1912. Unpublished, in ETMM. Reviewed in *Votes for Women,*

26 April 1912, p 467 and *The Vote* 4 May 1912.

Florence Hobson, *A Modern Crusader: a dramatic pamphlet*, National Health Week at King's Hall, 30 April 1912. London: A. C. Fifield, 1912. Reviewed, negatively, as propaganda by Rebecca West in *The Freewoman* 23 May 1912. On sanitation.

Christopher St John, *Pageant of the Stage*, Albert Hall 11 June 1912. Directed by Edith Craig. Unpublished.

Winifred St Clair, *Juliet Strikes* in *The Vote*, June 8 and June 22, 1912. See Carlson.

Winifred St Clair, *Two of the Odd Boys*, Caxton Hall, 3 July 1912. Unpublished. See also July 1913.

E.Ion Swinley, *The Aspirations of Archibald*, Bohemian Fete, Hampstead, 13 July 1912. Unpublished.

Charles Brookfarmer (pseud. Carl Bechhofer) *Suffragette Sallies* in *The New Age* 25 July 1912. Satire. Characters include Evelyn Sharp, Miss M.Slieve McGowan, Laurence Housman and others.

H.S. *A Speech: Justice to Women* in *VfW*, 24 Aug 1912. Version of Mark Antony's oration for Julius Caesar. H.S. also wrote a suffrage parody of a scene between Rosalind and Celia from *As You Like It,* in *The Vote* 31 Oct 1913.

E. Weir, *Those Antis!* in *VfW* 12 Sept 1912. 'Mrs Higgs tells her cousin from the Market-Town all about the Anti-Sufferin' Meeting in the Village Hall', a monologue.

Isabel Tippett, *Women Old or New?* Published in *The Vote*, 31 August, 1912 pp 325-6 and 6-7 Sept 1912, p341-2 and in Cockin, Norquay and Park. Isabel Tippett was the mother of composer Sir Michael Tippett and was on the Executive Committee of the WFL. See: Carlson.

Jess Dorynne, *The Telegram*, Little Theatre, 18 Oct 1912. Unpublished, in LCP. One-act, Nicoll. Suitor and heiress are fooled into admitting their love through amateur theatricals. In double-bill with *The Sacrifice* by Alfred Crocker.

Ethel Ayres Purdie, *A Red-tape Comedy*. Published in *The Vote*,

16 Nov, 23 Nov and 30 Nov 1912, and in Cockin, Norquay and Park. Purdie was a Certified Accountant and auditor to the AFL, WFL and others.

Charlotte Perkins Gilman, *Three Women*, Pioneer Players, WFL International Suffrage Fair, Chelsea Town Hall, 13 Nov, 1912. Published in *The Forerunner* 2, no. 5 May 1911 See Cockin 2001. Play deals with whether a woman should marry, pursue a career – or both.

Margaret Chick, *In a Watteau Garden*, International Suffrage Fair, Chelsea Town Hall, 13 -16 Nov, 1912. Unpublished. Part of the extensive series of entertainments at the Fair including an opening pageant of nations, Glover's *Chicky*, Tippett's *'Eroes*, scenes from 19th Century Women Writers, Irish sketches, Ju-Jitsu demos and international dances.

Constance Clyde, *Mrs Wilkinson's Widow*, AFL, Lyceum, 29 Nov 1912. Unpublished. Presented with St John's *The First Actress* and Glover's *A Chat with Mrs Chicky*. Review *The Stage*, 5 Dec 1912 and *The Vote* 7 Dec 1912.

H.M.Harwood, *Honour Thy Father*, Pioneer Players at Little Theatre, 15 Dec 1912. Published in *Three One-Act Plays* London: Ernest Benn, 1926 and in Cockin, Norquay and Park.

Edith Lyttelton, *The Thumbscrew*, Pioneer Players at Little Theatre, 15 Dec 1912. Published NY: Longman's, 1912 and in *Nineteenth Century* 69, May 1911, pp 938-960. Lyttelton was on the Executive Committee of the Women's Unionist and Tariff Reform Association, a Vice-President of the Conservative and Unionist Women's Franchise Association and of the London Society for Women's Suffrage. (see A.J.R.)

Hugh de Selincourt, *Beastie*, Pioneer Players at Little Theatre 15 Dec 1912. Published in *The Open Window*, 12 Sept 1911, pp.294-317 The De Selincourt family were suffrage supporters. Hugh was drama critic of *The Star* and literary critic of *The Observer*. His nephew Aubrey married Irene MacLeod (*WWW*)

C.J Tonsley, *Sir Robin Hall* or *The Fairy Suffragettes*. Published London: Boosey and Hawkes, 1912. Comic opera, set 1790-1800 where a selfish oppressive magnate Sir Robin Hall is reformed and converted to pro-suffrage and pro-Labour views.

1913

Ethel Richardson, adaptation from Whitelaw's translation, *The Antigone of Sophocles* in *VfW* 17 Jan 1913.

Susanne Rouviere Day and **Geraldine Cummins,** *Broken Faith*, Abbey, Dublin, 24 April 1913. Unpublished, in Cork Archive Institute. Source: Nicoll. Day and Cummins co-founded the Munster Women's Franchise League with Edith Somerville.

Marion Cunningham, *The Hour and the Woman*, Advance Players, Cosmopolis, 25 April 1913. Unpublished. Source: Nicoll.

Alison Garland, *The Better Half*, AFL at King's Hall, Covent Garden for Liberal Federation delegates, 6 May 1913. Later given a public performance at the Royal Court, 14 Feb 1914. Janet Steer was in the cast. Review *The Vote*, 12 Sept 1913. Published Liverpool: *Daily Post* Printers, 1913. AFL annual report 1912-1913, p12. Full-length play, role reversal comedy.

A.L.Little *The Story* in *The Vote* 9 May 1913. Short dialogue.

Helen MacLachlan, *Mr Peppercorn's Awakening*, WFL meeting, Edinburgh, cMay 1913. In *The Vote,* 1 Aug 1913 and in Cockin, Norquay and Park. The author is identified in *The Vote,* 30 May 1913, p78.

'S', *Lady Butterby and Mrs Macbean*. WFL meeting, Edinburgh, cMay 1913. Published Perth: Wood and Son, 1912. See *The Vote*, 30 Dec 1913. A lady wrongly assumes her working-class neighbour to share her anti-suffrage stance and is challenged in her view. In Scots.

Mabel Lawrence, *The Salvation of her Sex.* Published in *VfW* 13 June 1913. Short dialogue.

Hilda Adshead, *Ten Shillings*, produced by the AFL at the Arts Centre, 93 Mortimer St, in triple bill, 8 July 1913. Unpublished. Source: Nicoll. Adshead published several stories in *VfW*.

Ruth Young, *The Iron Law*, Produced by the AFL at the Arts Centre in triple bill, 8 July 1913 Unpublished Nicoll. Member of WTGC. Nicoll misprints date as 8/17/13. Probably the third play was St Clair's *Two of the Odd Boys* (see Bensusan's AFL annual report, p12.)

H.S., *The New Socrates.* Published in *VfW*, 29 Aug 1913 and in Cockin,

Norquay and Park. See: Carlson.

Constance Maud and **P. Berton,** *A Daughter of France,*
Ambassadors, 21 Oct 1913. Unpublished. Review in *VfW* and *The Vote,*
31 Oct 1913. Maud published reviews etc in *VfW* such as *'Through
Shakespeare to Suffrage'* and published with her sister Mary,
Shakespeare's Stories (1914).

Kate Harvey *Hiawatha*, Cripplegate Institute, in aid of *The Vote,* 4
Nov 1913. Adverts and references in *The Vote*, Sept and Oct. A notice
on 19 Dec 1913 details plans for a special matinee for schools at the
same venue 24 Mar 1914, due to requests from headmaster and
headmistresses. Harvey was celebrated in the WFL at this time, having
just served 2 months for tax resistance.

Winifred St Clair, *The Science of Forgiveness* published in *The Vote,*
28 Nov 1913 and in Cockin, Norquay and Park. See: Carlson.

Henry W. Nevinson *The Cabinet Concert.* Published in *VfW*, 5 Dec
1913 and in Cockin, Norquay and Park. Journalist husband of Margaret
Wynne Nevinson and later of suffragist Evelyn Sharp.

Eugene Brieux, (tr. Charlotte [Mrs Bernard] Shaw) *A Woman on her
Own*, Women's Theatre, Coronet, 8 Dec 1913. Published London: A.C.
Fifield, 1911. Company was developed by Bensusan out of AFL. See
Holledge, Pfisterer

Henrik Ibsen, *Rosmersholm*, Irish Suffrage Conference in Dublin, 9
Dec 1913, produced by Elizabeth Young's company. Irish premiere of
the play. Unclear which translation was used. Probably edition tr.
Charles Archer, introduced by William Archer. Published London and
Felling-on-Tyne, 1906.

Mary Costello *Not Made in Heaven*, comedy, Irish Suffrage
Conference, Dublin, 10 Dec 1913. Published in Lynn and Harding and
in *The Tatler*, No 20, 13 Nov 1901, p. 329-33. "screamingly funny in a
typical Irish vein" *The Vote* (19 Dec 1913).

Bjornsterne Bjornson, (tr.R Farquharson Sharp) *A Gauntle*t,
Women's Theatre, Coronet, 11 Dec 1913. Published in *Three Plays*
London: J.M. Dent & Sons, 1912. Company was developed by Bensusan
out of AFL. Play had recently been done by Play Actors. See Holledge,

Pfisterer, reviews in VfW.

Joan Dugdale, *10 Clowning Street*, Men's Political Union, Cosmopolis Hall, Holborn, 19 Dec 1913. Published in *VfW* 23 December 1913 and in Holledge. Dugdale was Organising Secretary of the AFL. Production was organised by Mrs Victor Duval. Cast included Daisy Dugdale and A.S.Dugdale. *VfW* reproduced photos from the *Daily Sketch* with script.

A.L.Little, *The Shadow of the Sofa* published in *The Vote* 24 Dec 1913 and in Cockin, Norquay and Park.

Katherine Susannah Prichard, *Her Place*, produced by AFL 1913. Unpublished script in Australian National Library. Produced, according to Throssell (p264) and Pfisterer, however not listed in Bensusan's AFL annual report. About a jewel theft, it ends with a eulogy to the working woman.

Puppet Plays, Crosby Hall, Chelsea, in aid of the Working Women's Legal Advice Bureau and the Industrial Law Committee, no production date 'recently', *The Vote*, 19 Dec 1913.

Anon, *Wanted- A Lady's Companion*, Snowball Party, Chester, c22/23 Dec 1914. Unpublished. Possibly Margery Stanley Clark's *Wanted- A Companion* 1903. Performed by Mrs Crosland Taylor and Miss Mona Smith of Liverpool Rep. See *The Vote*, 2 Jan 1914

1914

Evelyn Glover, *Showin' Samyel*. Published London: WWFA, 1914. Monologue with working-class character.

Gladys Mendl (pseud. Mrs Harrie Schütze), *Su' L' Pavé Being Half an Hour in the Life of a Paper-Seller* in *VfW*, 9 Jan 1914, p224. Mendl wrote occasional sketches for *VfW*.

Marie Robson, *The Suffragette: a four act play*, Palace, Crewcrook, Ryton-on-Tyne, Newcastle, 15 Jan 1914. Unpublished, in LCP. Bensusan lists a production of a play of this name in the AFL report for 1913-14 but it seems unlikely this is the one. The Examiner of Plays described it, accurately, as a 'mixture of suffragette polemics and old-fashioned melodrama'.

Lorimer Royston, *Little Jane and Grandmamma Published* in *VfW*, 16 Jan 1914, p230 and in Cockin, Norquay and Park. See: Carlson.

Agnes Leigh, *The Lunatic*, Green,White and Gold Fete, Ipswich, 2 Feb 1914. Published London: Lacy Acting Edition, 1899. Performed with monologues and recitations. See *The Vote* 13 Feb 1914. Mrs Tippett was one of the organisers.

Lorimer Royston, *Fair Play: a Dialogue*. Published in *VfW*, 13 Feb 1914, p298 and in Cockin, Norquay and Park

James Sexton, *The Riot Act*, Playhouse, Liverpool, 3 Feb 1914. Published London: Constable, 1914. About Labour politics and a Transport Workers strike. Typist/clerk to the manager is a WSPU activist.

A.D'Este Scott *Daughters of Ishmael*, from the novel by R.W.Kauffman, Pioneer Players members only performance at King's Hall, Covent Garden, 1 Mar 1914. Unpublished. On white slavery, with Cathleen Nesbitt, Jane Comfort, Janette Steer, Marjorie Patterson among the cast. The play had been shown in NY where attempts were made to ban it. See *The Vote* 27 Feb 1914.

Constance Maud *Madame Marcelle*, MCH Dramatic Society, Cripplegate Institute, 3 Mar 1914. In aid of Mrs Despard's School Clinics at Nine Elms. See *The Vote*, 19 Dec 1913 and 27 Feb 1914.

Kate Harvey *Courage: a Dutch play,* in triple-bill with above, 3 Mar 1914.Unpublished. Reviewed *The Vote* 6 Mar 1914

Oliphant Down *A Maker of Dreams* in triple-bill with above, 3 Mar 1914. Published London: Gowans and Gray, 1913. A one-act fantasy.

Vernon Carey, *Kindly Flames*, AFL at Arts Centre in triple-bill, 24 Mar 1914. Unpublished. Part of first of two triple-bill performances at this venue. The play had previously been produced privately at Chelsea Town Hall. Cast included Irene MacLeod (see 1910).) *The Vote,* 24 Mar 1914 describes it as 'a satire on popular prejudice'.

Alfred Bucklaw, *The Suffragette*, AFL at Arts Centre in triple-bill 24 Mar 1914. Unpublished. *The Vote,* 24 Mar 1914 describes it as advocating to women a knowledge of ju-jitsu. Bucklaw had appeared in the Women's Theatre's *A Gauntlet*.

Evelyn Glover, *Which?* AFL at Arts Centre in triple-bill, 24 Mar 1914. Licenced for Concert Hall, Olympia, 23 Mar 1914. Unpublished, in LCP. Second of the two triple-bill performances at this venue, listed in AFL annual report 1913-14, p12. A woman struggles with her father over her wish to take up an important hospital job.

Unknown, *Overheard at* — As above 24 Mar 1914. Unpublished. Listed in Bensusan's AFL annual report 1913-14, p12 but not in *VfW* review.

Mrs Harlow Phibbs, *The Mothers' Meeting*, Woman's Kingdom Exhibition, April 1914. Published London: AFL, 1913 and in Gardner. Author may have been L.S.Phibbs. Played by Jane Comfort (see Holledge) as part of the event's several days entertainment programme, along with Glover's *Mrs Chicky*, act 4 of *A Doll's House*, Shaw's *Press Cuttings* etc. See *VfW*.

Marion Emma Holmes, *Brass and Clay*, Woman's Kingdom Exhibition, 22 Apr 1914. Unpublished, in LCP. The play was submitted anonymously to LCP and is on sexual double standards. Programme also included Glover's *Which?* and performance by children of Italia Conti school.

Marion Emma Holmes, *A Child of the Mutiny*, performed at suffrage events. Date uncertain. Unpublished. Crawford: 'a powerful dramatic sketch'. Holmes was a prominent activist in the WFL and in Croydon and served as co-editor of *The Vote*, initially with Cicely Hamilton, later with Mrs T.P. (Elizabeth) O'Connor (an American, and also a playwright.)

F. Sheehy Skeffington, *The Prodigal Daughter*, Irish Women's Franchise League, Daffodil Fete, Molesworth Hall, Dublin, 24 April 1914. Published in *The Irish Citizen*, 1915 and in Gardner. Journalist and editor of *The Irish Citizen*, husband of prominent Irish suffragist Hannah Sheehy Skeffington, co-founder of the Irish Women's Franchise League also a journalist.

Henrik Ibsen, *Ghosts*, Royal Court Theatre, 26 April 1914, produced by J.T.Grein for the New Constitutional Society for Woman Suffrage. Published: various editions. Bessie Hatton played main part. See *The Vote* 1 May 1914.

Mrs Alexander Gross *Break the Walls Down,* Savoy, 16 May 1914. Unpublished, in LCP. Sarah Hartley's biography of Gross's daughter, London A-Z mapmaker Phyllis Pearsall (*Mrs P's Journey,* Simon and Schuster, 2001), states that Gross's play was dismissed by critics as "Suffragette nonsense" (p51). Also reviewed in *VfW* and *The Vote* 22 May 1914.

Charles Brookfarmer (pseud. Carl Bechhofer) *Women Still At It! – God Bless Them!* Published in *The New Age,* 21 May 1914. 'Report by Charles Brookfarmer of a meeting of the Women Writers' Suffrage League, Thursday, April 30, 3.30 p.m. Tea 6d.' Features Mrs (Louise) Jopling-Rowe (well-known artist and supporter of the Suffrage Atelier) and Mrs Naidu.

Harold Rubinstein, *Consequences,* Coronet Theatre, 8 May 1914. Production by Gaiety Theatre, Manchester. Unpublished, in LCP. *VfW* describes suffrage movement as the background of action.

Lane Crauford, *When Women Get The Vote,* Pavilion, London, 3 June 1914. Unpublished, in LCP. Satirical farce: women have the vote and a Radical husband and Unionist wife are divided until each is converted to the other's party by beer and flattery.

Constance Campbell, *One Of The Old Guard,* The Church Institute, Strand-on Green, 13 June 1914. Published London: Samuel French, 1914. Mother and daughters intrigue to persuade father to support cause.

Magdalen Ponsonby, *Idle Women: a Study in Futility,* Pioneer Players at Kingston's Little Theatre 21 June 1914. Published London: Arthur L. Humphreys, 1914. A comic satire on bored fashionable London women and their latest intellectual fads. Suffrage is specifically excluded from those fads. Reviewed in *The Vote* 26 June 1914, (Ponsonby was member of Pioneer Players Advisory Committee and a friend of Gertrude Kingston, manager of the Little Theatre) Also with Guy de Maupassant's *The Duel.*

Mrs Herbert (Jennie) Cohen, *The Level Crossing,* Pioneer Players at Little Theatre, 21 June 1914. Unpublished, in LCP. Cohen was an active worker for women's suffrage with the WWSL and the Jewish League for Women's Suffrage and related to the artistic and pro-suffrage Lowy family, a supporter of Inez Bensusan's Women's Theatre and on their General Committee.

Anon, *For the Cause*, Camberwell Empire, 22 June 1914. Unpublished, in LCP. Topical tragic melodrama: a young wife blows up the Albert Memorial – and accidentally, her husband too. She is a member of S.P.E.W (Society for Political Enfranchisement of Women).

Mabel Ross Rees, *The Modern Woman's Soliloquy* i.e 'To be or not to be a Suffragist' published in *The Vote*, 26 June 1914. Rees was from Brooklyn, NY.

Flora Annie Steel, *Indian Sketch*, also *A Pageant of Famous Men and Women*, AFL Costume Dinner, Hotel Cecil 29 June 1914. Unpublished. See *VfW* 26 June. 30 tables were staffed by actresses or writers in costume inc. Lena Ashwell, Janette Steer, the Greins, Cicely Hamilton, Evelyn Sharp and Decina Moore. The event was directed by Edy Craig. Steel was a prominent suffragist.

Box and Cox and Scenes from *School for Scandal*, garden party, Clapham, 2 July 1914 in aid of Mrs Despard's birthday fund, organised by Winifred St Clair.

Katherine Susannah Prichard, *For Instance*, AFL Play Dept. for Grand Overseas Entertainment, Dominion Conference, Westminster Palace Hotel 10 July 1914. Unpublished, text lost. Source: Throssell (p264), Pfisterer. Described by the *Melbourne Herald* 'designedly a play with a purpose' showing 'skill in compacting together romance, politics and social economics' (p254), also reviewed in *VfW* 17 July 1914, p650.

Olive Schreiner, *Scene from The Story of an African Farm*. As above 10 July 1914. Script unpublished adaptation of Schreiner's novel. Australian Bensusan was in the cast for this entertainment focusing on the British dominions in aid of the International Suffrage Shop. Also performed 25 July, at a Garden Party at Fitzjohn Ave, together with Wentworth's *Allegory* and Annie Spong's and Italia Conti's dancers.

Charles Brookfarmer (pseud. Carl Bechhofer) *Give Us Women!* or *What are Men?* in *The New Age*, 20 Aug1914. 'Report of a meeting of the East London Federation of Suffragettes, Mare St, Hackney July 28'- Brookfarmer's satirical dialogue features Sylvia Pankhurst and George

Lansbury.

Janette Steer, *The Sphinx,* Royal Court, 3 Oct 1914, 9 performances. Unpublished in LCP. 'Purports to represent the mystery underlying the sex problem'. The script had been approved by Harraden, Laurence Housman, Madeleine Lucette Ryley and others. Steer advertised in *The Vote* for suffrage societies to subscribe for tickets and a bookstall operated throughout the run.

Millicent Wadham, *Eden Gate,* Highgate, London 1914. Unpublished. Crawford states that it was probably published by the London Society for Women's Suffrage.

---

1 *The Cause and Lady Peggy* by Muriel Crawley, for example, listed as a suffrage play in Crawford, is in fact a one-act comedy in which her fiancé persuades Peggy out of her superficial conversion to socialism.

2. Githa Sowerby's *Rutherford and Son* for example was reviewed in *The Vote* under the heading 'A Great Suffrage Play'. It can be found in Gardner and Fitzsimmons and elsewhere.

Anthologies Referred to in Publication Column

Cockin, Katharine, Norquay, Glenda and Park, Sowon S. ed. *Women's Suffrage Literature*, London, NY and Tokyo: Routledge, 2007 vols. 1-6. Vol 1. inc. Robins

Vol 3 inc: St John, Nevinson, Hamilton & St John, Bensusan, Hatton, Vaughan, Baker, McLachlan, Little, Purdie, St Clair, Tippett, G. Watkinson, as well as writers of unknown gender (H.S., N.A. Lorimer Royston) and male writers (Austin, Harwood, Arncliffe-Sennett, H.W.Nevinson, H.M. Paull, Pett Ridge)

France, Rachel, *A Century of Plays by American Women*, NY: Richard Rosen Press, 1979 inc. Hamilton & St John

Kelly, Katherine, *Modern Drama by Women: an International Anthology*, London: Routledge, 1996 inc. Robins.

Gardiner, Juliet, *The New Woman*, London: Collins and Brown, 1993 inc. Glover

Gardner, Viv, *Sketches from the Actresses' Franchise League*, Nottingham: Nottingham Drama Texts, 1985 inc. Bensusan, Hamilton, Harraden, Hatton, Jennings, Phibbs, Wentworth (and male writers P.R. Bennett, Israel Zangwill, H.M. Paull, H. Arncliffe-Sennett; F. Sheehy Skeffington.)

Hayman, Carole and Dale Spender, *How the Vote Was Won & Other Suffragette Plays*, London: Methuen 1984 inc. Hamilton & St John, Robins, Bensusan, Harraden, Glover, Jennings

Lynn and Harding, *A Book of Original Plays*, London: Lynn and Harding, n.d.(1910) inc. Costello

Holledge, Julie, *Innocent Flowers: Women in the Edwardian Theatre*, London: Virago, 1981, inc. Dugdale, Phibbs, Glover

Pfisterer, Susan, *Tremendous Worlds: Australian Women's Drama 1890-1960*, Sydney: Currency, 1999 inc. Bensusan

Bibliography

A.J. R, ed. *The Suffrage Women's Annual and Women's Who's Who,* London: Stanley Paul, 1913

Auchmuty, Rosemary, "By Their Friends We Shall Know Them: the lives and networks of some women in North Lambeth, 1880-1940" in *Not Just a Passing Phase: Reclaiming Lesbians in History 1840-1985* ed. Lesbian History Group. London: the Women's Press, 1989

Banks, Olive, ed. *The Biographical Dictionary of British Feminists* Vol. One, Brighton: Harvester / Wheatsheaf, 1985

Carlson, Susan, "Comic Militancy: the Politics of Suffrage Drama" in Gardner and Gale, 2000

Cockin, Katharine, "Women's Suffrage Drama" in *The Woman's Suffrage Movement: New Feminist Perspectives* ed. Maroula Joannou and June Purvis, Manchester: Manchester University Press, 1998

Cockin, Katharine, *Edith Craig (1869-1947) Dramatic Lives,* London: Cassell, 1998

Cockin, Katharine, "Charlotte Perkins Gilman's Three Women: Work Marriage and the Older Woman" in *Charlotte Perkins Gilman: Optimistic Reformer* eds. Jill Rudd and Val Gough Iowa City: University of Iowa Press, 2000 pp74-92

Cockin, Katharine, *Women and Theatre in the Age of Suffrage,* The Pioneer Players 1911-1925 Basingstoke: Palgrave, 2001

Crawford, Elizabeth, *The Women's Suffrage Movement: a Reference Guide 1866-1928,* London: UCL Press, 1999

Croft, Susan, *She Also Wrote Plays: an International Guide to Women Playwrights from the 10th to the 21st Century,* London: Faber and Faber, 2001

Croft, Susan ' "A new untravelled region in herself" : women's school plays in late nineteenth and early twentieth century Australia' in Schafer and Bradley Smith, 2003

Dymkowski, Christine, "Entertaining Ideas: Edy Craig and the Pioneer Players" in Gardner and Rutherford

Ferris, Lesley, "The Female Self and Performance: The Case of the First Actress" in *Theatre and Feminist Aesthetics* ed. Karen Laughlin and Catherine Schuler, Madison/Teaneck: Fairleigh Dickinson UP, 1995

Gandolfi, Roberta, "Edy Craig and Community Theatre in the 1920's" in Women and Theatre: Occasional Papers 4

Gandolfi, Roberta, *La Prima Regista: Edith Craig, fra rivoluzione dellascena e cultura delle donne* Roma: Bulzoni Editore, 2003

Gardner, Viv and Susan Rutherford, *The New Woman and Her Sisters: Feminism and Theatre 1850-1914* Hemel Hempstead: Harvester Wheatsheaf, 1992

Gardner, Viv and Maggie Gale, *Women, Theatre and Performance: New Histories, New Historiographies,* Manchester: Manchester University Press, 2000

Gates, Joanne E., *Elizabeth Robins 1862-1952; Actress, Novelist and Feminist* Tuscaloosa: University of Alabama Press, 1994

Hamilton, Cicely, *Life Errant,* London: Dent, 1935

Hirshfield, Claire, "The Suffragist as Playwright in Edwardian England" in *Frontiers* IX, 2,1987, pp 1-6

Hirshfield, Claire, "The Woman's Theatre in England: 1913-1918" in *Theatre History Studies,* vol 15, 1995 pp 123-138

Holledge, Julie, *Innocent Flowers: Women in the Edwardian Theatre* London: Virago, 1981

John, Angela V., *Elizabeth Robins: Staging a Life* 1862-1952 London: Routledge, 1995

Kemp, Sandra, Charlotte Mitchell and David Trotter eds. *Edwardian Fiction: an Oxford Companion* Oxford: OUP, 1997

Marshall, Beatrice, *Emma Marshall: a biographical sketch,* London: Seeley and Co, 1900

Melville, Joy, *Ellen and Edy: a Biography of Ellen Terry and her daughter*, Edith Craig 1847-1947 London: Pandora Press, 1987

Nevinson, Margaret Wynne, *Life's Fitful Fever: a Volume of Memoirs* London: A.E. Black, 1926

Nicoll, Allardyce *English Drama 1900-1930: the Beginnings of the Modern Period* Cambridge: Cambridge University Press, 1973

Nicholson, Steve, *The Censorship of British Drama 1900-1968* vol 1: 1900-1932 Cambridge: Cambridge University Press, 2003

Orme, Michael, *J. T. Grein: the Story of a Pioneer* 1862-1935 London: John Murray, 1935

Paddey, W.G., *The Suffragette in Plays for Amateur Actors* London: C. Arthur Pearson Ltd, 1911

Pfisterer, Susan, "Australian Suffrage Theatre" Unpublished Doctoral Dissertation, University of New England, 1995

Pfisterer, Susan and Carolyn Pickett, *Playing with Ideas: Australian Women Playwrights from the Suffragettes to the Sixties*, Sydney: Currency, 1999 [NB Pfisterer's later works are published under the name Susan Bradley-Smith]

Robins, Elizabeth, *Both Sides of the Curtain: an Autobiography* London & Toronto: William Heinemann, 1940

Schafer, Liz and Susan Bradley-Smith ed., *Playing Australia: AustralianTheatre and The International Stage* Amsterdam and NY: Rodopi, 2003

Sihra, Melissa ed. *Women in Irish Drama* London: Palgrave Macmillan, 2007

Stowell, Sheila, *A Stage of their Own: feminist playwrights in the suffrage era* Manchester: Manchester University Press, 1991

Throssell, Ric, *Wild Weeds and Windflowers: the Life and Letters of Katharine Susannah Prichard* North Ryde NSW: Angus and Robertson, 1975

Tickner, Lisa, *The Spectacle of Women* London: Chatto and Windus, 1987

Townsend, Joanna, *Elizabeth Robins: Hysteria, Politics and Performance* in Gardner and Gale

Whitelaw, Lis, *The Life and Rebellious Times of Cicely Hamilton*, London: the Women's Press, 1990

Williams, Antonia, *The Street* in *Three New Plays* London: T. Werner Laurie, 1908

The Modernist Journals Project: http://dl.lib.brown.edu:8081/exist/mjp/index.xml

Additional works of interest include:

Bird, Kym, *Redressing the Past: the Politics of Early English-Canadian Women's Drama*, 1876-1927, Montreal: MacGill-Queens, 2004

Blair, Karen, *The Torchbearers: Women and their Amateur Arts Associations in America*, 1890-1930 Bloomington: Indiana University Press, 1994

Engle, Sherry, *New Women Dramatists in America, 1890-1920* NY: Palgrave Macmillan, 2007

Fitzsimmons, Linda and Viv Gardner eds. *New Woman Plays* London: Methuen, 1991 includes *Alan's Wife* by Elizabeth Robins and Florence Bell

Friedl, Bettina, *On to Victory: Propaganda Plays of the Women's Suffrage Movement*, Boston: Northeastern University Press,1987 (American)

18TH CENTURY

1718

Sweden: Female taxpaying members of the cities' guilds are allowed to vote in local elections (rescinded in 1758) and general elections (rescinded in the new constitution of 1771)

1755

Corsica (rescinded upon annexation by France in 1769)

1756-1778

Colonial Massachusetts, Lydia Taft, Uxbridge, Massachusetts town meeting

1776

New Jersey (rescinded in 1807)

19TH CENTURY

1838

Pitcairn Islands

1861

South Australia (Only property-owning women for local elections, universal franchise in 1894)

1862

Sweden (only in local elections, votes graded after taxation, universal franchise in 1918, which went into effect at the 1921 elections)

1864

Women in Victoria, Australia were unintentionally enfranchised by the Electoral Act (1863), and proceeded to vote in the following year's elections. The Act was amended in 1865 to correct the error.

1869

United Kingdom (only in local elections, universal franchise in 1928)

1869-1920

States and territories of the USA, progressively, starting with the Wyoming Territory in 1869 and the Utah Territory in 1870, though the latter was repealed by the Edmunds-Tucker Act in 1887. Wyoming acquired statehood in 1890 (Utah in 1896), allowing women to cast votes in federal elections. The United States as a whole acquired women's suffrage in 1920 (see below) through the Nineteenth Amendment to the United States Constitution; voting qualifications in the U.S., even in federal elections, are set by the states, and this amendment prohibited states from discriminating on the basis of sex.

1881

Isle of Man (only property-owners until 1913, universal franchise in 1919.)

1884

Canada Widows and spinsters granted the right to vote within municipalities in Ontario (later to other provinces).

1886

Republic of Tavolara grants universal suffrage. Monarchy restored 1899.

1889

Franceville grants universal suffrage. Loses self-rule within months.

1893

New Zealand September 19 (including Maori women, although barred from standing for election.)
Cook Islands

1894

South Australia grants universal suffrage, extending the franchise to all women (property-owners could vote in local elections from 1861), the first in Australia to do so. Women are also granted the right to stand for parliament, making South Australia the first in the world to do so.
United Kingdom extends right to vote in local elections to married women.

1899

Western Australia

20TH CENTURY

1902

Commonwealth of Australia (The Australian Constitution gave the federal franchise to all persons allowed to vote for the lower house in each state unless the Commonwealth Parliament stipulated otherwise. Thus, South Australian and Western Australian women could vote in the first federal election in 1901. During the first Parliament, the Commonwealth passed legislation extending federal franchise to non-Aboriginal women in all states.) New South Wales

1903

Tasmania, Australia

1905

Queensland, Australia

1906

Finland First country to give both the right to vote and stand for elections. First country to give both rights to all women regardless of wealth, race or social class.

New Hebrides Perhaps inspired by the Franceville experiment, the Anglo-French Condominium of the New Hebrides granted women the right to vote in municipal elections and to serve on elected municipal councils. (These rights applied only to British, French, and other colonists, not to indigenous islanders.)

1908

Denmark (only in local elections)

Victoria, Australia 1910s

1913

Norway

Denmark (full voting rights, with Iceland)

1916

Canada (Alberta, Manitoba and Saskatchewan only, others later)

1917

Russia

1918

Azerbaijan

Austria

Canada on federal level (last province to enact women's suffrage was Quebec in 1940)

Estonia

Germany

Latvia

Poland

United Kingdom (see Representation of the People Act 1918: women above the age of 30, compared to 21 for men and 19 for those who had fought in World War One. Various property qualifications remained)

1919

Armenia

Belarus

Belgium (only at municipal level)

Georgia

Hungary (full suffrage granted in 1945)

Luxembourg

Netherlands (right to stand in election granted in 1917)

New Zealand (along with voting rights, women now allowed to stand for election into parliament)

Ukraine

1920

Albania

Czechoslovakia

United States (all remaining states)

1921

Lithuania
Romania (with restrictions)
Sweden

1922

Irish Free State - now known as the Republic of Ireland - (equal suffrage granted upon independence from UK)
Burma
Yucatán, Mexico (regional and congress elections only)

1924

Mongolia (No electoral system in place prior to this year)
Saint Lucia
Tajik SSR

1925

Italy (local elections only)

1927

Turkmen SSR

1928

United Kingdom (franchise equal to that for men)

1929

Ecuador
Puerto Rico (to vote)

1930

South Africa (only granted to white women on the same basis as white men; black women did not qualify for the vote even though some black men did)
Turkey

1931

Ceylon (Sri Lanka)
Chile (only at municipal level for female owners of real estate; Legislative Decree No. 320)
Portugal (with restrictions following level of education)
Spain

1932

Brazil - Berta Lutz
Maldives
Thailand (Siam)
Uruguay

1934

Chile (only at municipal level; Law No. 5,357)
Cuba
Portugal expands suffrage
Turkey expands suffrage

Tabasco, Mexico (regional and congress elections only)
1935
British Raj (same year as men) (Retained by India and Pakistan after independence in 1947).
Myanmar (Burma)
1937
Philippines
1938
Bolivia
Uzbek SSR
1939
El Salvador
1940
Quebec becomes the final Canadian province to give female suffrage.
1941
Panama (with restrictions)
1942
Dominican Republic

1944
Bermuda (property-holding whites only)
Bulgaria
Jamaica
1945
France
Indonesia (Dutch East Indies)
Japan (with restrictions)
Senegal
Togo (French Togoland)
Yugoslavia
Italy
1946
Cameroon
Djibouti (French Somaliland)
Guatemala
Kenya
North Korea
Liberia (Americo women only; indigenous men and women were not enfranchised until 1951)
The British Mandate of Palestine
Portugal expands suffrage
Romania (with restrictions)
Venezuela
Vietnam

1947

Argentina
Republic of China (includes Taiwan) (with restrictions)
Malta
Mexico (only at municipal level)
Nepal
Pakistan (Pakistan declared independence on the 14th of August 1947)
Singapore

1948

The Universal Declaration of Human Rights (adopted by the UN includes Article 21: The will of the people shall be the basis of the authority of government; this will shall be expressed in periodic and genuine elections which shall be by universal and equal suffrage and shall be held by secret vote or by equivalent free voting procedures.)
Belgium
Israel
Iraq
Italy
South Korea
Niger
Dutch Guiana (now Surinam)

1949

Chile (right expanded to all elections on January 8 by Law No. 9,292)
People's Republic of China
Costa Rica
Syria

1950

Barbados
Haiti
India (Same year as men)

1951

Antigua and Barbuda
Dominica
Grenada
Nepal
Saint Christopher-Nevis-Anguilla
Saint Vincent and the Grenadines

1952

United Nations enacts Convention on the Political Rights of Women
Bolivia

Côte d'Ivoire (Ivory Coast)
Greece
Lebanon (partial)

1953

Bhutan
British Guiana (now Guyana)
Hungary
Mexico (extended to all women and for national elections)

1954

British Honduras (now Belize)
Colombia
Gold Coast (now Ghana)

1955

Cambodia
Ethiopia (and Eritrea, as then a part of Ethiopia)
Honduras
Nicaragua
Peru

1956

Dahomey (now Benin)
Comoros
Egypt
Gabon
Mali (French Sudan)
Mauritius
Pakistan (right extended to national level, previously only literate women could vote)
Somalia (British Somaliland)
Tunisia

1957

Malaya (now Malaysia)
Southern Rhodesia (now Zimbabwe)

1958

Upper Volta (now Burkina Faso)
Chad
Guinea
Laos
Nigeria - South

1959

Brunei
Madagascar (Malagasy Republic)
San Marino
Tanganyika (now Tanzania)
Tunisia

1960

Cyprus
Gambia
Tonga

1961

Burundi
Mauritania
Malawi
Paraguay
Rwanda
Sierra Leone

1962

Algeria
Australia: franchise extended to Aboriginal men and women.
Brunei Revoked (including men)
Monaco
Uganda
Northern Rhodesia (now Zambia)

1963

Congo
Equatorial Guinea
Fiji
Iran
Kenya
Morocco

1964

Bahamas
Libya
Papua New Guinea (Territory of Papua & Territory of New Guinea)
Sudan

1965

Afghanistan (revoked under Taliban rule 1996-2001)
Botswana (Bechuanaland)
Lesotho (Basutoland)

1967

Commonwealth of Australia (Aboriginal women)
Democratic Republic of the Congo
Ecuador
Kiribati (Gilbert Islands)
Tuvalu (Ellice Islands)
South Yemen

1968
  Bermuda (universal)
  Nauru
  Portugal (claims to have established "equality of political rights
  for men and women" although a few electoral rights were
  reserved for men)
  Swaziland
1970
  Andorra
  Yemen (North Yemen)
1971
  Switzerland (on the federal level; introduced on the Cantonal
  level from 1958-1990)
1972
  Bangladesh
1974
  Jordan
  Portugal (all restrictions were lifted)
  Solomon Islands
1975
  Angola
  Cape Verde
  Mozambique
  São Tomé and Príncipe
  Vanuatu (New Hebrides)
1977
  Guinea-Bissau
1978
  Marshall Islands
  Micronesia
  Moldavian SSR
  Nigeria - including North
  Palau
1984
  Liechtenstein
1986
  Central African Republic
1989
  Namibia (South-West Africa)
1990
  Samoa (Western Samoa)
  Switzerland (the Canton of Appenzell Innerrhoden is forced by
  the Federal Supreme Court of Switzerland to accept women's
  suffrage)

1994

Kazakhstan

South Africa: franchise extended to black men and women.

1997

Qatar (municipal elections in 1999)

21ST CENTURY

2002

Bahrain (Bahrain did not hold elections prior to 2002)

2003

Oman

2005

Kuwait

Qatar (national elections in 2008)

2006

United Arab Emirates (limited; to be expanded by 2010)

WOMEN'S SUFFRAGE DENIED OR CONDITIONAL

Brunei (Women and men have been denied the right to vote or to stand for election since 1962).

Lebanon (Partial suffrage. Proof of elementary education is required for women but not for men. Voting is compulsory for men and optional for women)

Saudi Arabia (No suffrage for women. The first local elections ever held in the country 2005; women not given the right to vote or to stand for election, although suffrage may be reviewed and granted by 2009.)

Useful links

www.archiveshub.ac.uk/news/afl.html

www.news.bbc.co.uk/1/hi/uk/3153388.stm

www.bbc.co.uk/radio4/womanshour/timeline/1900.shtml

www.bbc.co.uk/threecounties/content/articles/2008/11/27/playing_
for_power_feature.shtml

www.guardian.co.uk/commentisfree/2008/feb/06/venusfrommars

www.historylearningsite.co.uk/suffragettes.htm

www.learningcurve.gov.uk/politics/g9/

www.museumoflondon.org.uk/English/Learning/Learningonline/
features/wc/world_city_5.htm

www.parliament.uk/parliamentary_publications_and_archives/
parliamentary_archives/archives____the_suffragettes.cfm

www.peopleplayuk.org.uk/guided_tours/drama_tour/1900_1945/
political_actresses.php

query.nytimes.com/mem/archive-free/pdf?
_r=1&res=9507E5DB173FE633A25750C1A9629C946296D6CF

www.romanbritain.freeserve.co.uk/SUFFRAGETTES.HTM

www.spartacus.schoolnet.co.uk/Whunger.htm

www.susan.croft.btinternet.co.uk

www.timesonline.co.uk/tol/news/uk/article654659.ece

Forthcoming:

o   An anthology of the best plays by female dramatists from
1600 - 2000 in the UK.

o   Historical overview of women's playwriting and extensive
chronology of plays by women in the UK.

o   Will become essential student source book for colleges,
universities and libraries.

o   Publication June 2009

ISBN 978-1-906582-00-5
Price £12.99
orders@aurorametro.com
www.aurorametro.com